TEMPTATION

THE IMAGE OF SOLAN ... passion, would not vanis ... d it,
to form a logical rep ... lips
moved he saw himself kissing them. When her arms lowered
and the comb released her hair, he saw himself buried in it.

He took a heavy breath. How could she not know? How could she not feel it too? She was no longer an inexperienced maiden. She had to realize what she was doing to him, that she was deliberately torturing him. It was enough to drive a sane man over the edge, and he had already been there too many times.

"Damon?" She placed her hand lightly on his arm.

The simple touch jerked him back to the present. He pulled away from her and turned, baring his teeth in a semblance of a smile.

Her eyes grew wide, fearful. He almost hated her for that, hated that she could feel fear of him, when all he had ever wanted to do was protect her, take care of her, love her.

Damon took a menacing step in her direction. "Now, what's amiss with you, Countess? You do not look yourself."

Solange shook her head in bewilderment. "I don't understand you. You are angry. Have I done something wrong?"

"Something recently, you mean? I don't know, you tell me." He was stalking her now, steadily matching each step, closing the space she put between them.

"Stop it! Why are you behaving in this odd manner? Are you feverish?" She halted defiantly, daring him to come closer. Brave, foolish little Solange, and so he caught her up easily.

"Yes, my lady," he drawled. "I think I must be feverish. It is the only reason I can think of to do this," he said. He covered her lips with his own. . . .

A Rose in Winter

Shana Abé

Bantam Books

New York Toronto London Sydney Auckland

A ROSE IN WINTER

A Bantam Book / January 1998

ISBN 0-553-57787-5

Published simultaneously in the United States and Canada

Bantam Books are published by Bantam Books, a division of Bantam Doubleday Dell Publishing Group, Inc. Its trademark, consisting of the words "Bantam Books" and the portrayal of a rooster, is Registered in U.S. Patent and Trademark Office and in other countries. Marca Registrada. Bantam Books, 1540 Broadway, New York, New York 10036.

PRINTED IN THE UNITED STATES OF AMERICA

WLD 10 9 8 7 6 5 4 3 2 1

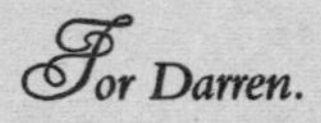

For Darren.

With sincere and heartfelt thanks to

Mom and Dad, Ruth Kagle, Stephanie Kip,

and Michael Palmer.

Prologue

FRANCE, 1287

THE KNIGHT KNELT AT HER FEET and took her proffered hand.

"My lady," he said. The irony of the words twisted his lips. He kept his head bowed.

Her hand was cool between his fingers, the smooth, alabaster skin a sharp contrast to his own roughened, dark palms. Her fingers were long and elegant, her nails pink and satiny. He noticed with dull surprise that she wore the garnet and gold ring he had given her all those seasons ago. The stone glowed subtly in the dim light.

A slight shiver shook her fingers—had he imagined that? Damon looked up, meeting her eyes for the first time this evening.

Even after these full nine years she appeared unchanged, beautiful, as youthful as the maiden he knew during their schooling together at the castle keep. All those long nights Solange had haunted him, and now he saw his dreams hadn't even done her justice.

Her face was perhaps a bit more drawn; her fine dark eyes contained a faint sadness now that was not banished even as she smiled down at him. The gold and silver circlet that graced her forehead seemed too heavy for such a slender neck.

Her hair was swept back into a regal roll beneath an almost transparent veil. He didn't need to see it again to remember the color of it: a rich brown so dark it fooled the eye until sunlight hit, and then it transformed to a halo of russet fire. Aye, he remembered that.

"My loyal friend," she finally said with a squeeze of her fingers. "I am pleased to see you again."

Damon remained kneeling, absorbing her presence, content and not content at once to stay at her feet. Her other hand covered both of his, and she raised him to stand on the step below her on the dais.

The chamber room was cold enough to frost their speech, for all the elaborate tapestries lining the walls and thick rugs on the floor. Behind him he could hear the hushed whisperings of her attendants, huddled around the fireplace. He could feel their speculative eyes on his back.

"You were sore missed," Solange added softly.

Damon felt the old familiar tightness in his chest and took a steadying breath. "I come out of duty, my lady." He kept his tone formal, hoping the reminder of his obligation would serve to ease this terrible ache she brought on.

A flash of emotion—pain? regret?—crossed her face. She released his hands.

"Of course," she said, then looked away.

The silence stretched between them, heavy with unspoken thoughts both knew neither could acknowledge. To distract himself, he studied her gown, embroidered pale gold cloth encrusted with pearls so luminous, they reminded him of dewdrops. The material captured and held the soft light of the torches above them.

His eyes were drawn helplessly to the cut of the bodice. He found himself counting her breaths, straining to see beyond the froth of lace edging her breasts.

What was he doing? Damon took control of himself and wrenched his eyes back up to hers. She was studying him, well aware of the nature of his thoughts.

The sting of blood heated his cheeks. He was a knight of the realm, and here he was acting no better than a rude young squire.

The corners of her lips tilted up slightly. She had always been able to read him so clearly.

"The lord, my lady?" he asked desperately.

The delicate smile vanished. Once more she looked at him with grave intensity.

"I have no lord," she replied.

"Madam?" He was stunned.

The world had taken on a shimmering edge, and she was the center, the sun, the moon, all the jeweled stars. He was falling, but there was nothing left for him to hold on to.

"There is no lord," she said very quietly. "There is only you."

He gaped at her, unwilling to believe what she said. The tightness in his chest became an unbearable pain. Unconsciously he pulled at the neck of his hauberk to ease it.

The muted chatter of the ladies behind him faded into silence.

Solange stood before him unmoved, unblinking. Her lips seemed very red against the paleness of her face, her eyes shadowed as she watched him. There was about her, as always, a fragility that drew him, even though he knew she had perhaps the strongest will he had ever encountered.

Now the stern purpose of her gaze was belied by the physical trembling he could see affecting her entire body.

She was mocking him. She could not be serious.

"My friend," she said, then paused. Carefully she reached out and placed her right hand on his shoulder. Her voice was low and sweet.

"Wilt thou have me?"

Chapter One

ENGLAND, 1279

As CHILDREN THEY HAD RARELY FOUGHT. Her elevated status as daughter of the overlord had placed her in a social restraint that even as a young girl she had fought to outwit. Solange hated embroidery, she loathed the lyre, and lessons in decorum sent her scrambling away to the remotest corners of the castle, where Damon would find her tucked away, spinning stories to invisible companions.

Many of the serfs whispered that she was an enchanted child, a changeling elflet traded in the cradle for the true human daughter. Perhaps some of her strangeness was the influence of her French-born mother, who had died giving Solange life without ever bothering to learn the language of the adopted country she had detested.

But there was no doubt that Solange had a solitary sort of presence, a singular completeness all her own.

From her mother she had inherited her milky skin, almond-shaped eyes, and fey demeanor. From her father, the stoic Marquess of Ironstag, Solange received her slender frame and the love of reading. And yet she was widely considered a child of mixed blessings, born of castle folk but not wholly one of them. Most of the servants avoided her, fearful of the unusual.

And indeed, even as a child Solange often seemed possessed of a sort of magic, ancient eyes in a young face, a crackle of energy ever present in her fingertips.

Damon didn't care. She was his sparkle, she was his life, even back then. And he was her champion, always defending her oddities, which he saw as proof of her unique beauty, teaching her the ways he knew to get on in the world.

Sometimes at night she would drift to sleep on his shoulder, her head tucked under his chin, the hot, sweet childish smell of her filling his senses. He would hold her close and let the feeling of satisfaction wash over him in great waves.

Adults of the castle regarded him as an older brother to her, which by his birth and status he was entitled to be called.

But he loved her, only her, always her. It never occurred to him to be a brother. He was simply waiting for her to grow up so they could be married. Solange belonged to him as surely as he did to her. Marriage was the only possible outcome, and in his youthful naïveté Damon never doubted the day would come when they would drink from the same cup as man and wife.

So he was content to wait for her, to wipe her nose in the drafty winters, to dry her tears over pets frequently lost in the hunts—for nothing could persuade her not to befriend the great dogs, who always doted on her. To take her hand and show her the safest way to climb the tallest tree in the ancient orchard, since she was determined to do it one way or another anyway.

She trusted him implicitly, she relied on him as the source of all possible good things in her life. She did love him. But the role of daughter of the castle had confines even she could not shirk.

As Solange grew older, Damon couldn't help but look at her with a possessive pride that he was careful to disguise. Although he realized his destiny was with her, he also knew it would take every ounce of his tact and cunning to win her from her father, Henry, the powerful Marquess of Ironstag.

Damon Wolf was not landless, but his parents, the Marquess and Marchioness of Lockewood, had died of cholera early in his childhood, leaving him subject to a harsh feudal system that crushed the meek and infirm. Solange's father had accepted the three-year-old boy as his ward, since Damon's father had been a close friend. He could not bring himself to leave the child to die at the hands of ambitious lords.

Damon's family castle, Wolfhaven, had been rapidly abandoned. It sat perched dramatically atop a rugged hill overlooking both land and sea, perpetually shrouded in mist and thick forest. Rumors had long since claimed it to be a place of pagan demons. Druid devils built the blackened base stones of it, it was whispered, and held their unholy rituals on its grounds. Indeed, the story wound on, the noble family itself was descended from these very pagans and had taken the name of Wolf as their own, from the familiars that they had used in their spells.

These stories turned both the castle and the family into curious objects of fear and fascination for the peasants. The last Marquess and Marchioness of Lockewood had held the village society together by sheer force of will. But by the time they had succumbed to the disease combing their castle, most of the population had either already died or fled. Surely, the rapidly disappearing locals pointed out, the place was cursed by God.

And so Wolfhaven stood alone, a spired monument to a nearly vanished family. True to its name, packs of wild wolves could often be heard crying amid the stones at night. Peasants would not go near it, nobles thought it too inconvenient to bother with. But the land was another matter altogether.

As the young marquess grew to manhood, he watched helplessly as his ancestral properties were slowly overtaken by encroaching lords. His guardian made little attempt to right matters. Henry was busy enough sowing and strengthening the boundaries of his own lands.

This left the child Damon in the odd position of being a noble orphan, ward of the overlord but not the son this family needed. Not quite impoverished, yet with no practical resources to speak of.

He slipped in and out of the cracks of the castle society, a chameleon of social status. Wellborn but powerless, his determination to find his own way won him a small but loyal handful of friends among the serfs and freemen, particularly the castle physician. But no one could say what would become of him.

Damon himself had long felt the call to be a healer. His persistent but unobtrusive presence on the professional visits of the physician merited him a sort of unofficial apprentice status. He learned the basics of medicine but soon discovered his growing thirst for knowledge was no longer satisfied by the aging doctor. So Damon branched out, speaking to villagers about home remedies, cornering visitors to the castle to learn whatever they knew, or had heard of.

By the time he was a youth, he had expanded his studies to include an array of herbology far beyond that of any for miles around. A steady trickle of patients, all of them peasants, began to come to him for help for their impacted teeth, broken bones, and various illnesses. His popularity grew, in part because his cures often worked, but also because unlike Henry's doctor, he charged nothing for his services.

Damon always did the best he could to help, but he knew there was so much more out there waiting to be discovered. If only he had the means, how much more he could do. . . .

Years were spent adding to his collection of pharmacopoeia. Solange often secretly accompanied him into the forests and bogs around the village, where they collected anything interesting they could find. He cherished her company not just because he loved her, but also because she had an unerring eye for detail and could spot the tiniest of plants which eluded him.

By all signs he would become a great healer. However, like the girl he loved, Damon could not escape his heritage. Nobles did not enter into professions. If he tried, he knew he would be shunned by his peers. To take his practice beyond a hobby would be inviting official disaster from Henry.

He was coming of age to inherit an empty, crumbling castle, the few feral remains of once-green fields, and a neglected village or two on the outskirts of civilization.

He never doubted he could put it all to rights. There had to be a solution that would allow him to both restore his castle and heal people, as he dreamed. He was waiting for Solange. They would do it together.

Their time was coming.

One early evening, a few weeks after she turned sixteen, Solange called Damon to her chambers. Ordinarily it would be forbidden to have an unrelated male of his age secluded with her. The fact that he was allowed this freedom made him uneasy, as he began to suspect that he was considered no threat to her maidenhood.

Solange sat by the open bay window, a dusky figure silhouetted against the sinking sun. She would insist on keeping her windows open in dry weather until the last slice of sun disappeared over the horizon, no matter what the season. She told him once she could not enjoy the fiery pageantry the sun put out every evening if she had to view it stifled behind a thick glass barrier.

The purity of her profile was etched clearly, reminding him of a lunar moth he had seen one night in the forest near the village: brilliant, graceful. Ethereal.

He walked over to her.

"Damon, what do you think? Lady Elsbeth says a woman is in disharmony without a husband. She says a woman is no match for the earthly temptations of sin, and that woman's natural weaknesses dictate she be controlled by man." Solange turned to look up at him, tilting her head curiously. "She says God made us this way for our own good."

Damon made an exaggerated grimace. "Lady Elsbeth is a pious old hag. Everyone knows she rules Lord Hatrone, not the other way around."

She smiled briefly, eyes twinkling. "Well, yes, that's rather what I thought too."

He sat beside her on the bower, letting the cool breeze from the open window drift over him. She scooted over and rested her head on his shoulder. Her arms twined around his waist, securing him closely.

Even this innocent touch sent his senses reeling. Her long hair draped over his arm and brushed his hand. He spread his fingers and then closed them again, trapping the silky strands against his skin.

"A man and a woman have a mutual need," he said slowly. "They create a balance between them."

He couldn't think of what more to say. She wasn't ready for him yet; in spite of his burning impatience, he knew she wasn't ready. He lifted his hand and let her hair flow freely over his wrist. The texture fascinated him. It was thick and soft, rich and brown and shiny, always smelling of her. The setting sun brought out the copper highlights glinting through it.

"Damon," she said, and then her voice trailed off. She sighed and shifted a little against him.

"Yes?" He tried to feel brotherly, but the dark spell she put over him was making him dizzy again, making him want to forget the promise he made to himself to wait one more year for her. She rubbed her face against his arm like a sleepy kitten. It made him smile in the gathering dusk.

"Damon, when are you going to kiss me?"

The surprise of it winded him as if he had been thrown from his horse. He couldn't seem to move for a long instant. Solange kept her face hidden in the full sleeve of his tunic.

Finally she looked at him, peering up through the thick fan of her lashes. She didn't speak again. She didn't smile to show it a girlish prank. She waited.

Damon had lost and he knew it. Even as he lifted his hand to cup her chin he was sharply regretting his loss of restraint. But he could not stop.

Her lips were full and sweet, had always looked to him like ripe cherries, or red roses, and more recently, like soft, forbidden feminine things. He watched his thumb trace their outline, watched them part gently, and felt her warm breath against his fingers. Her eyes were sleepy now, half-lidded, full of flames he should have recognized before.

All thoughts of caution fled. She was offering herself to him and he was powerless to hold back anymore. Nothing could be more right.

Damon tilted his head and rested his lips against hers. He was uncertain, breathless, and trying desperately not to frighten her. Her lips were softer than he imagined, tasting of some unknown delicious thing that could only be her. It was a potent realization that had him suddenly crushing her closer.

The kiss deepened, the blood pounded in his head, obscuring all but her. The taste and smell of her overflowed in him, added raw power to the embrace as the fire roared through him. *Solange, Solange, Solange . . .*

Solange helped him, wrapping her arms around his

neck and pressing her body tightly against his. Her firm breasts met his chest, her hair surrounded them both like a shadowed secret. She drew back to take shallow gasps of air, but he was beyond that, kissing her cheeks, the elegant line of her jaw, the tender throat. He heard a moan and realized only distantly that it came from him.

She responded eagerly, a little clumsy in her inexperience and haste. Her fingers caught in his hair, tugging at him.

He held her close and tried to show her all the pleasures she could have, but was distracted by the scent of her skin, the salty taste of her cheek beneath his tongue.

There were tears running down her face. Many, many tears.

The knowledge left him sick to his stomach. God in heaven, what was happening here? He was an animal, to use her like this.

He grasped her arms and pulled them free of his neck.

"Mistress?"

It was Adara, her maid, entering the chamber with tonight's dinner gown and bliaut.

Solange turned swiftly away to face the window, wiping her tears away with the tips of her fingers. "Leave it on the bed, Adara. I will be with you in a moment."

Damon felt the woman's scrutiny. He stood. "I must go. I will see you at supper, Solange."

She faced him, still sitting. She said nothing, merely searched his face with her eyes. For the first time, he felt uncomfortable with her. Her clear, penetrating gaze was unsettling.

Her lips appeared wet and bruised, glistening. He had to leave now, before he did something to completely humiliate himself.

"Yes," she said softly. "I will see you then." She lowered her gaze, freeing him to walk briskly from the chamber.

SOLANGE STOOD IN FRONT of the polished glass that reflected her image back to herself in wavy segments. She raised her eyebrows. The wavy Solange did the same, only the eyebrows were the thickness of caterpillars and reached up into the hairline of the reflected girl. She lowered them, and the girl in the mirror resumed her regular warped pattern.

The glass girl was strangely beautiful to Solange, an image of herself and yet not herself, dressed in an emerald green gown with an embroidered blue and gold bliaut over it. The bliaut hugged her figure, drawing in the gown underneath with girdled ties of gold that looked richly elaborate in the mirror.

She took a step sideways for balance as Adara tugged on the chained belt hanging low from her waist. The maid worked quickly, her hands as informal as always, but there was something different about her tonight, a suppressed excitement Solange could sense but not articulate.

Silently she stared at the woman working on closing the links of the belt. Was it odd, she wondered, that she had known Adara all her life and yet really knew nothing about her? It wasn't that she didn't care to know. Adara had the same aloof attitude that Solange had encountered in all the serfs. It seemed to be a combination of fear and condescension, and for the life of her, Solange couldn't figure out why.

"Adara," she said. "Do you like me?"

The woman's hands paused, but she did not look up from her work.

"Eh? Like? Of course I do, milady."

Solange studied the bent head curiously. "If that is so, why do you never smile at me?"

Adara released the belt. It fell into a graceful circle about her hips. The jeweled ruby tips of it settled into the folds of her skirt. Adara stood up without answering the question, and went to retrieve the golden net to bind Solange's hair.

"Have I done aught to offend you, Adara? Have I been cruel or unjust and not known?"

Her hair was bundled quickly into the net, twisted painfully tight against her neck. She dipped her head and touched the back of it, following the diamond-shaped contours of the delicate metal with her fingers. Her eyes found Adara's in the glass.

The maid shook her head, lips compressed. Solange decided to press on. "Have I offended any of the other serfs, then?"

"Nay, lady, where do ye get such talk?" She hurried on, before Solange could answer. "Supper is yet, milady. Ye ought to be below stairs by now."

Adara bobbed a brief curtsy, then turned and rushed

out of the chamber. Solange sighed, used to this reaction. She made a face at herself in the glass.

"No doubt you are some monstrous, ugly devil," she whispered to the reflection, "designed to frighten old women and little babies."

But then, why would Damon kiss her?

"Because you asked him to, foolish girl," she replied to herself. Obviously he would never have kissed her on his own. She had practically thrown herself at him. He must have been perfectly appalled.

Damon, her love.

Damon, with hair of raven's-wing ebony, the color that held all the rainbows in the world under sunlight.

Damon, with dark brown eyes so immeasurably beautiful that she knew in them all the mysteries of the stars could be revealed to her if she searched deep enough.

Damon, who had abruptly stopped her kisses, wanting no more of her.

But she had so much more to offer.

The intensity of his embrace had overwhelmed her. She had been waiting for it for such a long time, countless eternities. When it had finally happened, when he had finally enfolded her in his arms in a way that told her he thought of her as more than just a sister, her joy had flowed out of her heart to form silent tears down her face. That moment had been the happiest she could ever remember.

But that was over. Now she must set her mind to go about wooing him all over again. She had to salvage things.

Solange tugged despondently at the net in her hair,

then swept her skirts up in her hands, testing their weight. Too heavy to do anything that was not practical, like running or climbing. The older she became, it seemed, the heavier her clothing. She sighed and left her chambers to begin her plans to win Damon back.

The castle at night was a magnificent sight. Torches and braziers illuminated the meticulously embroidered tapestries which were the result of generations of noblewomen's stitches. The dancing shadows all around her reminded Solange of pleasant, unexpected things, like the taste of honeysuckle or the scent of autumn. Although drafty and damp as all castles were, Ironstag was placed on the trailing edge of a forest, which meant there were always plenty of fires burning to take away the chill.

The furniture, cloth, jewelry, and plate her father provided were all of the best quality. Some were handed down from pillaging ancestors, some he had obtained through careful maintenance of the harvest and trade of his crops and wool. His lands were fertile and extensive. He was often a favorite of the king's at tax time.

The Marquess of Ironstag lived well, and when he chose to entertain, he did so lavishly. The finest spices available from merchant traders were plentiful in his kitchens, obtained on yearly trips to London and Dover: from caskets of ginger and saffron to precious bundles of dried tea leaves from the Orient.

Everything about Ironstag was designed to impress.

Solange rounded the corner of the main staircase, then stopped. Below her the serfs bustled in an unusual frenzy of activity, and again she felt that sense of unease. No company was expected that she knew of. The usual group of minor nobles who lived in the castle with them were present, and she saw when she looked more closely, so were some unfamiliar figures.

Soldiers in orange and green tunics milled about in the crowd, jesting and drinking, examining the great stateroom curiously. They were all long-haired and bearded, with a wild, harsh look she instinctively did not like.

Someone saw her lingering at the bottom of the stairs, and elbowed his companion. The knowledge of her presence spread like wildfire throughout the crowded room, until she could see literally all eyes upon her. A hush descended.

Solange did not know what to do. She was unused to such widespread, meticulous attention and not schooled in the finer arts of court behavior. A furious blush stole up her neck and turned her fair cheeks to scarlet. Desperately she searched the crowd for a friendly face, but was met only with open, brash stares.

She took a step forward, and then another. She lifted her chin a little higher to hide the quiver of anxiety in her stomach. Where was Damon? Where was her father?

That question, at least, was answered for her.

"Daughter." The hearty, booming voice came from behind the backs of the soldiers. One by one they parted to reveal Henry, standing by the giant fireplace with another man. With great relief Solange slipped through the crowd to go to them.

Henry met her halfway, then escorted her back to

the man he had been talking to. "You look exceptionally fine," he muttered under his breath, as if to reassure himself.

Solange looked up at him in surprise. He had never complimented her on her appearance before, or indeed, on anything at all. She had the impression he thought of her as a sort of domestic pet, to be fed and stroked now and again but never deeply regarded. She opened her mouth to thank him, but the marquess cut her off. He clapped the stranger on the shoulder.

"Well, good sir, this is she."

Solange waited in vain for either man to complete the introduction, but they only stared down at her, both appearing lost in some deep thought. She felt her stomach clench tighter in the silence.

"I greet thee, kind sir," she finally murmured shyly, staring down at her hands. She was afraid to look up and confirm her thoughts that the entire population of the castle was eagerly watching this strange scene.

Without warning the man reached out and took her hand, pressing it to his lips. Startled, she looked up into his face, taking it in for the first time.

He had the brightest eyes she had ever seen. They seemed to reflect all the light in the room without revealing any of their own color. In fact, they appeared not so much like eyes at all, but rather like two shiny glass balls in a man's face. For an instant she felt a tingle of alarm as his lips gently touched her skin. A man without eyes has no soul, she thought whimsically.

But then he smiled, and the empty eyes shifted to a light gray color, and he was just an ordinary man after all.

Her father spoke. "Daughter, this is the Earl of Redmond."

"Lady Solange," the earl said with just the right French accent. In what seemed a peculiar trick of time, she watched his lips move before she heard her name. *Sol-ahnjh . . .*

Her own lips parted slightly in shock. She knew exactly who he was, of course. Stephen, Earl of Redmond, was the latest heir to a neighboring family of nobles that had been held alternately in either great esteem or great revulsion by her own family for centuries. The clashing dynasties held a continuous, and of late frigidly cordial dispute over land boundaries and tithings from the villages that straddled the lines of the two estates.

It had ultimately taken a royal decree to stop the fighting. Wily King Edward wanted neither of two of his most profitable estates to bankrupt each other in petty skirmishes, so he had claimed the disputed strip of land as his own and thus ended the feuding.

What astonished Solange was that the earl was here at all. The official feud was over but hard feelings abounded on both sides. Each remained convinced it was the fault of the other that the precious land was lost. Redmond's uncle, the late earl, was generally referred to by her father as "that bloated old goat," and when he had died five years earlier Henry had held a week-long feast to celebrate, inviting all the neighboring nobles *except* the new earl.

Solange surmised this Redmond must have looked little like his uncle. No one could possibly say he resembled a goat, she thought. A tiger, perhaps, or a lion, more like. He appeared at least a decade older than she, with long hair and a beard like the rest of the strangers, but unlike them, he was not swarthy. His hair curled in yellow ringlets down his back, almost as long as her own. His beard was rust colored and well trimmed, but still managed to conceal most of his face.

She noticed a strangeness about the man, a subtle haze that fogged her senses, made her slightly light-headed.

"Sun angel," Redmond said. She couldn't seem to stop staring at his mouth, mesmerized by the slowness of the sound coming from it. The lips closed in a smile, and she looked up again into his pale eyes.

"An apt name," he said, smiling still.

She realized he was talking about her, and lowered her head again to cover her disorientation.

For a frozen moment that stretched on and on, no one said anything at all. Solange twisted her hands together nervously, wishing for all the world she were back in her chambers, or the stables, or anywhere but right here, right now.

Henry broke the silence.

"Excellent. Let us sup."

The crowd in the greatroom erupted into noise, talking, whispering, bellowing for service from the serfs. Benches scraped the stone floor, servants scurried around with pitchers of mead and ale, platters of steaming roasted meat and vegetables, trenchers of bread, and thick wedges of cheese. Honey-glazed figs and other sugary treats were offered all round. Plates clattered on the tables, cups were slammed heartily against the wood.

It almost seemed to be a celebration.

Solange was escorted between Henry and the earl to her usual place next to her father at the head table.

Diners at her father's table were privileged enough to receive their own chairs instead of sharing benches, all set up on a stone platform overlooking the rest of the room.

To Solange's extreme embarrassment, Redmond was placed on her immediate right, which meant they were to share a trencher of bread. Ordinarily it was Damon who sat beside her. But where was he?

Solange scanned the hall anxiously, searching the crowd for his familiar form. He was nowhere to be seen.

Her appetite deserted her. She was filled with remorse and a terrible shame. She had disgusted him so much with her flagrant advances that apparently he couldn't even bear her presence. She swallowed hard at the lump in her throat. If she were to lose Damon, she didn't know what she would do.

He was her best friend. Her only friend, really.

For some time the earl had been patiently holding a small bite of meat between his fingers by the side of her face, waiting for her to notice. In the interim, the rest of the assembly had stopped what they were doing, one by one, to record the outcome of this choice offering. Once again the hall grew silent.

Solange slowly registered the change even in her misery. She looked up to find the thick fingers of the earl hovering inches from her lips, dripping with the juices of the meat.

Her eyes widened at this familiarity. Surely he didn't

expect her to eat from his hand? He gazed at her steadily, no expression on his face. He did not take the meat away.

Solange pressed herself as far back as she could into the ornate chair, throwing a desperate look to her father and then to the faces in front of her. Most of them watched her avidly, food forgotten halfway to mouths, goblets raised and arrested in mid-motion. A few of the women gazed at her with what looked like sympathy, even pity. But it was her father's look that frightened her.

His brows were snapped together, his mouth pinched. It made him appear years older than he was, and angry. She had never seen him look at her that way before. He nodded his head at her, indicating she should take the bite.

Her breath drew in sharply at that nod. She looked back at the earl, unwilling to do this, unwilling to show such obsequiousness in front of not only this man, but also the rest of these people who had never loved her.

Redmond met her eyes calmly, waiting. The meat was growing cold, the juices were congealing, but he did not move his hand.

Solange could only think that somehow her father had heard of her brazen behavior with Damon earlier and this was some cruel punishment designed to teach her a lesson. The scope of it seemed bizarrely out of proportion to her offense, but no other reasons for this humiliating situation sprang to her mind.

She had better do it. She couldn't risk angering her father further, lest he forbid her to see Damon.

Cautiously Solange came forward in her chair, leaning toward the hand and the meat. Her own hands gripped the carved armrests tightly. She could feel the anticipation rising in the air around her, a greedy energy that focused on her lips coming closer and closer to the earl's fingers.

As delicately as she could, Solange closed her teeth around the bite and pulled back.

The earl resisted her a little, holding on to the meat until she was forced to close her lips over his fingertips. As soon as she did so, he released her.

She sat back hastily, chewing and staring down at the array of food in front of them. The meat was tasteless in her mouth, dry. A sudden wave of chatter hummed all around her, rising and falling in cadence, settling down to nothing.

The hall was quiet once more, the third time this evening. The third time she had ever heard it this quiet in all her life.

Solange swallowed the meat. In an agony of self-awareness, she looked up again.

The earl was holding a goblet of wine in front of her to drink from.

It was his goblet.

For a long time she simply stared at it. She noticed his hand was tanned but the skin unbroken, unscarred by battle. She noticed the laced cuff of his tunic sleeve was sewn with minute, almost invisible seams. She noticed that his hand did not shake in spite of holding the heavy gold goblet, one of her father's finer pieces, in front of her face.

Instinctively Solange knew this offering was different from the last. Eating the meat from his fingers had been suggestive at best, lewd at worst. Drinking from his cup would mean another thing entirely. Something even more intimate. It suggested, to her, that he wanted to command her in some way. To possess her.

She could not do this. She would not. This man, this *stranger,* had no rights to her, and certainly had no right to force her to drink from his hand. Her lower lip began to jut out mutinously, her eyes slanted back and sparkled with resentment.

Henry shifted in his massive chair beside her.

Solange knew if she looked at her father that she was doomed to lose this battle. She kept her eyes on the goblet. Seconds ticked by.

A minute.

Henry moved again. He said her name once.

Her eyes shifted and were captured by the gaze of the earl. She saw intent there, her future meshing and dissolving in the flatness of his irises. She saw that ultimately, her game was futile. He had already taken measure of her spirit and defeated it with his own cunning. The pale eyes held determination, and some admiration for her too. But he would not let her win.

Henry said her name once more. His voice echoed away, falling heavy into the pregnant silence.

Redmond allowed her a little smile that only she could see, a subtle concession. He moved the cup over to her mouth and pressed the cold metal rim against her lips, tilting it up. She could drink, or she could allow the wine to spill down her face.

She opened her mouth and drank.

The crowd cheered wildly. Men pounded their fists

on the tables, ladies tittered in shrill voices. Even the serfs were smiling and chattering as they began to serve the supper again.

Very deliberately Solange wiped the back of her hand across her mouth. Redmond laughed out loud, then took the goblet and downed the rest of the contents. He turned to the woman on his right and began to compliment her lavishly on her outfit. The level of noise climbed to a delirious high.

Henry ignored her completely, talking in hushed tones with Lady Margaret, his latest mistress, seated on his other side. Solange was left feeling beaten, confused and utterly alone in an immense room brimming with people.

She was used to feeling alone, except for Damon. She thought perhaps everyone in the fiefdom, from noblemen to serfs, was there to witness her defeat at this game she could not name. Everyone except Damon. At least that was some scrap of comfort to her.

To keep herself from leaping from her chair and running away, Solange concentrated on the image of his face, square-jawed and handsome, wavy black hair brushing his forehead. She imagined he was beside her now, telling her what nonsense it was to care what these people thought of her. Telling her that he loved her and that was all that mattered.

She would go to him tonight, as soon as she could, she decided. She would steal out of her chambers and melt into the shadows until she reached him. Then she would beg his forgiveness for her actions this evening.

Perhaps he would hold her again, just hold her close to him, so that she could feel the strength of his heartbeat beneath her cheek. Perhaps she could convince him to love her as she loved him, not as a sister, not simply as a friend—

The tail end of a sentence containing her name chased randomly through these thoughts.

Solange is eager to start . . .

She frowned, deciphering what she had heard, listening for more.

". . . soon, I trust. The weather is uncertain this time of year, as I am sure you are well aware, Ironstag." Redmond leaned past her, talking to her father. "It would be folly to delay our departure any longer than necessary."

"I agree. The priest will be here tomorrow morning, according to my messenger. He's making the trip from Scallypeak even now."

The blood drained from her head in a sudden rush, and she was gasping for air, unable to speak out.

A traveling priest visited the castle once a year on his annual circle of fiefdoms. During that time he took confessions, baptized babies, married couples, and consecrated whatever dead had accumulated since his last visit.

There was no reason to have a priest come out on a special, and surely expensive, trip to Ironstag.

No reason at all, unless the Marquess of Ironstag wanted him very, very badly.

Solange closed her eyes and then opened them again. Her father was still addressing the earl.

"She'll go richly prepared, Redmond. Your soldiers had better be ready to defend her dowry."

Before he could answer, Solange spoke.

"Father? What are you discussing?"

Henry reddened. It was some measure of his ignorance of his daughter's nature that he felt annoyed with what he thought of as her unusually stubborn behavior this evening. His voice was curt. "We are discussing your marriage, of course. Do not interrupt me again, Solange."

She ignored that order, growing bolder with her rising panic. "Marriage to whom?"

God help her, she already knew the answer to that. It made all the strangeness of the evening come together with perfect clarity. She kept her face turned to Henry, even as she felt the earl beside her cover her hand with his own.

"Why, to me, angel. It's why I've come."

His low, melodious tone reverberated in her ear, echoing again with its peculiar delay. She snatched her hand back, still not facing him, and instead pleaded with her father.

"Marriage? Father, I am not ready for such an honor. I need time to—to prepare myself, to learn the proper lessons to become a wife! I am unworthy, I would surely disgrace the earl if married now!"

There was a pause as her father blinked down at her incredulously, as if seeing her for the very first time.

Redmond spoke softly in his velvet voice, but had overtaken her hand again. He pressed against it heavily. "Is that a threat, Solange?"

"No." She shook her head at him, trying futilely to escape his grip. "Not a threat, sir, a fact!"

Henry scowled. "Enough, child! You have had a full sixteen years to learn the ways to become a proper wife. Your maidenly *modesty*"—his emphasis on the word said clearly he doubted it was such—"is becoming, but this course has been planned and laid for many months now. You will become the wife of Redmond. He is a nobleman of excellent stock, equal to our own. His lands march along with mine for a good long border before splitting off. Our families will be united, as will our armies." Her father considered her thoughtfully for a moment, then shook his head.

"You should be grateful I have done so well for you, daughter. You will be the mistress of your own castle, and several smaller manors. Your sons will inherit a great combined estate."

A tight band of pressure across her chest was making it difficult for her to breathe, impossible to think. She had to leave, she had to find Damon. He would right things for her. He always did. She could not outwit the two of them by herself.

"I must go—" She began to rise from the table.

The earl pulled her back down beside him with a grip of steel at her elbow. He was smiling at her gently as he crushed the flesh at the tender crease of her arm. Haltingly she obeyed him, furious at his show of force, more furious at her inability to stop him.

"Solange," he said softly. "Look at me."

He waited, then took his other hand to physically turn her face to his. He was careful not to bruise her cheeks.

Solange met his eyes reluctantly, keeping her chin tucked down. The curious sense of light-headedness enveloped her again, the haze of him now surrounding them both. The earl gave her a wide, attractive smile. He had large teeth.

"An angel so lovely should not spoil her looks with disagreeable tempers. It is neither becoming, nor wise. You are a true beauty, Solange. You may depend upon me to see to it that you are always thus." The grip on her cheeks became a caress. "You will see me tomorrow morning bright and fair, as a blushing bride is always eager to meet her husband."

Once more it seemed to her that his eyes had no color, no life of their own, yet they held her spellbound, drew her into their bottomless depths.

"You will be there, Solange. I promise it."

His thumb traced the outline of her lower lip in a terrible parody of the loving stroke Damon had given her earlier. Redmond leaned down toward her, his fingers now framing her mouth.

She pulled away, shaking her head. "You go too fast, my lord." Her cheeks flared bright red, not with embarrassment, but anger. She gestured mutely to the attentive crowd below them.

The earl followed the wave of her hand, then sighed. "Perhaps you are right. We will save the fastness, then, for another time."

She stood quickly, before either man could think of something else to stay her. "I would retire early, Father."

Henry stared at her, then at the earl. His face was inscrutable. "Go, then. Tomorrow will be busy enough."

She dipped a careless curtsy in the general direction of them both, then fled the great hall. The earl watched her slender form silently, noting the naturally graceful sway of her hips, the proud set of her shoulders.

"She will be there," he said again quietly.

"Aye," said her father.

Chapter Two

She could not get warm. The fire had died in her chambers while she was gone, leaving only smoldering embers in the bed of the fireplace. None of the servants would come to relight it, since they were all busy downstairs helping with the feast.

Not that she wanted them there anyway. Her primary concern, the thought that kept her chilled feet moving, was getting to Damon.

Solange stripped off her confining clothes as quickly as she could, tossing the belt and garments in a tangle on the covers and furs of her feather bed. From the bottom of a huge leather clothing trunk she pulled a pair of thick woolen stockings and a large tunic, followed by a pair of soft-soled leather boots. All were dyed to muted, dark colors.

These were her prowling clothes. Damon knew her penchant for stargazing from odd locations, and had presented them to her the previous spring when he discovered she was tying her skirts up past her knees for ease of movement whenever she sneaked out.

He told her he had been haunted by visions of her

being discovered that way by a guardsman, or worse, the cumbersome skirts making her lose her footing on any of the narrow ledges or trees she liked to crawl about. He had given her the clothes one night as she came to visit, cautioning her to always wear them instead of her usual feminine garments when she wanted to venture out unnoticed.

Solange had been completely delighted. The men's clothing had freed her in a way she had never imagined. Her entire life she had worn only the finest of garments, but they were still the heavy skirts, the tight oversleeves, the multiple layers of cloth on cloth common to noblewomen. Her gowns were designed for fashion and modesty, not comfort.

Now she shivered into the men's clothing as quickly as she could. The tunic settled over her shoulders in a cloud of soft cotton. She added a dark brown woolen vest from the trunk for warmth. A cape might be too noticeable, and certainly too much material to worry about. The boots came on last, hugging her legs up past her knees.

The window by the bower had been left open, and now a chilled breeze circled her, wafting through the silver wedge of moonlight slanting across a patterned Turkish rug on the floor.

It was a clear night. But the weather could shift in a heartbeat. The following day could bring rain or snow, or perhaps the last of the fair days of early winter. But of all things, it absolutely could not be her wedding day.

She didn't bother to stuff a pillow under the covers of her bed to substitute for her sleeping form as she usually did. Haste made her impatient, and so she was almost discovered by the grumbling guard outside her room before she discovered him.

She backed away from the entrance as quickly as she could, holding her breath. Lord, she hadn't even been careful in opening the heavy wooden door. The sheer weight of it necessitated her inching it open, which is what saved her.

Solange pushed the oak door shut again, praying the hinges would not choose just then to let out a squeak for oiling. The door swung closed with an almost silent click.

She pressed her ear to the crack but heard nothing unusual from the guard. Her breath came out in a silent rush; she leaned against the door for strength until her knees quit shaking.

A guard, indeed! One of her father's men, looking none too pleased to be pulled away from his supper. A serious strategic move on the part of Henry, but she wasn't beaten yet. He obviously expected her to try to bolt, but in honesty Solange hadn't considered anything that drastic. Damon held the key to right this problem. But how to get to him?

Solange went over to the bed and sat down, reconsidering her options. She drew her legs up to her chin and wrapped her arms about them, trying to warm herself in the cold air. Another breeze drifted past the leaded glass window.

Her lips pursed thoughtfully, but she had already made her decision. It was her only choice, really. She hadn't climbed out there since one moonless night a few years before, when she had almost fallen to the cobblestone courtyard below. She had grabbed a loose stone as a handhold and it had nearly meant her death. No one but Damon ever knew of it, but the incident had put enough fear into her not to venture out that way again.

She imagined the stones had not grown any tighter over the past few years, but circumstances were desperate and so was she. She bit her lip for courage.

This time she was careful to tuck two pillows beneath the covers before she left, just in case.

The view from the window was breathtaking. Her chambers occupied not quite a full fifth of the upper floor of one of the four walls of the castle. Directly below her was the usually raucous inner courtyard, which bustled with village folk and nobles alike during daylight hours. At night it was deserted except for an occasional soldier on guard duty, making lonely rounds.

Beyond the castle gate was the meandering cluster of squat buildings that made up the village, a sizable one by common standards. Past that spread the gracious landscape of England in its full beauty. Even in winter Solange saw wonder in the frosted grass, the bare limbs of the trees softly glowing in the moonlight. The line of the forest trees was cut back unevenly, giving tantalizing glimpses into the darkened world beyond.

It was a world Solange had visited many times, but never enough to satisfy her love of nature and of all living things. The wild forest paths were as familiar to her as her own face, but she always managed to discover a new marvel whenever she went out.

Of course, Henry knew nothing of this. To the best of his knowledge, his daughter spent her time doing all the proper things a young gentlewoman should. Occasional reports of her absences reached him, but whenever he bothered to summon her for questioning, she always assured him she was off reading, in private.

At least Henry himself had scoffed at the notion of keeping his only child uneducated and had hired a tutor specifically to teach both her and his ward to read not just English but Latin, in addition to the regular studies of science, mathematics, and religious philosophy. It would prove to be one of the few occasions in his life when he broke with tradition, but nevertheless it remained a godsend for Solange, who, along with Damon, had already devoured most of the scrolls, manuscripts, and books available in the castle.

The meetings between Solange and her father were invariably the same. She would be summoned to his private study, alone. The marquess remained seated behind an enormous table of mahogany, framed on either side by two giant royal family crests draped from the fringed tapestries behind him. The crests held dancing green and yellow lions and griffins—all with fearsome teeth—on a background of royal blue. It was an intimidating effect for any visitor, and Solange was not immune to it.

The study always reminded her of the things she was expected to become; things that held infinite rules that all circled back on each other, as inescapable as a Celtic knot.

Her father would ask why she never arrived for Lady Matilda's sewing lesson, or Lady Josephine's singing lesson or whatever it was. Solange would wait for her list of transgressions to end, then state simply that she had been reading and had forgotten about the lessons.

Henry would rub his beard and then nod absently. He would tell her for the thousandth time that although the ladies of the castle didn't approve of her literacy, he didn't see anything wrong with it. Then she was dismissed. Until the next time.

Tonight the forest looked blackly obscure, even to Solange. A shiver overtook her as she leaned uncertainly out the bower window. An examination of the stones below her revealed nothing. The moonlight created harsh shadows that left the rock looking pitted and scarred, manifesting the illusion of niches in the wall where actually there were none.

It was going to be a perilous climb, no doubt, but she only had to go down one floor to get to an unguarded room. Right below her chambers was the library, which would almost certainly be empty at this hour.

She hooked one leg over the sill and then paused, listening. She could swear she heard horses, several of them, running for the gate of the castle.

The guard below heard them too, and summoned help to open the gate.

Solange pulled her leg back in quickly, then ducked down to watch the courtyard unseen.

Men were greeting one another in cheerful tones, although she couldn't quite make out what they were saying. The horses clattered through the open gate and onto the cobblestones, snorting and prancing about impatiently. It was a hunting party, from the looks of it.

One rider had a familiar posture, ramrod straight in the saddle but without stiffness, powerful and in control of his giant sorrel gelding.

Damon! She raised her head farther, confirming it was he. No one else seemed such an innate extension of his horse but Damon, a naturally gifted rider.

He turned his head and looked up toward her window, the moonlight bringing to bold relief the planes of his face, the waves of hair curling down to his collar. Solange remained where she was, willing him to see her, unwilling to draw the attention of the other men.

He didn't see her.

He dismounted with the other men and disappeared into the castle, talking with the others. A group of stableboys led the horses away.

She withdrew from the bower and ran lightly to the door, again pressing her ear to the wood.

The volume of the party in the hall decreased momentarily, then swelled anew. That would be the mark that the riders had entered the hall, and were probably now reporting to her father. Over it all she could hear the restless footsteps of the guard, moving away from her door.

Slowly, so slowly she closed her eyes and measured the time and space with her whole body, Solange pried the door open a scant inch. A rush of heated air pushed through the opening, lifting wisps of hair off her forehead, warming her cheeks. She pressed her face against the crack.

She couldn't see the guard. Her narrow field of vision included just the wall opposite, and part of a burning torch. The door opened enough to let her see with both eyes now; she tilted her head sideways to get a better angle.

There he was, standing down the hall at the top of the stairs. He obviously wished to be down there with the new arrivals. The guard shifted from foot to foot, then leaned over curiously to hear better.

He threw a glance over his shoulder and Solange pulled back swiftly. This corner of the door was in shadow, and there was no noticeable light coming from her chambers. The guard, who had been well into his fourth cup of ale before he was ordered up there, noticed nothing unusual.

Solange silently counted to thirty in Latin, then braved another look.

He had taken several steps down the stairs. He was visible only from the knees up, his back to her.

She saw her chance. Before she could reconsider, she slipped out the door and shut it gently behind her. The guard still did not turn. As soon as she heard the familiar click of the latch closing, she dashed down the hall in the opposite direction from the guard, running on her toes for silence. There were no cries of alarm, no sounds of pursuit.

She paused, panting, at the entrance of a narrow tunnel that burrowed through the spine of the castle, all the way around. It was old, and seldom used. Solange knew it by heart, which was fortunate tonight, since the length of it was utterly black.

The darkness didn't bother her. She walked forward

confidently, supporting herself on both sides with her arms outstretched against the stone walls.

Damon's chambers were in the wing adjacent to hers, one floor down, but not too far away. Several times she had to clear away the cobwebs that stuck to her face, and more than once she stumbled over an uneven stone in the floor. Nothing broke her pace, however. Damon was close, and so salvation was near.

Finally she reached the narrow stairs leading down to the outer rooms of the main hall. Here and there torches began to appear again, leaning away from her in their gutters, following the draft.

"Almost there, almost there," she chanted under her breath. Ahead loomed a giant hallway that led to the main artery of the castle. She moved cautiously now, observing the flow of people passing by the opening, intent on their own business. An occasional burst of drunken laughter rebounded down the tunnel. It seemed even the torch flames shivered.

Here! She had reached Damon's door. Her fingers clenched on the latch and squeezed. It was locked—no, only stuck, for the door moved slightly when she put her shoulder to it.

Someone was coming.

A man and a woman appeared at the end of the hall, holding each other close. Their coy laughter carried, and she knew that she had to disappear now. In desperation, Solange heaved at the door with all her might. It opened. She fell inside, then whirled and shut it just as the couple passed.

They walked on down the hall, his low tones mingling with her giggles until they could be heard no more.

Solange leaned her head against the wooden planking, breathing heavily from an equal combination of exertion and fear.

After a moment she turned, taking in the details of the room, noting the low fire, the simple arrangement of Damon's few belongings scattered neatly throughout. The familiar goodness of the surroundings began to seep into her system, calming her.

Damon kept his room deliberately spartan. There were, for example, none of the plush luxuries that decorated her own, like the sumptuous curtains and tapestries, the polished oak bed frame, the numerous carpets she loved with colors so deep and vibrant they seemed to eat up the chill from the stones beneath them.

No, nothing very much like that here, although he could have had those things if he so desired. But Damon preferred his surroundings more stark. Even so, Solange could appreciate the easy harmony of it. And there were a few drops of whimsy here and there.

Here, on the table by the window where he liked to study, was a collection of colorful stones laid out in a straight line from one end of the tabletop to the other. Solange recognized each one of them, since all had been her gifts to him over the years. No two were alike—some crystalline, some fancy colored, striped or spotted, others plainer, yet all contained a beauty she had been compelled to share with him. He had received each one as a solemn treasure, always discussing the merits of each as she found them.

He kept them by the window, he told her, because when the sun laid across them they lit up his room like a symphony of nature.

There, by his pillow, was the linen handkerchief she had embroidered for him with his name over a year before. In honesty, Solange thought it a pitiful example of needlework, but at the time she had been proud enough to present it to him. It was almost embarrassing to look at now, the sloppy stitches, the uneven lines. Yet he kept it always by his pillow.

And here, on a group of sturdy tables placed against the far wall, was his vast collection of herbs, all neatly jarred or kept from the light in leather pouches. There were well over two hundred of them, a botanical array that added the spirit of decoration to his chambers, if not the intent.

Propped up outside each container was a stiff piece of vellum folded in half, naming the leaf or flower or root within. She had labored over the labels for weeks, writing both the Latin and English names, attempting careful little drawings on the edges to illustrate each herb.

She noticed absently how faded the ink had gotten. She must see about starting some new ones for him.

The dwindling fire drew her to crouch by the hearth. She was sweating and shivering all at once, holding her hands out to absorb what she could from the sullen flames. But the shaking would not leave her body.

Solange stared blankly ahead, seeing not the cherry glow before her, but the empty, colorless eyes of the earl. Her father's words reverberated all around her, announcing her marriage to this person . . . her marriage . . .

You will become the wife of Redmond . . .

And the earl's chilling smile, his quiet voice: *You will be there . . . I promise . . .*

Her teeth began to chatter convulsively, but she didn't notice.

The door to the chamber slammed open, hitting the wall with a startling *crack!* Damon strode into the room still wearing his riding cape, rage apparent in every step. He kicked the door shut behind him, not seeing her small form by the fire.

He looked magnificent. Gone was the shadow of his youthful years. Solange saw a man coming toward her, a man with a bitter look she was unaccustomed to seeing on his face.

She stood.

For a moment Damon was dumbfounded. He halted abruptly, simply staring at her, then squinting, attempting to see if she was a trick of his will.

Solange stood awkwardly, as if unsure of her welcome. She was wringing her hands together, something she did only when she was unusually nervous. The slender elegance of her figure was outlined by the firelight.

He didn't know what to do, what to think. The news of her engagement to Redmond was being toasted again and again in the great hall, and he had been turned away by the guard at her door when he went to confirm the story with her. His stomach was a sick ache; he couldn't believe she would refuse to see him.

But here she was, not in her chambers after all. The truth of that thought slowly drifted though his mind, coalescing on the image of Solange standing there, in front of him. She was here. She had come to him.

A log in the fire popped loudly and fell apart, releasing a shower of sparks around her.

The pleasure of her presence overwhelmed him, making him drop the longbow and sack of arrows he had been carrying from the late-night hunt. He stepped away from them and opened his arms to her.

Solange needed no further encouragement. She flew to him.

Her embrace was a heady relief.

Damon leaned his cheek against her hair, closing his eyes, inhaling her scent. He turned his face and kissed her hair lightly, over and over.

He smelled of horses and sweat, an earthy odor that she appreciated more than she ever thought she would. He was here, he was holding her, and everything was going to be all right. The shivers had stolen the momentum that brought her there and left her body empty, but Damon gladly took her weight.

She would not cry. She would not.

She did anyway.

His fingers caught on the golden net binding her hair, she had forgotten to take it off. Carefully he pulled the pins loose from the sable strands, capturing the net and then tossing it aside.

Her hair unfurled, cascading down in a glossy waterfall, clinging to them both. Her shoulders shook with her quiet sobs, and it began to register on Damon that they had a true problem, despite the bliss of comforting her.

He led her over to the bed and sat her down gently. She wouldn't let go of his tunic until he knelt in front of her, and even then she clutched his sleeve with one clenched fist. He might have murmured sweet words to her, he wasn't certain.

Her distress consumed him. He had to stop it. Her head remained bowed, but the sobs were diminishing. He stroked her hands, her face, until she quieted.

"Solange," he said softly.

Her name on his lips nearly brought her to tears again, absurdly enough. The longing in his voice was such a contrast to the strangeness with which the earl had said her name.

She stifled the panic building in her throat. "Did you hear?" she asked instead.

He concentrated on wiping away her tears. He couldn't answer right away, the emotions were still too raw. She waited.

"Yes," he admitted finally.

Her breath came out in a rush; she pulled his hand down from her face and held on to it. "What are we to do, Damon?"

Her implicit trust in him warmed him as much as it created a fear of failure. He needed to get facts. "You really knew nothing of this plan before this evening?"

"Nothing, I swear! Father has never mentioned marriage to me before now. He barely speaks to me at all. And none of the others would speak to me of it, as you know. I met the man for the first time tonight and even still they did not consult me, but began to bandy about the word as if it were a foregone conclusion." She shuddered, remembering her humiliation. "I would never marry a man like him!"

"Who would you marry, then, Solange?"

She looked away. Her fingers plucked at the folds of the quilt on the bed.

"Who?" he asked again, his entire being waiting for her answer.

Her face grew troubled once more, but then she gave an uncertain smile. "There is only you."

It was the answer he craved, the one he needed to go forward with his plan, but it still left him momentarily winded. He folded both of her hands together and pressed them against his forehead, thanking the Lord, thanking her. After a moment he got off his knees and went to one of the large trunks resting against the wall by the bed. He opened it and reached in, feeling through the clothes for the small leather pouch that he had been worrying about for months now.

He found it and shut the trunk, coming back to her. With her large, solemn eyes and loose hair draping her shoulders she seemed to him a kind of saint, a beauty too fragile to remain long in this world. The thought chilled him, but he brushed it aside, coming again to kneel before her.

"This is for you," he said simply, and placed the pouch in her hands.

She gave him a questioning look but said nothing, turning the little bag over in her hands to get the feel of it. She loosened the drawstring at the neck of it and shook out a ring into her open palm.

He was sorry he couldn't do better. It wasn't a grand ring, in his opinion, but he had immediately thought of her when he saw it for sale at the summer festival several months past. It did not sparkle and shine like the jewelry women usually favored. Rather, it had an unusual design and a bloodred stone that glowed like the sunsets Solange loved. It had taken all his spare coin and several head of sheep to get it, but he thought it worth it now for the look on her face.

The ring was delicate but ornate, gold with an oval cabochon of garnet in the center and two small pearls surrounded by raised golden petals on each side. The rounded cut of the deep red garnet drew the weak light into itself. It gleamed mysteriously, set off by the silver-white pearls.

It was the most beautiful thing she had ever seen. She touched the gilded patterns of it reverently, contrasting the slickness of the garnet with the hard, intricate shapes of the gold. Finally she looked up at him, incredulous that he could give her something so obviously rare.

Damon plucked the ring from her palm and slid it onto her finger. "I got it when I went with the wool-selling party to the festival last summer. A Gypsy was selling gold from his cart, and this ring was in a basket with some other things, not nearly as nice."

Still she said nothing, so he added, "I was hoping you would like it."

"I have never seen anything so fine as this," she said, and meant it.

Together they stared at the ring on her finger and considered what it meant to them now. How odd that a band of gold, even one as lovely as this, could change her life and fortune, Solange thought. She welcomed the newness of it, closing her fingers in a fist.

A sense of rightness filled Damon, as if seeing the

ring at last on her hand was as natural as breathing. She was wearing his troth now, and both of them knew it.

Solange slid off the bed onto her knees in front of him. She rested her head on his chest and held him as close as she could manage.

"I will speak to Henry tonight," he said, gathering her closer. "I'll tell him how we feel about each other. I'll tell him we were waiting to announce it to him a little later, and how his plans with Redmond have taken us by surprise. He must understand."

"He wants the lands," Solange said into his chest. "Father indicated the match would join our lands together, forming an alliance."

Both of them knew the importance of this. Alliances between neighboring nobles could make or break a fiefdom, and if the lands were already bordering each other, so much the stronger could the alliance become.

"He can have my lands for an alliance," Damon said fiercely. "He can have them in *forfeit,* if he wants."

"Damon, no—"

"Yes! But I think he'll realize how much smarter it would be to have us living there, working with him. I'll give him a portion of the crops, of the herds, the rents, whatever he wants."

"Truly?" His generosity of sacrifice for her was unbelievable.

"Truly. I will persuade him to see reason. He cannot be so cold to keep us apart. We belong together, Solange, and no man anywhere can ever change that."

"I know," she replied. "I've always known."

The depths of her eyes told him it was true, she did feel the power between them as he did. He kissed her lips once, then once again, relishing the sweet taste of her.

The dark magic was beginning to weave around them again. Damon broke the hold, unwilling to surrender to it yet. There were too many plans to make right now. And there was the marquess to consider.

That sobered him. Despite his determined words, Damon realized it was going to be extraordinarily difficult to persuade her father to let him have Solange as his bride and leave the earl empty-handed.

In fact, Damon was certain Redmond would not be willing to leave with nothing at all. He would demand respite for his troubles, for traveling out in expectation of a wedding that never took place. He would demand compensation of some sort, for that was the only way he could salvage his pride.

Damon had to come up with something to offer him, something so impressive, he wouldn't miss marrying the daughter of a powerful, wealthy nobleman. Hidden deep in the corners of his mind was a nagging, malicious voice that told him he really had nothing to offer either the marquess or the earl in exchange for Solange, nothing at all.

He stood, and pulled her up with him. "We must get you back to your chambers. You need to get some sleep tonight, for we don't know what tomorrow will bring."

Solange felt a chill at his words, which echoed almost exactly her own thoughts earlier. When she had thought it, a sense of resolution had filled her. Now, hearing Damon say it, all she felt was foreboding.

He was ushering her toward the door, one arm

around her waist. She stopped him from opening it by stepping in between him and the handle.

"Damon. It will work, will it not?"

He cupped her cheek with one hand. She was his hope, his future, his whole life.

"Aye," he said. "It will."

Chapter Three

True to the earl's words, the morning dawned bright and fair, if crisply cold. Golden lances of sunlight reached across the room to warm Solange's bed cozily. She was used to this effect and had perfected a way of sleeping with her head under the covers to block the early morning sun. Solange was a typically heavy sleeper, and it took her maid several minutes to rouse her enough to accept the mug of bitter tea that she liked to drink every morning upon awakening.

" 'Tis a shame to sleep so late, especially on this morning, milady." Adara seemed in an excellent mood for a change, even chipper.

Solange rubbed her eyes and wondered at that. "What is so special about this morning, then?" Was it her birthday? Was it someone else's?

The old woman clicked her tongue. "Tch! As if ye could truly forget, little slypuss! Why, mistress, the priest is already in the chapel. He came before dawn. Today is the day of yer wedding to the man!"

Everything came back to Solange in a rush, causing

her to choke on her tea. Indeed, how could she have forgotten?

Last night marked the beginning of the rest of her life as far as she was concerned. She quickly checked her hand, and yes, there it was, the glorious ring Damon had given her. She had not dreamed it after all. Her heart filled with exultation.

After Damon had escorted her back to her room—he distracted the guard while she slipped through the door—he must have sought out her father, as planned. As she lay in her bed last night, she had prayed and prayed for her father to accept Damon's suit, until exhaustion had at last swept her into unconsciousness.

Please God, let it have worked.

Adara had gone to the dressing chamber and was busy fussing over something Solange could not see.

"A pity," the maid was muttering to herself. "Look at this hole here. The thread is loose enough to cast a net, I'll warrant."

Suddenly Solange leapt out of bed and ran over, grabbing Adara by the shoulders and spinning her around. "Tell me! Tell me who it is!"

Adara eyed her wildly, backing up. "Eh? Who?"

"The man! Who is the man I am to wed today?"

Solange could not know how she looked at that moment to the superstitious peasant woman. The devil's magic she was said to possess surely flowed around her now, with her hair crackling and her eyes like golden flames. Without meaning to, Adara crossed herself.

"The man, mistress, the man from Redmond, of

course. He is the man ye met last night, do ye not recall? A fine man, a fit husband for ye."

"Redmond," Solange repeated, aghast.

Adara moved over to the chair taking up most of the dressing chamber. She indicated a stiff bundle of scarlet cloth draped across it. "This be yer mother's gown, mistress, from her wedding these years past. My lord himself wanted ye to wear it today. I've done the best I could with it, I have," she added defensively. " 'Tis an old gown, and not in best repair. A French thing, no doubt. But it will fit ye."

"Redmond," said Solange again before her knees gave out and she sank to the floor. The woolen skirts of her nightgown pooled around her waist. She buried her face in her hands.

Adara rolled her eyes fearfully and began to curtsy her way out of the chamber. "Yer father bids ye to dress quickly. I will return in a few minutes to help ye."

"Wait!" Solange scrambled to her feet and caught the woman before she had made it to the door. "I want you to deliver a message to my father. I want you to tell him I must see him immediately."

"Milady, the marquess is off preparing for the wedding—"

"I don't care about that! Tell him that I will not dress, I will not be ready until he comes to me, do you understand? I will not do one little thing until he arrives. You tell him for me."

The maid gaped at her.

"Please," Solange begged. "Go tell him."

Adara collected herself and nodded, eager to leave.

Solange let go of her arm. As she exited, Solange noticed a new guard outside her door, standing firm with bored resolution.

She was trapped there until Henry came. Her mind raced in circles around the mystery of what was said between Damon and her father. Poor Damon, he obviously had not been able to convince Henry of the sincerity of his offer for her. She would do it herself. He would listen to her, the child of his flesh.

He would not be pleased, no, to give up the Redmond lands, but she would show him how Damon's holdings would be vastly more suitable, in the long run, for an alliance. Somehow.

She could not marry the earl. All that she was lived with the spirit of Damon. Redmond had nothing of his soul, nor his beauty. Damon had been there her entire life. If she were separated from him, she surely would wither away to a dry cusp of herself, a starving specter.

She paced the room impatiently, then caught a flash of herself in the standing glass. Her hair was disheveled, her feet bare, and she was still in her nightgown. She realized that she would make a better impression if she were a little more presentable.

She hurried over to the ceramic basin and splashed her face with the cool water, then dragged a comb through her thick tresses, throwing the mass of it over her shoulders when she was finished. She didn't have time to change clothes, however, for by then Henry had arrived.

He didn't bother to knock.

"What is this, daughter? Your woman comes to me

in a frenzy and tells me you will not dress, nor do aught, until I come. Well, I am here. Explain yourself."

He was already wearing his wedding finery, a fancy blue and green tunic with split puffed sleeves, all stitched with threads of gold. A heavy gold belt, studded with lapis and malachite, secured the long tunic over his dark blue hose. Solange approached him cautiously.

"Father. I have an urgent matter to speak to you of before this morning's events can go forward."

He walked over to her bed slowly, taking in her room with an exacting eye. He had not been in here for years, it seemed, since she was a child. Apparently it had gotten no neater since then. He removed the comb from the edge of the bed and sat down amid the tousled covers and furs, crossing his legs.

"Yes?"

"Did Damon speak with you last night?"

His expression did not change. "Yes."

She waited, but it appeared that was all he had to say. "Well, then, may I ask what occurred? Did he tell you we are already betrothed to each other?"

"Yes, he did."

Solange raised her winged eyebrows, attempting to match his coolness. "And, what happened?"

"I told him it was inappropriate, of course. Neither of you has the right to contract a betrothal on your own."

"The *right*?"

"In addition to that," he continued smoothly, "a marriage between the two of you is completely out of the question. You are my daughter, Solange. You will become a great heiress someday. Damon is a good boy, of noble stock, but his lineage is tainted with rumors of druid blood. Redmond's line is pure. Most certainly Damon's lands cannot even come close to the earl's. When it does come time for the boy to marry, he will do fine with one of the minor noblewomen hanging about the castle." Henry waved his hand in the air.

"No," said Solange very calmly. "He will not. I love him and he loves me. Bloodlines mean nothing to me. We cannot be married to anyone but each other."

"You are quite wrong, my dear." The marquess stood up. He sounded almost indifferent. "You are going to be married to the Earl of Redmond on this very morning, in just over an hour, I think. The preparations are nearly complete."

"I won't do it," she said, fighting to keep the fear from her voice.

"You will, Solange." Suddenly his temper snapped, betraying the anger that had been buried under his casual demeanor. "By God, I have put up with your tempers and your moods long enough! Perhaps it is my fault for allowing you so much freedom growing up. It has poisoned your mind and spoiled your sweetness. That will end today. I am taking in the reins with you, daughter, and passing them on to a man who knows full well how to control your willfulness. You are fortunate that Redmond is eager to have you, not just the lands."

Her heart was pounding. "Father, please, just listen to me—"

"I have heard enough! You will do as I bid, and that is all!"

She threw herself at his feet. "Please don't do this! I can't marry him—"

He shook her off. "You can. You'll see."

"No." The hated tears were starting again.

Henry picked her up off the floor and pushed her gently over to the bed. "Let me say it this way to you, Solange. This match means a great deal to me. A great deal. My father, your grandfather, dreamed of owning the land Redmond now controls. A good many men died in those days, your grandfather's men, trying to claim it. Now, through you, we will at last have what they gave their lives for. Our descendants will rule Wellburn Castle, and all the lands with it. A lifetime of wishes is about to come true, through your body."

"That's what I am to you? A body?" She had stopped crying. "Have you no heart at all?"

Henry scowled at her.

"Land is what matters, foolish child," he snapped. "Land is power. Did I waste my good gold on those tutors I hired for you? Remember your history, Solange. Men with land are men with money, and money equals power. Power like mine, and Redmond's." He paused, and lowered his face level to hers.

"Power like Damon of Lockewood wants but does not have."

Their eyes met and clashed, exactly matched in both color and pride. But Henry had an unbeatable advantage, and he chose now to play it.

"You will marry Redmond this morning." He bit off each word, measuring their effect on her. "You will do it without tears, without sighs and moans. You will do this, or I will toss your Damon out of the castle this very minute with nothing more than the clothes on his back."

"You would not," she gasped.

"You know I would. He is a man now, and I have no further obligation to him."

It would be a death sentence, and they both knew it. No villager, no peasant, would dare take in someone who had so displeased the Marquess of Ironstag. There was no other shelter for miles and miles around, several days' worth of traveling. He had nowhere to go; he would live only as long as his skills allowed him to. True winter was only days away; no one caught out in the open would survive the savage storms that whipped over the fields here. No matter how many precautions were taken, seasoned men were lost every winter due to the sudden blizzards. Damon could never make it to safe haven in time, much less his own lands.

"I would give him nothing, Solange. Not food, not water, not clothing, not bows nor arrows, not a horse. Nothing. All his herbs, that impressive collection, would be burned in the courtyard." He cocked an eyebrow at her ill-concealed surprise. "Oh, yes, I know about his pharmacopoeia, and about his imprudent ambitions to become a physician. I am not quite so isolated from castle society as I seem to be."

Her limbs were numb, as if they no longer were a part of her body, but rather just pieces of flesh belonging to someone else. She pressed her fingernails into the palms of her hands, trying to feel some other pain than her father's words.

"And were you to devise some foolhardy plan of running away together . . . well, I think we both know how easy it would be to find you. And my punishment then would be much more severe."

"Father." Her voice was a thready whisper.

"Would you do that to him, my dear? Would you sentence him to die like a stray dog in the wild?"

It smothered her: the image of Damon in rags, living in the dirt, worse than the most wretched of serfs. Succumbing to the inevitable. Lying dead in the snow, his perfect face frozen, his body left to be picked apart as food for scavengers . . .

Henry noted with satisfaction the torment etched on her face and resumed his indifferent air. "You decide, Solange. But before you do, let me tell you something else."

He backed away and walked over to the window, as if to admire the view. Leaning his weight against his elbow, he addressed his remarks to the square of hard blue sky outside.

"If, on the other hand, you do as I command you to, Damon will have quite a different life from the one I just described. You know I can see to that as well. If you wed Redmond today with no more fuss, then I will use my power to help Damon. I will supply him with horses and men, food, armaments, whatever he needs to ride to Wolfhaven, or even to the king himself, to reclaim his lands. I will give him all these things for free, for as long as he needs them. I will use my influence—influence about to be made significantly more powerful by your marriage—to help oust the lords who have stolen the fringes of his estate. I will also inform the king that Damon Wolf has my full support in these matters."

A long pause.

"I see," Solange said.

"And, in his own castle, with no one else to rule over him but our good King Edward, he will have a measure of freedom he has never tasted before. He may cultivate his own crops, collect his own rents." Henry cleared his throat delicately. "He may even practice medicine all he wants. Who knows? Perhaps one day, with enough experience, he would become a truly outstanding healer."

She stared at him wordlessly.

"And naturally, if you choose this path for Damon, you will not mention this conversation to him. We wouldn't want the boy to go off and get himself speared to death by one of Redmond's men over some youthful, misguided devotion to you, would we?"

Her eyes were glazed and vacant. Her father smiled to himself, tracing his fingers into the dust motes on the windowsill.

"Only you may say, Solange. You hold the power of not just his future but his very life in your small hands. What will you do with it? I wonder. How much do you really love him?"

THE WEDDING WAS MERCIFULLY SHORT.

The castle chapel had been built two centuries earlier by a more pious lord of Ironstag than the present one. No expense had been spared to make it one of the most lavish around, and the result was an overbearing mix of marbled suffering saints, depictions of scriptures on stained glass panes, and endless curlicue swirls on anything wooden. In the center of the pulpit hung a tremendous crucifix of gold leaf and rounded gems. The painted eyes of the hanging Christ were cast up mournfully to heaven, meant to remind that salvation was never painless.

Solange had never been comfortable amid all the fussy somberness, but now all she felt was emptiness where her heart and mind used to be. She concentrated on the cool, musty air filling her lungs in rhythmic expansions, on the abstract patterns of colored light falling all around her. What relief to feel like this, what blessing after the torment she had endured giving up the one thing in her world that had ever really mattered to her.

Damon was not there to witness the event. At least, she had not seen him as she walked down the chapel aisle on the arm of her father. The gilded room was far from empty, however. Every pew was fully crammed, and more people crowded in the back and spilled down the sides, all eager to witness a royal wedding. They gawked and whispered in a moving mass of ruffles and lace, wondering at the paleness of the bride, the fixed stare of her father.

Only the groom seemed truly pleased, regarding his bride with the proper sort of satisfaction that made several feminine hearts flutter with envy.

Except for one.

Lady Margaret had no envy in her heart today, only complete and utter satisfaction. Today was the end of a long series of events she had taken exquisite pains to begin over a year before. She watched the back of the bride stiffen as the marquess handed her over to the earl. Her lips curled into a cat's smile.

It was almost done now. How clever she was, she crowed silently, how terribly clever. It had been so much easier than she had hoped. Her hands smoothed the rich mauve velvet of her best overskirt on her lap, then reached up to adjust the fine veil covering her favorite headdress, one composed almost entirely of pearls.

Her eyes were green and bright, her cheeks flushed as a young girl's with self-pleasure. A flattering beam of pink light from a stained glass prophet's skirt cut down by chance though the chapel to surround her angelically. Many agreed among themselves that Henry's mistress had never looked better. She rather thought so herself.

It had been Lady Margaret who had first brought to Henry's attention the fact that his young daughter was rapidly budding into full womanhood. It was time, she declared one night in his bed, to give Solange what her heritage deserved: a hearth of her own to manage, a husband to provide her with sturdy, noble children.

Many of them.

It was for her own good, she argued in a voice rich with mock concern. The girl was growing up wild and unsupervised, surely he could see it? It would not be fair to Solange to allow her to continue like this.

Eventually, after more than a few nights of these soft

persuasions, coupled with Margaret's rather limber personal charms, Henry decided he agreed.

When she proposed the Earl of Redmond as a suitable candidate, Henry had more than agreed. It was a match he had been considering for some time. To have his mistress, a woman with her finger firmly on the pulse of society, confirm his thoughts cemented the idea in his head.

But he did not know that Margaret had already contacted Redmond regarding Solange.

She was a woman who understood men, and she had understood what Redmond wanted two years earlier, when she had first met him in London on a visit to court to wrap up the affairs of her recently deceased husband. A brutally handsome man, Redmond's strange, magnetic manner attracted the court ladies in droves. Yet he had rebuffed them all.

Margaret knew why.

The earl, with his cunning eyes and curling hair, had no use for women jaded by court life. Even the maidens there, simpering with their painted faces, held no appeal to him. He wanted someone fresh, someone completely innocent.

Her reasoning was close enough to the truth to hold the earl's attention when she approached him. Soon she had woven enough insinuations regarding Solange into her conversation that he was asking questions of his own, probing her further.

They had continued the conversation for months afterward, using his men as messengers, men who came to Ironstag as travelers, pilgrims, or tinkers.

It was no matter at all to have him come out to take a

look at Solange for himself. Margaret had offered to send him a miniature of the child, but Redmond had cordially refused, noting that more often than not painters would flatter their subjects until they became unrecognizable in person. His message to her stated he needed to evaluate Solange with his own eyes.

And he had insisted on anonymity to do it. Margaret was not to inform even the marquess that the Earl of Redmond was posing as a simple traveler in a rough group of men, all of whom were really his soldiers. Redmond claimed the ruse necessary in case he decided the girl did not suit him. He wanted no further ill feelings between the two families, he said.

Lady Margaret had politely sent back her full agreement to his condition, chuckling bitterly to herself at the notion that Solange would not suit the man. She knew what the odds of that were: none. Half the men of the castle were openly lusting after the girl, and the other half were too wary of her father to even be seen near her. For a good while now Margaret had watched enviously as grown men, men older than Henry, fell into strained silence whenever the child walked into a room. Amazingly enough, Solange never seemed to notice how none of the men could tear their eyes from her.

It was yet another sign to Margaret that the girl had no sense at all, but that was beside the point. The earl would prove to be no different from the others, Margaret thought, and she was correct.

Actually it had all been delightfully amusing at the time. There was Redmond, hunched in his plain brown hooded cloak over a meal of mutton stew and bread, eating with the common men in the greatroom.

And there was Solange, her nemesis, at the head table. Her silken hair was rolled loosely around her head, her perfect little body shown to ideal advantage in a flowing gown of pink and white. She laughed, she positively glittered during the meal, keeping up a steady flow of conversation with the ward of the marquess. She couldn't have looked more pure and virginal if she had tried.

Margaret was no fool. She understood the subtle power of this young woman, and she recognized the danger it represented to her. This was something that had to be eliminated as soon as possible. Fortunately the solution to her problem had been unable to stop gaping at Solange all evening. Margaret had a splendid time monitoring them both from the main table. Really, she could feel the earl's hunger for the girl all the way from there.

At the end of the meal, as they rose to retire, Redmond gave Margaret a brusque nod. She had merely smiled demurely in return.

After that, the rest was mere formality. Henry had already heartily embraced the notion of an alliance between the two families. Since Redmond had satisfied himself with examining the girl personally, the negotiations were conducted via messenger, the deal sealed in wax long before Henry thought he met his future son-in-law in the flesh. As far as Ironstag knew, he first saw the earl only an hour before his daughter did at that fateful supper the previous night.

Yes, the earl had been delighted to take Solange off her hands. That left only one real problem: Damon Wolf, Marquess of Lockewood, ward of Ironstag.

Naturally Margaret had noticed the way the two of them clung together. She noted his innate tendencies to protect her, his far from brotherly looks when he thought no one watched. For a good while she had even considered Lockewood as a marital possibility for Solange.

Solange, daughter of Jazel. Solange, the living porcelain image of her dead mother. Solange, with that breathtaking face, that translucent beauty, reminding Henry every day of his deceased wife, the French coquette.

Margaret had her heart set on the royal coronet of a marchioness, and she was convinced her lover's reticence to marriage was really due to some latent devotion to Jazel. The logic of it seemed simple enough. Get rid of the daughter, and the reminder would be gone. Henry would then reconsider his marital status, she was positive.

Therefore Damon Wolf would not do. Oh, his castle and his lands were dismal enough to wish on her worst enemy, but still on English soil, and therefore still conceivably close enough for visits.

Ah, but Redmond had promised her he would banish the girl to his French estate at his earliest possible convenience.

It had been Margaret who suggested to Henry to send Damon out with the hunting party for extra provisions last night before the earl arrived.

And it had been Margaret who suggested to Henry his terms of agreement for Solange, after Lockewood had left Henry's study in a fury over having his suit denied. Ironstag had come to her chambers full of shocked anger over the boy's proposal—he had not seen it coming, really, the man was as dense as his daughter at times—but he had left her later in a much better mood.

The cat's smile curled broader. Margaret lifted her hand and tapped her fingers lightly against her chin. The priest was still mumbling on in a monotone, putting half the congregation to sleep in spite of the importance of the moment.

But Lady Margaret was fully awake, enjoying the denouement of the show she herself had orchestrated. And it was stunning.

Solange concentrated on holding on to the feeling of nothingness that floated inside her. It was growing more and more difficult.

Her mother's wedding gown was cut from stiff velvet, designed for a different generation. It had a fitted waist formed by a thick satin sash that tied just under her breasts. The material had held up well over the years, hidden from light in a leather trunk so that the deep, rich red of it was as brilliant today as it was the day Jazel wore it. The ruby-colored velvet was as excellent a foil for the daughter as it had been for the mother, setting off the clarity of her skin and the darkness of her eyes.

Solange did not know, nor would she have cared about, what an exquisite picture she presented to the gathered assembly. Her chestnut hair tumbled freely down her back, as brides were allowed this one day to show off whatever beauty they may have regularly hidden under cones, veils, and headdresses. On her head was an elaborate full crown of flowers created from spun gold, with petals of sapphires, amethysts, and rubies, and leaves of emeralds. In the center of each flower was a large pearl. It was Redmond's bridal gift to her, she later discovered, a thing so delicate, she barely felt the weight of it.

Under her hand was his arm, solid, immovable. She felt the rigidity of it with the muscles in her palm; she felt how useless it would be to try to adjust things in any way. Redmond used his other hand to hold her fingers fixed on him, as if even now he did not believe she wouldn't run away. How different he felt from Damon's sinewy strength.

Oh, God, she could not think of Damon now. Not now.

Not after this morning, when he had come to her one final time.

She had been almost done dressing, ostensibly aided by a throng of women present to help prepare her for the wedding. Solange knew as much as anyone else that they were there to make sure she did exactly what she was expected to do. She did not require twelve women to help her dress.

She let their fawning attentions flow and eddy around her. They were the embodiment of her father's will, and so she allowed the women to giggle and touch her, adjusting her body, her arms, and legs like a wooden doll. They straightened her undertunic, slipped her feet into satin shoes, bedecked her with bracelets, rings, and a necklace, dabbed her body with perfumed oils that she would never ordinarily wear. Solange kept her gaze fixed on a point far outside herself, of this room.

From the hall came a duo of raised masculine voices.

She honed in immediately on Damon's tones, deep with anger. The bevy of women swirled to surround her with collective squeals of dismay as the door swung open.

Damon brushed past the still-protesting guard, knocking his hand away easily. He took in the protective cluster of women, then motioned them away.

"Leave us," he commanded.

None of the women moved, though several exchanged nervous glances.

Damon looked impatient, and took a few steps forward. The women backed up together, jostling Solange along with them. She struggled free, slapping away their restraining holds on her.

"Everything is fine," she said to them. "Go now. You may wait outside the door."

The leader of the group spoke. "We're not to leave you alone, milady. The marquess has so commanded it."

"Well, I will not be alone, will I? The Marquess of Lockewood will be here with me. Go."

Still they did not move. Solange threw up her hands in mock exasperation. "Merciful heavens, what do you think will happen? I am hardly likely to crawl out the window, now, am I?"

The women muttered uneasily among themselves, but with her urging were now shuffling out the door.

"Only a moment, my lady," called out the leader as Damon shut the door in her face. "We must be ready on time!" she yelled through the wood.

Solange and Damon faced each other across the expanse of her chambers. She was wearing an undertunic that was composed of layers of thin cotton and lace. It was demure enough but nevertheless provoked evocative thoughts in him. She rubbed absently at the collection of gold and pearl bracelets covering her arms. She wasn't wearing his ring.

"Talk to me," he commanded in that deep voice again. "Tell me what I am seeing is some sort of scheme to get out of the ceremony."

Solange steeled herself for her part in this charade. She turned around and wandered over to the dressing chamber, where the wedding gown was laid out in full splendor. "This is no scheme, I'm afraid," she said, running her fingernails through the scarlet velvet. They left a trail of ragged little furrows in the thick pile.

Damon stalked over to her and pulled her around to face him. "What are you doing, then? Are you going to marry him after all, after everything that happened between us last night?"

She stood stone still in his grip. "Yes, Damon, I am going to marry him. Father came by this morning and convinced me of it. I'm sorry."

"Sorry? You're sorry? What the hell has come over you? You can't marry that bastard, he wants only your money and your lands, you know that! He cannot love you. *I* love you, Solange."

He gripped her shoulders tightly, willing her to look into his eyes and read the truth there. But she was changed, different in some sly way he could not fathom.

"Love is irrelevant for marriage," she said. "I am well aware the earl is interested in my dowry far more than my person right now. That simply does not matter. Father has reminded me of my familial bonds. I will be strengthening the family with this union, and that is of tantamount importance." She shrugged. "We cannot control fate, and my fate is cast."

"What are you doing?" he rasped. "I cannot believe this is you talking."

"Damon, last night was an impetuous mistake for both of us. If I had been thinking clearly, I never would have bothered you at all. I'm afraid that the suddenness of it all overcame me, and naturally I turned to you for help. You have always been, after all, my older brother. I have always counted on you as such."

Her words cut him to the quick, as they had been designed to do. She broke away from his grip and went over to her night table. She closed her fingers over something, then glided back to him, graceful as a swan on water. In her outstretched hand she offered him the ring he had given her.

"Take it back," she said. "I cannot accept it."

His life was shattering to fragments around him, cutting him deeper and deeper, bleeding his very soul dry. She held her arm motionless, waiting for him to take the ring from her palm. His throat closed; he had to blink to clear his vision. She was making the choice for him, he realized. He could not fight for her if she did not want him.

She did not want him. She did not want him, when he would have gladly given his very life for her with the snap of her fingers.

She was choosing to become the plaything of a stranger rather than accept him. His pride finally rebelled at this indignity. Ignoring her offering, he snatched her by the waist and pulled her roughly against him.

She recovered her balance quickly and attempted to escape his hold, but he grabbed the hair at the nape of her neck and held her head in place as his lips claimed hers.

The garnet ring hit the floor with a muffled chime and rolled, unnoticed, in a wide half-circle away from them. It tumbled over against the bedpost, masked in the pattern of the carpet.

He put his anger into the kiss, along with the anguish he couldn't conceal. He was ruthless, plundering her mouth again and again, trying to force her to reveal something of her true self. He would conquer this foreignness in her, he would make her respond to him with the passion he knew she felt for him.

It was almost her undoing. She held her arms out stiffly from them both, her fingers spread wide. With every last ounce of her willpower Solange fought the drugging desire he produced in her. This was Damon, the other half of her soul. How easy it would be to just give up, to submit to the darkness washing over her, to let go of it all and kiss him back. And what could her father really do to them that would be worse than separation? Her own life was of little importance to her without Damon, but his survival depended on her now. . . .

Damon ended the kiss by pressing his face against her neck, a rough feeling that made her shiver. "I am not your brother, you know that," he whispered harshly. "Run away with me! Come away and be my wife."

He couldn't see, but her face twisted in pain, her

mouth opened on a soundless cry of grief. Her father would hunt them down, she knew, aided by Redmond. They would be caught and punished before they got far, she would be forced to marry the earl anyway, and Damon—

"Solange, I need you. You need me in spite of what you say." Damon shook her gently, then rocked her close again. "Come with me. We can do it."

"No." She struggled to push herself away from him. "You ask too much! It's not *worth* it to me!" She pushed her hair back with trembling hands and said wildly, "Don't you understand? You are not worth the sacrifice! I don't want you!"

His face turned ashen before her eyes.

"It is impossible. Please go now." She tucked her hands behind her back to keep them from reaching for him.

He stood mute, unmoving. She took another step away from him.

"I'm sorry, Damon. I must prepare for my wedding now. You must go."

Time suspended, brittle as December grass. Seasons of knowledge of each other tumbled and fused with dreams of their future together. Gossamer dreams, so fragile. Then the moment shattered, everything blown away with her unyielding refusal.

"My apologies," he said presently. "I didn't mean to disturb you."

He turned and left the chamber, walking quietly into the midst of the waiting women outside.

He closed the door behind him.

Solange stood still amid the rubble of her dreams. She felt an aching pride at her performance, just before the choking cry trapped in her throat overtook her. She ran over to the bed and smothered her face in the furs, burying the sound in the pelts. Her body bowed with racking, dry sobs.

Soft hands touched her shoulders; hushed voices urged her to rise.

Solange collected herself. She raised her head from the bed. Her eyes were feverish and bright, her cheeks like parchment.

"Enough, I am fine. Let us continue."

And the marriage ceremony dragged on. The Earl of Redmond repeated his vows in that mellow voice that had the ladies sighing. Solange watched him with curious detachment, the wetness of his lips, the way he grasped her fingers, using his whole hand to control her.

The priest now turned to her, and she said the words after him without thought, her mind on the clouds outside, flying with the hawk over golden fields.

Her voice was so muted that the members of the congregation had to lean forward to catch the words at all. Redmond listened thoughtfully to her melodious inflections, marking the absence of life in her voice.

Not that it mattered. She would revive soon enough, he knew.

The priest gave the final blessing upon them both, and declared them husband and wife in the eyes of the Lord God, amen.

Redmond turned to his bride and lifted her chin with one finger. She appeared dazed, unaware of what was happening. He lowered his head and kissed her lips.

Approving murmurs broke out in the crowd. Redmond raised his head and threw the audience a rakish grin. Many of the women were wiping tears from their eyes. The gentlemen looked relieved it was finally over. Now was the time for the feast.

Solange followed the earl back down the aisle through the patchwork of colored sunlight, heedlessly crushing the flower petals strewn beneath her feet. Behind her a choir of young boys soared into an aria, the sound resonating throughout the chapel.

How strange it all was, she thought. How unreal. Here was the earl by her side now as her husband, instead of the man she had always expected to see in that place.

Here was her father congratulating them both, joining them to accept the felicitations of the gathering group that crowded around them.

Here were all the people who had made up the folds of her life, yet who had never seemed to like her, suddenly all smiles and charms in her direction. Here was her father's mistress, a woman who had openly and deliberately ignored her, now kissing her cheek and telling her how much she would be missed.

Perhaps it was all just a bad dream, Solange thought remotely. Yes, a bad dream, the worst dream possible, really. She would wake any moment now to her normal life. She would find Damon and tell him about it, ask him to interpret all the nuances of it for her. He was so good at that.

But to be a true nightmare, surely Damon himself would appear now. He would be staring at her, the new Countess of Redmond, probably shaking his head at her folly. She would begin to realize just what it was she had sacrificed for this future, and the pain in her would reawaken.

Solange shook her head, fighting back that treachery.

"Are you tired, my angel?" Redmond pushed his hand under her hair to cup the back of her neck. She hated the creeping chill of his touch.

"A little," she replied, taking a careful step away from him.

His fingers tightened, holding her firmly. He greeted another couple cheerfully as they filed into the greatroom for the banquet, then leaned down again. "You may sleep in my arms during the ride. I'm afraid I brought no carriage for you, since a carriage would not make it through some of the paths on our journey home. But you will be comfortable with me, my lady."

Her attention flickered to life. "We leave today?"

"Of course. You heard the conversation last night. We will be off as soon as the feast is done. Your women are packing your belongings for you now."

The last of the guests entered the hall and were seated. Redmond escorted Solange up the pedestal to the main table, where her father and the rest were waiting for them.

Henry raised his goblet.

"To the happy couple, the Earl and Countess of Redmond. God bless their union!"

Everyone cheered, raising their goblets in return, pounding the tables. The world was taking on an unreal edge for Solange; last night's events were repeating themselves before her. They couldn't leave today! How could they possibly leave today? It was too soon, too abrupt. She was not ready to say good-bye yet.

The earl pressed the rim of his goblet to her lips. This time she automatically opened her mouth and swallowed the contents. Why fight now, she thought wearily. The battle is over.

Servants dressed in festive colors offered delicate treats that must have taken days to prepare: baked pheasant, glazed duck, roasted venison and boar. Marzipan treats in the shape of two crowns interlocked were given to each man and woman, honeyed nuts and sugared fruits were offered freely. Even the kitchen servants, it seemed, had known of her fate before she did. Throughout the meal she caught herself searching the room for Damon. He was gone, pointedly absent from the entire affair. She supposed she would never see him again.

She dropped her head into her hand, unable to bear the weight of it any longer. Redmond quickly stood.

"My bride is eager to begin our journey," he called out, then added suggestively, "As am I."

A chorus of whistles and shouts greeted this announcement. The earl's men, in particular, roared their appreciation.

"Finish your meals, then." Redmond grasped the hand of Henry, who had stood with him. "My wife and I will go now. I have scouts already in place for the journey. We will gain a head start. My steward"—he indicated a bowing man who had appeared behind him—"will take care of the details of the dowry, and my wife's personal items."

Henry ignored the man, addressing the earl. "Are you certain you don't wish to wait an hour more?"

"No, we will leave now. Come, Solange. It's time to go."

She stood up and looked at her father, saying nothing.

Henry coughed uncomfortably. "Well, my dear. I wish you good journey. Obey your husband and you will lead a happy life, I am certain."

He leaned over and embraced her awkwardly. Solange did not return his hold, but when it was over she spoke quietly.

"Keep your promise to me," she said.

Redmond took her arm and led her away down the great hall and out the main door, where they were swallowed up by the daylight.

Among the crowd watching them leave was a trio of minor noblewomen, seated together at one of the far tables.

"A thorn from Lady Margaret's paw, plucked out once and for all," observed one.

"Aye, but not the thorniest rose in her crown," said another. "Margaret sets her aim too high this time. I have heard on good authority that Ironstag is interested in a fair dame from Lincolnshire as his next wife."

"I have heard that same story, but of a damsel from Leeds," added the third. "It's said that Ironstag has an eye for both her person and her lands."

The first one laughed. "Indeed? I think my Lady

Margaret will be fair surprised by the news of *both* these ladies."

The third patted the scarves of her headdress and replied, "Oh, no, my dear. Everyone knows she's as barren as a fallow field. Ironstag would never risk marrying that."

Chapter Four

SHER NEW HUSBAND BARELY ALLOWED HER TIME to hand over her jewelry to one of his attendants before ushering her to the mounting blocks. She had to lean down from the saddle to give the crown of precious flowers to the page holding the horse.

Redmond would not allow her to ride her own horse, which he left behind to follow with the rest of his retinue. Instead, he insisted she sit sideways in front of him on his own steed, a strutting stallion with rolling eyes.

"We shall both be more comfortable like this," he told her, settling her in his lap. He had not even stopped to get her cape, so now he gathered his own about them, tucking the ends around her.

She was swaddled as a babe, tightly bound to him. "My lord," she said. "I urge you to reconsider. I am an adequate horsewoman. It will be no problem for me to keep up with you. If you'll simply give me a moment to change my dress—"

"Keep up with me on that mare of yours? I think not. You will ride with me. I wish to reach our first encampment before nightfall. And your dress is fetching enough." He cut off her reply by digging his heels into the flank of the stallion, which bounced forward eagerly, jostling her into his chest.

"Hold on to me," Redmond ordered. She had no choice.

The gray stallion with the two riders galloped from the courtyard past the gate, then kicked up dust on the eastbound path from the castle.

And that was the end of it. Her life at Ironstag was over that easily. Solange didn't try to look back. She didn't want to see what she was leaving behind.

From his solitary post on a turret, Damon Wolf watched the horse with the two riders until it vanished in the forest outside the town. Then he went back to his room and resumed the packing of his belongings.

THE STEED WAS WELL BRED, his gallop smooth and airy. But once they entered the trail of the forest, Redmond reined in the animal to a steady trot, and then a walk.

Neither of them spoke. Solange was fighting off the heavy-lidded sleep of exhaustion. She would have dearly loved to succumb to it but resisted leaning any more of her weight against the earl. Pride kept her upright as long as she could stand it, but as the hours passed she lost this battle too, and slumped against his chest in deep slumber.

He studied her face at leisure, fascinated with seeing her this close for the first time.

She really did resemble an angel in her sleep, he thought dispassionately. Her features were relaxed and peaceful, her coloring a dramatic contrast that pleased the eye. Dark, long eyelashes, slanting brows, full red lips, and a faint, becoming blush on her pale cheeks.

Redmond smiled to himself. Yes, he was quite satisfied with Solange. She would be perfect for his needs. He let her sleep on, steadily increasing the distance from Ironstag to her.

She drifted through layers of sleep to become aware that she was being carried in someone's arms, someone with a beard that pricked her cheek. She opened her eyes as she was being settled upon a pallet of furs.

A strange man leaned over her, a man with a muddy red beard and shining eyes. She gasped, startled, then scrambled backward on the pallet to escape him.

"No." He shifted his grip to hold her down firmly. "Don't be afraid. Tonight you will sleep alone in your tent."

She blinked up at him, placing the voice and the face, remembering the events of the past two days.

"I will be with my men. There is a guard outside if you need anything. I bid you good night, Madam Wife."

Redmond left the tent, having to duck to exit through the low flap. She heard him talking to the guard, and then his footsteps crunched away on the fallen leaves littering the ground.

Solange sat up, rubbing her head. Her entire body ached, even as she rested upon the thick furs. It was nighttime; she had no idea how late exactly. She had been left no candle or lamp. The half-moon outside added a faint light to the walls of her tent but not enough to see clearly.

She fumbled with the satin sash around her waist until it came free, then reached under the bodice of the loosened gown to rub circles on a section of skin beneath her breasts. The small, hard object had pressed a ring of red into her flesh, and she was thankful to finally be able to untie it from the ribbon drawstring of her undertunic.

She pulled out Damon's ring and slipped it back onto her finger on the hand opposite the one that wore the signet ring of the earl. She had searched for it frantically on hands and knees that morning before the wedding. It was the one thing of Damon's she could take with her, and she was determined to do so since he hadn't wanted it back. If Redmond asked her about it, she would say it belonged to her mother. Surely he would have no objection to that.

The fog in her head would not leave. Solange felt neither hungry nor thirsty, and the siren song of falling back to sleep lured her. She thought vaguely of standing up, seeing where she was, talking to someone about how much farther there was to go.

Instead, she curled up on the furs and listened to the music of the crickets outside until she fell into a heavy, dreamless slumber.

THE NEXT DAY'S RIDE was almost identical to the one the day before, except now Redmond and she traveled surrounded by a small army of men; his soldiers had caught up with them late the previous night. They carried with them her belongings, and so Solange now wore a more comfortable gown of soft green wool. She had pulled her hair back into a simple plait. It was all she could really manage to do without a maid, but Redmond didn't seem to mind one way or another. His demeanor reflected neither admiration nor condemnation when he saw her. All Solange could perceive was his strong sense of possession of her, and his anticipation of something she could not guess.

He had shaken her awake that morning at dawn and informed her she had only a few minutes to get ready to leave camp. She had wondered at his haste but had no opportunity to question him, since he left as soon as she had sat up. He had tossed her gown down on the furs before exiting, and she had dressed as quickly as she could through her yawns. The thought of this man catching her in her undergarments was mortifying.

Solange sat aside the gray stallion in Redmond's arms and considered that. The party of soldiers alternated between a walk and a brisk trot, which joggled her so much that her head soon throbbed. The end of her braid bounced up and down in her lap. She caught it and held it, stroking the tip, wondering what it would be like to be intimate with the man holding her.

She tried to imagine anything beyond the chaste kiss they had already shared.

Impossible. All she knew was Damon.

Logically she understood her body now belonged to the earl, and that ultimately—probably very soon—she would be surrendering it to him. But that was all it could be for her, a surrender. She would fulfill her end of the bargain with her father, but her heart and her mind were still her own to command.

Her hair picked up burnished highlights from the sun and threw them back to her eyes, a weave of glinting colors twined in her fingers. She had always hoped that her children would have Damon's glossy black hair.

"My lord," she said, breaking the silence of the woods, "is your holding far from here?"

Redmond took his time answering. "Not much farther," he said finally. "We'll be there tonight."

She let the silence rest between them.

He slid one arm around her waist and held her closer. "I have taken pains to welcome you to your home," he said in a low voice. "You will appreciate my work, I think."

She closed her eyes against the sun and tried not to think of her real home, many miles behind them now.

The horses plodded on. At noon they stopped to eat a plain lunch of bread, cheese, and tart autumn apples. Solange sat by herself on a boulder near a meadow, in plain view of the earl. He ate with his men, talking of the route they had left to travel and where the next scout would be found.

A cardinal scolded her from the branches of the closest ash. She scattered her bread crumbs beneath the tree for the bird to eat later.

It was another fine day. Lucky, she thought. A few thin clouds threaded the sky, foaming and dissolving in the wind. But Solange could smell the change in the air, had known of it since the morning before. Snow was coming very soon. She could taste the dull metallic flavor of it on the breeze. Whatever else awaited her at Redmond's keep, she would be glad not to travel through a snowstorm.

Lunch ended and they mounted up again. Many of the horses had a tense prance to their steps now. Solange thought they sensed the coming change as well.

By sunset they had reached the first of the sod huts that made up the outer boundary of the village of the castle. Her first view of Wellburn itself came upon them suddenly through a clearing of trees.

It was the endtime of dusk, when the last light glowed on the horizon, silhouetting all things in darkness against it. Through the hanging branches she saw the western sky drenched bloodred, and against it rose a sloping hill with a dun-colored wall that circled five dun towers: Wellburn, fortress keep of the family of Redmond for generations.

The earl stopped his steed and let her look.

"Magnificent, isn't it?"

"Yes."

"It has stood five centuries of war, with only my ancestors to conquer it. I have made a few . . . improvements to the original design. You must tell me what you think of them."

"How will I know what you've done?"

"You will know, Solange. It's one of the reasons I've brought you here."

This rather mystifying remark was the last thing he said to her until they had reached the inner courtyard. The soldiers, who had entered ahead of them, were waiting in rows, along with a plethora of peasants and a few nobles who hung in groups near the main doors.

All chatter ceased as Redmond pulled in his steed and dismounted.

Solange attempted to smooth her gown, but then Redmond grabbed her by the waist, swinging her down to the ground.

He stood away from her, faced the crowd.

"Behold," he called. "My lady wife."

There was a long silence in the smoky twilight. As curious as the boisterous noise of her first meeting with Redmond was, she found this hushed watchfulness even stranger.

There were no welcoming smiles, no bowing servants. Even the horses were still. Solange kept her face blank, attempting to match the looks she was receiving. She scanned the mass of people, but there were no exceptions, not even her husband, who was also staring at her as if she were some foreign thing.

Fine, she thought defiantly, let them take good measure of me. If I am not liked, it will not be the first time in my life. She straightened her aching shoulders with cool disdain. But her hands were clenched tight in the thick folds of her skirt.

Redmond's stallion snorted behind her, jerking his massive head away from the boy who held his reins and rearing up to scream and paw the air by her head.

She turned but did not step back from the hooves. In an instant the horse was down again, the stableboy lunging for the fallen reins.

The stallion was docile now, head hanging, eyes mild. He blew through his nose at her. She fancied she could even see him give a crafty smile.

The noise behind her made her face the people

again. They were talking now all right, talking and pointing, as if there were someone else standing right behind her, a devil.

Redmond came over, his mouth downturned.

"Were you frightened, my angel?" His hands pinched her shoulders.

"No," she said.

"Of course you were," he chided her. "We must get you inside so you may recover."

He pulled her past the hissing crowd into the hallway. Solange had a blurred image of dozens of faces following them into the castle, of the uneven stones of the courtyard changing to smooth marble beneath her feet. Redmond kept his arm about her shoulders, steering her past a cavernous hallway, up a set of stairs that crawled the outer wall to a second floor, and then up again to the third. They passed colorful tapestries in the dimness, doors that were closed with ornate iron locks, statues of armor in platform niches.

"My lord, could we not slow down? I am breathless to keep up with you."

He answered her request by sweeping her up into his arms and carrying her with him. She grabbed up her trailing skirts as best she could to keep him from tripping on the steep stairs.

The curve of the steps tightened considerably. She knew this meant they were actually in a tower now. Still, he did not slow until they had reached a door at the end of the steps. It was open a crack. Redmond pushed at it with his foot until it opened the rest of the way, then crossed the threshold with her still in his arms.

He deposited her near the center of the circular room, then backed away from her as if to admire his placement of some bauble on a table. He was breathing heavily from the climb.

"Yes, yes." He raked his hair back from his face with a peculiar laugh, staring down at her.

Solange stood perfectly still, aware of dangerous layers of meaning in the moment that were beyond her. Her eyes shifted from the right to the left, but the room appeared quite ordinary except for its roundness. She couldn't fathom what the earl was excited over, but there could be no doubt something was making him act so oddly. He was sweating and smiling at her in a way that brought back the chill of his touch at the reception. He said nothing now but watched her closely.

She touched her hand to her throat, a nervous gesture. "My lord?"

"My name," he said in his mellow voice, "is Stephen."

"I think I might—"

"Say it."

She swallowed. "Stephen."

"Again."

"Stephen. It feels a bit—"

"You have no idea how long I have waited for you, Solange." As soon as he said her name, the time displacement came rushing back to her, swimming in her head, forcing her to follow the movements of his lips closely to match the sound with the action. She lifted a hand to press against her forehead. She felt hot suddenly, crackling hot, though she saw no fireplace in this room. Her mouth was so dry.

"You will rest now, Solange. You will rest, and when you are through you will be prepared to receive me tonight. Tonight, Solange, I will come to you. Do you understand me? Do you understand what I am saying, Solange?"

With every repetition of her name her sense of displacement grew, until she found herself sitting on the edge of a great posted bed, unaware that she had moved or been moved there. She was so tired.

"Tell me you understand, Solange. Tell me how happy you are that tonight is the night we will be together."

She tried to speak, but it was too complicated. She could barely keep her eyes open.

"Solange," he said, and it reeled through her.

"Yes," she whispered, only wanting him to stop.

"Good. Sleep now." The palm of his hand pressed into her forehead, and she pitched back onto the bed against a mound of covers.

The spinning darkness consumed her, but it was not complete. She was caught in a whirlwind of voices and faces, the unfamiliar mixed with the familiar. Her father, scolding her for disobedience. Adara, the maid, mocking her with her eyes, sneering. The nodding head of the stallion, disembodied, with a sick smile that grew and grew.

She was caught helpless in the middle of the storm, struggling to speak to them, reaching out for them to have the images vanish through her fingers. Nothing mattered, she could not stop them, they would not stop circling her—Lady Margaret, Lady Elsbeth, her father's men, all the people she had once known laughing at her, spinning and spinning.

Damon was there, not laughing. Damon was talking to her, but the hurricane of others drowned out his voice. She reached for him.

What, she cried, *what are you saying to me?*

Her pleas didn't matter; still he spoke under the madness of the sounds, and she could not hear him, but she had to, because it was Damon, and he wanted her to know something, she could feel it. Something important, important enough for him to shout it now, his face literally changing from the effort, his hair lightening to yellow, growing longer, a rusty beard sprouting from his chin.

He was screaming now to be heard, Damon and not Damon, and she was weeping because she could not understand him. The heads of the others became long and monstrous, their mouths gaping holes of blackness.

The chorus of noise died at once.

Awaken now! howled the Damon-thing.

She sat up with a gasp.

She was alone in the tower room, tangled in the covers of the large bed.

"Lord have mercy," she said under her breath, removing herself from the layers of quilts and furs with very shaky hands.

She had to grasp the post of the bed for balance at first, but soon she was able to take rapid steps to the door. She didn't know where she could go, but she had to escape this room.

The door would not open.

She tried the handle again, jiggling it furiously, but it remained locked, latched from the outside. She bent down and peered through the keyhole. There was nothing but darkness beyond.

Something unusual did catch her attention though. The pads of her fingertips felt it first, clutching the cold iron latch.

She pulled away and examined it curiously. Far from being a simple handle, it had been fashioned into a sort of animal, she saw, a horned animal. Perhaps it was a cow, or a hart, she thought, but it was not.

It was a gargoyle, a hideous one, one of the worst she had ever seen. She pulled her hand back and looked again to confirm it. A gargoyle with bulging eyes and two horns that attached it to the panel on the door. Its arched body created the curve of the handle, the tips of its scaly wings meeting under the horns.

But the worst part was the face. It was almost human, too human, but with clawed hands shoving the remains of another human into its mouth.

Solange backed away, filled with disgust. Why would Redmond allow such a repulsive thing in his castle, much less on her door? She shook her hand out away from her body, as if to rid it of any trace of the gruesome handle.

She examined the room once more, and this time noticed immediately something else that was wrong: There were no windows in the walls, not one. Tapestries hung in the circle, eight of them by her count, each filled with scenes of the moon and sun, of hunting and feasting, and some that seemed to show odd religious ceremonies. All of them featured twin animals of red and white, fighting dragons, flying griffins, and strange, monstrous creatures she had never seen before.

Solange pushed aside each one to examine the stone beneath. She found two arched squares of stone that did not match the rest in either color or size.

A tiny bubble of fright was forming under her lungs. Why would a man stone in the windows to a room? Especially a tower room, where views were vital to the security of the castle? There was no logical reason, she thought. It seemed completely mad to shut out the light of day like that. The only reason at all could be that this room had been redesigned to hold . . . a prisoner.

And this was her room.

The bubble expanded. She took deep breaths to control it. She was not a prisoner, she told herself sternly. Perhaps Redmond dislikes the sunlight, or the night air. He would tell her why he did this and all would be well. She must have faith that all would be well.

Wasn't it odd, though, that the bed stood in the exact center of the room? It made movement around it rather awkward. At the head and the foot of the bed were branches and branches of unlit candelabra, a score of them at least. And on the floor directly beneath it all, created in intricate marble tile, spread the points of a star that reached to the walls. The star was black against a white background. There were no rugs on the floor.

The door opened and two women came in carrying trays, followed by four men who carried a wooden tub of hot water.

The men placed the tub on the floor, then bowed their way out the door. The women both came over to her, standing uncertainly by the bed.

"Countess," said one softly. She had light hair wrapped in intricate braids. "We are here to prepare you." She placed her tray on the table against the wall and the other woman did the same. One tray held food and drink, the other, colored glass vials of bath salts and oils.

Solange didn't realize how hungry she was until she smelled the steaming dishes. The thirst in her reawakened to accompany it.

"Thank you," she said, reaching for the goblet of wine.

It had a strange bittersweet flavor that drew her. After three swallows the blond woman stopped her by gently pulling her hand down. " 'Tis a special blend, milady, made here at the keep for only you. But you must not drink it too fast."

"For me? Surely not. I have only just arrived."

"Aye, milady, for you." The other woman, a redhead, spoke. "We have known of your coming for years now."

"Years?"

"Yes," said the other. "It was for you, the wife of our lord, that this wine was crushed."

For the first time, Solange realized that both these women were not only well spoken but also extraordinarily beautiful. They were dressed alike in gowns of blue and gray, one with red hair, the other yellow, like the earl. Their features were almost identical in delicacy and Saxon fairness. In fact, Solange thought she had never seen two more lovely people than these.

"Pray, are you sisters?" she asked.

The women exchanged amused glances. The redhead answered. "Not by blood, Countess. Now you must eat, and then we will bathe you. Your husband awaits."

"Yes, of course, I . . ." For some reason Solange was having trouble finishing her thoughts. But it did not matter, for the women were helping her now, feeding her bites of bread and fowl, peeling off her bliaut, then her gown and undertunic.

She closed her eyes, letting the familiar dizziness overtake her. These women, whatever their roles were here, were taking great care with her. The servants in her own castle had never been this friendly, had never chatted with her quietly about silly nothings such as clothes and jewelry. They had never washed her hair as sweetly as these two women did, taking care not to get the soap in her eyes, rubbing her scalp with skillful fingers.

It was heavenly. Solange leaned back into the tub of water, smiling at them both.

"What are your names?"

"I am Celeste, and this is Mercedes," said the fair one with a nod to the redhead.

Mercedes leaned over the water with a confiding smile. Her eyes were pale gray. They reminded Solange of someone, but she couldn't think who. The goblet of wine was offered again. "It's delicious, isn't it, Countess? You'd like some more, wouldn't you?"

Their hands slid over her, washing away the grime

of travel in a perfumed rinse that Solange thought she could live in forever.

"No, no," laughed Celeste. "You must get out of the water. The earl will be here soon."

Her thoughts were becoming a mire to her; Solange was uncertain of the difference between what she said and what she thought. Perhaps it didn't matter, perhaps they could read her thoughts without the bothersome knot of her tongue.

They helped her step out of the tub, rubbed her briskly with strips of dry cloth until her skin glowed pink and white, until her hair no longer dripped. She wanted more food, but it was all gone. She wanted more wine, and they allowed her this, but only a little, hardly enough to ease her parched throat.

A distant part of Solange watched this scene unfold with detached wonder. She saw herself standing naked, shivering barefoot on the circular marble-tiled floor while the two women looked her over, turned her this way and that, murmured to themselves approvingly. They threw a robe of white silk over her shoulders—surely they didn't expect that to keep her warm? And then the men came back in to remove the tub and the trays.

Solange watched herself being led over to the bed. A blaze of candles brightened the room; Celeste had lit the candelabra while Mercedes had dried her hair.

The women laid her down on top of the covers, and then she saw what they had given her was not a robe, but a cape. A cape of silk, very fine. Very cold to the touch.

Each woman lingered for a moment, adjusting the

cape, the curls of her hair. They covered her bare skin with furs. Then they were gone.

She was alone.

Awaken now, she thought, but the words no longer had the power to break this strange spell. This was more than nervous exhaustion brought on by the wildly shifting events of the past few days, she knew. The wine, that special wine, had evaporated in her mouth to cloud her brain. She could not tell how much time had passed since the others had left. A rational thought intruded through the haze: It wasn't right, she should know the time, she should be aware of this simple thing.

She tried to lift her hand and couldn't. She tried to lift her head and managed to roll it to the side a little, enough to witness the door to the room opening again.

The earl entered. For an hour, or a minute, he simply stood by the entrance, still as a statue. The glow from the candles obscured his features so all she saw was the black shape of a man, but she knew it was he. A loose-fitting robe flowed around him, belted at the waist. She was reminded of a picture of Merlin the magician she had seen in one of her father's books.

The thought stuck in her head. Merlin, the sorcerer. Merlin was here, a traveler through time. He had come to take her away—no, he had married her. She was the wife of Merlin!

He came closer, past the candles, so that the light now fell full on him. The magician shifted into the features of Redmond; that was right, she had married her father's enemy to make him her father's friend. She had agreed to become their shared pawn in the elaborate game they played.

Why had she done this thing? Solange frowned, trying to remember. Something about sacrifice . . .

The man in front of her wore a robe of bright red, silk like the cape she wore, but with designs embroidered on it. She couldn't make sense of them, circles and squares, moons and suns, outlines of hands and eyes too. It was the earl, and his hand reached out and lifted a lock of her hair. He brought his head down into it, inhaling.

Strangely enough, Solange saw that her hair was completely dry. Redmond dropped the strand and moved to touch her face.

She could not avoid him, but she wanted to. Something was terribly wrong. This was her wedding night. Why was she caught frozen in her own body like this?

"You may move, my angel," said her husband, sitting beside her. "You may move for me."

So she did. Her lips parted on a deep breath, and she sat up. He supported her back, pulled her forward so that the furs fell beside her, and the cape opened and revealed her body in soft shadows. She clutched the edges of the cloth together.

"No," said Redmond. He pushed her hand aside, letting the material flow free. "You may not hide from me."

He was breathing heavily, as if he had run up the stairs again. He pushed the cape completely over her shoulders, baring her to the cold air. She felt his eyes devour her.

"Please," she whispered, finding her voice. He was

relentless; his bold appraisal embarrassed her to the bone. Her head bent forward, bringing down a curtain of her hair where the cape had been.

"Silly girl," chided Merlin. "What did I just tell you? You are going to learn to obey me. All good wives obey their husbands." He reached in through her hair and caught her nipple with unerring accuracy. "Pull your hair back."

When she did not comply immediately, his fingers tightened and twisted, sending a sharp jab of pain through her breast that brought her head up. She quickly gathered her hair in one hand and tossed it back. A bright red blush was stealing over her body.

He let go of her, leaning back to take her in again. "You are everything I knew you would be. You were made for me, little wife. You belong to me."

No, she wanted to cry, I am not yours.

Redmond snaked one arm around her waist and nuzzled her neck. With his other hand he put her arm around his shoulders, then lifted her to sit on his lap.

The blush was banished to frigid cold. She felt her skin prickle as his lips closed on the tender flesh under her ear. He locked her closer, biting her now, his free hand creeping up her thigh.

"Stop," she said clearly. "This is not right."

"Solange," said Merlin.

Time did its dance again. The quivers of his voice rumbled through her, knocking out her protests. He rubbed his beard against her skin. When he pulled back she saw herself, tiny and round, shining in his eyes. A cry caught in her chest. He ate it up with his mouth over hers, swallowed it whole with a moan of his own. His grip tightened to pain.

She couldn't breathe, she had to breathe, he was smothering her, he would kill her now, oh, God, and she couldn't stop him. The weakness was back in her, her arms and legs flopped uselessly. The haze tilted her head back, left her swimming without logic or reason.

"Now, my wife," he said lightly against her. "Now I will take you somewhere I vow you never thought to go."

He pushed her down into the bed and straddled her in one motion. From under the folds of his robe he pulled something, something long and thin and bright.

A dagger. A silver dagger in his left hand.

His smile was gentle now. The sliding light on the blade hypnotized her. He handled the dagger lovingly, as tenderly as he did her arm, which he lifted up.

As if it were happening to someone else, Solange watched as the blade met the inside of her wrist.

A line of blood welled up, crimson rich in the candlelight. It gathered and hung as a drop in perfect balance at the bottom of her wrist, growing larger as he pressed on her skin.

Pinpricks of blackness became a rushing tide that overtook her. She surrendered to the welcome darkness without a sound.

Outside the walls of Wellburn the first of the long winter's snow began to fall.

Chapter Five

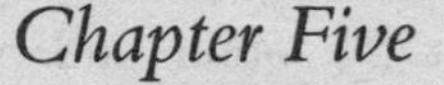

FRANCE, 1287

SHE WAS SO DIFFERENT.

The memory of her childhood companion refused to agree with this hard man in front of her now. Oh, his features remained nearly the same, she could have drawn them from her memory and matched them now with ease. The same chiseled lips, the same strong jaw, the flowing blackness of his hair just as pure.

He surely was the object of admiration from the women across the room. Solange could understand why. There could be no doubt he was larger than the youth she knew, taller and much more muscular, with the solid confidence of a man who is certain of himself in any situation. The lines in his face had deepened, but this added only a mature handsomeness to his features.

Perhaps the main difference had more to do with his bearing, she thought. So stiff and formal, no trace of the familiar comfort of old. Those lips she loved were flattened into a grim line, and his eyes slid off hers too easily.

Solange swallowed a trace of panic. She could not afford to lose Damon now, not again. She needed him much more than he could appreciate. She could not let him know how much. She could not let anyone know.

The women at the other end of the room were openly watching them, silent to record every word spoken between them, every little gesture. They were a school of sharks, ready to shred her later, when she could not escape.

"My lady," Damon repeated softly.

She came back from these thoughts with a guilty start. Damon shifted his feet on the dais. She still touched his shoulder with her hand.

"Can you explain this to me, that you have no lord?"

"The earl took a grave illness," she said. "It was a fever that lasted three days and three nights."

Damon studied her now. "He is dead?"

"He died tonight."

She was lying. He knew it as surely as he knew anything. Oh, she did it very well, much better than she had as a child, but his sensitivity to her had not abated during their separation. The signs were fairly shouting out at him: the deliberate set of her lips, the pale pinkness high on her cheeks. She didn't shift her eyes from his. What sort of fool was she playing him for now?

And her question, that unbelievable thing she had asked him: Would he have her? He would never have trusted that the words left her lips had he not seen it for himself.

It was a part of her game, he saw suddenly, this unfathomable game she was choosing to subject him to. The idea that she would even consider giving herself over to him, in any form, for any reason, was ridiculous enough to be laughable. Aye, and that must be what she was doing right now, laughing at him, turning him into some mockery for her own wicked amusement.

Time had made her harsh indeed. He did not travel all this way to be ridiculed.

The line of his mouth grew thinner. "My sympathies on your loss, Countess. You must be distraught with grief. I am sorry I carry only more bad news for you."

Now she blinked and took her hand away.

"What news?"

"Your father, my lady."

Her hands clamped together, but her face showed no signs of emotion. "Yes?"

"The marquess died a fortnight past, my lady. It was a hunting accident."

She stared down at him, speechless.

"He lingered for a week. That was when he sent for me and bid me to come to you personally with the news."

"He sent you?" she whispered.

"Aye. It was a deathbed wish. I could not refuse him." Anger tinged his voice, alive again at the memory of the imperious old man, commanding him even now, long past the time he had thought to be free of Ironstag.

Damon had been knee-deep in the autumn harvest at Wolfhaven when the messenger arrived. He had not communicated with Henry for many seasons now and had no wish to begin again. But the messenger had convinced him of the peril, so he had ridden back to Ironstag with him.

It had been a bad accident, breaking an arm, a leg, several ribs, and the physician couldn't say what more. A chill had settled into his chest. Damon could tell from the first glance there was no hope for survival. The old man must have been pushing death away with all his will, waiting for Damon to arrive.

Or perhaps he had merely ordered death to wait, Damon thought sardonically. Henry surely had enough arrogance for it, even now.

The marquess lay flat in his sprawling bed, alone, as he had been for years now. Lady Margaret had long ago left to hunt for less reluctant prey, leaving behind her a succession of women to fill his bed. Eventually he had married again: the gentle damsel from Leeds, who bore several miscarriages until finally succumbing to the perils of childbirth, taking the stillborn child with her. After that Henry had sworn off remarriage, growing cantankerously old, keeping his cronies beside him as he counted his gold and mapped his lands.

Damon was inwardly shocked by his appearance now, although he was careful to let none of his emotions show. Henry had aged more than two decades in half as many years, a frail figure with waxy skin and fiery eyes.

The physician by the bed was a man Damon didn't recognize. He left the room protesting that his patient must not speak more than a few words. Henry ordered him furiously out the door, then fell back into the pillows from the exertion of raising his voice.

Damon said nothing, simply stood by the bed. He brushed some dirt from his boots.

"Go to Solange," Henry commanded in that gasping voice. "Tell her yourself what has happened."

"It is not my place," Damon responded evenly.

He never wanted to see her again. He couldn't see her again. Just the mention of her name brought him to a cold, unpleasant sweat.

Henry took a ragged breath. "Lockewood, it is my final request of you. I have raised you. I have provided for you. Now you must do this one last thing for me. She is my daughter. I have heard nothing from her for almost eight years." His eyes grew dim. "Nothing at all."

Damon paused, considering this. He knew that Solange and her husband had removed to Du Clar, the earl's French estate, about a year after the wedding, but then he, too, had heard of nothing more.

He had not bothered to investigate further. In fact, he had shunned all offers of assistance in finding news of her. He wanted no reminders of Solange.

But to cut off her father? That seemed unlikely. Damon had always assumed the two of them had remained in communication.

Henry coughed, a terrible wet sound from the bottom of his lungs. "I have sent her greetings every year, Lockewood. Every year I get no reply. She turns my men back from the gate of the estate; she won't even allow them entrance! She turns them away with nothing, nothing to bring back to me."

Damon shut his eyes. He did not want to be a part of this.

"Eight years," hissed the marquess. "What has happened to her? Does she have children? Is she dead? Is her heart so hard that she could ignore the mortal farewell of her own father?"

Is she dead? Against his will he felt his soul clench at the words. She could not be dead. He would have known that.

Would he? mocked a familiar voice inside him. It was vanity to think he could maintain a connection of any sort with her over such a long time and distance. *Anything could have happened to her,* continued the voice, *anything at all. And you never bothered to find out. A brave knight indeed.*

"I've heard rumors," said Henry softly.

Damon waited, then asked, "Of what?"

"Unmentionable things. Alchemy. Devil worship."

Damon's mouth grew dry. He didn't want to hear this. He didn't want to know. But the marquess rasped on.

"I cannot believe this. I won't. Go to her. See for yourself if she is still alive."

Damon walked away from the sickbed, paced the room impatiently. He did not want to do this. Not a single particle of him wanted any part of this. But God, Redmond, an alchemist! Performing those forbidden experiments, mixing chemicals and devilish sacrifices with the worship of the profane, a member of that hidden society of men who would sell their souls for the secret of making gold. And Solange, wed to this. It could not be true.

He did not want it to be true.

"You fooled me, boy," croaked the old man suddenly. "You fooled all of us."

"And how is that?"

"Didn't think you had the nerve. Didn't think you'd leave to solve the problem on your own. You circumvented all of us, by God, went straight to the king." A weak chuckle interrupted him, and then Henry continued. "You knew where the heart of the power lay, didn't you, boy? Took care of Wolfhaven all by yourself."

A faint stirring of the old wrath welled up in Damon's chest. He focused on that, pushing aside the worry that thinking of Solange had conjured. "I was hardly likely to ask anything further of you, my lord. You made it clear I was an unwelcome presence in your demesne."

Henry's voice got stronger. "Yes. But I was wrong about you, Lockewood."

"Perhaps. Perhaps not."

"Got yourself knighted. Got your lands back. Fought right beside Edward himself, I heard. Fought like all the demons of hell were inside of you, that's what they said. The Wolf of Lockewood, they called you. No fear. No fear at all."

"Fear accomplishes nothing."

Fear was reserved for those who cared about living through the battle. One of the supreme ironies of his life, Damon had always thought, was that the lack of caring for it seemed to ensure its perpetuation. He had thought his life worth nothing without his love, and somehow that worthlessness had stretched on and on, carrying him along with it. How long, he thought bitterly, how damn long it had taken him to crawl out of that despair. And now this man wanted to plunge him back in without a second thought.

Henry was silent, watching, inert in his bed. He missed nothing of the expressions on his visitor's face. He bided his time, waiting for the anger to play out, waiting for it to thin enough to feed his plot further. He had lived a long enough life to know he was doing the best thing.

Finally.

"Go to her, Wolf of Lockewood," he said for the last time. "You're the only one who can reach her now."

Damon rubbed a hand across his eyes. What choice did he have, really? None. In the course of a few minutes this old man had managed to destroy the years of defense he had created, slaying his guard with a few carefully chosen words. Years, he thought acidly, spent building a wall against her that had proven to be no more sturdy than cobwebs.

Solange, he thought, you she-devil, for bringing me back.

"She'll not thank me for bringing her this news, nor will her husband."

"No," replied Henry with a sigh. "But I will thank thee, Damon Wolf."

He had died that evening before Damon could think of a rebuttal strong enough to release him from Ironstag's mad command.

He was needed at his own home. This crop would carry his people though the winter, and it was essential that it be harvested in time to beat the first frost. He could not spare the time to travel across the ocean to deliver a message to the woman who had spurned him. The ocean, for God's sake. It would take a month at least. It was an insane idea.

But of course he went. Ironstag had managed to trap him one last time.

The duration of the journey was actually slightly less than he had originally considered, since he had caught a fair wind across the channel and the earl's estate was not far inland. Damon traveled lightly and swiftly, with no accompaniment to slow him. He had chosen to travel alone despite a plethora of offers from the men at Wolfhaven to accompany him. He had politely refused them all with the excuse that he would be returning soon and that right now each of them was needed at home for the harvest, which was true enough.

But the real reason was buried deep within him, buried so well he couldn't even acknowledge it to himself: His secret fear was that he would crumble at the sight of her. He wanted no witnesses for that, and therefore he had to see her alone. She was a ghost that had lived in his heart every single day for the past nine years. Now it was time to exorcise her. He was not the callow youth she knew. He was a man, a knight, even, by the grace of the sword of the king himself.

A knight with no heart, for Solange had stolen it wrongfully a long time past. Now he would gain it back.

Every day he spent on this journey became a torture to him. He was eager to simply have it done. Thoughts of her that he had managed to suppress for years came winging back, just as he had dreaded.

Her laughter, for example. How her laughter had infected him, had tickled him in some ridiculous way until he had to end up laughing with her. Her sense of joy and wonder at the details of nature . . .

Her smile. The warmth of it spread everywhere, blinded him. Her hair, her long, silken hair, her delight at running through meadows, her intensity in her work—painting, reading, helping him with his studies.

But what Damon remembered most while riding toward Solange through the French countryside was her scent.

Yes, the scent of Solange, her fragrance, that flowery spice of her that owed nothing to perfumes or oils. It was the essence of something truly magical, of moonlit mist and fairies, like one of the stories she would tell.

It maddened him at the campfire he built every evening, chewing on the smoky meal of the hare or quail he had bagged that day.

It bothered him astride his horse, going through the plowed fields and empty woods of this foreign land.

But at night it was the worst. At night, when he lay on the hard ground with just a blanket between him and the endless sky, she would come back to him on the breeze, a hint of magic he could never contain.

Of all the flowers and herbs he had memorized, none came close to her sweetness. Now, on this trip, she haunted him more than even the first few years without her. It made him clench his teeth until the muscles in his jaw ached.

His mood swung from despair to hope and ultimately to anger for having these feelings at all. His fury was aimed at her, at her father, but mostly at himself. He had been doing so well without her. He had almost managed to forget the pain.

That thought seemed ludicrous now. The instant he saw her again he knew he would never be able to truly forget.

This hard journey had led him here to the French estate, where, somewhat to his surprise, he had gained immediate entrance. It all happened too fast. He thought he would have time to prepare. He thought he would be able to at least change clothes before gaining an audience with her. But no, they led him straight here to the chamber room, a frozen place, where she had risen to greet him from the dais, sending her women over to the fireplace, showing no more surprise at seeing him than if they had just parted a few hours before, not years. His spurs clicked against the marble floor as he crossed over to her.

Solange.

At last. It was a moment of epiphany. Here she was in front of him, a grown woman, a widow by her account. His mind was having a difficult time taking it all in.

But his body was not, by heaven. He wanted her as fiercely as he ever did. He nearly could not breathe for the want.

He would not crumble, no matter the cost. He wanted to shout at her, he wanted to know why she had rejected him, why she had rejected her father, her homeland. Instead, he kept his lips tightly shut, marking her reaction to his news.

She turned away from him, took a few blind steps to the thronelike chair topping the dais. She did not sit, however, merely stood next to it, arms crossed over her chest. He saw the shiver take her again and again. Her head dipped low.

"My lady," he began.

"My father is dead. The earl is dead. I find—" Her voice broke, a tremulous waver before she recovered. "I find that I cannot think right now. I must rest."

As if on cue, the court women swarmed over to her, taking her arms and leading her down the steps. In frustration, Damon watched them go. He felt robbed of his moment after coming all this way. It couldn't be over this quickly. He would not allow her to disappear just yet.

"Countess," he called.

Solange stopped, then turned. The women fanned around her.

"I am weary," Damon said clearly. "I have traveled far to reach you. I require food and a place to bed for the night."

His words seemed to snap at her, drawing her spine straighter. "Of course. Forgive my poor manners. I'll have one of the men show you to your chambers and arrange to have dinner brought to you. I'm afraid it is past the evening meal, but there is always plenty of food in the buttery."

She murmured instructions to one of the ladies, who curtsied and fluttered away.

"Someone will be with you shortly," she said. "Good eve to you."

They left as a group out the chamber door, a flash of gold in a wash of pastels.

The fire popped and sizzled behind an iron grate, echoing off the emptiness around him.

HE WAS AWAKENED FROM A SOUND SLEEP by a hand placed over his mouth.

In an instant he had drawn the stiletto from beneath the pillow and pressed it against the throat of his attacker. It was a move so deeply ingrained from the years of battle that it took him a full minute to realize that both the hand and the throat belonged to a woman.

To Solange, to be exact.

The dimming fire allowed just enough of the delicacy of her features to stand out in the darkness. She showed no reaction to the sharp dagger but looked down at him calmly, waiting for the recognition to sink in.

He drew the knife back, then pushed her hand away. "Are you mad?"

"Shhh. You must speak quietly, lest they hear you."

He tossed the covers off himself and climbed out of the bed. He was almost fully dressed, another habit learned from battle.

"What is the meaning of this, Countess? You have no place here."

"Please, Damon, lower your voice. They must not find us!"

He stared at her in the darkness, baffled. Her urgency was real enough; he reckoned if the newly widowed countess was discovered with another man on the very night of the death of her husband, her reputation would not survive.

The Solange he knew wouldn't have given a shrug of her shoulders over something like her reputation. Yes, she was the countess now.

"Leave," he ordered curtly.

She approached him slowly, hands held out in appeal. "It is my every intention to leave. That is why I'm here."

"What?"

"I want to go with you back to England. I want us to leave here tonight."

He laughed softly. "Your wits are addled, Solange. Go back to your women."

She made an exasperated sound. "The hounds of hell could not drag me back there. I have to go with you, tonight, right now."

She looked so thin and lovely, and very serious. A heavy black cloak swirled around her ankles, but as she moved toward him he saw to his amazement that she was wearing a tunic, hosiery, and buckskin boots: men's clothing. She was still talking.

"We need to leave as soon as you may be ready. I'll help you if you like." In the darkness she took on the earnestness of a young girl, breathless and beguiling. "I can pack very quickly."

He shook his head. "You'll not go anywhere with me, Countess. I'm not courting that kind of trouble. Seek your adventures elsewhere."

She paused, looking as if his barb might have actually hurt. He ignored the flash of guilt. She would not use him, damn her, for whatever game she was playing. He would not submit to that.

"You don't understand." Her voice was subdued. "I have to go."

"And why is that?"

She chewed on her lower lip, another girlish habit he found suddenly annoying. But then her face cleared, became resolute. "If you will not help me, then I will go alone." The cape billowed to life as she swept past him toward an opening in the far wall he had not noticed before.

He caught her before she could vanish into the blackness.

"What is this, madam? You have deliberately put me in a room with hidden doors and secret tunnels? Is it so that you may creep in here in the disguise of nightfall? Is that your amusement these days, Solange?"

"Of course. I knew you would bolt your door closed tonight. How else was I to get in?"

Her look was so innocent, he practically could believe in her virtue again. Amazing, this acting ability she had discovered.

How convenient for her to have a room to keep her lovers nearby, tucked away from prying eyes. What sort of husband had Redmond turned out to be, to allow his wife this unusual freedom in his own home? Damon was almost sorry he could not question him for himself.

"But the man is dead," he muttered. Very interesting.

"Pardon?"

"Your husband. I have just remembered myself. You are a widow driven mad with mourning, no doubt. Someone should be watching over you."

She shook him off with supple strength. "You have changed greatly, Marquess. You should not be surprised to learn that I have changed as well. You speak now of things you could not possibly know anything about. My apologies. I didn't mean to disturb you."

Before he could think to respond, she was gone, her footsteps fading away down the tunnel.

"Damn. Damn, damn, damn."

It was no accident, he knew, that she had chosen to throw back at him his own words from their parting those years past. She was too clever for it to be anything else.

She wasn't really fleeing the estate. She wouldn't act so rashly, he reassured himself. She had nowhere to go that he knew of. It would be a folly beyond belief to think she could make it back to England on her own—a woman, a gentlewoman, who really knew nothing of the ways of the world. She could not be that foolish.

With a muttered oath Damon picked up his scabbard and secured it around his waist. It took only a few minutes to toss his scant belongings back into the traveling sack, but he could feel each second slipping by.

He hurriedly shoved his boots on and laced up the sides. She would be at the stables by now, or who knew where that tunnel let her out of the house. She might have already had a horse waiting in some hidden location, in which case he would have to track her either by sound or wait until dawn, when he could see her horse's prints.

By dawn the entire houschold would realize their mistress was missing. And who would they first suspect in this dangerous mystery?

Damon flung his cape over his shoulders, grabbed the sack, and strode out the door. As quietly as he could, he picked his way over the sleeping bodies of the pages and serfs who lay on the floor on the way to the main doors. A brace of hounds raised their heads inquisitively as he passed, but made no move or sound.

"Good dogs," he mouthed. He wondered fleetingly if Solange had trained them the way she had the hounds of Ironstag. And then he was past them all, out the doors and into the night. No guard challenged him, a fact that registered at the back of his mind but that he did not take time to heavily consider. He had to find the stables.

It didn't take him long. There was no sign of Solange, however, either outside the wooden building or in the steamy darkness. He saddled his stallion on his own, keeping a hand over his muzzle to quiet him as he led him outside. Curious that the stableboys had not awakened; and neither had the pages in the hall. A strange coincidence that Damon was beginning to suspect was no coincidence at all.

Tarrant was well trained, and stood obediently as he mounted. Once more Damon paused to listen for any sign of Solange to betray her presence, but he heard nothing save the crickets singing to each other. At his signal the stallion began an eager canter around the walls of the estate. He wanted to be certain she had not slipped out some hidden way on foot.

"Hsst!"

He pulled up and turned at the sound behind him. She was on a roan mare behind a crook of trees. One pale hand waved him over to her. Tarrant covered the distance in no time. She greeted him before he could speak.

"Have you changed your mind, or are you merely searching for me to return me to Redmond?"

"I believe you said the earl had passed beyond this mortal coil, Countess."

"Redmond's men, then. They are one and the same. Well?"

The hooded cloak lent her an air of mystery he did not need tonight. His head was still fogged with the ache of slumber, yet it seemed he had not slept for weeks. The reason for this inconvenience was now sitting before him, astride, bold as a fishwife, demanding his allegiance to whatever scheme she had created. Damon thought her flight ill advised at best and criminal at worse. He could think of no good reason for a wife to run away from her dead husband's affairs.

The mare whickered and pawed the ground, exciting Tarrant to snort and shake his head. He calmed the beast with a steady hand. "I will not accompany you unless you fully explain what this is about."

"Fine. God be with you."

She wheeled the mare around and took off at a gallop. Whatever else she had become over the years, she was now an excellent horsewoman, Damon saw. It was almost a pleasure to watch her, except for the fact that he was having to dodge branches and roots to keep up with her.

"Dammit, Solange!" He made an attempt to grab

the reins from her as soon as he had drawn even, but she maneuvered the mare to artfully dodge his attempts. Then suddenly she stopped, pulling her mount up into a clearing of the woods. He followed, slowing to match her pace, then stopping beside her.

"That was a foolish risk, Countess! These woods are so thick, it would take nothing at all to knock you from your mount, or worse, trip her up to land on top of you! I cannot believe you have developed such a disregard for the care of your animal!"

Solange pushed her hood back impatiently. "You are the one who has taken the foolish risk, Lockewood! Both Iolande and I know these woods all too well! I have lived here many years, in case you do not remember. We could find our way out of here blindfolded if need be."

He couldn't think of what to reply, and so stared at her in frustrated silence. She hadn't turned out at all as he thought she would have. She was not needy, not broken by the sight of him as he was by her, not desperate, except to leave.

"You actually think you can make it back to England on your own, don't you?" He didn't give her time to answer. "Of all the idiotic notions you've ever come up with, this is the zenith."

"I require neither your approval nor your censure, my lord. I am not interested in your opinion of my wits. I have a long trip ahead of me. I'll thank you to leave me in peace and let me go on my way."

"There are thieves, Solange! Hordes of men cut loose from the wars, scattered about with no homes and no loyalties. They prey on travelers far more seasoned than you! What do you think would happen to you if you were captured by one of their gangs?"

"They will not catch me."

"As simple as that, is it? Well, if you do make it to the docks alive, just how were you going to cross the channel? No one but scoundrels and rogues would take your money for passage."

"If you really must know, I am going to disguise myself. As a boy. If they won't take my gold, I will work for my passage."

He uttered a short laugh of disbelief.

"You really have no concept of the world out there, do you?" Damon took in her long lashes, her soft mouth. "They'll take your gold, all right, and your body as well. It will please them mightily to have such a pretty hostage, boy or woman."

"I will come up with some other strategy, then! I will think on it on the way there."

"And winter will arrive before you can make it back to Ironstag. How do you plan to survive the storms? Don't you remember how sudden and fierce the snowstorms would rise and take over everything in their paths? Don't you remember all the good lives lost to them each winter?"

"Yes," she said quietly, "I remember."

"Then God in heaven, woman, what are you thinking? The chances of you reaching Ironstag alive are as good as none! You would risk your life for this adventure of yours? Is your frivolity so great?"

"Damon Wolf, I will say this to you only once more. I have to go. The reason I have to go is simply that I cannot stay. I *will* not stay." Her voice rose in pitch, and the mare took a fretful step sideways. Solange patted her neck and continued. "There are no ties to bind me here any longer. I am a free woman and have the right to travel as I see fit."

"If that's so, why not travel with a contingent of the earl's men to protect you? Why this need for veiled exits and secrecy?"

"What concern is it of yours?" she burst out. "Leave me in peace, I pray you! I wish no ill upon you, but leave me in peace!"

"Would that I could," replied Damon grimly. "But I fear your flight of fancy has already rendered us quite unpopular with your people back at the estate, who will be stirring soon, no doubt. I cannot return there without you. Let someone else explain that their mistress has taken it in her head to run away."

She stroked the mane of her horse, running her fingers through the coarse dark hair. She spoke down to her hands. "So, my lord, are you saying you will accompany me?"

"Aye, I will, though it goes against all my good sense. God protect us, woman, from the repercussions of this deed."

"I do not rely on God to protect me any longer," she replied. "I will protect myself."

SHE HAD A tent rolled up in one of the packs on her horse, a heavy green cloth that she insisted would blend in with the foliage of the landscape.

"It's too awkward," Damon said, dismissing the bundle without a glance.

The late afternoon sun shone down with little warmth through the canopy of the forest top, creating a patchwork of shifting shadows for the travelers. They had clung to the woods as much as possible, not wanting to be noticed on any of the main roads or empty fields. This made their progress much slower than Damon thought it should be, and that irritated him. They had been riding for hours, to him it now seemed like days, and he could not keep his eyes open any longer.

If it weren't for her, he would have gained a full night's rest before beginning his trip home.

Hell, if it weren't for her, he wouldn't have had to make the trip in the first place.

They had agreed to stop and rest until nightfall in the heart of an oak wood, with nothing around but trees and brush. Even the sky was missing, hidden behind the tangle of branches above them.

Solange waded over to him through the thick covering of leaves on the ground, waving the tent cloth in the air.

"It is necessary," she insisted, "for protection against discovery."

"And what will prevent your mount from being discovered? Did you bring a tent for her too?"

She closed her eyes and took a deep breath. Without her unsettling gaze Damon let his guard down for an instant to admire her beauty, even through his exhaustion. Her slight form was set off by the melted mix of scarlet, gold, and green leaves around her. Even in a shapeless cloak and with circles under her eyes, she was undeniably the most attractive woman he had ever seen.

Her eyes snapped open. "Iolande is a good horse. She will make no noise while we rest. She will not move from where I place her."

"Would that you were so biddable," he muttered under his breath.

Solange threw the tent down by his feet.

"I had no idea it was going to be so difficult to travel with you," she exclaimed.

He ignored the wad of cloth and walked over to Tarrant, loosening the girth and removing the saddle with a grunt. The great stallion stood patiently, allowing Damon to remove the bridle as well.

"Use your head, Countess. I am assuming that one of your priorities right now is to make haste, with as much secrecy as possible, correct?"

She gave him a little frown. "Correct."

"Supposing, then, while we are dozing in your fair tent, a meandering group of pilgrims comes our way. Or better yet, a parcel of your dead husband's men, looking for us. What then? Will we ask them nicely to wait for us to escape from the folds of your tent before mounting up and riding away?"

"Why, I—"

"You're going to have to trust me on this, Solange. We will sleep in the leaves, with leaves for covering. I am going to hope your mare is as well trained as you indicate, for our horses will be the only things that may call attention to us."

"Is yours?" she asked a little defiantly, hands on hips.

Damon shrugged. "Tarrant is a warhorse of the finest stock. He has kept me alive through too many battles to remember. He is trained to my specifications, and follows what I order."

She walked over to the stallion before he could warn her to stay away and cupped his chin in her palm. She said nothing, only stared into his liquid eyes for a long while. Tarrant didn't move, locked to her eyes. He allowed the caress with calm patience.

Damon swallowed the protest on his lips. The stallion was trained to kill strangers. He had seen pages and squires literally shake with fear at having to handle him. He had personally attended to at least two lost fingers from men acting too hastily around Tarrant's mouth, dammit, and here was Solange casting her strange charm over his horse. His horse! Was there nothing she could not tame with her touch?

It infuriated him so much that he had to look away from the scene before him. He scuffed his feet in the leaves.

"He is devoted to you." Solange gently released his muzzle. "What does his name mean?"

"Thunder," responded Damon gruffly. He was gathering a bed of leaves together, bent over with his back to her. "Thunder. It's all I heard back then."

The cry of battle was always lost to him, lost in the pounding of the hooves and of his own heart. With every gallop forward he had focused more and more on the sound of it, the combined deafening power of it. It drowned out the fear in him, it hammered over the revulsion he felt at lifting his arm against another human being.

He had lived in the thunder because it was what he had to do. His lands depended upon it. His men depended upon it. His king depended upon it. And the thunder took his weaker feelings and drowned them, let him live in the rhythm of battle, let him survive again and again when those around him had long ago fallen.

The thunder had even obscured the image of Solange at the time, which was his saving grace. Nothing before or since then had shown that power. Only battle, only death and destruction took him away from her. So many times he had been afraid it would poison his soul, this path he had chosen. But it was too late to worry. If he became blind to pain, so much the better.

"Thunder," said Solange. "A fine name, I think."

"I do not care," he ground out, "what you think. Attend to your horse so that we may rest."

She said nothing to his brutal tone but instead went over quietly and began to unsaddle her mare.

Damon's hands were clenched into fists; he made a conscious effort to release them. He did not want that thunder now, not now. He sought to distract himself with a question to her.

"What happened to your other mare, the one that left Ironstag with you? What happened to Gytha?"

He sensed rather than saw her careful tensing.

"She was put down," she said after a pause.

"Why? What was wrong with her? She was sound enough when she left."

"She had an accident. She had to be put down."

Solange pressed her face briefly against the neck of Iolande and tried to breathe soundlessly through her mouth. She fought to stem the torrent of feeling that swelled at the mention of her previous mount.

Noble Gytha, the only living friend of either man or beast left to her from home. A brave little brown horse, following her from Ironstag to Wellburn and then all the way to France, carrying her faithfully until Redmond came back.

Iolande snorted softly, impatient with her mistress's slowness in attending to her. Solange bit her lip and then patted her mare on the shoulder. She pulled off the saddle and began to rub the horse with the curry brush she had been certain to pack. She could feel Iolande's preening pleasure, she had always loved being curried. Solange did it personally whenever possible.

"Good girl," she murmured. "Thou art such a lovely girl."

The mare nodded her agreement.

Damon shook his head and wondered why he should be at all amazed at the scene. Even now, as a fugitive, when she should be half out of her mind with either fear or grief, Solange calmly talked to animals as if it were the most normal thing in the world. Perhaps she *was* a witch, as it was always rumored. He wouldn't be surprised.

But no. She turned a careful glance to him over her shoulder as she moved around the horse, a shy look from her dark eyes, her braid unraveling down her back; he could see that she was just a woman. A woman no different from any other.

It still pained a part of him to think this, so he deliberately did it again. She was an ordinary woman, a fair one, no doubt, but as mortal as he, and as full of folly.

He had seen dozens of women just like her since he had broken away from Ironstag. Hundreds. And what was so fair about her anyway?

Since she had abandoned him, he had found a bounty of English roses: women with eyes the color of the summer sky, or greener than mountain lakes, women with hair brighter than gold, brown as a fawn, or burnished like copper. Tall or short, thin or plump, the most celebrated beauties of the land had all flocked to him at Edward's court, had sought him out and flattered him, invited him to their beds with the most blatant advances. They had wanted him, those court beauties known for their fickle ways and exquisite tastes.

None of them talked to animals, he wagered.

None of them had been Solange.

She was humming now as she finished brushing her horse, a simple tune he recognized from childhood. She seemed buoyant, almost cheerful, in spite of the odd circumstances. Damon honestly didn't know what to make of it.

The humming stopped. "Shall we take turns at a watch? Do you think it necessary?"

"No. If aught approaches, Tarrant will warn me."

"Of course," she said, giving the stallion an approving look.

Damon busied himself with settling into the bed of leaves he had formed for himself. Solange gave her mare whispered instructions. He could have sworn he saw the animal wink at him. He rolled to his side, throwing more of the dry leaves on top of him, deciding he would just ignore her. He was certain that after he had gotten some sleep, the world would seem a much clearer place and he would be better able to make some sense of it. He simply needed sleep.

Solange came over to her leafy bed not far from his. She could see his features hardened in a deliberate attempt to shut her out. She lowered herself into the pile, nestling into it. The leaves were softer than she had imagined they would be and smelled wonderful. What a delightful way to retire, she thought. What a pity it could not be done all the time.

With her head resting in the crook of her arm, Solange stared at her rescuer, for that was how she saw him, bitter looks or no. She kept her breathing slow and even and was rewarded with the eventual relaxation of his face.

First his jaw unclenched. Then the furrow between his eyes smoothed away. Finally he slipped into complete slumber, a heavy doze. A single curling lock of ebony graced his forehead. He must have been quite tired, she thought. She hoped that might also account for at least some of his bad mood. How she longed to see his smile again.

She was not tired. She wanted, in fact, never to sleep again. She felt she could go on forever, feeling the wind in her hair, the sun on her shoulders, the moonlight in her eyes. Every breath she took became more precious to her; every time she filled her lungs she tasted freedom.

Freedom. A smile lit her eyes as she watched the face of her beloved. For almost a decade she had been dead, a prisoner in body and soul. This new life tingled in her body. It shucked off the dead skin that had covered her whole being and brought forth the newness that she longed to feel.

Her future was uncertain, she knew. She had done a daring thing, a perilous thing, but she would not regret the consequences. She would never do that. Her eyelids slowly closed.

In one of her last conscious thoughts freedom became a sparrow, sailing up into the endless sky.

Damon opened his eyes. She was finally asleep. He pondered her for a moment, then closed his eyes again.

Chapter Six

OVER THE COURSE of the next few days Damon became convinced that he was traveling with more than one woman.

In fact, he was discovering a plethora of Solanges, each as different from the last as could be.

There was the countess, of course, the newest to him and most foreign part of her. The countess kept a stoic silence, a commanding look so reminiscent of her father, Damon sometimes had to marvel. Solange put on this mask whenever his casual questions probed too deeply for her comfort. No doubt she would not have been happy to learn the haughty flash of her eyes served to amuse rather than intimidate him.

There was her bashful, girlish mask as well. This was much more recognizable to him as a leftover from their old days: the sideways looks, the way the tendrils of her hair fell forward to hide her face as she bent her head down, the hesitant pauses between sentences. Her words became simple and sparely descriptive, a prose of talk that lured him with its natural rhythm. The ease of his familiarity with her in this guise both amazed him and repelled him. She seemed to seek something from him with this show; he couldn't guess what.

She could be bold too. Confident and at ease on her horse, sure of her catastrophically flawed plan to reach England, blind to the almost infinite dangers that faced them every minute, every second, as far as Damon was concerned. It was more than exasperating, it was exhausting, defending her from her own reckless path. He worried for them both constantly. His warrior's eye scanned the surroundings, always on the ready to defend them even as she would cajole her mare to a gallop ahead of him, laughing cheerfully as he made to catch up.

Aye, and there was the most puzzling thing of all: her inexplicable joy, which could flash like summer lightning, there and gone before you could blink. Countless moments Damon would watch her covertly, following the moving shifts of shade and light across her profile. More than a few times he had seen a dimpled smile given to the air ahead, or heard a quiet laugh that rang like chimes in his ears.

She offered no explanation for her mirth. He demanded none. Almost as soon as her happiness could be noted, it was gone, melted into the typically solemn look she wore. Indeed, sometimes she shifted so quickly from one mood to another, he was left with just the fleeting impression of what had gone before. It was a hollow feeling he didn't like.

He wondered sometimes quite seriously if her mind had been touched. It had been a very long time, after all, since he had seen her last, and God knew her behavior then had been anything but rational.

But time itself took care of that concern for him. Careful and continuous observation revealed the final sadness beneath her outward appearance of serenity. Still, as the days went by, he thought he could see a lessening of the lines around her mouth. Even her eyes seemed to be opened a little wider, not as wary of what the day or night could hold for her.

The many faces of Solange. She mystified him, entranced him, irritated him beyond reason. There could be no question of her continued hold over him in some deep way. Damon was eager to find a solution to his imprisonment by her.

The sooner they could part company, the better.

One of his worst fears came to pass only three days into their journey. They had been traveling mostly at night, since Damon was still suspicious of pursuit. He pushed them as hard as he dared, but as much as he wished to end the journey, he could not risk losing a horse to injury. The nights were mostly cloudy and light was dim at best. To go beyond a steady trot would be inviting trouble.

Tucked away in a snug valley between tawny hills, they came upon a rural village neither could name. Damon vaguely remembered seeing it on his way out, but that time now seemed an eternity ago and he could not recall if the residents had been friendly or not.

Most likely not. His encounters with the French had shown them to be a disagreeable people who tended toward suspicion of outsiders to an unpleasant degree.

And unfortunately enough, they came upon the ring of squat houses without warning, cresting a ridge just after dawn to behold the community well only a few lengths away.

The sun was behind them, hiding their features to the cluster of women gathered beside the well, drawing water for the day's demands. Without a word Damon snatched the reins from Solange's hands and guided both horses back down the ridge as quickly and as quietly as he could manage.

Even more unfortunately, Solange was in one of her daring moods.

"What—" she began indignantly.

He silenced her with a harsh look, willing her not to speak until they were well out of range of the women. Somewhat to his surprise, she fell back with a fitful frown but kept her peace until they had taken refuge behind a grove of wild crabapple trees.

The trees edged a small stream. Both horses waded in to drink.

"Why did you pull us away?" Solange asked in a hushed voice. "We might have had eggs, or milk from them. We could have had fresh bread."

"Oh, yes," Damon replied scornfully, in part to quash the wistfulness he heard in her tone. "What a fine idea, to have the widowed Countess of Redmond ride up with her male companion to some peasant women and demand food. I'm certain it would go quite unremarked around here."

"I wouldn't *demand* it, I would pay for it. I have coin. And there is no manner by which these people could suspect me to be the countess, as you say. I appear to them to be a boy. I am your squire, my lord!"

Damon shook his head helplessly. "Solange, no man on earth, nor woman either, could think you a boy."

Her eyes sparkled with amber fire. "You are mistaken!"

"No, you are. All it will take is one close look to reveal your gender. Very few boys, however young, have such womanly features. Your voice is too high. Your hair is too long. And," he added bluntly, "your chest is too round."

She blushed, and shifted in the saddle. "I have taken measures to hide my figure, sir."

"Not enough. Give it up, Countess. Our best plan is to stay hidden from the populace, at least until we are safely on your father's land again."

She looked so pensive, so damned pretty in her rough tunic and stockings. How absurd to think she could ever be anything but a female. One look into her eyes was enough to give her away.

Now she turned them to his, soft brown with golden depths, thickly lashed, utterly feminine.

"Fresh bread," she sighed.

"Try some crabapples," he suggested heartlessly. "They should be ripe enough."

Instead of answering him, she stiffened, turning to the left of him at the exact moment the horses raised their heads and pricked up their ears. Now Damon heard them too, raised voices, coming closer, coming straight at them from across the dale.

He dismounted and dragged her out of her saddle, holding on to her waist until she found her footing in the creek bed. Both horses walked docilely behind him as he led them deeper into the grove. The crabapple trees mingled with the drooping fronds of a willowleaf. Solange hurried ahead and pushed branches aside, clearing a path for them.

The voices were clearer now, speaking French in high-pitched tones. It sounded like an argument.

The heart of the grove was a mass of twisted branches of both trees; it was behind this that Damon thought they would have the best hope of remaining undetected. They hunched over amid the leaves, peering out where they could.

He heard the hiss of Solange's indrawn breath. In a flash she was gone, around the thicket, in a running crouch over to the muddy banks of the creek. She kneeled and patted the mud flat with her hands, then scooped up a clump of leaves and scattered them over the bank.

The people were now just beyond the line of mulberry bushes growing on the other side of the creek. He could see the colors of their clothing; he could almost make out their features.

Damon abandoned the horses and went after Solange, but she was already coming back.

"Are you deranged?" he uttered through clenched teeth. He grabbed her elbow and yanked her the rest of the way back to the thicket.

"There were tracks," she panted as they dove for the cover.

The crash of their bodies blended with the noise of the strangers walking through the foliage. Two women and a child approached the water. The women were busy quarreling, holding between them a heavy basket of clothing. The child stood apart, thumb in mouth.

The nature of Damon and Solange's arrival into the thicket had left both of them sprawled on the spongy ground, tangled together and covered with debris. Chance had placed his right leg over both of hers, with her head pressed up against his chest. His right arm was pinned under her, her left arm under him. His body half covered hers.

Neither could move without betraying their presence amid the twigs and leaves. The squabbling women knelt by the water, pulling out the clothing piece by piece to pound against the rocks. As each one was done, it was wrung out thoroughly, then slapped up against the mulberry branches. The child spread the material out as evenly as possible to dry.

Solange was lying with half her face pressed into the dirt. A fallen crabapple under her cheek was growing remarkably painful. Slowly, carefully, she eased her head up, but the unyielding pressure of Damon's chest would let her move only a little, no matter how she pushed at him. She could feel his heart thudding hard against her temple, his rapid inhalations betraying his anxiety. She decided to remain where she was, to calm him.

It was agony. He couldn't move, he was paralyzed to the bone. She surrounded him, she was on top of him, below him, on all sides, inside his body. She was killing him and he could not stop her.

With every breath he was forced to draw in the essence of her, that intimate magic that was as heady as spiced wine. The silkiness of her skin caressed him, the softness of her body followed the hard lines of his own relentlessly. He could feel every outline of her, every sweet curve. Her breasts were crushed against his arm beneath her.

She stirred a little under him; fresh shivers of desire coursed through his veins. He held himself immobile, eyes squeezed shut above her, rigid as stone.

This was his old nightmare, to be trapped with Solange, to be tortured with desire for her and unable to act upon it. To have it come true now was almost laughable, but that it hurt so much. He tried desperately to think of something else, anything that would distract him, but even the old call of the thunder was too distant to save him now.

Her hair stirred under his breath. His lips dropped down, as inevitable as the snowfall, to rest upon the chestnut strands. He lingered there, unable to think of doing anything else. It was hell, it was heaven. He hated the part of him that thought if he never moved again, he would be content, soaking up the fragrant heat of Solange. But that didn't change the truth of it.

Damon was pressing down harder now on her head. Solange tried to bear it unflinchingly. She must have given him quite a fright, she mused, for he was clenched around her tightly and was showing no signs of letting go.

If she moved her chin down just a fraction, she could make out through spaces between the vines the feet and skirts of the women, who had ended their argument with much splashing and muttering. They now slapped the wet clothing around in mutual silence.

But the child, a girl of perhaps four, was squatting in the mud across the creek, staring back at Solange with wide-eyed interest. She kept one grubby thumb in her mouth.

All Solange could do was smile at her.

After a thoughtful moment the thumb was removed. The child smiled back.

Very slowly Solange raised her free hand to her face. She pressed her index finger against her mouth, making the universal sign of silence. The girl tilted her head and then mimicked the move, an action Solange hoped meant that she understood the meaning. To be extra sure, she winked.

The little girl winked back. Then she placed her thumb in her mouth again. One of the women cuffed the child and scolded her loudly. She seemed to take the blow in stride, merely standing up and returning to spread the clothing over the mulberry branches. She did not look over at Solange again.

Damon seemed not to notice any of what just took place. He remained frozen above her, a great portion of the weight of him, she noticed, placed squarely on her torso. Her legs were tingling, and the arm trapped under him had gone completely numb. How long were those women going to loiter over their wash? Solange was positive she could have finished up in a quarter of the time they were taking.

Finally they were ready to leave. The last of the clothing had been cleaned and spread to dry. The women picked up the empty basket and clumped back though the bushes to the village. The child followed obediently, throwing Solange one last look and a little wave good-bye.

Solange waved back with her free hand. The girl

skipped ahead, catching up with the others. Solange waited until she could hear nothing more of them.

"Damon."

He lifted his head off hers.

"Damon, it's safe now. We should go before they return."

He didn't answer her, so she wiggled around to pull her arm from beneath his chest. He exhaled deeply, as if he had been holding his breath for a very long time.

She had gotten her arm free and was trying to roll over to look at him, but he rose abruptly and walked away from her, over to the horses.

She sat up, and then stood, wincing at the rush of feeling that poured through her limbs. Twigs and leaves decorated her, and her hands were muddy. Ruefully she examined her new leather boots, now soaked through and sure to shrink. She was brushing herself clean as best she could when he spoke.

"Enough of this. It is unseemly."

She paused, staring at his back.

"What, pray, is unseemly? I admit I appear now to be more a straw figure than either man or woman, but—"

"Hold your tongue," he ordered, swinging up on Tarrant. "Time enough for talking later."

She flashed him her regal look to hide the hurt his words caused. "I am not the one who began the speech, my lord."

He ignored her and rode past the thicket, away from the village, leaving her to follow or not. She shook her head at his retreating figure. A strong part of her actually considered continuing her journey alone, but soon she mounted and caught up with Damon without incident. They continued the ride in silence.

"BUT I THOUGHT YOU SAID we should avoid people," Solange said in a puzzled voice.

She pointed to the battered wooden signpost marking the fork in the road ahead. "Calais is close, true, but it is the largest port in the area. If you wish us to remain unseen, that is certainly not the place to do it."

Damon shifted uncomfortably in the saddle. He had decided, upon reflection of yesterday's near encounter with the women at the creek, that perhaps more important than anonymity was the need to finish this journey with all possible haste.

It was not a smart thing to do, he knew. It was certainly not the strategy he would have chosen in a battle, for instance. It shirked all of his instinctual warnings and would plunge them into an unpredictable situation with almost endless possibilities beyond his control.

If this were a war, he would have laughed at the man who dared to suggest such a plan.

Solange was looking at him, waiting for him to explain his logic. But how could he explain to her that she was killing him, taking him apart piece by piece, a little more every day that passed?

How could he tell her that he was sending them both into danger simply because if he didn't, he would surely lose control of his sanity?

He kept thinking about that moment in the crabapple grove with an almost crazed intensity, remembering the whole of it as if it were happening to him all over again. Even now the early morning breeze danced up and tossed about the loose locks of hair surrounding her face, and it bedazzled him. It intoxicated him, watching the silky strands brush her cheeks, cling to the moisture on her lips. He could stare at her all day, forever, but for the fact that he wanted her so badly. He did not think he could continue indefinitely to convince himself that keeping his distance from her physically was a good idea.

He was already living in a dangerous situation, it was clear. He didn't know how much longer he could just watch her and not touch her again. And once he touched her, he was grimly afraid he would not be able to stop. The need for her was overwhelming everything else, including his logic.

Solange brushed back the hair from her cheeks and tucked it behind her ears. Her hands were graceful even in this spare movement.

He wanted them on him, caressing him. She was making him insane.

She spoke again. "I say we keep going, my lord, follow the path you originally laid out. It seems the wiser course."

"No," he said, fighting his senses. He stared out at the signpost, at the fork in the road. "This way is better. We will go into the city and find passage from there."

"But—"

"Just follow me," he snarled, and pushed Tarrant into a gallop down the road to Calais.

The city was filled with shadows and people, stinking of fish and refuse, just as he remembered from his journey over. He kept his focus on the surroundings, the tight buildings, the darkened alleyways, the strangers with curious glances.

Solange rode with her head shielded by the hood of her cloak, yet to him she shouted out femininity despite the hose, despite the way she sat like a man in the saddle. Every now and then he could feel her glance to him, and even though it reflected his own mounting unease, he ignored her. He was taking them to the docks. The docks would lead them to England. In England he would be free of her.

The wharf was seething with people. They had arrived in the midst of the fishing boats returning with the morning's catch. Great mounds of dead fish, crabs, eels, anything the nets could snare, were piled up high under the cloudless sky, surrounded by the fishermen and the marketeers ready to buy the catch. Wheeling flocks of sea birds circled them all, shrieking and diving, perching and waddling and snapping up whatever they could. The noise of the surf and the birds and the people mingled in an almost steady boom.

When the ocean breeze stilled, the stench was almost unbearable, and Damon wondered how anyone could live this way. But it was not his business. He would be away from this place as soon as possible.

They walked the horses slowly down the narrow street edging the docks and piers, jostling with the crowd. Damon was looking for a small boat like the one that had brought him over but with room for the horses. He passed one because it looked too rickety, another because the owner looked too greedy. He would find the right one. There had to be a craft for them.

Beside him Solange rode quietly, keeping her gaze pinned on the harbored ships as well. He noticed her hood had fallen back, revealing the thickness of her braid, the perfect feminine features of her face. He was about to instruct her to pull it back on, when she gave a little cry and pointed to the sea.

He followed her gaze and saw the boat that had captured her attention. It looked good. Not too small nor too large, solid wood, with an old man mopping down the deck.

He turned to Solange. "Wait here."

Without giving her time to answer, he handed his reins over to her and dismounted, approaching the man.

Solange watched him go, feeling the apprehension in her grow with every step he took. Iolande was fitful as well; she didn't like the crowds and it took more than Solange's usual efforts to calm the horse. Tarrant stood obediently beside them with his reins in her hands, but she could tell he was disquieted also. Both horses shook their heads, rolled their eyes.

The people jostled past but looked up at her curiously, at the fine horseflesh, the lone woman mounted and waiting. Belatedly she realized her hood had fallen back, and so she reached around to pull it up again. As she did so her eyes fell on the movement of a familiar form walking through the mass of people.

A profound chill stole over her. Time seemed to slow, every movement she made counted out in eons.

Casually she lowered her head, keeping the hood as

far down as it would go, while she pulled her hands back in close to her body. Iolande responded by taking a step sideways, allowing Solange to turn her head and scan the crowd again from beneath the edge of the material covering her face.

Where was he? Had she imagined that man who looked so like the captain of Redmond's guard? It had been so quick, she wasn't certain she had actually seen anything at all. There were so many people. She was jumping at nothing.

Nevertheless, she dismounted to be less conspicuous. Damon was still speaking with the old man, who was shaking his head with pursed lips. That didn't look good. She walked between the two horses, keeping them as buffers against the passersby. Stroking the nose of Iolande, she gradually turned her head again toward the buildings and warehouses lining the docks. The crowd was finally beginning to thin, taking the loads of fish with them.

She looked back at Damon, who was doing the talking now, obviously trying to persuade the reluctant fisherman to take them over the channel, then back at the wharf, where the people were slipping away down the streets, into the buildings.

Except there, back the way they had come, was a small knot of people surrounding something she could not see—a man, or several men, and a few were shaking their heads, but some were nodding and looking around, looking toward her. They parted, and she saw the familiar orange and green tunics.

At that instant the world became very quiet. There was her heartbeat, pounding so hard it flooded her senses. There was the gasping of her breath, the labored breathing of fear. Above her circled a pelican in a lazy spiral, a seemingly harmless quirk of the winds and its own inclinations, drawing the eye right to her.

She ducked her head and walked the horses past the boat with Damon on it, down the wharf. She could not let them see him as well.

It took all her willpower not to mount up and flee, but she couldn't leave Damon behind. She had to pray he would notice her moving off and guess the reason for it. She had to hope he would be clever enough not to come chasing after her.

A quick glance over her shoulder showed him still talking, the old man still shaking his head, pointing to the mast, to the deck of the boat.

Her heartbeat thudded over the words, over all the noise. She couldn't get the breath to scream, she couldn't inhale deeply enough to shout at him. She was having trouble moving her feet, her hands.

She paused as if to check the shoe of Iolande, and as she bent over she looked up again, risking a direct look at where she had seen Redmond's men.

And they were looking back at her.

There was no help for it now. Still holding the reins, she scrambled up onto Iolande and turned both horses around to the ship with Damon on it at a full gallop, scattering people in her path.

He had seen her. He was running toward her, asking her something she could not hear, and because she couldn't speak over her heartbeat, she threw the reins down at him, looking wildly past him to the soldiers, who were running on foot now, coming so close.

Damon needed no further encouragement. He vaulted up into the saddle and followed her lead, though she didn't know where she was going. She steered Iolande past the last of the crowd with a delicacy of footwork that left Damon filled with a combination of admiration and dread.

The hood was free, her cloak billowed back behind her like a banner, the tail of her braid unwinding in the wind. She was heading for a side street, one of the many leading into the town, the closest one to them. She was almost upon it, when from the shadows of the building stepped a woman holding a child.

No, oh, no, she thought, but it was far too late to stop. Even as the woman screamed in fright and turned to run, Solange felt the familiar tensing of Iolande's powerful muscles, felt the neatness of the jump that carried them over the woman and safely down again past her.

Behind her, Tarrant followed in their wake, but the woman had retreated to the wall of the alley, still screaming. Damon and his horse pounded harmlessly past her.

They were in a circle with a fountain in the middle, a meeting of streets that was all but abandoned. Damon caught up with her and motioned her to slow down. She didn't want to—hadn't he seen those men? Didn't he know they would find their own mounts and follow? Didn't he realize they would do anything to get her?

But he didn't realize, because she hadn't told him. She slowed Iolande to a walk down a long cobblestone lane and then stopped.

Her breath was coming in short, staccato bursts. There was a deafening buzzing in her ears. She could see Damon's mouth moving but still could not hear him. He appeared angry, but she was unable to explain. How could she, when it was all she could do to drag the air into her lungs?

Damon paused, looking at her, then reached over and took one of her hands which had clenched around the reins. She could see his lips form her name, an inquiry. The anger had melted into something else, something she did not have the presence of mind to identify. His eyes became hooded and bright.

She felt his hands rub hers. Slowly her fingers uncurled, and the warmth returned. The buzzing around her faded as she stared up at him. She could hear again.

". . . better?" he was saying. He let go of that hand and took the other, rubbing it as he did the first. She blinked at him.

"We have to go," she said abruptly.

"Aye," he agreed, not letting go of her hand. "We'll go."

But they didn't move. Tarrant shifted on his feet, crunching on his bit. The alley smelled strongly of garlic and brine.

"They'll come after us," she said somewhat desperately.

"Don't worry," Damon replied. "We're safe for the moment."

His fingers massaged hers in a way she found suddenly disturbing, the way he drew out the movements, followed the lines of her palm to her wrist with long, deep strokes. Wherever he touched her it felt peculiar, a tingling sensation that warmed her whole hand and traveled up her arm. He said nothing now, just studied her, moving his hands around her own in that way that was making her short of breath again.

But it was not fear that made her heart pound so fiercely now.

Oddly enough, she felt like crying. It was the shock of things, she told herself sternly. Don't you dare cry. Keep your wits about you.

She stared down at their joined hands and felt the tears well up. It was baffling, this turn of events. She was angry, yes, angry that the touch of the man she had longed for for so many years would have to come in this way. It was not fair. It should have been so different.

She looked up at him again and watched his face change back into his usual hard mask. He released her hand.

"We'll go now. Follow me and don't stop until I tell you to, and for God's sake, keep that damned hood on."

He took them back through the maze of alleys of the town, always a casual walk when there were people nearby, otherwise a trot.

Once they accidentally stumbled across a duo of men in Redmond's colors, and only the overheard snatch of conversation saved them from rounding the corner, where they stood talking to a group of peasants.

"Are you positive they have not passed by?" one asked. "A dark-haired woman on a roan mare, a man with her on a black stallion with a white blaze?"

Another man spoke. "The reward is rich, my friends. Think it over. . . ."

They retreated slowly, cautiously, and wandered around a few more of the twisted streets until she realized where they were going.

They had reached the gateway to Calais they had entered what seemed a lifetime ago. They were headed back for Du Clar.

"THEY WILL NOT THINK to look for us coming toward them," Damon explained patiently. "We have been spotted in Calais. They will comb the city, and when they cannot find us they will either assume we secured passage to England or that we fled farther north."

"What makes you so certain of this?" Solange was visibly upset to be backtracking. She didn't trust his plan, and that bothered him, though he didn't want to admit it. A part of him could understand her reluctance to follow his reasoning, given the fiasco Calais had turned out to be. But he wanted her to trust him. He would not have turned his life upside down for anyone but her, dammit, and the least she could do was trust him.

They had traveled on through the day and night; now dawn was breaking again. It seemed he had not slept in weeks, months.

"It will work," he said gruffly. "I passed a fishing village on my way out to Du Clar. They had boats, sizable ones. We will gain passage from there."

"It is too close to Du Clar."

"You are exaggerating. It is some distance from the estate, and perfect for our needs. I should have thought of it before. Your dead husband's men will have passed it already."

"'What makes you think there won't be soldiers still there?"

"There won't be." He prayed there wouldn't be. His entire plan hinged on the fact that they had passed by the village days earlier. The soldiers would surely have already been there and gone, if they had even noticed it at all, it was so small. All he could recall were a few miserable boats and some squat houses lined up along a beach. But it would do. It would have to. He tried to inject some authority into his voice.

"If you want to get to England, Countess, you had better listen to me."

She gave him a cold look. He edged Tarrant a little closer to her mount and tried a diversion.

"Or you could tell me why those men are so intent on finding you."

"I am with you, Damon Wolf, on the promise that you will get me to England. If you wish to make inquiries into my former life, please feel free to do so. But I will not be here to answer your questions."

She gave her horse some invisible signal and they bounded ahead into the countryside. Well, at least he got her going in the right direction.

By noon they were both too exhausted to continue. Damon kept pushing them, however, even as Solange complained she simply couldn't stay upright in her saddle any longer. Besides, she said, the horses needed the rest more than they did. It had been more than a full day since they had last slept.

She was correct, of course, but he told himself there were no suitable locations to stop. The fields they traveled now were too exposed. And the more land they could put between them and Calais, the better.

The landscape was gradually changing as they went on hugging the coast, growing wilder, rockier, less fertile. They encountered a slanting wall of limestone that stretched far ahead. Damon remembered it from before, a good sign.

Solange finally stopped him by refusing to ride farther. She had found a secluded meadow of tall, wild wheat grass that had been unharvested. The dry fronds waved in the breeze invitingly. There was a grove of trees for the horses, she pointed out. It was ideal for their needs. She was going to stay there and sleep and didn't really care if he wanted to or not.

With that, she led her mare to the grove, patted her down, and then stretched out in the meadow wheat. She closed her eyes and rolled away from Damon, wrapped in her cape.

He contemplated her from atop his steed. She was right. He knew she was right. There was no reason for them not to stop here for their slumber except the nagging reluctance that kept him immobile, watching her. He simply didn't want to lie next to her. He didn't think he could take that. Despite the peril of the past few days, his attraction to her had not abated. It was more than a nuisance. Seeing her stretched-out form on the grass made him think of her lying in a different place.

Like his bed.

He sighed and rubbed his eyes, as if to rid himself of the vision. She was right, they had to rest.

Grudgingly he joined her, setting Tarrant loose amid the trees with the mare, making a bed for himself as far from Solange as possible while still keeping her within a safe distance. The wheat stalks surrounded him in a fantasy of delicate reeds. Slowly he relaxed.

He dreamed of her.

He woke once and thought he heard her singing: a sweet, clear voice reflecting the heavens. But perhaps it was part of his dream.

When he woke again it was to moonlight and crickets. Solange was already up, feeding the horses and herself some of the leftover apples from an orchard they had encountered two days before. Both horses crowded close to her as she murmured to them, a string of soft syllables he couldn't make out.

He stretched and strolled over to them, helping himself to one of the apples in an open pouch. It was hard and sweet, just the way he liked them.

Solange greeted him without turning around.

"Sleep well?"

He grunted in response, intent on finishing the apple. Somewhat to his surprise, he discovered that he was ravenous. He tossed the core over his shoulder and reached for another.

"Damon, how much farther, do you think, to your village?"

He had been calculating that from the moment he started eating. He adjusted for the possible time they would lose for caution, traveling a circuitous route. It wasn't too bad, actually.

"Another day or two, I suppose." He couldn't help but add, "Are you so eager to be rid of my company, then?"

She shook her head. "It's just that . . . bad weather is coming. Very soon, I think."

He stopped chewing. "Are you certain?"

"Yes."

"What kind of weather?"

"Sleet, perhaps snow as well. That's all I can tell."

Wonderful. It was all they needed, to be caught in France in the miserable flush of winter. It didn't occur to him to doubt her words. She had always had the knack of predicting the weather. As a boy he had seen her proven right again and again. Her attempts to inform the adults had been rebuffed, but she had always let him know exactly what to expect outdoors. Damon rapidly finished the second apple and this time gave the core to Tarrant, who was nudging him.

"How much time before it hits?" He almost didn't want to know.

She shrugged her shoulders.

"Solange, how much time?"

She turned to look at him. The moonlight gave her a ghostly air. "A day. Two days. No more."

She had been generous in her estimate. The storm hit almost eighteen hours later, a driving, greasy sleet that pelted their skin like bee stings. They were soaked immediately in the frozen slush, skin red and eyes tearing. The path they had to follow led them directly into it; the horses kept their heads bowed low with each plodding step.

When it grew so fierce it became impossible to see, they took shelter in a small cave Damon discovered in the cliffs, with just room enough for all of them. They formed a huddled, dripping mass. Damon had to stoop to avoid hitting his head on the low ceiling, then gave up trying altogether and slumped on the ground against the rough limestone wall. Solange sat beside him, peering out from beneath the legs of Iolande. All four watched the storm rage by the oval mouth of the cave.

From the scraps of wood that littered the floor of the cave they managed a sullen, smoky fire. It was shielded from the winds by a small outcropping of stone, but it offered little real heat.

The next day was no better. It was cold comfort to think that the men searching for them were enduring this weather as well.

The sleet remained constant, but now there was a thick coating of ice over everything. There was plenty of water and they ate the last of the apples, but their stomachs were not full by any means. Damon could not hunt when the game stayed hidden, and so they waited, while the skies emptied above their heads.

He had finally found the one thing that could blunt the sharpness of his desire: exhaustion. And it affected her too. He could see it in the purple smears under her eyes, the way she slept like she had melted onto the rough ground, no matter how awkward her position, no matter how cold it became.

By the morning of the third day he would wait no

longer. The small cave had been tolerably warm, thanks to the fire and the body heat of the horses, and so they were mostly dry but starving. Solange had developed a translucency to her skin that made him deeply uneasy for her. He could not sit around and watch her vanish before his eyes. Or, worse, go into that deep sleep she had found and not wake up again . . .

Damon could make no sense of dying in a cave, not after all he had been through already. If crazed men with battle-axes could not bring him down, he wouldn't let a sheet of frozen water beat him.

At his urging, they struggled on. Before they left the cave, Solange had pulled a sharp knife from one of her packs and sawed the green tent in half, then sliced a ragged tear into each half. She placed one piece over each horse, fitting their heads though the holes. The cloth hung down to the horses' knees and halfway down their backs. Damon thought it would be no real protection against the storm, but she retorted it was better than nothing, and he was too tired to argue with her. The tent would never have withstood the force of the winds anyway.

Now the green material flapped in the gales, making a wet, slapping sound with every step. Damon tried to follow the line of the limestone cliffs in case they needed to shelter again. His sense of direction was growing blurry, and time slipped past without his being able to mark it. Was it the same day or the next? Did the steel-gray clouds indicate dawn, or sunset, or mid-day, or moonlight? He didn't know. After a while he found he didn't really care.

Each moment extended, flowed without interruption into the next. The wind was an incessant howl in his ears. He was frozen, and he couldn't feel his body any longer. He thought the dim gray line ahead was the blur of the horizon, almost indistinguishable from the sky.

And still the sleet came, always slanting into his eyes, always pelting his already-unfeeling body. Did the Lord have no mercy left for him? Had he truly sinned so much to deserve this purgatory of ice?

He couldn't remember why he was out there. He couldn't remember where he was supposed to be going. Sometimes he recollected he had a companion, a dark figure beside him, but mostly he saw his own hands, the leather of his gloves black with wetness and coated in ice, solidified to the reins he held.

Damon sensed an inner humming stillness he longed to reach. If he could let go, he would make it. It would be warm and dry. It would be pleasant and calm. He kept his eyes closed, wanting it, searching for it. Everything was easier with his eyes closed.

It was wartime again. He was leading his men into battle against the rebels. Half of his troops were dead from exhaustion, from the bitter cold of the Highlands. But here was Edward beside him, forcing him to march on, damning the odds and all sense. Edward, that bastard king who held Damon fast in the fist of his iron glove, squeezing the life out of him as it pleased him. He was wearing a crown of gold over his helmet, the arrogant fool. He would be singled out and killed in the battle, and where would that leave the rest of them?

Edward was determined to defeat the rebels. It possessed his soul. He would drag his loyal men to the depths of hell to do it, and Damon was utterly his to command.

Who could have known hell would be so cold?

Something was shaking him, forcing his eyes open. It was a woman mouthing words he couldn't hear above the wind. She was familiar to him. He squinted, trying to make her out more clearly. Yes, she looked a little like the girl who had destroyed his passion and his heart years earlier.

But no, this woman was plainly a banshee, with streaming hair and witch's eyes, an unkempt creature of the night.

Banshees predicted death, wailing and weeping. He wanted no part of her. There was death enough around him. He tried to knock her away but for some reason couldn't release his hands from the reins. He would ignore her instead.

The banshee wasn't making it easy. She seemed excited about something, reaching out to shake him again with both hands on his shoulders. How annoying she was. He wanted her to leave him alone, to go away. Let her cast her dire predictions on men who cared about life. He had no use for banshees.

The banshee let go of his shoulders and slapped him, a hard right.

Damon blinked, then scowled at her.

"Look!" she shouted into the wind, and turned his head for him.

Below them, sloping gently to the sea, was an array of thatched stone and wood houses, many of them shining a warm yellow light under doorways and through cracked window shutters.

Damon blinked again, and the image remained steady. The village, the fishing village, by God. That meant . . . He frowned, trying to piece the logic together. That meant there would be a tavern, with food. A shelter, and food!

He pressed his knees into his horse and began the descent.

It wasn't difficult to find the local tavern. Damon and Solange took care of their horses themselves, finding two empty stalls in the stable. In the pungent warmth of the solid little building he began to regain his composure, along with most of the feeling in his extremities. He was all for remaining there, staying with the horses and the clean hay. It was warm and safe. It was familiar. But Solange insisted they go seek food.

The bleached wooden door of the tavern had a crooked plank nailed above it. It read, in faded letters, *Le Chat Noir.*

And indeed there was a large black cat sprawled on the bar, which hissed at them as they entered. A gust of wet wind blew past them, prompting the cat to leap down behind the bar with an angry growl.

"Idiots!" screamed a woman behind the bar in French. "Shut the door!"

Solange was already pushing it closed, allowing the smell of ale and the smoke to gather inside once more. Damon approached the woman.

"Good evening to you, mistress," he began in French, roughening his accent to match hers. From the corner of his eye he saw Solange glance at him in surprise.

"I do not see what is so good about this evening," the barmaid responded sourly. Coming closer to the bar, Damon saw that she was not as old as he first thought. Indeed, under the grime she appeared to be only in her thirties, a buxom woman with mousy blond hair and cracked nails.

She was examining him too. It was almost comical how her demeanor changed once she saw him up close. She wrinkled her nose at him, a coy maneuver that ill suited her. "Even wet to the bone, I do not believe I have seen you before, monsieur."

Damon gave her the full force of his most charming smile. "You are extremely bright, mistress. That is because I have not been here before, wet or dry."

Her smile stretched wider than his. "I am Ghislaine, your hostess. How may I . . . serve you, monsieur?" She leaned over the bar, letting her ample bosom fall forward in her stained blouse. Damon smiled appreciatively. He was beginning to warm up already.

Solange came up and gave the woman a disgruntled look. She had remembered to tuck her hair under the cloak and kept it fastened up to her chin.

"My brother and I"—he clapped an arm around Solange's shoulders—"have had a rough time of it, kind mistress. Could you find us some food, a warm stew perhaps, and some ale?"

Ghislaine cast her eye over the bedraggled waif by the handsome man's side.

"You do not look alike," she observed.

"We share only the same father," responded Damon smoothly.

"Ah. Your brother is tall for his age, yes?"

"Yes. It runs in our family."

Ghislaine was silent, tapping her nails on the wooden bar. There were a few coughs from the men at the tables behind them.

"The food, mistress?" Damon asked gently.

She seemed to make up her mind about something. "I have only fish chowder."

"I am positive it will be the finest fish chowder I have ever tasted, Ghislaine."

"Yes," she replied. "I am also positive that it will be, monsieur."

With that, she disappeared behind a door, leaving them to drip on the bar. Solange clutched his cloak.

"We fooled her! I told you it would work! She thinks I am a boy," she whispered.

Damon leaned against the bar and scanned the rest of the room. "Does she?" he asked impassively.

The tavern was simple and stark. There were no decorations, and the rough stone walls were pitted and stained with the residue of a thousand fires, a thousand nights of salty winds. A few long tables with benches were placed squarely in the center of the room, which was uninhabited but for a table of grizzled old fishermen with mugs, and two others sitting over a game of chess by the fireplace. They all watched the newcomers with unconcealed interest.

He wanted to go sit at one of the tables, or better yet by the fire, but was uncertain of the mood of his legs. The bar was holding him up now, and he didn't want to show his weakness to the men watching.

The black cat bounded back up to the bar, landing

gracefully by his elbow. Solange released his cloak to pet it, running her hand through its fur. The cat shined a yellow glare at Damon, then let itself be picked up by Solange. A raspy purr filled the air.

"Never heard the likes of that," one old man muttered.

"Philippe has a way with animals," Damon responded in a casual tone. "I am certain he will do well as a stableboy on a fine estate."

The group of men guffawed together.

"A fine estate, is it? Well, you've come to the right place. And which one would ye be considering?" asked one of the fishermen over his ale. "We have so many."

The men burst into fresh laughter over this.

"It's true, we are strangers to these parts," admitted Damon. "I know of no estates near here."

"None ye'd want to send the boy to anyways," another man said. "Go home. There's no chance here of a job for your animal charmer."

Some devil in him prompted Damon to say, "What estate are you referring to, good man? We have heard of none nearby."

A sullen silence gripped the table of men; they swallowed their ale and looked down. Damon pressed on. "Because any estate will do. My brother is not particular." He glanced down at Solange to find her scowling at him, equaling the glare of the cat.

A man by the fire spoke around his pipe. "You don't want to send him there, man. Du Clar's no place for the innocent."

"Du Clar, you say? Du Clar. I believe I have heard of this before. . . ."

Solange took a step nearer to him and pressed down on his foot with the heel of her boot quite hard. He pushed her off by shoving away from the bar. His legs continued to hold him up, much to his relief.

"You do not want to send the boy there," repeated the man with the pipe stubbornly.

"An estate is an estate. Philippe will do his work without complaint. I cannot take him back to my cottage." He took an empty seat at the table beside them, smiling sheepishly. "I have promised my wife to send the boy out on his own. You would not believe it to look at his size, but he eats like three grown men! She will skin me alive if I return home with him. You know how women are."

At the bar Solange stiffened, then turned completely away. The oldest-looking man at the table jabbed a finger in the air near Damon's chest to gain his attention.

"Listen to me, son. Wife or no, it is to your peril to visit Du Clar. I cannot tell you more than this. It is no place for a God-fearing Christian. You don't want to risk your young brother's soul, do you? Of course not. Stay away from that place."

All the men muttered in agreement, nodding their heads at the words. Despite his cajoling, none of them would offer anything more on the subject. Solange kept her back to all of them, running her fingers across the bar for the cat, who batted at them furiously.

Although his interest was firmly caught, Damon

recognized the resolute looks on the weathered faces. He gave in with apparent good humor and started in on the bowl of chowder and mug of ale Ghislaine placed in front of him.

"Yours is on the counter, boy," she said to Solange as she draped herself over the bench next to Damon.

Solange reached for her bowl silently. She separated a sliver of fish from the chowder with her spoon and gave it to the cat, who had been watching her movements with fixed interest.

"So," said the barmaid, pressing her thigh against Damon's under the table. "You are looking for work for the little one, but there is none here for him. What, do you plan to cross the channel to find your grand estate?"

A few of the men snickered into their cups. Damon smiled—a sharp, feral look. "Yes. That is exactly what I plan."

Ghislaine let out a hoot of laughter. Then: "You're serious," she cried, aghast.

"Yes."

"You'll not get a boat any day soon, son," said one of the men.

"Not in this weather," added another.

"Oh, we don't need to leave tonight, gentlemen. Tomorrow morning will be soon enough."

From the bar Damon could see Solange turning her head to watch them. Her eyes were narrowed, once again matching the cat's beside her.

"Tomorrow!" they were exclaiming, shaking their heads.

"Impossible!"

"Insanity!"

"In the sleet, on the channel? You will never make it."

"Try Calais, traveler. There's men enough in that city to take on a death wish."

Damon took the handful of coins he had been concealing under his cloak and scattered them on the center of the table. The pattern of the coins fell in random circles of brightness against the dark oak. One of the gold sovereigns rolled in a lazy circle before knocking into a mug and clattering down against the scarred wood.

It was thrice the amount of the reward offered for them. He had made sure of that.

"Calais is too far," said Damon mildly in the ensuing silence. "My brother and I are of a mind to cross the channel first thing tomorrow."

The woman's hand darted out and picked up the stray coin. She bit down on it decisively, revealing a set of uneven yellowed teeth.

"Monsieur, for this price, I would take you to England myself if I had a boat of my own."

"Well," added the man with the pipe, who had stood up to see the sight. "I suppose my boat is sound enough for you and the boy. After all, what is a little snow to stop me?"

"It is sleet, Alain, and storm winds," said one of the other men flatly. "You are fool to sail in it."

"No, you are mistaken, friend." Solange spoke for the first time, lowering her voice to an attractive huskiness that made Damon wince. She went to the door and opened it for them to see out. "It is only a light snow. It will be gone in the morning."

Outside, the white flakes fell to earth in a gentle drift. The winds were gone.

Damon sat back and grinned.

Chapter Seven

BY THE NEXT MORNING he did not feel like grinning. He did not feel like crossing the channel, he did not feel like eating or doing anything but sleeping, and sleeping and sleeping. His head was stuffed with wool, his tongue was swollen and parched, his entire body was on fire.

He stood against the mainmast, back to the wind. There was no place to sit.

" 'Tis only a cold," pronounced Solange, her hand on his forehead.

"I know what it is," Damon replied irritably. "And, if you will recall, I even know how to treat it. If I were at Wolfhaven, I would have the proper herbs to do so."

"You'll be there soon enough," she snapped back.

"Not soon enough for me," he grumbled.

"Nor me!" She stalked away from him and went below deck.

The fisherman with the pipe operated his vessel with the help of his two sons, both of them blond and nameless. They treated Damon with the respect due a moneyed man and Solange with the contempt reserved for younger boys. Alain, the father, spent a good deal of time tacking the sail and scanning the skies. But their luck had held so far; the leaden clouds hovered low but that was all. The snow had stopped.

Damon tried to focus on what he had to do next, but the image of Solange's impatience burned in his mind. Perhaps he shouldn't have lashed out at her like that. It was hardly her fault he had fallen ill.

Of course it was her fault, he reminded himself. This whole debacle was her fault and he should not forget it again. He squared his jaw, gazing out over the steely waves. But still, what Damon saw were her eyes, dark with some unidentified emotion as she felt his skin.

In his traveling bag he always carried a medicine pouch filled with the bare essentials of herbal remedies for emergencies. It was below with the horses and the rest of their belongings. He would have to go get it to see what he actually had. He thought there would be a few things that would help him now, cinnamon, ephedra. He could decoct them into a tea once they landed. . . .

Solange's eyes—was that worry he had read in them? Damon paused, considering.

Worry for herself, perhaps. Worry that she would not be able to reach Ironstag without him. No, he thought wryly, she hadn't enough sense for that. With or without him, she would continue until either she made it there or died trying.

It hadn't been worry he saw. Just some faint concern. Why should she care about his health, other than how it affected her? Why should her view of him have changed at all over these past few days? Only a fool would think such a small amount of time spent together would make any difference after nine years of absence.

He pushed away from the mast, grimacing at the aches that gripped his joints. He felt bruised all over. Most of that was due, no doubt, to the fact that his polite refusal to share a bed with Ghislaine had meant he spent last night huddled on the hearthstones in front of the tavern's fireplace with his back against a definite draft. Solange, taking up the other half of the hearth, had seemed to rest peacefully in spite of that—the woman could probably sleep through the Apocalypse. But Damon had tossed and turned, roasting on one side and freezing on the other. If he had slept at all, he couldn't recall it.

Below deck was a cramped space for cargo, and in this case the horses. At least it was out of the chill breeze. He found Solange sitting with her arms wrapped around her knees and her back propped against the slanting inner hull. She was staring moodily into space.

He debated about what to say to her, whether he should even venture a word. Her frosty look was not encouraging. He walked past her to the pile of their belongings, searching until he found the right bag. Tarrant greeted him with a soft neigh.

Solange watched him silently.

He opened the saddlebag and felt around until he found the medicine bag, a thick leather pouch with separate compartments sewn inside it. Each compartment contained an herb, securely wrapped in lambskin.

It was his own design, one that he had made improvements on over the years as he gained practical experience. It had proven its worth again and again to him, his soldiers, his people.

"You should try to stay out of the wind," said Solange suddenly.

He looked up at her.

"And keep your head covered," she added. "If your hair becomes wet and you're outside, you won't get better. You should stay down here until we reach land."

"As you said, Countess, it is only a cold. I will be fine."

"No, you need to ensure that it does not grow to be anything worse. It's quite easy to have a simple cold develop into any number of serious things, like consumption."

Something in her voice put him on alert. Instead of telling her he already knew these things, he decided to gently prod her, to see where she would lead him.

"Do you think so?"

"Yes." She stopped, looking hesitant. After a moment she offered, "One of the women at Wellburn fell ill once. It began as a little thing, a slight irritation. But she . . . wasn't careful enough. She was exposed to the cold every day without sufficient protection, and eventually she couldn't leave her bed. It was even thought . . . she might die."

Damon leaned back against the pile of bags. "So, what happened to her? How was she treated?"

"Oh, well, they bled her, of course. The physician was very adamant that she be bled."

"They bled a woman with consumption?"

Solange stared him straight in the eye. "Yes. They said it was to rid her of the bad blood."

Damon shook his head. "Leeches are appropriate in certain cases, of course, but I am surprised they continued to bleed her after she showed no improvement. Did they not try herbs? Mustard packs? Tonics?"

"I am uncertain of the full treatment. I didn't know her very well. But I believe once she became bedridden she was . . . removed from the elements that caused her harm. She was kept warmer, and dry. They fed her broth and such."

"Broth." Damon found himself watching her hands, watching them repeatedly clench and relax around her knees. "How long was she bedridden?"

She leaned her head back against the hull. Her reply was muted. "A long time, I think."

"How long?"

"About . . . a year, I suppose."

Her hands clenched, unclenched.

Clenched.

He was going to change the subject. He wasn't interested in the rest of the story.

"A year in sickbed. That's a long time for anyone," he said instead.

"Yes."

"I am surprised she was able to pull through that."

"Many were." She seemed lost in thought, curled up tightly into herself. He watched her carefully as he asked his next question.

"And tell me, did they continue to bleed her until she recovered?"

"Oh, yes," Solange said softly. "They always bled her."

Something inside him was taut, stretched to breaking. It was a deep thing so fragile and frightening, he would not, could not, examine it. It was the thread that held the core of him together, now brittle as glass.

Looking at Solange, at the simple fall of brown hair twisted casually over her shoulder, tightened the thread unbearably. He knew looking into her eyes would break him.

Perhaps she sensed it. She flashed him an overbright smile. "But as I said, this woman recovered. Everything was fine. Today she is hale and hearty, I'm certain."

He couldn't reply. He couldn't think. He didn't want to. She continued to speak in a cheerful voice, ignoring his silence.

"But you can understand now how important it is to take care of your health, especially when it is already compromised. I think we shall buy you a hat in Dover, to cover your head."

Footsteps thumped down the short set of stairs from the deck above. Solange hastily tucked her hair back under her cape. She had been avoiding the crew at Damon's insistence, staying below for most of the voyage. Now she stood up and walked over to the horses, keeping her back to the doorway. The younger of the two sons appeared.

"Papa says to tell you the Saxon cliffs are in sight."

Damon stared at the boy, mute. He couldn't absorb what had just been said. The words bounced around him without meaning. The boy stood still, then shrugged. "Don't you want to come up?"

Solange answered him. "Yes. We'll be up soon."

The boy left. Damon stared at the space where he used to be, then it was filled with Solange herself, on her way out. Without thinking, he caught her arm to stay her.

"This woman," he began, and then was stopped by the severity in her face. He could find no mercy there; in fact, he thought he could see some of the brittleness singing inside him right now.

"It is over," she said firmly. "That woman is much better. I didn't wish to upset you. Don't make me regret telling you such an insignificant tale. I am certain you will fare much better than she did. You're stronger than she was." She twisted out of his grip. "We will buy you a hat," she said once more, and then hurried up the stairs.

A hat.

Damon began to chuckle, an acrid, painful sound. He had to bend double to contain it, but it grew, slicing his belly as it went. Certainly, a hat was what he needed. A hat would fix everything.

A hat to cover his head. He concentrated on that, imagined a hat that Solange would pick out for him.

For his health.

The boat jarred beneath his feet, sending him swaying to the opposite wall. The strait was growing rougher as they came inland. He should be above. The walls of the hull were growing closer and closer. He needed air, fresh air, to fill his lungs.

The sea was indeed rougher now. Outside, he saw

whitecaps topping the brownish-green waves, row after row of them. Solange stood with the others by the forward mast, all of them watching the chalk cliffs of Dover loom closer and closer out of a hazy mist.

He joined them just as the man and his sons broke away to guide the rig into the port. The wind whipped his hair across his face, stinging his skin, but the sensation was far from unpleasant.

Beside him stood Solange, leaning into the wind with a joy as bright as the day was desolate. A fierce smile lit her face as the ship drew closer inland.

The wind picked up tears from her eyes and blew them away. Or was that just his imagination? It was difficult to look at her directly; that pulled the cord tighter in him. Like her, he turned to face Dover, to the odd comfort of the sight of the busy port.

He was worried about the very real likelihood that Redmond's soldiers would be there, waiting for them, and so he scanned the shore anxiously as they docked, searching each face, looking for that one hint of betrayal in the eyes of strangers.

Solange kept close to him, kept her face turned down as much as possible. They were surrounded by the shouts of the seamen, but nothing seemed out of the ordinary. No reason to gallop out of the town, which was what he wanted to do anyway, to run and blend in with the familiar countryside of his native land, to gain the advantage once again by fighting her demons on his own soil.

Yes, it was good to be back. Wolfhaven was miles yet from Dover, and Ironstag farther still, but Damon could not pretend to be anything but relieved to be out of France.

And Solange . . . He could not tell what she felt. She had transformed to her now-usual impenetrable look as soon as they had reached the harbor. If he had not seen for himself the exhilaration she displayed earlier at sea, he would have thought she felt nothing at all to be back.

But he knew better. He was becoming more and more adept at reading her again. She was careful to hide her true self, he noticed. It had to be something she had learned as the countess.

He was eager to leave the city; the littered streets and row after row of buildings crowded in on him the way cities always did. And there were too many faces to search all of them. They were vulnerable here. They had to leave.

Screeching cries of children mixed raucously with the hawking of the marketers, the bleating of sheep, screaming roosters and chickens for sale. He was never comfortable with so many people around him. It seemed unnatural, stacking people and animals on top of each other, mingling the garbage and filth with homes and markets.

Damon was born and raised to a different life, one that cities could not touch. It was space and land, the steady cycle of planting and harvest, room to breathe. Dover or London, it made no difference. City life held no appeal for him.

But to his chagrin, the first thing they did was shop for a hat. Solange would not think of leaving, she said, without getting him one. When he pointed out the danger of lingering in the city, she gave him an astonished look.

"Oh, but this is *England,*" she said. "They won't catch us here."

The naïveté of that statement left him stunned enough to allow her to lead him into the nearest shop.

Despite her confident words, she had decided to continue her charade as a boy, keeping her hair hidden and her cloak buttoned closed.

Ragged as they were, the hatmaker was delighted to see customers on this dismal day. Solange explained politely what they needed. Her brother had lost his hat to the winds and needed a replacement. She remained unswayed by the man's displays of velvet, feathers, and lace. It had to be sturdy, she instructed, a good, plain hat for a good, plain man.

Damon hid his smile when he heard her. They settled on a hat with an unadorned black brim, much to the hatmaker's open dismay. When Damon paid in gold, however, the little man's smile returned, along with the fancier goods.

"Something for the young sir, perhaps?" he suggested encouragingly.

Solange shook her head, but Damon walked past her over to examine again the man's display of wares. His smile became fulsome as Damon lingered over a particularly ornate, ruffled beret complete with blue velvet trim. Solange rolled her eyes and was still saying no as he paid for it, then clapped it on her head.

"My brother, you see, is neither good nor plain, and is properly suited to a fancier style than I," Damon said, smiling at her scowl beneath the lacy brim.

"Yes, yes," cried the shopkeeper. "A delicate boy! The ladies will much admire him thus!"

"No doubt," agreed Damon amicably. "It brings out his better qualities, don't you think?"

"Quite so, yes, indeed, it does! Those eyes! Such refinement!"

"You have feathers for brains, my brother," muttered Solange. "We have what we came for. Let us quit this place."

Damon nodded, bowed to the hatmaker, who bowed in return so low that his nose nearly touched his knees.

"A pleasure, a pleasure to serve you," he exclaimed as they left.

She tried to take the beret off as soon as they left the store, but Damon laughed and stopped her. "You must admit it hides your face well, Countess. You appear to be quite the city dandy now."

"I do not wish to be a dandy," she said clearly.

"Come, come, don't be so modest. Your rather amazing hat was perfectly made for a lad of your exquisite refinement."

"You are ridiculous!"

"You will slay all the ladies with one look, I vow."

"They will die laughing, no doubt."

"You have entirely the wrong view of it, Philippe. No, I suppose I should call you Philip now. Leave it on, I pray you, at least until we leave the city. It does set off your looks, you know."

She shot him a suspicious glance from atop Iolande, but all he did was smile guilelessly. He was telling the truth, so help him. The frills and lace both framed her face and concealed her features, a double advantage as far as Damon was concerned. He could see her all he wanted, but from a distance all was obscure but for the hat.

He settled his own firmly about his head, then brought Tarrant to a trot, deciding that he was feeling much better, all in all, than when the day began.

Dover was a bustling place, even this late. At Solange's insistence, they stopped for a mediocre dinner at a tavern near the entrance to the city. Perhaps he was getting soft in the head, he thought, allowing them to flirt with jeopardy like this. But there was no denying he enjoyed watching her pleasure over a tableful of food. He needed to see the shadows under her eyes fade completely. He wanted that, a sign she was better now that they were so close to home. Now that it was almost over.

Damon requested hot water from the tavern girl and brewed a strong tea from the herbs in his medicine pouch.

Solange followed the process avidly even as she devoured the boiled mutton and pigeon pie. It was as if she had not eaten in weeks. There was some satisfaction in seeing her eat her fill, but what charmed him was her complete delight over the fresh hot bread and creamy winter butter. She ate her share and another, then looked around hopefully for more.

He gave her his.

"One would think," he said mildly, "that they did not bother to feed you at all in France."

She didn't reply at first, but then said, "I find myself exceptionally hungry, that is all."

"I see that."

She lowered her eyes but did not stop until the last morsel was cleared from their table.

They purchased extra provisions for the journey, two blankets, an extra flask for water, and four more pigeon pies. Despite her pleadings, he refused to stay the night in an inn, citing the obvious hazards of giving too many people an opportunity to remember them. As much as he would like to have slept on a real bed again, even the thought of her sharing it with him could not make him stay in town.

Their goal, he reminded her, was to reach Ironstag as rapidly as possible. Unless she wanted to risk the chance of the Redmond soldiers finding them again? He would, in fact, be interested in hearing what they had to say to her. . . .

"But I have nothing at all to say to them, my lord. You are correct, it would be much better for us to continue on this evening. I am ready now, if you are."

And that was that. They made good time out of the city and were quickly into the countryside of Kent. Damon began to breathe a little easier, embracing the smell of the land. The moon was waning, casting a shallow glow that was little brighter than the starlight. They met no other travelers on the road.

They rode in companionable silence, each deep in thought.

Damon's mind wandered, from childhood to manhood, from innocent moments in apple groves to not-so-innocent moments at court. How strange the path his life had taken. He had ended up where he had begun, at Wolfhaven, but the winding way to get there had proven to be torturous. The Church would tell him the ways of the Lord were mysterious, and he had to agree. All he had to do was look over at his companion to confirm it.

She rode easily beside him, pensive but not grim. She had kept on the silly hat he bought her; she claimed it kept her head remarkably warm and was truly sorry they had not bought the same one for him.

The lace jiggled in time to the horse's steps, creating a fanciful dance around her face and down her neck. How beautiful she was, Damon thought, even dressed so strangely. How uncommon she was, how striking.

How he loved her.

He turned his head and tightened his jaw, but he couldn't deny it any longer. He loved her undeniably, loved her still after all that she had done to him.

It split him into two different men, two men with two minds. The Marquess of Lockewood, Knight of the Royal Court, was in a fury over it. How dare he abase himself to her after what she had done? What kind of man would want to return to a woman who had spurned him to marry another, who had ruthlessly and effectively cut him out of her life after deliberately leading him to believe she cared? And who even had the audacity to pretend she still cared today? It was intolerable.

The warrior in him refused her, refused all she stood for, all the humiliation and pain of the past that she alone had created for him.

But the other man had a different view. It was quieter, all the more determined behind the bluster. Damon was not certain who that could be, the other man in him who looked at Solange and saw his own completion, the perfect complement to who he was and wanted to be. This man had grown up with the girl, knew her gentle heart, her strengths and foibles. He knew her soul, because it still matched his own.

This man ached for her, for the whole of Solange, in all her passion and glory and false pride. But with it came a price. Damon was desperately afraid that the identity of this part of him would turn out to be his true heart. And then he would be lost again, for who was to say that Solange would ever want him in return?

She had scorned him once and it had been enough to shatter the boy he was then to dust. Deep down, Damon was afraid she still wielded that power over him. He had come too far, worked too hard, and had too many lives depending upon him to ever risk losing himself like that again. He simply could not do it. To have to start over again would kill him this time, he was certain.

It meant he would live the rest of his life alone. Constantly surrounded by other people, yes, and certainly even with a wife someday, but ultimately and utterly alone.

He needed an heir for Wolfhaven, and so he would do his duty to his forefathers, but there could be no joy in him for the fulfillment of it. He planned to be a good husband to his bride. He would provide for her and protect her, father children and admire the mother she would become. He still intended to keep that pledge to himself. But she would not be Solange, so she could not be his soul's mate. He knew now finally that he would not be able to love the woman he took in marriage. He was never going to get his heart back from Solange.

God worked mysteriously, indeed. For all intents and purposes, the woman riding beside him now was as free for remarriage as any widow of means could be. In fact, how delighted Edward would be to gain a portion of the treasury and estate of a woman as rich as Solange surely was now. She would have to remarry soon, Damon realized. Edward would insist on all her assets being properly protected.

Odd to think of her as a titled widow, a wealthy woman, this unkempt gamin in her voluminous cloak and frilly beret. Her hands poked out of the cloak to handle the reins, looking like nothing so much as a little girl's holding on to her mother's leading strings. The only jewelry she wore, he noticed, was his ring.

His ring. She hadn't taken it off since he had seen her, from the estate through the storms and the cold passage back to England, she wore it always.

Damon smiled bitterly to himself. Should he be flattered or apprehensive? If only he knew.

"What are you thinking, my lord?" She had been watching his feelings chase one another across his face and could contain her curiosity no longer.

"I was thinking of God, and the strange ways in which He works," Damon replied.

"I did not realize you were so religiously inclined."

"Religion finds you when you need it," he said cryptically.

"Does it? Then I am unenlightened, I think."

He didn't respond, so she let the silence carry them

for a while. He seemed to be struggling with something in himself, something dear, she guessed. Poor Damon, it could not be easy for him to deal with her again. It would be much kinder of her to simply let him go, she knew. The way to Ironstag was clear cut from here, even if it was not close. She was positive she could make it on her own.

Then Damon could return to his castle and his lands. To his life. His duty to her was done long ago. It was either pure chivalry or sheer obstinacy that kept him with her. She was being selfish to want him to stay. It was awful of her to make him continue on just to have the fleeting pleasure of his company, to memorize him all over again to last her for the rest of her life.

She thought she had done it once, all those years ago. What a gift it was to have another opportunity to see him, even if the pleasure of it was solidly intertwined with the pain of knowing he did not want her. And why should he? He was a man now, a knight even. He had a life and a world far outside of her own. His future was firmly planted at his beloved Wolfhaven, while hers was really no more rooted than a milkthistle wafting in the breeze.

Leaving Du Clar had been an act of desperation that had built over years of suppression. It was over, it was done, but all she had considered at the time was escape. She was fleeing to Ironstag because it remained her home in her memory. But her welcome there was not assured, she knew.

Her father's death dealt her a serious blow. After her marriage, after Redmond had removed her to France, she had tried to be at peace with the notion of never seeing Henry again, but she knew now her resolution had been self-deluding.

She had never really believed it. Even though he had never bothered to see her, to send inquires of her or to answer her carefully reviewed missives, she never believed he would cut her off so ruthlessly. Time had proven her wrong. Her father was gone now and forever, ironically so close to her bid to break away from Redmond. She could never see Henry again, save in marble effigy on his tomb.

She would never be able to ask him if he had known anything of the man he had given his daughter to save his name.

Of Damon she had expected to hear nothing, and was not surprised over the years to have this thought confirmed. Indeed, a large part of her wanted to hear nothing of him, could not bear to even think of him. Far more painful than the loss of her father was her separation from her love, especially knowing that what he thought of her could not by any means be considered loving. But nevertheless, it was Damon who had kept her alive all this time.

How he would laugh to hear it, she knew. The knight riding beside her would not appreciate the information; in fact he barely resembled the Damon who had advised her in her dreams, the Damon who had whispered to her in her heart to be brave, to be cunning and resourceful. It was embarrassingly clear that the man he was now wanted nothing to do with her.

So she would cling to the memories and soon create new daydreams from the moments she shared with him now. It was better than nothing, and she was grateful.

She was greedy, she would take what she could get of Damon Wolf. Ashamed and yet shameless, she would not release him to his world just yet. They would have him for the rest of his days. She wanted to hold on to him for just a while longer, to fill herself with him until she could take no more. That was all. It wasn't too much to ask.

"Tell me of Wolfhaven," she invited him.

He seemed to come out of some reverie, shaking his head. "Wolfhaven? What is it you want to know?"

"Anything. Anything you wish to tell me."

"You know the history of Wolfhaven."

"I want to know about today. Tell me what it's like to live there. Tell me what you do there."

"Do?" He was overwhelmed with answers. "I do what any lord should do for his manor and villages. I plant crops—"

"Which?"

"Mainly wheat, also barley, rye. Some oats and flax." He made an impatient gesture. "I fail to see why you should be interested in this subject, Countess."

"Why should I not be? I grew up with you, hearing the stories of your castle. I think it's only natural I would wish to know of the fulfillment of some of those plans we made."

Solange grimaced, regretting the words as soon as they left her tongue. She had not meant to remind him of their shared past, especially of the youthful dreams they had built together. She could feel him retreat from her.

"What I mean to say, my lord, is that I am curious—"

"I understand full well your meaning, madam. You

need not elaborate. Wolfhaven is a working system consisting of the castle, the villages, and all the inhabitants therewith. We are largely an agricultural society, relying upon a series of crops to support the population and provide trade with neighboring lords. We also raise sheep for wool, much like Ironstag but on a smaller scale, of course." His voice was flat and emotionless; he spoke to her as if lecturing a pupil.

Solange gave a little sigh. This was not at all what she really cared to hear about, but she understood that his dry recital of facts was all he was going to offer her unless she queried further. She wasn't feeling daring enough for that.

"I see," she said meekly. "Thank you."

They bedded down for the night against a haystack, one of many dotting the constant fields of stubble left after the harvest. Solange slept with her hat beside her and Iolande hovering nearby, as if standing guard over her sleeping mistress.

Even Tarrant seemed uneasy over something, waking Damon with soft snorts and restive steps in the hay. These were not the signs of danger, however, and so after each disturbance, Damon sank again into a weary slumber, only half wondering what was bothering his horse. Probably the stallion was just as ready to end this trip as he was.

To be certain, he asked Solange about the impending weather the next morning when they awoke.

She stared intently at the sky, and then at the ground, then shook her head. "Fine, I think. No snow, no storms coming soon. Today should be clear and fair."

He grunted an acknowledgment, giving Tarrant an accusing look. The horse only stared back at him placidly.

Perhaps they were not as alone as it seemed, Damon thought as he prepared for the day's ride. Perhaps all his senses had failed him, after all, in his careful scouting of the land, his listening to the winds. Was this what Tarrant was trying to alert him to? Was there danger afoot?

They had to go. He turned to Solange, opened his mouth to tell her to mount up, but then he closed it again.

She was perched on a stone with her legs tucked under her and the sunlight behind her, combing out her long hair. It was something she did every morning before braiding it up again, but usually Damon tried to be elsewhere when she began. He stayed where he was, paused in adjusting the girth and stirrups on his horse.

It was hypnotic, following the stroke of the ivory comb through the heavy tresses. She started at the top and worked her way down, having to stretch her arm out full-length to reach the ends before allowing the captured strands to tumble back down against her body. In the morning light her hair glowed with auburn fire. He remembered so clearly how it felt in his hands, against his lips.

She parted another section of hair and began on it, the same pattern, the same results: thick, glossy locks falling to curve against her, molding to her shape. She tilted her head and the sun shone with it, a shifting halo of brilliance that surrounded her, deep reds and coppers, rich dark browns. The ivory comb worked through so slowly, so rhythmically, he could count the pace. She used her free hand to smooth the locks after each passage.

It was unusual to see a woman's hair so openly displayed. Even Solange kept hers tucked away when she could. He felt he was intruding, watching her perform this simple task. He thought absently that he should not be looking, that he had been about to tell her something, but the stroking of her hand and the comb swept away that thought. He could not stop staring.

Again the comb separated the strands, again it slid down the tresses with silky ease, leaving a wake of softness behind. Every time she moved, the cascade of hair moved with her, rising and falling with each breath.

Without the cape to hide her body, her femininity was plainly revealed under the gray tunic she wore. It had a simple drawstring at the throat to tighten or loosen. The knot was free now; the strings hung limply to the tips of her breasts. He could see a wedge of creamy white skin where the cloth fell to the sides. He could see her hair brushing the tunic, lying trapped between the folds of cloth and her skin. He could feel the tantalizing stroke of her hair, the tender delicacy of her body. He could feel her wrapped around him, all of her at once—hair, skin, scent—pressed against him, welcoming him, wanting his touch as he wanted hers.

They were collapsed together on the ground, and her tunic was open to him, baring her breasts to his lips. He was tasting her, the shocking sweetness of her body, the fullness of her embrace as she writhed under him. She was covering him in kisses, she was twining her long legs around his waist, moaning with desire.

He was tugging the tunic off her, the hose, impatient, eager to feel her hot and bare against him. She was helping him, lifting her arms up to be free of the clothing, then clutching him closer, pulling him into her, gasping his name . . .

"Damon? Damon?"

He realized Solange was still seated on the ground before him, comb paused halfway though her hair. She looked concerned and very fully clothed. "What's amiss, my lord? I spoke to you and you didn't reply. You were looking at me so strangely."

Fortunately, life at court had taught him well how to say one thing while thinking another. His mouth was responding before his mind had fully caught up with him.

"I was . . . contemplating other matters. What did you ask me?"

"I said, do you think it wise of us to travel by day now, instead of by night?"

The image of her beneath him, naked, alive with passion, would not vanish. Damon struggled to focus beyond it, to form a logical reply to her question, but when her lips moved, he saw himself kissing them. When her arms lowered and the comb released her hair, he saw himself buried in it. He turned away stiffly, checking the already tightened girth to his saddle.

He heard her stand up behind him. "Are you well?" she asked uncertainly.

"Yes." He took a heavy breath. How could she not know? How could she not feel it too? She was a widow, by heavens, no longer an inexperienced maiden. She had to realize what she was doing to him, that she was deliberately torturing him. It was enough to drive a sane man over the edge, and he had already been there too many times.

"Damon?" She came up behind him and placed her hand lightly on his arm.

The simple touch jerked him back to the present. He pulled away from her and turned, baring his teeth in a semblance of a smile.

"Day versus night, you ask? It doesn't matter now. We are close to the conclusion of this little sojourn, aren't we?"

Her eyes grew wide, even a little fearful. He almost hated her for that, hated that she could feel fear of him, when all he had ever wanted to do was protect her, take care of her, love her.

Damon took a menacing step in her direction. "Now, what's amiss with you, Countess? You do not look yourself."

Solange shook her head in bewilderment. "I don't understand you. You are angry. Have I done something wrong?"

"Something recently, you mean? I don't know, you tell me." He was stalking her now, steadily matching each step she took to put space between them. One hand was raised as if to push him away; the other was grasping the folds of the tunic together. The fear in her eyes became stronger.

"Stop it! Why are you behaving in this odd manner? Are you feverish?" She halted defiantly, daring him to come closer. Brave, foolish little Solange, and so he caught her up easily. She crashed into his chest, helpless because her arms were pinned and he would not let her put her feet down firmly to the earth. He held her tightly against him until she stopped struggling, until she only stared up at him in almost comical disbelief.

"Yes, my lady," he drawled. "I think I must be feverish. It is the only reason I can think of to do this." He covered her lips with his own.

She didn't fight him. She didn't do anything but hang there in his arms and let him kiss her. It didn't matter. He was beyond caring about any objections she had.

Nine years he had dreamed of these lips, nine years of longing for one more chance, just one more, to savor her again. No man should have had to live like that. He would not spend the rest of his life regretting a passed opportunity.

For a heartbeat all he felt was the closeness of her. Her lips were warm and succulent, and completely still under his. It was too much like that fateful kiss they had last shared on her wedding morning, and his heart cried out with anger and despair.

But then she moved. He instinctively tightened his arms to prevent her from escaping, but she wasn't trying to back way. She was attempting to move higher in his arms, to match herself more equally to his height.

She was kissing him back.

The last remnants of reason retreated into the roaring hunger that gripped him. A part of him knew this was the moment he had been waiting for all this time, her response to him, proof she was not immune to the desire that flamed to life between them.

Sweet Lord, she was not. Her hands inched out from between their bodies to hold on to his shoulders, enabling him to pull her closer, his fantasy becoming reality faster than he could take it in. His body knew what to do, however. It answered hers with a surging heat. He bent her almost backward over his arm, bracing her against his legs. She was light, so light he barely noticed her weight. Her hair slid silkily under his palms as they traveled up her back, down to cradle her thighs, then up again.

Their lips meshed and parted, sharing the same breath. The maidenly shyness she had been treating him with had vanished as if it had never been. Before him now was a woman, a siren, arousing him with a bold lushness he wanted to drown in. He kissed her jaw, her neck, straightening to lift her higher to reach the hidden softness beneath her ear. Her head tilted back, helping him.

Slowly he released her, allowing her body to slide over every muscled plane of his own. Her tunic caught on his and rose to her waist. He slipped his hands under it and felt the satin of her skin beneath his palms. They traveled up to cup her full breasts, softly squeezing their roundness. Solange gave a startled gasp and then moaned in pleasure, arching farther into his hands. Her reaction was like a thunderbolt running through him.

Damon was intent on getting her to the ground. He had to find a good place to lay her down, anywhere without the stubble of cut hay. She was panting for him, ready for him, and he was more than ready for her. He would toss her onto the haystack, it didn't matter, he had to be inside her soon or risk losing his thin grasp on the resolution not to make love to her in the dirt.

She stiffened suddenly, trying to pull away from him with a muted cry. He held her immobile against him, confused—she couldn't want to stop now, she wanted him, he knew it—but Solange braced her arms against his shoulders and shoved, looking wide-eyed at something behind him.

"Damon! Thieves!"

The agitation in her tone penetrated the haze of passion fogging his mind. Immediately he released her and turned, reaching to his waist for the stiletto he always carried there. His fingers groped at the empty sheath; the dagger lay on the ground next to that morning's breakfast of pigeon pie, much too far to reach in time.

Close behind him, right next to the haystack, was a half-circle of four mounted men dressed in rough, dirty clothing. Two of them were leering at the couple, but the others just stared at them blankly.

The man closest to them, a bearded fellow with a long scar down one cheek, followed Damon's glance to the stiletto and back again to his empty hands. And then the thief gave a wicked smile.

Chapter Eight

"MY GOODNESS GRACIOUS," said the scarred man. "It appears we have caught the couple unawares."

Solange took a step forward around Damon, as if to block him from the strangers. "We have nothing of value. You waste your time with us."

The man effected an exaggerated look of surprise. "Oh? I think perhaps our time has seldom been better spent, eh, boys?"

The group broke into muffled chuckles. Damon scowled at them and then took her gently by the shoulders. "Solange—"

At the mention of her name the men choked into an astonished silence, but she didn't notice. She ignored the warning of Damon's tone and faced them, hands on her hips. "What manner of men would creep up upon a pair of pilgrims, to rob them of what little means they possess? You are cowards, all!"

Damon pulled her back to him. "Solange," he said again.

"So be it," she said haughtily. "Take it all, then. But leave us our steeds; they will not serve anyone but us."

The men were staring down at her from atop their horses, dumbfounded, although Damon couldn't say if it was at the speech of the lady or the fiery beauty she radiated.

Amazing, he thought reluctantly. She stood in front of him, vehemently defending both of them from a group of men, all of whom were more than twice her size, and on horseback. It was a touching scene, if a ludicrous one.

"Solange, listen to me," he said firmly.

She whirled around and whispered, "I will not let you fight them! There are too many, you would be killed! I won't allow it!"

"Fight?" echoed one of the thieves, a giant of a man with white-blond hair. "Did she say she wants us to fight?"

"Fight who?" asked another.

"There will be no fight," Damon said loudly. "My lady, allow me to introduce my men"—he looked up and glared at them—"who will have an excellent reason to be out here looking for me, rather than at Wolfhaven, where they belong."

Her jaw dropped. "Your men?"

"Yes. Gentlemen, I present Lady Solange, Countess of Redmond."

Slowly, deliberately, she broke away from his hold on her shoulders. Her cheeks were flushed. She turned around and took in the group, who were now looking somewhat abashed, except for the leader, the one with the scar.

"My lady," said that man, dismounting. He gave her a sweeping mockery of a bow, waving about an invisible hat.

"Godwin, my steward," said Damon with a freezing look.

Solange gave no reply. Her back was ramrod straight, her lips pursed. Damon could hardly blame her for her lack of civility. He was ready to strangle the group of them himself. He watched helplessly as she finally nodded, then excused herself in a quiet voice and went over to her horse. The sight of her long hair swaying against her thighs made him grit his teeth. He stalked over to the others.

"Please do enlighten me," he ground out, "as to why I am seeing any of you here at all, especially at this particular moment."

The other men shifted uneasily in their saddles, but it was Godwin who coughed discreetly behind his hand. "We came with urgent news, of course, my lord. As to this moment, all I may say is we were quite unaware of your . . . intimacy with the lady. We were merely following your trail."

For the first time since he had known him, Damon found his steward's blithe sarcasm annoying. "You are fortunate, Godwin of Lockewood. Any other man who dared insult the countess would feel the cut of my blade."

Godwin arched his brows. "Indeed? Well, perhaps I am fortunate, as you say, my lord. Although you would just have to sew it up again, as you did for me before." He fingered the thin scar running down his cheek. "Rather a lot of work for you, I would think."

"Enough. Why are you here?"

The steward dropped his careless pose, assuming a grave demeanor that portended trouble. "We came to intercept you, my lord. We had no idea you would bring the countess with you."

The others were dismounting, walking over to him with covert, awed looks in the direction of Solange. She was busy packing her bags.

Damon felt the inexplicable forces of his life pulling together for one strange moment, uniting him with the vision of his past and the hard-won efforts of his present represented in each worn, loyal face around him. He shook his head to rid himself of the effect, then pinched the bridge of his nose to relieve the pressure mounting in his head.

"It was just as unexpected for me, I assure you," he said.

"She's the one?" asked Aiden, a dark-haired man in his thirties.

"Aye," answered Damon.

Again the men grew silent, now openly watching Solange loading up Iolande with prim precision, marching through the broken stalks of hay in her old tunic and hose with the dignity of a young queen. Only Damon could guess how much it cost her to hold on to her mask. He knew she was probably quite embarrassed.

She was mortified. Her treacherous hands refused to stop shaking, so she kept her back to the group as much as she could manage. She had finished packing the bags, so now she pulled out the curry comb and began to groom Iolande. She didn't care that the horse didn't need it. She didn't care if they thought it strange. She didn't care what they thought of her! Indeed, Solange thought wrathfully, she wouldn't care if she never saw any of them again in her entire life, including Damon Wolf.

To be caught like a common trollop trysting in a field by a group of sneering jackanapes! And worse yet, to have the man she was trysting with not only know them, but *introduce* her to them as well . . .

All she wanted, she told herself, was to go home. Things would become clear to her once she was safely back at Ironstag. If they would not take her there, she would think then about where to go next. She had options. She was not destitute.

She would think of something.

Across the field the men huddled in a single clump, all eyes aimed at the woman brushing her horse. Godwin was the first to break the silence.

"My, how cozy! Are you two—"

"No," Damon interrupted before he would have to hear the dreaded question. "Do not place too much importance on whatever you thought you just witnessed, am I clear? The countess and I are nothing to each other."

"Very well," continued Godwin after the barest pause. "Then certainly you won't mind me inquiring of the rather unusual travel arrangements the lady has chosen to make? She is a countess, after all. Her husband must surely be an accommodating man. . . ." Godwin grinned. "Unless you have killed him, of course."

A few of the others smiled nervously at this, but Damon only shook his head. "Not I, my friend.

Apparently the earl took care of that problem for me by ending his miserable existence the day I arrived."

Amid the exclamations of the others, Damon gave a summary of events leading up to their discovery by the haystack. He kept it as brief as he could manage, but was still bombarded with questions.

"Why would she want to leave?"

"She was going to run away alone?"

"What do Redmond's men want?"

"You been posing as brothers all this time? And people believed it?"

"You're headed for Ironstag?"

"You slept in a cave?"

The last question was from Braeden, his fifteen-year-old squire, who revealed a good deal of envy in his tone.

Damon held up his hands. "You know all that I know now. No doubt the circumstances of my lady's departure from Du Clar are unusual, but as I said, she would have left alone if I had refused to accompany her. It is readily apparent that she is quite eager not to meet Redmond's men, and equally apparent that they do want to meet her just as badly.

"I am escorting her to Ironstag and no farther. What she does with her life from then on is none of my concern. Now, tell me this"—he surveyed the group with an acid glare—"what required four of my best men to intercept me against my specific orders to stay at home and tend to the harvest?"

Only Godwin met his gaze with pure innocence; the others looked away at the sky or at their own hands. "Why, I carry a message for you, my lord," he said.

"A message? Four of you to deliver a message?"

"You couldn't expect me to go alone, my lord? What, with thieves and rogues around every corner?" Godwin gave an exaggerated shiver. "I would be their fodder in a matter of days!"

"He needed a guard," said Aiden stubbornly. "We all insisted upon it, didn't we?"

A chorus of affirmatives answered this question. "And the harvest is sound," added Robert, the blond giant. "It was all but finished when we left. You needn't worry."

Damon knew when he was defeated, and he didn't want to waste time arguing with them. They were already here; nothing was to be done about it but accept it. In truth, he was relieved to see them. If they did meet up with the soldiers, it would be a fairer fight.

Behind them, against the bright blue sky, he could see Solange, who was beginning to pace impatiently beside her mount.

"Tell me, then. What is it?"

"Well, you see, we expected to greet you in Dover in a few days, but you made much faster time than we anticipated. I'm not sure how you managed that. Your clandestine traveling modes would seem to slow you down rather than speed you up. . . ."

"Yes, yes, Godwin. The message?"

"I'm afraid, my lord, that Ironstag must wait for your company."

Damon felt an uncomfortable foreboding.

"Why is that?"

"It seems, my lord, that the king's emissary is waiting at Wolfhaven to see you. He's waiting right now."

The foreboding sharpened to dread, which made

his voice curt. "If you do not tell me what you are talking about, Godwin, I will personally see to it that you are confined to duty in the buttery for a month doing nothing but scrubbing pots and talking to old women—"

"The emissary is awaiting you to read the royal parchment declaring that Ironstag is yours."

"What?"

Godwin smiled, enjoying the effect of his announcement. "The Marquess of Ironstag left his castle and all his lands to you, the Marquess of Lockewood."

Robert clapped one meaty hand on his shoulder. "Congratulations, my lord."

Denials rose to his lips, but he knew his men would not dare play a prank such as this. So help him, all Damon could think of was how this news was going to affect Solange. Was the estate supposed to go to her? He remembered the family tree well enough to know that Solange represented the end of her line. There were no cousins or uncles to inherit. When she had married Redmond, everyone had assumed the marquess planned to have Ironstag go to his eldest grandson through Solange. How did Henry get around the entailment?

Godwin, as usual, answered his thoughts. "Apparently Ironstag had no wish for Redmond to inherit, my lord, in any capacity. He is specifically excluded from the entailment. Ironstag paid our king a goodly sum to ensure it."

"And the countess?"

"Ah, yes. The countess is also excluded."

Damon muttered an oath under his breath. It appeared the old man had the last laugh after all. By forcing Damon to take over Ironstag, he had effectively tied him to Solange whether he willed it or no. What had possessed him to make such a drastic move? Had the pain of his final days driven him to madness?

Damon shook his head, perplexed and annoyed all at once. He would have to work out this problem, see about how he could reverse the marquess's order and give Ironstag over to Solange. He sure as hell didn't want it. Time was what he needed.

"I must take the countess to Ironstag before going home. The king's message can wait."

"I don't think so, Damon," said Godwin seriously. "It took all our resources to get them to permit us to travel alone to fetch you. Howard wanted to send out a small army after you. We didn't tell him why you'd gone to France, only that you'd be back soon."

"Howard? Howard Longchamp? Bloody hell."

Damon's dealings with the king's minions had taken an unforeseen turn for the worse when Longchamp had decided to make an enemy of him. Longchamp had been, and Damon supposed still was, one of Edward's closest advisers. Typical of Edward's twisted sense of humor to send him out to deal with this.

Aiden rubbed his beard. "Perhaps Howard's still vexed that his wife invited you to her bed more often than him."

"Or perhaps he's still upset over that time you humiliated him in front of Edward, when you pointed out the flaws in his plan to take the castle Glencairn," added Robert.

"Or perhaps it was all those times you defeated him in the joust," said Braeden with pride.

"Or perhaps the man is simply an ass," stated Godwin. "It doesn't matter. He was frothing at the bit to send out a contingent of soldiers to bring you back to Wolfhaven in all haste. Fortunately, I was able to dissuade him."

Damon raised a brow. "Dare I ask how you accomplished that?"

"I merely pointed out that Edward wouldn't be pleased to have the Wolf of Lockewood angered by an excessive show of force, implying a lack of trust in one of his most loyal warriors. And that our king would not be pleased to learn Howard would be the one who usurped his authority in this matter. I reminded him of how Edward can be a little touchy on the matter of authority."

"Beautifully understated." Damon shook his head. "But what I fail to understand is why Howard is at Wolfhaven at all. Why couldn't he read the declaration to you, as my proxy?"

"Ah, well, you see, in addition to the fact that Edward declared that you must be there personally for the reading, there is a little matter of gold to be paid, my lord."

"Edward is a greedy bastard," threw in Aiden. "He's charging you an inheritance fee for Ironstag."

"On top of what Henry paid to him already? This is getting worse and worse."

The rest of the men grunted in agreement. Damon stared bleakly at the sky, then let his eyes rest on Solange, now mounted up and waiting with poorly concealed irritation to ride.

"Mention nothing of this in front of the countess, understand? I must think about how to tell her."

"The marquess left a provision for any offspring of my lady . . ." Godwin let his voice trail off suggestively.

"No. She has no children. At least, I don't believe she does." Damon was appalled at himself, at his lack of basic knowledge of this woman he claimed to love. His world was turning upside down. "Let's go," he said brusquely.

"I was beginning to wonder if I should continue my travels alone, my lord," said Solange with just a hint of sarcasm as he climbed into the saddle. "I wouldn't wish to tear you away from your men."

"My apologies, Countess," he replied. "We had urgent business to discuss."

She looked ready for a fight, but he wasn't going to give her one. All the weariness of the past few days caught up with him at once, coupled with the news of Ironstag and, of course, the still-startling fact of Solange reentering his life. For the first time in his life Damon felt at an utter loss as to the best path to choose for his future. It had seemed so clear before, and now the choices were too confusing. In the center of all the conflict stood Solange: delicate, obstinate, captivating Solange, made, it seemed, to be his ultimate, final temptation. In the battlefields of life she remained his sole weakness, the golden icon he both cherished and reviled. She was the perfect rose in the winter of his heart. He wanted to crush her, he wanted to adore her, but thanks to her father, he now could no longer settle on the solution of ignoring her.

She rode slightly ahead and to the left of him, carrying on a hesitant conversation with Godwin, who was at his most ingratiating. Her cloak and hat covered all her features to him, but he needed no visual aid to picture her face. She would be giving Godwin her solemn, slightly suspicious look, since he was a stranger to her, albeit a voracious one. Her chin would be tucked down, her eyes clear and unblinking. She would be carefully dissecting every word he said to her, examining each for hidden meaning. She would be using her clever mind to analyze Godwin's smile, his posture, even his horse for clues to unwrap his motives. She might yet decide to play his game and lead him on, Damon thought with amusement.

Well, Godwin couldn't say he hadn't been warned. All the men here knew of Solange and her role in his life. All of them had heard the tales, had listened to the growing legend of the girl who had broken Damon Wolf's heart. Some of the reports that had gotten back to him had made her into something no longer resembling a woman at all, but sometimes a mythical creature of celestial beauty, too pure for the earth. Or more often, a soulless siren who had drained away his tender feelings, leaving the shell of the Wolf behind.

Neither version was true. Solange was actually somewhere in the middle, but Damon of Lockewood could not pinpoint exactly where. Wherever it was, she was definitely on the human side. He had felt the proof of that today.

His true musings of her, late night memories over

ale and campfires, had been entrusted to only those closest to him, and Godwin was one of those. No doubt the steward was on some mission of exploration of his own, out to discover the workings of this woman he had heard of for years but never met.

"I myself prefer the color pink," Godwin was saying. "A man who wears a pink hat, I say, is a fearless man indeed."

"Ah," said Solange.

"Would you be surprised, my lady, to learn that I once owned not only a hat of the finest pink wool, but also a matching doublet and cape? It is a fact. The ladies were quite impressed, I assure you."

"Really."

"But no more so than the men! Why, when I entered a room, the conversations ceased immediately! Crowds parted as I walked through, men and women both held mute in stunned admiration!"

This won him a small, dubious smile from her.

"But, alas, I lost my handsome set of pink in a game of chance," he continued. "A rigged game! The men at court became so jealous of my clothing—none could match it, you see, this color pink coming from only the rarest of Persian cockleshells, each more costly than the last—that they decided to divest me of my set publicly and permanently. They plied me with wine, wom—er, wine, and befuddled me so that I had no possibility of winning against their wicked plot. When I was out of coin, they would take nothing else but the hat, cape, and doublet. And that was that."

Solange was intrigued in spite of herself. "Did you not attempt to win them back?"

"Oh, yes! Naturally! But they would hear nothing of it, my lady! Those villains burned my outfit that very eve! I was devastated!"

"It was a merciful plan from heaven itself, the night we burned those hideous clothes," injected Aiden. He had dropped back to listen to the tale and monitor the lady's response. "You should have thanked us for sparing you the embarrassment of wearing such foolish things. 'Twas a merry bonfire we had in the courtyard that night!"

"You see, my lady," said Godwin mournfully, "how the scoundrel still does not repent his sin against me. A shameful state, indeed."

"You burned his clothes?" Solange asked Aiden.

"Aye, all of us. But it was my plan."

"It was *my* plan, Aiden Gerard!" Robert looked indignant. "The rest of you just helped me out with it!"

"Ho! And who decided to get Godwin drunk that night?"

"Well then, who rounded up that tavern wench with the red hair and the magnificent pair of—"

"Gentlemen!" Damon had heard enough. "Suffice it to say it was a mutual effort. Do not attempt to bore my lady with the details."

"Oh, no, my lord. I am not bored. Pray, do continue, sir," she said sweetly to Robert. "The tavern wench had a magnificent pair of what?"

Robert blushed to the roots of his pale hair. Aiden snickered audibly. Even Braeden looked abashed.

"Of teeth, my lady," answered Godwin. "She had two perfectly formed, white teeth, right in front, here. She was actually quite famous for them. They were so magnificent that one barely even noticed the absence of the rest."

Solange gave a knowing smile. "How unusual. I would enjoy meeting a woman like that."

"As entertaining as that would be, I'm afraid the lass lives in London. It would be a far way to go from here."

There was no mistaking the twinkle in Solange's eye. "What a pity. But someday, perhaps, I shall go to court and find this unique woman. Shall I tell her you sent me, good sir?"

"Not if you wish to get past her door!" laughed Aiden. The others joined in.

The rest of the day passed with the same casual, easy banter that marked the familiarity of old friends. Solange spoke little but listened closely, happy to learn whatever she could of Damon and the life he had lived these past few years, summing up what she could of the circle of men around her.

Damon had chosen unusually loyal men, she surmised. From the good-natured teasing passed around, she would have thought them more friends to him than servants. Although he laughed and joked with them, it was clear he was the leader of the group, and the others always deferred to his judgment. He radiated power; it was far more than the pure muscular strength of him, more than the image of the handsome, black-haired knight on his stallion. His power stemmed from an inner confidence, Solange thought. From the top of his hat down to his spurs he appeared to be a man of action, a man accustomed to leadership.

And he was taking nothing for granted. He kept his

unfathomable eyes pinned to the horizon, or making quick sweeps of the surroundings as they passed through each knoll, each valley. His men, she noticed, did the same, following his cues. It was the extreme opposite of Redmond's relationship with his men. They had respected him only as far as they feared him, and emulated him only to flatter him. It was a pattern she had seen again and again. Thank God she would never hear another fawning word spoken of the earl. She doubted she would be able to keep her silence in the face of such insincerity again.

As night fell, they camped at the base of a small hill, the men unpacking their steeds with rapid efficiency. Solange kept her distance by making up a bed near Iolande, politely refusing an offer of extra furs from both Godwin and Aiden. She wrapped her cloak around her and fell asleep almost immediately.

Damon kept up a desultory conversation with Godwin on the status of Wolfhaven after the others retired, occasionally poking a stick into the fire to send sparks flying up into the velvet sky.

"Why don't you just bring her closer?" asked Godwin bluntly after watching Damon's eyes linger worriedly on the sleeping form of Solange for what seemed to be the hundredth time. "It must be cold over there anyway."

"She won't like it," Damon muttered.

"She won't wake up," countered the steward.

Another shower of sparks flew into the night. With an air of resolution Damon tossed the stick into the fire and strode over to Solange. She was curled up into a tight ball, one arm tucked under her head as a pillow.

She had kept her hat on under the hood.

Carefully he knelt and scooped her up in both arms, moving as smoothly as he could so he wouldn't jar her awake. He had wondered when the hard traveling would finally drain her, and the fact that she didn't even stir in his arms confirmed his fears. All she did was give a little sigh as her head came to rest against his chest. He carried her back to the fire, then stood uncertainly, unwilling to let go of her just yet.

"I believe it is time for me to withdraw for the first watch, my lord," said Godwin in a low voice. "Good night." He stood up and walked away to the perimeter of the camp.

Damon watched him go, then looked back down at the face of the sleeping woman in his arms. He crossed to his own pallet, made up of the extra furs garnered from his men. He had been going to cover her with them after she fell asleep. Now gently, slowly, he lowered them both onto the pile, nestling her into the warm softness. He would sleep across from her, he decided, close enough to gather warmth from the fire.

But when he tried to remove his arms from her, she whimpered and frowned fretfully, still fast asleep. When he tried again, she had the same reaction. He had no choice, he told himself. She obviously needed to rest, and if she awoke now, she might be too disturbed to fall back easily into slumber. It really was for her own good, Damon thought as he lay beside her. She would rather freeze from her own stubbornness than admit weakness, he knew. He had to protect her from herself.

He lay on his side, facing her, her backside pressed

against him. His arm against the ground cushioned her head while the other drew the furs over them both, then curled around her waist. Solange took the arm holding her and wrapped her own around it, hugging it to her chest. She let out another sigh, and this one sounded like contentment.

Right now, for this stolen moment, he knew how she felt.

SOLANGE AWOKE IN a different place from where she fell asleep. And although she woke up covered in furs, she had a distinct impression that something was lacking, something she couldn't quite articulate. She presumed she had been moved closer to the fire at some point during the night, and she couldn't help but be grateful, since the nights were growing colder and colder. Still, it was odd. Something was missing, but she had no idea what.

It was early yet. Dawn broke with rising color to the eastern horizon, already tipping the treetops with rosy gold. Thrushes were trilling off in the forest, announcing the new day.

Solange sat up, stretching. All the men were off a good distance, sitting on a fallen log, talking in low voices, and sharing a breakfast of hard biscuits. Damon rose and came over to her when he saw she was awake. His hair hung loose in smooth waves, setting off the tan of his face in a way that left her curiously short of breath, reminding her abruptly of that moment in Calais when he rubbed her hands. He seemed to search her eyes for something, a line of worry creasing his brow.

Wordlessly he handed her a biscuit. She accepted it, thanking him. He hesitated, then asked, "How did you sleep?"

"Very well, thank you," she replied cordially. The morning air left puffs of frost hanging between them.

He frowned, then turned on his heel and went back to the others.

What a mystery the man was. She had thought from the kiss they shared yesterday that perhaps he did feel something for her, after all, but then with the change of a few hours he was back to treating her like a barely tolerated stranger. She could not make it out. Well, she refused to dwell on it. Never mind that the kiss had been one of the most amazing things she had ever experienced. Never mind that she thought she might have died in perfect bliss right then.

She would pay it no mind, because Damon obviously didn't. Her heart hurt just a little at that, but she concentrated on getting ready to ride.

Solange devoured the stale chunk of bread while checking on Iolande, then rushed through her morning ablutions, wanting to be ready to go as soon as possible.

It didn't take more than two days for her to realize they were headed in the wrong direction.

She had planned this journey long enough to realize the problem was subtle but persistent. To be certain, she checked the path of stars repeatedly, and compared them to both the sun and the direction they were traveling. They weren't much off the proper route, but it would be significant enough to make them miss Ironstag entirely by miles. Should she say something? It seemed peculiar that none of the men, seasoned soldiers, she presumed, had noticed. Solange was slightly shocked to think that she would be the only one who knew how to navigate.

Perhaps they were caught up in the worry of watching out for the enemy. She hoped that was it.

To make matters worse, the weather was about to change. That old familiar smell was back, as well as the numbness in the tips of her fingers. Snow was coming. She decided they couldn't afford to waste time meandering simply because she had to placate masculine pride. They had to reach sanctuary very soon. She would speak to Damon privately, and let him set the correct course.

That evening after a meal of roasted pheasant, Solange approached him instead of bedding down immediately, as was her habit. He was alone, off staring at the stars while his men argued cheerfully over the last hen.

"May I have a word with you, my lord?"

She glided silently into his view, the witch's element in her alive again. Starlight gilded her hair silver, lit her cheekbones, glistened on her lips. He found it painful to meet her eyes, impossible not to remember her kiss, her body, or that long, innocent night they shared of which she remembered nothing. He didn't reply to her question, merely nodded his head in acquiescence.

"Damon, I am uncertain of how to say this to you."

His attention honed in on her with jagged speed. "Yes?"

She tilted her head to look up at him. "I believe we

are headed the wrong way, somewhat too westerly. I didn't wish to say anything in front of the others, but if we keep going this way, we won't reach Ironstag in time."

He fought against the disappointment, telling himself he had no right to expect anything else from her. Certainly nothing personal. Certainly nothing so outrageous as an admission of attraction, or love. Still, he had been expecting this particular conversation from her sooner or later, knowing how observant she was. He would have preferred it to have been later.

"What do you mean, 'in time'?" he asked, stalling.

"Winter is here. Snow is coming. We'll want to reach Ironstag before the first of the storms hit, which means we'll need to ride longer to make up for the lost time. We'll have about four days before it begins."

The solution leapt out at him. It was so simple, he wanted to laugh with the discovery of it. He turned away from her to study the stars again. "If what you say is true," he said finally, "then Wolfhaven is much closer."

She paused, considering this. "You would take me to Wolfhaven?"

He heard the quiet wonder in her voice, and closed his eyes to hide the relief he felt. *Let it work,* he prayed, *please, Lord, let it work.* "It would seem to be best, don't you think?"

She said nothing, but turned her head to follow his gaze to a slanted row of three glimmering stars: Orion's belt. Right now the constellation hung low in the sky, so close that it seemed on top of them, the eternal hunter returning with each winter season. It was her favorite constellation, had always been. He knew that.

"At Wolfhaven," said Damon in his peaceful voice, "the spires touch the heavens. It's easy to believe you can reach out and sweep the stars from the sky into the palm of your hand."

Longing filled her, a violent yearning for a place she had visited ten thousand times over in her dreams. *I want this,* she cried in her heart, *please, let me have it now, at last. Let me have it for this small time and I'll be good forevermore.*

Oh, please.

"Wolfhaven," she whispered, and it was all he needed to hear.

Chapter Nine

IT WAS THEIR SECRET PLACE. None of the adults knew of it, none would guess that it was there, the thicket of briar bushes, a miniature valley of the richest green tucked up against a crumbling old Roman wall. They had to make a tunnel through the brambles to reach it and were rewarded with a long, hidden blanket of grass containing wondrous things: shiny ants, beetles with iridescent shells, quartz pebbles both smooth and rough. Above them tiny birds with speckled throats sang in short, piercing bursts.

She was young, very young, with Damon still a full head taller. He sat beside her, cross-legged in the grass. Blades of grass tickled her chin. But she wasn't happy. Damon was angry with her. Damon was upset, and that meant she was upset.

Tears welled up in her eyes and rolled unchecked down her rounded cheeks. For once he did not comfort her, he would not hold her.

I'm sorry, she sobbed, I'm sorry I did it. Please, Damon, I'm sorry . . .

His boyish face was unchanged, condemning. You knew

better, he said, I told you not to do it and you did anyway. That was very bad.

No, she cried, and thought her heart would break.

Bad girl, scolded Damon, but now he was a grown man, here in the thicket beside her, a huge man without the warm brown eyes of the boy she knew. The man's eyes were hard, glittering. They were filled with disgust.

She reached out to touch him again, and now she was grown too, a woman's hand stretching for him, a woman's voice pleading with him. Please . . .

He changed again, the boy and the man shifting, but remaining the same person at once. Both of them rebuffed her, made her sit alone in the well of thick green grass, made her feel her punishment with the keen sharpness of a knife. Was it so bad, she wanted to say, was it that unforgivable? I had to do it! You are my life, please hold me again . . .

But all he did was shake his head.

No. Never again, never again . . .

And in the distance, she heard the lonesome howl of the wolf . . .

SOLANGE JERKED AWAKE, covered in a cold sweat that molded her nightgown to her form and chilled her to the bone. The wolf cry she had heard in her dream came again, a haunting echo of forlorn depths, sending shivers to her soul.

It was her first night at Wolfhaven, the first few hours still, she would guess, and the first time she had had the dream in many months. She hated waking up this way; she hated reliving the pain of loss over and over again. She had hoped this dream would have stayed behind at Du Clar, where it had been born. She didn't want to go through that again. Foolishly she had thought it would be vanquished now, but she was wrong.

To calm herself, she wrapped a warm quilt around her and climbed out of the bed, going over to the gabled window overlooking a misty forest. The window was already open; she had left it that way deliberately, uncaring if the cold air came in. At least there was air flowing, a breath of life in the room. She pushed the panes open wider and leaned her elbows on the sill, enjoying the briskness on her face. Beyond the forest and curving around to the south was the ocean, crashing against steep granite cliffs. The steady boom of the pounding surf carried over the treetops.

Wolfhaven.

Poised between the land and the sea, more savagely beautiful than even she could have imagined, Damon's druid castle felt right to her from the moment she set eyes upon it.

It felt like home.

Not like Ironstag, of course, that physical home of her birth and unsuspecting youth. Wolfhaven felt like the phantom home of things she barely remembered, times so far past she could never name them, ghosts of friends, companions. She recognized the blackened towers, she knew the elegant, sharp lines of the castle even as she looked upon them for the first time. Her spirit had cried out in gladness to be back here and she didn't question that. She didn't want to question anything at all, no doubts, no fears in her new life. She wanted to embrace everything joyfully, she wanted to replenish her life's blood here in these ancient halls. She didn't know how long she would be allowed to stay, but she would relish every moment.

It was what she was supposed to do, she was sure of it.

Damon's arrival at Du Clar had been an unexpected shock, doubled by the news of her father's death. Her knight's timing, however, could not have been more fortuitous as far as she was concerned. She had already made plans to leave the estate as soon as possible; his visit had merely speeded her decision by a day or so.

She had planned to seek sanctuary in a convent, an English one if she could manage it, and had collected enough gold to ensure her welcome at any of them. But Henry's death ripped a sudden hole in these long-awaited plans, and then the decision to go to Ironstag instead had seemed natural.

She would never have returned to the castle if her father were still alive. It was a sullen grudge, childish, no doubt, but anchored in a woman's fear of being returned to Du Clar without being heard, or, worse, without caring.

Well, perhaps she had merely wanted to say goodbye. Looking back upon those final moments at Du Clar, Solange realized she had acted without much thought at all but rather on pure instinct. She supposed Ironstag would have belonged to Redmond now, but she was certain she could have made it there and been gone again before his men showed up.

But with a sudden turn of the stars Wolfhaven became home. She didn't miss Ironstag. It felt as if she was supposed to have been here all along. It had just taken her a few extra years to achieve it.

Her room was open and airy, filled with things she naturally loved, as if someone—no, she amended to herself, as if *Damon* had placed each piece of furniture, each thick rug, each glowing tapestry with her in mind. Even the window, the large, gorgeous window, faced west into the sunset, her favorite view. It was an impossible thought, of course. She wasn't so vain as to think he actually did decorate a room for her, since he could not have known she would ever be here. But perhaps some of her taste did reflect in this magical room. Perhaps he had remembered, and thought enough of it to, well, emulate it a little.

Or perhaps she was just a stupid dreamer, she told herself firmly. He probably had nothing to do with the furnishings of any of the rooms. He was the marquess, after all, and decorating was women's work.

Which led her to an interesting question. Was there a current Marchioness of Lockewood? She cupped her chin in her hand. He would have told her, she decided. She would have known somehow.

She turned and gave a speculative look to a tall wooden door in the wall by the bed. It was not the door to the hallway outside, that one was over by the fireplace. This was a connecting door leading to another chamber. Another bedchamber.

They had arrived long after the household had gone to bed, so late that the moon had already left the sky. Solange had been in a strange daze of excitement mixed with exhaustion. When she had her first view of Wolfhaven, satisfaction was added to the myriad emotions within her. But for all the glory and wonder the castle evoked, she barely had time to take it in, for by then the gates were being raised by the nightguardsmen and Damon was ushering her inside, assuring her that Iolande would be well provided for.

She had declined food or drink, wanting only to lie down somewhere, anywhere, and sleep forever. The other men looked as tired as she felt and scattered to their own corners of the castle almost immediately. Damon did not press her for refreshments, but instead took her straight to this chamber. He lit the fire for her himself while she stood swaying wearily in the center of the room. Then he took her gently by the shoulders and led her over to the bed. He looked closely at her, unsmiling, and bid her a good night.

Then he left.

Solange tried now to remember which door he had exited. She thought it might have been the connecting door, but at the time she had paid no attention. All she had wanted to do was strip herself of her dirty clothing and fall into the softness of the feather bed. A maidservant had come by—or was that her imagination? No, because she was wearing a nightgown, a pretty thing of fine pale blue wool, and she had brought none to wear. Also, she didn't feel the grime of the trail as she should. She had taken a quick sponge bath, that's right. The maid had brought the gown and pitcher of water, yes, there it was, on the table, and then left without saying a word. She had definitely left through the hall door.

With the quilt trailing behind her, Solange walked over to the connecting door. It had a plain iron handle, she noted, which opened easily to her touch.

Behind it was a second bedchamber, just as she guessed. If anything, it was bigger than her own, sparsely furnished, and as familiar to her as could be. The figure in the bed was silent, unmoving, a dark shape she couldn't make out. Nevertheless, she had no doubts about who lay there sleeping. This was Damon's room.

It had the spareness typical of his style, a simplicity of design both masculine and elegant. He had a matching window here to the one in her room, with the same view. She saw a few scattered rugs of muted colors, solid wooden furniture, one or two massive trunks, and—this was new to her—a rather daunting collection of weaponry on the far wall, from crossbows to gauntlets to spiked morning stars.

But he had also kept the things she remembered. There was his vast pharmacopoeia, now taking up an entire wall. He had made a clever rack for them out of jointed, crisscrossing wooden planks that reached from floor to ceiling. Some of the jars and pouches still had her inked cards in front of them, balanced in the nooks.

She also saw the row of stones, placed on a far table, and beside them was the handkerchief, a small square banner of her love for him, faded and frayed but still kept after all this time.

Of all the things to keep, she thought regretfully, I left him with that sorry little bit of cloth. It should have been so much more.

The sadness overtook her without warning, the bittersweet heat of it blurring her vision, making her press both hands over her mouth to stifle the cry. She turned back to the door, grabbing up the quilt with hasty hands, trying to make no noise at all as she retreated.

"Solange," came the quiet call from the bed.

She stopped, stunned to the core.

"Come here," Damon said.

She didn't move. She couldn't move.

"Please," he added in a ragged whisper.

She had to do something. She had to decide. Behind her she heard him move the blankets off him, heard him stand up.

She was out of time and out of options. *This was what you wanted all along,* whispered a knowing little voice inside of her, *this is the real reason you opened the door. You should at least be honest with yourself.*

Solange straightened her shoulders and dropped the quilt. It fell in cushioned folds to the ground at her feet.

She was breathing rapidly, though from fear or anticipation she couldn't tell. *Turn around,* the voice scolded, *turn around and face him, he deserves that.*

So she did, standing in the well of the fallen quilt. The nightgown twisted at her feet, forming a sheath that hugged her body with sudden appeal, leaving him to halt halfway between her and the bed. To her extreme embarrassment, she saw that he was nude. After one mortified glance downward, she kept her eyes trained on his face.

"Solange," he said again, and this time all the raw need he felt was apparent. "If you don't want me to shut that door behind you forever, you had better leave now."

She licked her dry lips. "I don't want to leave."

Still, he didn't come over to her. His eyes glittered with an inner heat in the darkness, his hands clenched to fists at his sides. "You don't understand what I'm saying to you. I made a mistake when I called to you. Go back to your bed."

She responded by taking one careful step out of the quilt, then the other. The nightgown swirled free, briefly highlighting the outline of her figure as she came forward. She closed the short distance between them, stopping a foot away to search his face.

"I understood what you said, Damon Wolf. I don't want to go back. I want to be here. With you."

His jaw clenched tight. He was speechless, part incredulous, part ravenous. Damon had awoke from a dream of childhood hiding places to find her standing in the darkness of his chamber, and for a time the dream lingered; she had seemed a part of it. When she had moved to leave, he had called to her without thinking, only wanting.

That was his weakness, the want. He would never be able to escape it.

"Please." A soft shiver took her, causing her to hug her arms to her chest. "I'm so cold."

He had no resistance. It was Damon who took the last step needed to bring them together. As he pulled her into his arms, all she felt was a fervent elation to be doing this at last, no regrets, no sorrows to trail her. Tonight she would live again, she would do the thing she was meant to do from before time, when the stars were just a thought in the universe.

He kissed her with all the passion he had shown before, and she relished it, returned it to him twice over. She kissed his face, his neck, used her arms to pull herself higher, to reach all of him that she could. Before she knew it, he had picked her up, cradled her to his chest as he carried her over to the bed.

She didn't want to let go of him when he bent over to place her amid the blankets, but he gave a crooked smile and allowed her that, moving in beside her and then lifting her tenderly up to his body. She gasped in wonderment at feeling the length of him against her, all hard muscle and sinewy lines. Her hands found his head and held him for her kiss, meshed with his silken hair. The clean scent of him surrounded her, intoxicated her.

His hands caressed her body through the gown, leaving a heated trail wherever they went. She wanted more, the nightgown was confining her, so she began to tug it off. Damon stopped her by capturing both of her wrists in one hand and pulling her arms gently above her head.

"Not yet," he said huskily. "Let me do it."

He kissed her again, a heated lingering, and outlined her lips with the tip of his tongue. She opened her mouth willingly in response and he groaned with approval, plunging in deeper. She thought she would burst into flame at his tantalizing rhythm, but he wasn't going to give her what she wanted yet. She tugged lightly against his grip on her wrists. Damon shook his head with a teasing smile. Instead, his free hand began to trace a sensitive path up her legs, stroking her skin in velvet sweeps, exploring every part of her that his fingers could reach. He pushed the nightgown up to her waist, then resumed his quest, drawing lazy circles farther and farther up her legs until she was trembling with anticipation.

When he found her delicate center and began to rub, she gave a breathless cry, half embarrassed, half exalted. He silenced her with his lips, keeping up the relentless plunging of his fingers again and again into her moistness, always withdrawing to renew his caress on the little bud of her pleasure.

He watched her face, captivated by her response. She was everything he had dreamed she would be. Her eyes were closed, as if she could hide herself from her own reaction to him. She was gorgeous, highly erotic in spite of herself, her lips full and wet from his, her mouth slightly open. He had never seen such a natural response given in passion; she was innocent and wanton all at once, a combination that aroused the blaze in him immeasurably. He was stiff and throbbing, already on the brink.

Without releasing her hands he shifted until his head was at her breasts. He blew on the finely woven gown, finding her nipples delightfully hard. He covered one with his lips and began to suck through the material, tugging at her lightly with his teeth.

The effect upon her was immediate. Her back arched up to meet him while her head turned to the side. "Please," she whispered, over and over. "Oh, please . . ."

He couldn't wait any longer. In one smooth motion he released her wrists and pulled the gown over her shoulders until she was free of it, tossing it aside. She was magnificent, just as he had known she would be. Her breasts were firm and full, inviting him to take their rosy tips into his mouth. Her stomach was flat but still soft, her downy triangle of dark hair led to long, lean legs, legs that he envisioned cradling him.

"My God, you are so beautiful," he said reverently with every ounce of truth in him.

Her eyes opened. "You are more beautiful," she replied seriously.

He gave a muffled laugh, but her hands were on him then, skimming his body until she found his manhood. His laughter soon gave way to an anguished moan as she began to caress him. After a few seconds he had to stop her.

"Solange, you are driving me insane. I cannot be responsible for the consequences if you keep that up."

Her voice was filled with admiration. "You are the most amazing man ever created. I want to know all of you. . . ."

He moved on top of her with an urgency he couldn't disguise, pushing her legs apart with his knees until he found the wet entrance, trying to go as slowly as he could manage. She was so tight, so incredibly tight around him. He gritted his teeth and pushed all the way in, burying himself to the hilt. He thought he might die right then from holding back, the pleasure and the agony were so great.

She clung to him but remained very still, as if aware of his precarious hold on his will. Both of them were breathing in rapid, shallow pants. He began to move in short thrusts, drawing out each stroke a little longer than the last. Her legs drew up and her arms tightened around him. She pressed her face into his shoulder.

At that instant everything else melted away: all the anger, all the misery of the past, all his fears for the future. There was only her beneath him, only Solange in his whole world, only the movements they shared, the building peak of liquid fire between them, leading forward in a harmony of kisses and murmured endearments. She was as fragile as etched crystal, as hot as the blue heart of a flame, he wanted to fill her with himself until she was nothing but him, could never be anything but his.

Her hips twisted to match his rhythm as she gasped his name and threw back her head, clenching around him in pulsing ecstasy, and he thrust deep and hard, learning her, loving her, giving himself up to her in a blinding moment that peaked and shimmered throughout his entire body, so deeply inside of her, he could not tell where he ended and where she began. It didn't matter anymore.

"Damon," she said against his shoulder. He rolled them both over carefully, still joined, facing each other. He stroked her back, felt her body relax, grow still, her breathing slow to a steady deepness. He withdrew from her slowly, pulled the blankets over them both.

Hazy thoughts of getting up, of returning her to her room buzzed through his head, but before he could gather the strength to leave her arms, Damon himself slipped away into a heavy slumber, lulled by the precious feel of her breath against his chest, comforted by the warmth of her body against his, right where she belonged.

SOMEONE WAS POUNDING on his door.

No one should have been at his door at this hour, partly because the gray light of the room indicated that it was still indecently early, and partly because Braeden, his squire, was supposed to be sleeping on a pallet blocking the entrance to prevent just such a thing from happening.

Damon covered his eyes with one hand and groaned inwardly. For some reason, the lassitude of sleep would not leave him. He felt warm and safe and completely unwilling to leave his bed. Had he retired last night so late? He didn't usually need very much sleep—

Solange! He bolted upright, heart pounding, but there she was, beside him still, curled up tightly against him with the blankets pulled up to her chin, showing all the trust of a child. She stirred and stretched, let out an adorable yawn. He couldn't take his eyes off her. Solange was in his bed, here, at Wolfhaven.

Solange had spent the night with him.

"My lord! My lord, please wake up!" It was the voice of his squire and the mutterings of others. The pounding continued unabated.

Solange had spent the night with him and now someone, several someones from the sound of it, was about to find out about it.

Damon climbed out of the bed, grabbed a blanket for warmth, and strode to his door. "Go away," he said distinctly.

"Lockewood, is that you? I demand you appear this instant. I have awaited your leisure long enough!"

"It is Longchamp, my lord," came a new voice

heavy with irony. That would be Godwin. "I think he wants to meet with you rather badly."

"For a month I have endured the somewhat questionable hospitality of your castle, Lockewood, and I have had enough! I told your men to awaken me as soon as you returned, and yet they deliberately disobeyed my command! It is outrageous!"

"I will be out shortly," Damon said. "Go away."

"You will be out now, by order of His Majesty King Edward!" Longchamp blustered.

Across the room, Solange was sitting up in the bed, wide-eyed, holding the blankets up to her chest. She began to look around frantically for a place to escape.

"Stay," Damon mouthed to her, then turned back to the door. "Howard, I have told you I will be down soon. That will have to be good enough."

"It is not good enough! I was told you would be back from France soon, as well, but it took you three weeks! I wish to quit this accursed place the moment I have discharged my duty! If you do not open the door right now, I will read the royal parchment here in the hallway, and collect the gold from your coffers myself!"

As soon as the man mentioned the parchment, Damon was working the lock on the door, furious at both Longchamp's audacity and the possibility that he would spill the secret of Ironstag to the unwitting ears of Solange before he was ready to tell her.

He swung the door open and blocked the entrance with his body. "As you may see," he said coldly, "I am not yet ready for an official meeting with His Majesty's emissary. I require time to dress."

Howard Longchamp was a thin man with narrow eyes, which were now even narrower in anger. "I will await you inside your chamber! I want no wily tricks to keep me pacing downstairs for you. The day is already clear for traveling, and my men and mounts are ready. All I need is your attention—" With sudden force Longchamp pushed against the door, taking Damon by surprise with his rudeness. The handle pulled free from his grasp and Longchamp shouldered forward triumphantly, followed by a jostling mass of his men and Damon's.

The entire tableau froze at a feminine cry of distress coming from the bed, and a flurry of blankets covering the form huddled there. Longchamp paused, taking in the scene, then finished his sentence. "—and your gold."

"Get out," Damon ground out, coming toward him.

"Really, man." Longchamp affected a pose of indifference he was far from feeling. "Your whore can stay or go, I care not."

Without a word Damon picked up the man by his tunic and threw him across the threshold, where he slammed against the wall in the hallway.

"Oh, dear," said Godwin mildly. "He's going to have such a headache when he awakens."

"All of you, out!" Damon ordered, infuriated. "Godwin! See to it that this thing"—he indicated the crumpled form of Longchamp—"is attended to *below stairs*. Gather up the damn gold and give to him! I will be down soon!"

"Aye, my lord." With a respectful bow Godwin left, pushing the others out in front of him. He shut the door with a quiet click. Damon locked it.

God, what a mess. From under the blankets he could make out the shivering form of Solange. He hurried over to her, eager to reassure her, doubly eager to find out what she had managed to put together from the conversation she had heard.

The blankets quivered and shook, alarming him. It must have been an appalling experience for her, to be exposed like that to a coarse group of men. He would be lucky if she wasn't in hysterics.

He sat on the side of the bed and placed his hands firmly on her trembling form. "Everything is all right. They're gone now, all of them."

She didn't reply, but did raise her head to show just her eyes peering out at him from the covers. He tried a reassuring smile. "You can come out."

The eyes were followed by the rest of her, but she doubled over with her face to the bed. He was presented with the smoothness of her bare back framed by long, dark hair.

He felt completely inept. "It's my fault. I was a fool to open the door in the first place. Damn that man, he's been a thorn in my side since—well, for years now. But don't take what he said to heart, my sweet. He was just—"

Solange drew in a great whoop of air, and released it in a gale of laughter that rang to the rafters.

He stared down at her, astonished. She was laughing so hard that tears sprang to her eyes. She reached out one hand and held on to his arm, then withdrew it quickly back to the covers, giggling still. "If you had but seen his face when he saw me," she began.

"He saw you?"

"Aye! But only for a moment. But his face, Damon! He looked as if you had punched him full in the stomach! I've never seen such bulging eyes!"

Damon had to smile a little at the picture she described. "Well. You do somewhat resemble his wife, you see."

"Really?"

"Only in the most superficial way. You are far lovelier than she could ever hope to be."

"Poor lady, to be married to such a pompous fool. I quite feel sorry for her."

"Don't," he said curtly. "She has plenty of diversions to entertain her."

Solange tilted her head and gave him a penetrating look. "I see. Tell me, who was that man?"

"Howard Longchamp. He is emissary to Edward, here only on royal business. He will be gone soon."

"Yes. That was abundantly clear."

She said nothing more, only continued to examine him in that disturbing way. She was a charming witch, a cloud of tousled hair framed her face, her skin as pure as cream in the morning light. Without conscious will he found himself staring at her lips, wanting to taste them again.

"You should go," he said slowly.

"Should I?" She raised a winged brow.

His body responded to her unspoken invitation immediately. Longchamp, he thought. "I have to get downstairs before he comes up again. We don't want him coming up."

"No," she said.

His mind was thick as soup this morning. She wasn't behaving like she was supposed to. She wasn't acting like a noblewoman who had just been compromised. She wasn't shrill, or overwrought, she didn't cry or scream in outrage; just the opposite, she seemed both relaxed and in good spirits. Amazing for a gentlewoman who had just been called a whore by a strange man when she was caught in another man's bed.

But this was Solange, and she had always managed to surprise him. Damon shook his head to clear his thoughts. "I will send a maid to your room with something appropriate for you to wear. I'm sorry, I must get ready or risk offending Longchamp, and thus Edward, further."

He stood, picked up her nightgown and gave it to her, then politely turned his back as she put it on, even though he felt foolish doing it. When she was done, he offered his hand and walked her to the connecting door. They reached her room. Damon simply stopped and stared down at her.

Solange was here, he thought again. His mind couldn't break that thought. She had come back to him, shared herself with him in the most intimate way a woman could with a man, and all he could do was tell her to go back to her room and dress. He was an idiot. He should be thanking her on his knees, telling her he worshiped her, that what they had shared was beyond anything he had ever known. None of the pretty phrases would leave his tongue; all was lost in the sheer improbability of the moment.

She watched him struggle for words, golden eyes under a dark fan of lashes. Finally, what he said was: "This was my mother's room."

He wanted to kick himself. *Oaf,* his mind chided, *what a stupid thing to say.*

But she nodded. "Yes. It's perfect."

He cleared his throat. "I'm glad you like it."

The moment grew longer. They could both hear people out in the hallway again, greeting each other, starting the day.

"Well, good-bye," he said, letting go of her hand.

She held on. "Damon. Thank you."

He could feel himself blushing like a schoolboy. "Thank *you,*" he responded without meeting her eyes. He left.

HOWARD LONGCHAMP WAS A notoriously bad loser. Damon expected to have to pay dearly for the morning, and he was not disappointed. When he arrived in the greatroom, he found Longchamp sprawled in a chair, nursing a black eye with a piece of raw mutton. Godwin stood beside him, weaving his clever blend of fact and fiction, as usual. The rest of the hall was uneasily divided between Damon's men and the king's soldiers, each group clustered along either side of the main table, all of them grumbling.

Damon was not worried about his side. Though a somewhat motley team of men, each was unquestionably loyal to him and none would act without his signal.

The king's soldiers, however, might be a problem. Their pride had been stung with the blow to Longchamp, and men who had openly disliked the emissary before now smacked their fists into their hands and muttered that he had been done wrong. Thank God they were significantly outnumbered.

And there was also the little matter of Damon's reputation to be considered. Although the years had significantly exaggerated his skill at battle, his talents at conquest, and his tactical prowess in general, there was a grain of truth or more in every rumor, and Damon was smart enough to make use of the legend when needed. Now looked like as good a time as any. Fortunately for him, the one part of the legend that was no exaggeration was the part about the demons inside of him. They drove him forward now, taking the stairs two at a time to reach his prey.

Careful, he thought, attempting a mastery he wasn't feeling. He couldn't afford to alienate Longchamp completely, not in light of the mystery of Solange's departure from Du Clar. It was a weakness he didn't want exposed yet, not until he found out what actually happened. Once he had the facts, he could determine a course of action. Until then, his hands were tied. There could be no doubt the story would spread sooner or later. He needed it to be later. If Longchamp met Redmond's soldiers, there could be hell to pay. He would have to placate the man as best he could.

Damon was richly dressed in his usual black, the heraldry on his chest a silver wolf under a crescent moon. The conversation filling the room ceased as he appeared. He towered over most of the men around him. Many of the king's men were more than a little in awe at their first sighting of the Wolf of Lockewood, who walked as if he commanded the entire kingdom, and not just this wild, unsettled portion of it.

Longchamp saw him coming and removed the mutton from his eye. "Lockewood! Your conduct is scandalous, even for you! Edward is going to learn of this first thing! That you would attack a peer of the realm over nothing more than a common whore is insufferable!"

All thoughts of tactical caution fled. Without breaking his stride, Damon came up to the emissary and picked him up again by his tunic, a deliberate repetition of his earlier actions. The men he passed shifted forward as one, but no one made a sound.

"The lady is not a whore," Damon said in a deadly voice as he dangled Longchamp in the air. "If you refer to her once more, in any way whatsoever, you will find yourself on the far side of hell, am I clear enough for you?"

The other man's face was changing from bright red to purple. "Yes, yes," he cried. "Quite clear!"

Damon dropped him back into the chair. "Excellent. Now, read me your damned parchment and then get the hell out of my demesne." He crossed to the head chair at the main table and took his seat, where a servant immediately placed a mug of tea and plate of food before him. He ignored the crowd and began to eat.

Longchamp cast a fearful but determined glance at a

chest near his chair. "I will, of course, be taking the required payment with me to the king."

"Of course," interrupted Godwin with a grin. "It is all there for you, my lord, the same as when you counted it earlier."

"Get on with it," Damon commanded in a bored voice.

Longchamp had regained his composure enough to realize he still had the backing of Edward's men, which brought some of the former brashness back to him. "As the king's chosen man, it is up to me to decide the proper moment to begin." He reached hastily into a pocket of his cape and withdrew the parchment when Damon began to stand. "And that moment is now," he added. He broke the wax seal and unfolded the paper.

The first part had to do with Damon's deeds on the field, a recounting of his infamous victories which Longchamp read in a suffocated voice. This was pure politics, a standard way to boost the recipient of any sort of royal gift. A vanity of Edward's, since Ironstag would not be a gift from him at all, and another example of his humor, to have Damon's bitter enemy recite his triumphs aloud before depleting his coffers. The scroll continued by going on to the Marquess of Ironstag, naming him a loyal and worthy servant, a good man who had requested a boon from his bountiful king. This was the part that interested Damon.

"Hear ye, hear ye," Longchamp read loudly. "Be it known that Our faithful servant Henry of Ironstag did request to break the entailment of his estate as a great favor from Us, and We did grant it to him afore he died. Therefore let it be known that Damon Wolf,

Marquess of Lockewood, is hereby the sole heir to the grand estate of Ironstag. As penalty to this break, however, We decree that Lockewood bestow upon Us the sum of one full year's profit from the estate of Ironstag, to be paid to Our emissary by none but the marquess himself, at the time of the reading of Our decree by Our royal emissary."

Damon sat back and continued eating.

"Be it also known that at the behest of the late Marquess of Ironstag, the Lady Solange, Countess of Redmond and sole offspring of Henry, shall be disinherited for as long as she shall remain wed to Stephen, Earl of Redmond, with the exception of any legitimate children from that marriage, who will each receive a single payment of a sum not to exceed the annual profit of the estate of Ironstag.

"Furthermore, it is a condition of this royal decree that if she yet lives, the Lady Solange shall be wed to Damon Wolf, Marquess of Lockewood, in the unfortunate event of the earl's death, and being that the Marquess of Lockewood has not already wed."

Damon choked on his tea. The rest of the men in the room erupted into comment, drowning out Longchamp's voice. Of all the faces in the room, only Godwin's remained unchanged, his inscrutable smile firmly in place. Longchamp pounded petulantly on the arm of his chair, trying to regain control.

"Read that part again," commanded Damon in a thundering voice, stilling the crowd.

Longchamp obeyed, barely able to conceal his glee that the Wolf of Lockewood had been trapped into wedlock with a woman he surely had not seen since childhood. May she be fat and pockmarked, he thought vengefully as he read. May she have a brood of unpleasant children to reduce his estate to nothing! May she always remember the touch of another man, her first husband, and so will slowly kill Lockewood by breaching his damnable pride!

Damon couldn't believe it. He searched his memory, trying to recall any hint in his last conversation with Henry that he had planned something like this. Nothing, not a single clue could have prepared him for this blow. Marry Solange! She would never stand for it. She would run away first, rather than be tied down again, he knew it.

But underneath the initial shock grew a pool of cool, collected thought. It was the Wolf in him, rescuing him once more.

Why not marry her? asked the Wolf. *You want her, and now between them Edward and Henry have ensured that you may have her. She really has no say in the matter at all. She is only a woman, and so has no legal right to decide her future. It was in her best interest to have her father and her king look after her.*

And they had chosen him to do it.

If you have to, continued the ruthless Wolf, *you should lock her up until she sees reason. Convince her of the soundness of the plan. Explain to her logically that she has no alternatives. Ultimately she'll have no choice but to do it. She needs your protection now, and this is the best way to give it to her. It will be for her own good.*

Longchamp had stopped reading aloud, mouthing the last words of the document to himself in delighted disbelief. Damon was alert to this, but Godwin was on top of it, reading over Longchamp's shoulder the final section of the decree. His face tightened unpleasantly. He threw Damon a warning look.

"Furthermore, We take it upon Ourselves to announce," called out Longchamp, resuming his role, "independent from the will of the late Marquess of Ironstag, that if the Lady Solange be eligible, and if the Marquess of Lockewood be eligible, that should either party refuse the lawful union of them both, one or the other or both shall be brought to the royal court to deal with Us, and shall be taken by force if need be."

"What union?" asked a clear, resolute voice.

All heads turned. Solange stood still at the entrance to the hall, silhouetted by a patch of sunlight from the archer's hole high above. She had been given the gown of someone's wife, a bliaut of cranberry-colored brocade with black corded trim. The gown underneath showed a deeper red as she walked farther into the room, toward Damon.

It took him a moment to adjust to the sight of her dressed as a woman again, but the color and the flowing lines of the gown suited her immeasurably. She had left her hair to hang in one thick plait down her back, but had placed two combs of silver on either side of her temples to hold the soft strands in place. She appeared regal, dignified, and puzzled.

"What union is he referring to, my lord?" she asked Damon again.

"This matter does not concern you, woman," said Longchamp arrogantly with a cautious look to Damon.

"I think it does," she countered, giving him a frown. "You spoke of a union for the Lady Solange."

"So?"

Damon was up and out of his seat already, but he couldn't reach her in time. Even Godwin was attempting to catch her attention. She spared them both a wary look, then faced Longchamp with her hands on her hips.

"I am the Lady Solange. Tell me your news."

Chapter Ten

"YOU ARE THE LADY SOLANGE?" Longchamp dropped the royal parchment to the stone floor.

All hell erupted in the hall. Everyone was talking at once, some shouting to be heard, while Longchamp had risen to his feet, staring at Solange with an open mouth.

Damon and Godwin reached her at the same time, both of them taking her arms and trying to get her to leave before the noise died down and Longchamp could question her further.

"What is happening?" Solange tried to shake them off.

"A little time, my lady," Godwin pleaded.

"Go back to your chambers, Solange, and I will come up and talk to you when this is settled." Damon was practically dragging her away.

"No, you will talk to me now, my lord! Or I will talk to the emissary myself!" With a quick twist she wrenched free of them both and whirled around, headed back to the center of the room.

"My lady! My lady!" Longchamp's voice could now

be heard above the roar. The men calmed almost immediately, all wanting to hear what would happen next.

Godwin looked at Damon and shrugged. Damon walked to stand beside Solange, his look flinty.

"Do you mean to tell me," Longchamp was saying incredulously, "that *you* are the Lady Solange, Countess of Redmond?"

"I am."

"Daughter of Henry, late Marquess of Ironstag?"

"That is correct." Impatience tinged her voice.

Longchamp shook his head. "This is beyond anything. Lockewood, do you comprehend the sin you have committed? You've taken another man's wife! Openly! Shamelessly!"

"It wouldn't be the first time," said someone from Damon's side, and muffled laughter wound its way around the room. Longchamp turned beet red.

"I am no one's wife," Solange called out. "I am a widow, visiting an old friend on the way to my father's estate."

Damon sighed, partly with relief. It was all over now, he supposed. He took Solange by the hand. "My lady will agree to the terms of Edward's decree, as will I. There is no need for force."

"What terms?" she demanded.

The countess did not look pleased with the turn of events, Longchamp noticed. Perhaps she was not enamored of Lockewood after all. If he were lucky, she would resist the marriage, and he would have the pleasure of her company all the way back to London. It would be small pittance against what Lockewood had put him through, but better than nothing.

She was quite lovely. And if she was willing to share her body with the Wolf, then why not with him too? After all, Longchamp thought, he possessed a certain masculine charm that pleased the ladies, or so he had been told. Yes, it could be quite a diverting trip. . . .

Damon looked down at his future bride and decided to answer her question. "Marriage," he said succinctly. "King Edward has decreed that you and I shall be wed. Would you care for some breakfast?"

"What!"

"My cook sets a very fine table. You must be famished. Your last meal was lunch yesterday. Allow me, my lady?" Without giving her a chance to respond, he pulled her to his table, bending his head low to whisper in her ear. "Don't fight me now, Solange. Just let me get this man out of here and I will tell you everything."

"Marriage," she repeated aloud. "Marriage to you?"

"Breakfast for the countess," Damon instructed a nearby serving girl. "Yes, to me. May I suggest a special tea to accompany your meal? I blended it myself."

"My lady, have you any children?" inquired the emissary hopefully.

"No. No, I don't. Would someone please explain to me what is going on?"

Godwin was there, reassuring. "Our astute and good king has decided my lord would make you a fine husband, my lady. He has sent his man to tell us so himself."

Damon handed her a mug of steaming tea. "Take a sip," he encouraged.

She put the mug down. "But this makes no sense. Why would the king bother with me?"

Longchamp gathered the parchment and his cape

together. If he couldn't have the woman, then the least he could do was to see to it that Lockewood would have to fulfill his sentence as soon as possible. "I think it far past the time you were wed, Marquess. We wouldn't want anyone to cast aspersions on the countess's honor, would we?"

"Anyone who did that would be a dead man as soon as I discovered it," Damon said silkily. "But I am in full agreement with you for once, Longchamp. Fetch the priest, by all means."

"The priest?" Solange echoed faintly.

Damon held the mug up to her lips. She stared down into the steamy contents and saw the reflection of a frightened sixteen-year-old girl, a girl who had been sold off into marriage in a manner much like what was happening to her now. But that girl had been an innocent, nothing more than a pawn between two pitiless men.

That was nine years ago. The woman today pushed the mug away from her face. "I will not be coerced like this."

"Then I shall be forced to take you to London with me, my lady, to meet with King Edward himself. And he will be *most* unhappy to see you, I am certain." Longchamp stomped back to the table with the mutton on it and slapped the meat back over his eye.

"He cannot make me go with him?" She made it a question to Damon.

"Aye, he can. Edward granted him that power. I believe you heard that part of the reading." He placed the tea in front of her and covered her hands with his own.

This couldn't be happening to her again. She wasn't

ready for this. Never in her most fanciful dreams had she imagined that Damon would take her to bride. Even after last night she had not expected it. Things were unfolding here too fast. Damon had no real idea of what he would be getting with her. She needed time to consider what would be best.

"I shall go to Ironstag. I shall seek protection there."

Longchamp let out a laugh. "Ironstag is no haven for you, my lady."

"What does that mean?" She frowned at the emissary.

"Ironstag is not yours, Lady Solange," he said condescendingly. "It now belongs to the Marquess of Lockewood, who would not be so imprudent as to allow you to go there against the wishes of our king."

"Dammit," said Damon.

Solange turned a bemused face to him. He dreaded having to explain the loss of her ancestral home to her. She was so tenderhearted, it was bound to wound her. He cursed Longchamp inwardly again for blurting out the news. "Your father didn't want the earl to inherit. He entailed Ironstag over to me instead."

She was shocked, it was plain to see. "I had no hand in this, I swear," he continued defensively. "Your father gave no indication that these were his plans."

"Redmond cannot have it?" She appeared confused.

"He would not have had it were he alive," Damon clarified.

Incredibly, he saw the faintest smile inch across her face.

Longchamp stood up again. "My lord, if you please! I need an answer for His Majesty now! Will you or will you not wed this woman?"

Damon leaned down to her. "They won't allow you to leave. If you try, they will follow you and then take you to Edward anyway. You will have to explain to him why you fled Du Clar." He ignored the stab of guilt he felt when he saw the fear in her eyes. "This is for the best, Solange. Trust me, it is not wise to cross the king. He has no patience for such things."

He gave her such a warm and tender look that she recalled her dream suddenly, vividly, the anguish she had felt when he rejected her, the desolation of being alone again.

Here was the man in the flesh, willing to sacrifice himself for her, to save both of them from the inexplicable whim of a sovereign she didn't know. To spend the rest of her days with him, every night beside him, building a future together—it was too good to be true.

If St. Peter had descended from heaven's gate and asked her the one thing she wanted most in her heart, ever, she could not ask for more than what she was being offered right now.

Damon raised her hand to his lips. He deliberately used the words she had asked him in France, but it seemed like years ago now.

"Wilt thou have me?"

It was a command from the king.

But it was a request from her love, and she knew that. Of course she would give in. She was not virtuous enough to let him go a second time.

"Yes," she said quietly. "I will marry thee, Damon Wolf."

"Excellent!" Godwin clapped his hands on both of their shoulders, then approached Longchamp. "Did you know, my lord, there is a monastery not more than a few hours' ride hence, and I am positive they will have a priest to spare us . . ." He led Longchamp and a core of his men away to the courtyard, while the rest settled down to break their fast in the hall. A regular din ensued, the sounds of men rehashing what they had just witnessed for the retelling again and again. It was the next chapter in the legend.

"How is the tea?" Damon asked Solange. "I remember how you enjoyed your tea at Ironstag."

"It is delicious. I haven't had tea for a long time."

And there it was, the first of the many questions that popped into his mind when they referred to the past. Why not? he wanted to ask. What stopped you? Who stopped you?

But he was loath to erase the half-smile she wore, sipping delicately from the mug. A single lock of hair was slipping from the silver comb. Without thought he captured it and put it back, adjusting the comb in the heavy tresses. She held motionless for him, as if it were the most natural thing for him to perform this personal service to her.

After breakfast she agreed to adjourn to her chamber to wait for the priest to arrive. Damon explained he had a few details of the castle to catch up with, and wouldn't she like a warm bath, a chance to rest an hour or two?

She said she would, and left gracefully enough. He sent a group of maids after her with instructions to provide her with a tub of hot water and whatever else she needed. And then he sent a guard to watch her door.

Just in case.

The maids reported the countess was relaxing in her bath and that she had requested to bathe in privacy so that she could align her will with God's in order to be married in peace and absolution.

Damon sent another guard up.

The priest arrived at midday with the rest of the party. He was a quiet young man who nevertheless took immediate charge of the planning. Damon pointed him in the direction of the castle chapel and was told to be ready within the hour, as both the priest and Longchamp's party were eager to ride.

He went up to his room and knocked on the connecting door.

"Yes?"

"They're ready for us," he said.

"Oh. I will be out soon."

He tried to analyze what he heard in her voice. Was that trepidation? Nervousness? Acceptance? He was driving himself mad, jumping on clues that didn't exist. Behind the door he heard faint footfalls, the rustle of cloth, and then humming. She was humming! That had to be a good sign, the buoyant little tune that reached him.

He didn't know what to wear. He had never used a valet, and most of his clothing was either serviceable or court wear. He had no idea where the trunk with the court wear would be. He hadn't been to London in over a year. In the end he kept what he already had on, but combed his hair back into a small queue, tied with a leather thong. He wondered if she was ready yet. Probably not.

He knocked anyway. "Almost done," she said. "Don't come in."

This was extremely trying. He paced his room aimlessly, examined his collection of herbs, studied the view from the window he had memorized from the first night he had spent here. It wasn't that long ago. It had taken him six years to make it back here, and another three to rebuild the castle, retill the soil, restock the sheep, and repopulate the village. It had been an uphill struggle from the beginning, even with Edward's public blessings.

Ironically enough, getting rid of the encroaching lords on his lands had been the easiest part of all. None of the lords had wanted to infringe on the Wolf of Lockewood's rights, none of them wanted to risk the mythic wrath it was said he carried with him. When news of his arrival at Wolfhaven sped over to them, he had received apologies aplenty, gifts of grain and gold, and all of his lands back in his control within a sennight.

It was what he had set out to do. But that young man who boldly charged to London had never anticipated the tests ahead of him. It was a blessing. He might have never gone forward had he known what lay ahead. Or maybe he would have. He didn't know. It was over now anyway. The price had been exorbitant, but the prize . . .

Behind him the door between the chambers opened. Solange was framed in the archway, standing still as a portrait as she greeted him shyly.

His prize was worth everything. She was exquisite. Somehow, somewhere, someone had found a gown of the purest white, a fitted bodice that clung to her tightly, a narrow skirt that trailed to the ground in a simple train. A singular row of pearls edged the deep neckline all the way around her shoulders. Her hair was loose and full, cascading freely down her back. The material fit her form as if it were made for her, the whiteness almost blinding, an icon of winter ice and beauty.

She tilted her head. "Will it do?"

"Yes," he whispered. "It will do very well."

"Two very nice women brought it to me, I didn't hear their names, but they said I was welcome to wear it. I thought it very sweet. They were both my age."

He had nothing to say to this; he didn't know who the women were, nor did he care. He had instructed Godwin to see to her clothing, and apparently he had. Damon's only thoughts now were of getting her down to the chapel before she vanished, before he awoke from this prolonged dream.

She waited a moment, then said helpfully, "One spoke in French."

"You will meet everyone later. We should be going."

She glided into the room to join him, lowering her eyes once she reached him. He took her arm and led her out, down the main hall, past a waiting crowd of servants, who cheered at the sight of them. The group followed behind them as they walked.

The chapel was separate from the main section of the castle, a secretive nook hidden away in one of the corners, buried beneath an avalanche of ivy. Belatedly he remembered that it had not been fully refinished yet, being of lower priority than most of the other rooms. The ivy was almost all gone, he recalled, but he knew nothing of the remaining progress other than that his first look of the shrouded, cobwebbed interior of the little room had been his last. There had been too many other problems to deal with first, and eventually, he supposed, he had forgotten all about it.

Please, he thought, let it at least be dusted.

But it was far more than dusted. Solange's mouth formed an O of wonder as they entered. In a season that stripped the leaves from the branches of trees and withered all vines, the chapel was a greenery of life. Pine boughs decorated each polished, chipped pew. Clean-smelling hay crunched under their feet as they approached the altar. Colorful hollyhock and mistletoe were everywhere, hiding the cracks in the walls, covering the faults of age and neglect. In front of them, beside them, were scores of friendly faces, curious soldiers, beaming women who had dropped everything and gathered to clean and decorate the chapel when they had heard of the impending nuptials.

It was simple and rustic, fragrant, a true welcoming gift from Damon's people.

The ceremony was equally simple, over almost before Solange had a chance to realize the import of what was happening. Damon looked so serious, so intently focused upon the priest and then on her. She smelled the piny boughs, curled her toes in the thin satin slippers into the crisp hay, and thought it the most wonderful place she had seen, a place filled with warm wishes, meant to cheer and encourage, not to intimidate or inspire fear.

She was open to it all. This is what God has intended, she thought, this is His great plan.

Damon kissed her with barely held passion, a complete enfolding of her to him. The crowd burst into cheers and then laughter as she wouldn't let him go after he released her, but rather leaned up and kissed him again.

The banquet hall had been decorated as the chapel had, and the cook had managed to scrape together a fine luncheon on short notice.

Longchamp, with a sour look, refused to stay and partake of the meal. His plan to entrap his old adversary had not gone at all as he had planned. He would have thought Lockewood, a confirmed bachelor, would be miserable at a forced wedding to a widow! But no, he looked anything but miserable sitting beside his bride. He looked pleased, even ferocious. He seemed to have grown another foot since the ceremony, Longchamp thought in disbelief, to become larger and more formidable than ever.

And the woman! Far from showing any of her earlier reluctance, she was actually glowing, a quiet dame whose beauty increased with every glance he took of her.

It was bitterly unfair, Longchamp thought. But at least he had done his duty and was leaving with the Wolf's gold. That was something.

Lockewood and his men insisted upon seeing the delegation off, and gathered in the courtyard to do so.

"Tell Edward I send my respects," the marquess said, "and also many thanks."

"I shall if I remember to," answered Longchamp

spitefully, looking down at him from atop his horse. "To be sure, he will hear of your bountiful harvest from me. Perhaps he will increase your taxes next year." He pulled his mount around to leave.

"And give my regards to your lady wife," Damon could not resist calling out as the group galloped away.

"Well done," said Godwin.

"And good riddance," added Robert. "The stench of the man was giving me an ill stomach."

"I for one wish him a good journey," said Damon mildly as they walked back inside. "He'll return to Edward with a tale that will delight the court for months, of how his enemy was forced to wed the widowed countess."

"He'd best not spread too wide a rumor about my lady," added Aiden. "If he wants to live, that is."

"Nay, I wouldn't worry about that," replied Godwin. "Edward will take care of it."

"Aye," said Robert with a grin. "Edward knew about her all along, didn't he, Damon?"

Damon took in the sight of his new wife conversing with a group of his men by the stairs. "Edward, that conniving old bastard, was the one who confronted me on my marital status years ago. He was determined to wed me off to the chinless daughter of one of his earls. After I saved his sorry hide at Glencairn, he owed me a boon."

"Really? I never heard of this," said Aiden.

"He didn't want it known he was so careless as to let a group of rebels sneak up on him during the night. It was just luck that had me passing by his tent at that moment, and my broadsword and I evened the odds."

"Routed them," Robert interjected with satisfaction.

"But my boon was for the king to let me be as an unwed man. Naturally he wanted to know why."

Solange was looking across the room at him now, a still and striking beauty amid the curious throng of people.

"So I told him," Damon concluded. "I told him that my heart was taken by a married woman and I wasn't free to marry until I could resolve it, one way or another."

"Edward let you by with that?" Aiden asked incredulously. It was common knowledge that the king was eager to populate his realm with loyal subjects, and was notorious for matching up the daughters of his nobles with any eligible lord.

Damon smiled. "Beneath that grim exterior our king has a very soft heart for romance, I fear. He wanted the entire story, and I gave it to him. After that he left me alone about it. Until now."

"Oh, wise king," Godwin said.

"Yes," Damon agreed, and then went to join his bride.

"Good day, my husband," she greeted him. "I was just learning of a few details of court life from these good men."

Damon's glance encompassed the group of suddenly quiet soldiers, who scattered as soon as he turned back to Solange. She didn't seem upset, so he didn't think they had told her anything too scandalous. He realized there were a few things he needed to go over with his men about what to say and what not to say in front of his extremely astute new wife.

"I had no idea there were so many beautiful women in Edward's court," Solange was saying. "And so many of them kind enough to, let me see, how did they put it? Oh, yes, to 'guide' you when you first arrived."

"Contrary to popular belief, none of those women 'guided' me when I showed up at court. Instead, I was put right to battle with a contingent of other unseasoned young men that marched north and stayed north for at least a year. And it was only after that assignment that Edward was willing to see me at all to hear my request for Wolfhaven."

Something in this speech gave her pause, more than the closed look on his face, more than his defensive response to her teasing. "Edward put off hearing your request," she said carefully, "even though my father backed you?"

Damon wanted to ignore her question. He wasn't ready to get involved in this bitterness so quickly, not on his wedding day. All that he wanted to do this day, he decided, was to investigate more thoroughly the charms of his bride. He took her arm and began to escort her up the stairs. "Allow me to show you to your rooms, my lady, where you may change into something more comfortable."

He got her halfway there before she stopped, staring up at him. "Damon Wolf, answer me." Her voice was a little too high. "Edward refused to hear you out, even with the Marquess of Ironstag behind you?"

Damon sighed. "Solange, your father had nothing to do with it. I went to London alone the morning after you left with Redmond."

"Alone?"

"Your father didn't know." He began to pull her up the stairs again. "So when I arrived to see Edward, it was just a brash youngster demanding his time and attention. He said he would hear my petition after I had fulfilled a quest for him, so that's what I did."

She said nothing in response, allowing him to lead her back to her chamber. She seemed stunned by what he had said, and although he considered it carefully, he didn't know what would be so surprising. The story of his arrival at court had become just another segment of the legend. It was no secret.

But she was laughing, laughing with wide, teary eyes, a strange thing that sent a chill up his back. It was not amusement that made her hiccup into her hand, it was not happiness that sent big, silent tears spilling down her cheeks like nothing he had seen since she was a child. She kept one hand over her mouth as if to keep in the sound and moved over to the windows.

He followed her, appalled, reaching for her. "Solange, what is it? What's the matter?" Her body was stiff in his arms, not resisting his embrace, but more as if she were unaware of him altogether, which was far worse.

He rocked her gently, murmuring her name down into her hair, willing the strangeness to leave her, willing her to talk to him, to tell him the problem so that he could fix it for her. Finally she relaxed enough to lean her head back onto his shoulder. A great sigh took her, leaving her to wipe her face with her fingers.

"All this time," she whispered. "I was misled."

"Misled about what?" He began to stroke her hair,

absently enjoying the smooth feel of it against his palms.

"It doesn't matter now. It's over."

He wasn't willing to let go of it that easily. "It matters to me that my bride would dissolve into odd fits and tears at the most innocuous of conversations. Tell me what made you cry."

She debated about this, wondering what the best course would be. She knew he would be too stubborn to yield until he was fully satisfied with her answer. If she had been more in control of her emotions, he never would have realized what he said to her had devastated an assumption that had sustained her for so long.

Ironstag had not been there for him! After what she had done, what she had thought would be such a noble thing to do, all her father's words had been rendered moot by Damon's impulsive bravery. Instead of supplying him with all the wonderful things he had promised her, Henry had allowed Damon to slip away with nothing, or, rather, next to nothing.

And Damon had survived. He had survived London, and the battles, and he had done all this alone. She shook her head at the thought.

The enormity of this new discovery left her almost breathless with a combination of emotions. Ridiculous, that it would make her laugh like this, but she had to laugh, because it was so ironic, and because if she did not laugh, she would surely crumple to pieces, or explode, or just start screaming.

She wanted to hate her father anew for this freshly discovered betrayal, but that wouldn't accomplish anything. That wouldn't help her deal with Damon right now, and her foremost concern had to be him. It was her responsibility to protect him. She couldn't let him know what his carelessly spoken words had just cost her. She needed something to tell him to satisfy his worried curiosity without upsetting him in turn.

But perhaps he had a right to know the truth. She had kept her silence to satisfy the terms of her father's requirements. She had done everything in her power to meet that deal. That faithfulness had been for naught; she couldn't be held responsible for breaking a bargain that had never even been met.

Damon was quiet with her now, just calmly stoking her back, her hair, waiting for her to decide. She reached a hand up to him, wanting to cup his cheek in her palm. His eyes caught the movement, then narrowed in on her wrist with the swiftness of a hawk.

Too late, she remembered. She tried to snatch her hand away, but he caught it before she could, holding her still as he pushed back the white sleeve.

"What," he asked in a terrible voice, "is this?"

She felt as helpless as a small creature might when captured by that hunting bird. Her heart filled her chest, and irrationally what she most felt was fear, a mindless fear brought on by his anger, and a strong desire to run away. It was instinctive in her now, a built-in reaction to the deep-voiced fury she heard. She tugged again at his grip, hard, but he wouldn't release her.

"Solange," he said, and then it was Damon with her again, Damon behind the anger, and Damon would not hurt her. But oh, she was so ashamed.

He pushed the fitted sleeve higher up her arm, following the marks all the way up to the inside of her elbow: narrow, straight lines, sometimes with pointed dots beside them, thin white scars making a ladder up her arm.

He hadn't noticed them the previous night, or that morning. He hadn't noticed them in the moonlight, or in the many days of travel he had spent with her. He hadn't noticed how she kept her clothing as close to her as she could, how, beginning that night in France, he had never seen her in anything that was not long-sleeved and concealing.

He hadn't noticed.

There was a blush stealing over her now, making the scars stand out further, thin dashes and dots of white against the rose of her arm. She let him take her other arm and examine it as well, no longer fighting him, but quiet, almost trembling in his grasp.

The other arm was marked almost identically. He wanted to see more, he wanted to follow the lines up her arm, but the sleeves of her gown wouldn't let him.

Her eyes were calm and light, detached as they met his. He couldn't think of what to say, the horror filled him up.

Solange ended the silence. "He had a very sharp knife," she said, and nothing more.

The rage that took him was like nothing he had known before. All the anger, all the frustration and hurt he was familiar with were now dwarfed by this new feeling, the blackest part of him he had never touched before. He wanted to kill, and kill and kill, he wanted to destroy the thing that had done this to her, and the fact that the thing was already dead left the anger growing wildly, without recourse.

He didn't know what he was doing; he was carrying her to the bed, pushing up her skirts around her ankles, and she was saying, *no, no* in a tearful voice, but he gently pushed her hands away and examined her legs, her thighs, for the marks, feeding the blackness with every new one he could find, a dot, a dash against the purity of her skin, thin, faded lines that marked him as permanently as they did her.

His own hands were broad and dark against her, tracing the lines, and a part of him noted this, the broad contrast between the rough, marked skin of his hands against the pearly, marked skin of her legs. She appeared so helpless, God, even next to his own hands.

Solange couldn't bear to watch his abhorrence of her, to see the disgust grow on his face, so she lay back against the feather mattress sedately, trying to remove herself from this awful moment, trying to imagine what she would do now, after he was going to make her leave. He wouldn't be able to bear to be with her after this, she knew.

She would find a convent, yes, just as she had planned. She would find a remote place to hide forever, and when the papal papers came announcing the annulment, she would be glad, and wish him wholeheartedly to the devil for throwing her away like this, for valuing her on just her looks alone, when looks were such a fragile thing and Solange was sure that the heart of her was not fragile at all.

Damon stood up and crossed to the door. She didn't watch him go but heard the click of the latch as he shut the door behind him. Part of her still expected to hear the sound of a lock turning after that, but all that reached her were his footsteps going away down the hall.

So that meant she was welcome to leave on her own. Fine. She sat up and brushed the white skirts down to their properly modest fall. She would change into her own clothing, gather what she needed, and then go, and no one would stop her, no one would dare enough or care enough to.

That's what she would do.

But instead, she sat on the bed. The room was surprisingly warm, cozy even, with bright diamonds of sunlight falling through the window, and a very pleasant scent wafting about. It smelled like—Solange frowned, trying to place it. Like roses, perhaps. Like lavender. Something sweet and summery, something out of place in this winter season.

A drowsy feeling stole over her. She decided to rest a little before leaving, they wouldn't begrudge her that, and so she lay down on the bed with her face to the sunlight, letting the rays warm her body and the smell of summer surround her.

From far away she heard low feminine voices, kind, not talking to her, but still comforting somehow, almost indistinguishable from the regular sounds of castle life. They were familiar in some indescribable way, familiar enough to tease the back of her mind yet not be worrisome. Soft, loving voices that were well matched with the warmth of the room, the perfumed air . . .

Probably some women in a sewing circle, talking about life and the weather. Something normal and sane, Solange thought languidly; they would be discussing something women were supposed to discuss, something happy and light and trivial. The color of thread, the taste of a pudding, the toddling steps of their children . . .

The steps grew louder outside, then paused. She heard the door open and shut again.

Damon came and knelt beside her, bowing his head to her on the bed, placing an arm around her waist to pull her into him slightly. The sunlight picked out the rainbows of black in his hair, melting into the fall of curls that escaped the queue.

She extended her hand and placed it on his head lightly, still in a drowse, wanting to feel what he thought if she could. He kept his head bowed but reached up and grabbed her hand, pulling it beneath him to his lips.

She felt his tears. A singular solace came over her. He still cared. If he was sad, then he did still care. If he cared, then she could stay. It might work.

"What did you mean when you said you were misled?" He kept his head down. She felt the words against her hand.

"Father promised me that he would support you in front of Edward if I married Redmond. That's what he told me that morning."

He held her hand tighter.

"He also told me he would throw you out with nothing if I didn't marry him. He said he would do it that very morning." She took a deep breath of the summer air in the room. "And a storm was coming, you see."

"Aye, the storm came and went, and I made it safe out in spite of your father."

"I know. I know that now."

She didn't seem inclined to speak further to him, and it was just as well. He wasn't ready to handle much more. The emotions in him were tearing him apart, and he didn't know what to do about it.

She hadn't wanted to leave him! She hadn't wanted to marry Redmond, and that night before the wedding when they had planned to be together had not been a sham after all! He couldn't seem to take it in, this new reality that laid waste to the old one that had tormented him all those years.

But what he felt right now, more than any other thing, was relief.

He was half ashamed that this would be his first reaction, but there it was, the relief that coursed through him that he had not been wrong all this time, that his love for her had not been some simpleton's dream, or some madman's folly. For years he had held her close to him in spite of the deep, festering wound she had created, and now he saw the wound had been false, his anger at her had been based on a horrible misconception.

She had made the choice to abandon him because she had thought it would save him; she had not wanted him to suffer. It had been a sacrifice, an act so generous he could scarcely believe it. This new knowledge soaked up that old anger, transformed it into a humbleness that brought him to his knees.

And yes, what he felt was relief.

He struggled to focus on that, because he knew now

what lay behind that selfish feeling was a black pit, and Damon could not see the bottom of it. That pit threatened to suck the rest of him down into it, and he didn't honestly know if he could climb back up.

She hadn't wanted to leave him, but she still did. What had happened to her after that, after he had allowed her to go so easily, was what created the pit.

Retribution, whispered the blackness, *you must pay for the consequences of your pride. . . .*

He fought that voice by speaking again.

"Henry sent me to you, after all that. Maybe he felt remorse."

"I don't know."

Damon lifted his head. "He said he tried to reach you, every year. He said you turned away his men at the gate."

Of course, Redmond would see to that, she thought sadly. "I never knew. I thought—I thought he no longer cared about me."

"I am trying," Damon said through a locked jaw, "to understand something. I am trying to understand how you could stay with a man who did these things to you."

"I didn't stay with him," she pointed out soberly. "I'm not with him now."

"But you were with him until he died."

"All of that is the past. In truth, after that first year at Wellburn, I hardly saw him at all. He sent me to France after I—"

"Stop. I don't want to hear anymore." The string that held him together was about to break; he couldn't stop it from breaking if she told him one more thing.

He thought he wanted to know the whole of it, but he had been mistaken, he didn't really want to. He couldn't bear knowing more right now than what he had already discovered.

The pit yawned beneath him, mocking him. *Retribution . . .*

Solange, his beautiful, sensitive Solange, had been brutalized in a way he would not have allowed the most base of animals to be treated. He couldn't stop the images now, and they left him gagging in the blackness, a deep wound in his heart that screamed and screamed in pain.

He was appalled for her, he was in a fury for her, but underneath all that was the guilt. Aye, there was his punishment.

The guilt told him he should have sought her out, he should have made an effort to find out what happened to her. He should never have let her go as he did, nor been so late to help her. The guilt said he could have stopped this atrocity somehow, that he had been honor bound to do so, but all he really did was fail her, when she had given everything to help him—

Solange read him again, easily guessing where his thoughts were going. "Damon, it's over. There's nothing to be done about it."

The greasy mixture of the anger and guilt clogged his throat. He was falling, falling down forever into the blackness.

He had failed her. Not the other way around. *He had failed her.*

Everything he had built himself to become had hinged upon his honor, the one thing that he had thought he could never lose. But now it seemed that base was a false one, something that had been tainted by his pride and carelessness from the beginning without his even knowing it.

The misery was so great, it blinded him. He was unable to stop his descent into the darkness. But then Solange sat up and pulled him up to sit beside her, and he felt a tremulous hope.

This time it was she who held him close, rocking him peacefully, warm in the sunlight, tasting fragrant lavender on her tongue. She pressed her lips to his temple. "There's only the present now, and the future to nourish."

The hope quivered and sustained, a single cord to pull him to safety. She had sacrificed herself for him, but now she was with him again. Whether he deserved her or not, she was there.

Her arms around him were sure and strong. And so perhaps the pit could wait.

Chapter Eleven

"AND THIS, MY LADY, is the second buttery."

"A second one?"

Godwin nodded. "This one is used primarily for the preparation of cold foodstuffs in the winter and warm in the summer, since it was attached at a later date than the original castle keep, and therefore is prone to, er . . ."

"Drafts," contributed the cook, a blunt woman with flour dusting her face. She was surrounded by a gaggle of kitchen maids who nodded enthusiastically at the assessment. "The whole room is as windy as an open sea in a storm come winter."

Solange glanced around the room, which was admittedly colder than any other part of Wolfhaven she had visited, even with a fire roaring in the enormous hearth. "Well, then, perhaps I could speak with the marquess about shoring up some of those chinks in the stone—"

"Oh, nay, my lady," interrupted the cook. "For this is the most pleasant room of all come summertime, what with the nice breeze ablowing in."

Since this was the longest sentence any of the inhabitants of Wolfhaven had spoken to her yet, save Damon and a few of his men, Solange merely smiled and nodded her agreement, then allowed Godwin to lead her out to the next chamber, or hall, or wherever the tour led next. Even into her second week as the new marchioness, Solange had not seen the entire castle. This was mainly due to the fact that Damon insisted she not go exploring alone, since more than a few areas of Wolfhaven had not yet been entirely restored, and also to the fact that the man he had assigned to escort her had been busy all week.

And indeed, whenever Godwin did manage to find time for her, they were inevitably interrupted by someone seeking him to tally up a harvest payment, or supervise a masonry dispute, or something else that only the castle steward could work the kinks out of.

It had meant she was left to her own devices for a goodly portion of her time, even though Damon would have had it otherwise. He had seemed truly torn: wanting to be with her more but knowing his duties had been neglected for over a full month already, and there was much to prepare for the winter stretch. If Godwin was busy, then Damon was ten times that as the overlord, even though for the first time since taking over Wolfhaven he wished it otherwise.

Solange had insisted he go do what he needed to do, she would be fine, she would meet a few of the women, she would begin her wifely chores, whatever those may be.

But it appeared she had no chores. Wolfhaven had a very capable chatelaine, a brisk, harried woman who commanded the legion of servants in cooking and cleaning. Although she listened courteously to Solange's request to help, and had even gone over the list of duties she fulfilled, neither of them could think of what the marchioness could do that was not already being done. The cook, also, had made it quite clear she needed no guidance from the new mistress.

Her attempts at befriending the scattering of noblewomen residing at Wolfhaven had not gone well, and although it was most likely her fault, Solange couldn't help but feel annoyed at the entire scenario.

She had maintained a casual contact with at least their maids, since many of the ladies had been kind enough to send over a selection of their gowns to their lord's new wife. No one had said one word to her face about traveling to Wolfhaven with nothing more than the clothing on her back. It made her remotely anxious to clear herself, to show them she was not so odd as her arrival must have seemed.

She had found the sewing circle one lazy afternoon, a cluster of quietly chatting women working on a tapestry together in a corner room of the main tower. To Solange, hesitating by the doorway, they appeared to be a group of delicately nodding flowers, dressed all in genteel pale colors, blondes and brunettes and a redhead with flashing needles and comet tails of thread floating between them.

Instantly she was back at Du Clar, seeing the group of women there who had betrayed her, who had never looked her quite in the eyes yet followed her relentlessly with their own, a spying party paid by Redmond, who wanted to control her even a continent away.

Sweet-voiced, false-faced women who feigned care for her even though they locked her up at night.

But that was ridiculous. This was Wolfhaven, and the ladies here were now looking up at her in polite inquiry. She saw no wicked designs among them, and they greeted her with murmured welcome.

However, to her dismay, Solange discovered she couldn't judge their sincerity. It was her own judgment that was impaired, she realized. She found she couldn't sift through the intricate layers of meaning around her in the room, the steadfastness of their gazes, the width of their smiles, the subtle tones in their voices.

In response to her uncertain inquiry, all of them denied with gentle bewilderment any knowledge of the identities of the two women who had brought the white gown to her, whom Solange had wished to thank. Were they telling the truth? Why should they wish to lie to her?

She pretended the matter was insignificant, though she felt the heat in her face from her own sense of confusion.

She sat with them awkwardly, having been given a golden needle and an edge of the tapestry to mend, and listened to the silence that had settled around her. They had been talking before she arrived, she knew. What were those sly looks they exchanged now? Were they laughing at her, at the less than neat stitches she attempted? Or worse, far worse, were they laughing at something else about her, her history, her shame? Did they know about her scars?

She bent over the needle and pretended not to notice until she thought she had stayed long enough to escape without rudeness. And although she searched the faces of each of them—a Mildred, a Stephanie, a Jenafer, Gwendolyn, Jacqueline and Julianna, who were sisters, even a Mairi—she still couldn't read the depth of truth around her. It was more than disconcerting, it was frightening.

Still, she smiled and bade them well as she left, and they echoed it back to her with identical inflections, inviting her to come again if she wished.

She did not wish. Not until she had some measure of calm infusing her, or until she was able to understand better the people now around her. For although the castle itself was a balm to her, the folk that lived in it had, so far, treated her with varying degrees of respect and distance. It was a watchful situation, but that was not new to her. After all, she had spent a good many years of her life learning to ignore prying eyes and finding ways to make herself invisible to them.

The secret passages at Du Clar, for example, had been a discovery almost too good to be true. She had stumbled upon the first one not quite by accident, for she spent much of her time in the chamber they called hers, and had many a long hour to study the pattern of carved vines in the woodwork by the fireplace, to trace the dark corners with her fingers, pushing, pulling. She was someone who still believed in fairies and miracles; it had only been a matter of time before she managed the right combination of flowers and vines that unlocked the old hinges leading to her eventual freedom.

In any case, it had literally opened up a whole new world to her. During her stay at Du Clar, they had allowed her rides through the woods, allowed her to exercise her mounts with a closely monitored gallop in a group of people. It had been her only treat, the daily rides in the fresh air, but it was never freedom. She was never more than a few paces from any of her guards.

Nevertheless, she had used every occasion to improve herself: practicing her riding skills, testing her memory of the forest paths. She had no plans to stay forever. She was just waiting for the right opportunity to come to her.

Eventually it did. After she found the passageways she became a nocturnal creature, going out at night via the hollow walls of the keep, all clogged with cobwebs and dust. The only footprints she ever saw back there were her own, but she was always cautious.

At night, with the retainers and the serfs and those hated women fast asleep, she would leave Du Clar, wending her way through the woods on foot, memorizing paths and markers for her final run. It was a slow process, and she was determined not to make a mistake that might lead to failure.

The woods offered her another gift, humble and scorned by farmers and shepherds: a ragged clump of common henbane. The sticky, toothy leaves would act as a sedative if she used them sparingly. How often had she seen Damon take it to his patients, sometimes brewing it, sometimes having it smoked to relieve pain? Solange had gathered a handful of the leaves, then another, uncertain of how much it would take to douse the entire population of the keep. Three nights before she planned to flee she chopped the leaves into very fine pieces, crept into the buttery, and emptied all of it into the large barrels of mulled wine served nightly. The spiced flavor of the alcohol was strong enough to cover the faintly bitter taste of the henbane, and the tiny broken leaves would appear to be just another herb to the uncaring eye. It might just give her an added advantage when she fled.

And so it had. No one had awakened to hail her as she left with Damon. No soldiers followed them that night certainly, though that had proved not to last.

She had to take a sudden gamble that Damon himself would not partake of too much of the drugged wine with his dinner, but could hardly have ordered it not to be sent to his rooms without arousing suspicion. It was fortunate that his drinking habits had not changed over the years. . . .

"My lady? My lady, have you seen enough?"

Godwin was facing her, solicitously patting her hand to gain her attention. "Have you seen enough of the storeroom yet? We can go on."

They were standing in a cold stone room hung with slabs of meats and strings of sausages. Braids of peppers, garlics, onions, and other dried plants crept in rows down the walls.

"Yes. I have seen enough."

But as they were walking out to the bailey, a soldier intercepted them, saying that the steward was needed down in the soldiers' quarters to settle a fight between a local tavern keeper and a soldier accused of not paying for his drink, and that it was looking "a mite ugly" when he had left to fetch him. Godwin excused himself with all evidence of sincere regret, adding that he hoped to finish their tour sometime in the next millennium.

Damon was gone for the day, out in the village visiting the field workers, he had said, to find out first-hand about the harvest. Solange wandered about aimlessly, examining some of the rooms she knew already, avoiding those with people in them. The second time she passed the darkened archway set far back from the main hall, she paused to peer inside curiously, but she could see nothing but a spiral of stairs fading up into the darkness.

The young maid whom Solange cornered to ask about it shook her head fearfully, declaring, "Oh, no, my lady, you don't want to go up there!"

"Why not?" Solange asked, thinking perhaps the floor was rotted or the roof was missing.

The maid looked around, then lowered her voice dramatically. "Because, mistress, up theres be haunted!"

"Really?" That certainly sounded interesting. "Haunted by what?"

"Nasty ghosts, mistress, gibbering things what cry at night, or else laugh like the madness, and shift things around!"

"Is it locked?"

"I dunno, milady. I nevers been up there to see. No one goes up there, milady, not even his lordship."

"I see. Thank you."

The maid bobbed a quick curtsy and hurried off, late to whatever duties she performed. Solange walked back to her room to fetch a candle, a beautiful beeswax candle, she saw, not the smoky, smelly tallow ones she had been given at Du Clar.

She wondered, on her way up the darkened, lonely stairs, if Damon kept bees.

There was a door at the top of the stairs, and it was not locked, although if anyone had been past it in years, she would have been surprised. The hinges protested loudly at their use, and Solange opened it only enough to steal through the crack, leading with the arm that held the candle, then wedging her body past the ancient wooden frame. Although the candle flame flickered and dipped, it did not die.

She was in another storeroom, but not one built for food. In fact, she suspected it had not been intended for storage at all, but rather as a sitting room of sorts. She was at the top of one of the towers. High above was the inverted cone of the ceiling, lanced with blackened oak beams. Strange that the room would be so neglected; she wouldn't have thought Damon a man to let a few ghosts stop him from anything.

Battered trunks lay at every angle across the bare floor, three-legged chairs tipped drunkenly aside, chipped tables bore the weight of moth-eaten rolled rugs and tapestries, broken crockery, what might have even been petrified remnants of food. Set deep into the wall was a narrow window of grimy glass that allowed in enough sunlight to cast an eerie brownish glow upon everything.

"It looks likely enough for a haunting," she said under her breath. She walked forward carefully, picking her way around the broken furniture, inspecting a clay pot here, a faded sash there.

There was a noise behind her, a tiny scratching sound. She whirled, raising the candle high, but saw nothing, not even a mouse. However, right beside her was one of the dusty trunks filling the room.

This one looked no different from the rest, with dark, stained leather over wood that had seen better years before time and a menagerie of rodents had gotten to it. But it had no lock upon it, and the thick, stiff leather straps securing it had been unbuckled.

She knelt, wedging the candle upright in the narrow neck of a cracked vase. The lid was heavy, much heavier than it looked, so that when she managed to push it open all the way it fell back abruptly, releasing a cloud smelling of musty, dry lavender which made her sneeze and cough.

She waved a hand in front of her face to clear the air, blinking down at the contents of the trunk.

First, of course, she saw the dried purple flowers on their spindled stems, laid daintily across the folded cloth as if the owner might return at any moment to refresh her wardrobe. Solange removed them delicately and placed them to the side.

The bliaut on top was of finely spun wool dyed a rich royal blue, with tiny, perfect embroidered flowers of white around the neck and sleeves. Beneath that was the undertunic, thin wool bleached to pristine white. After that, more dried lavender, and after that, a black bliaut with silver stitching, a silver wolf on the shoulder, similar to the one Damon had worn for the wedding, but without the moon. A black undertunic to go with that, then a rose bliaut, a mauve undertunic, an emerald bliaut, a teal undertunic . . .

Each piece she lifted out held on to the faded lavender scent, rustling with clean folds as she shifted them to the inside of the lid, where there was no dust. At the bottom of the trunk she found what she had been searching for without knowing she had been searching.

It was a miniature, exquisitely done, of a black-haired woman with laughing dark eyes, and even though it was a tiny painting that fit into the palm of her hand, Solange had no trouble recognizing the subject.

It wasn't so much that her son resembled her, although he did to a great degree. But her recognition was based more on the fact that she had seen this woman not so long ago, and in the flesh.

Or she had thought it to be flesh at the time. And the woman's eyes had been laughing then too, not unkindly, as she presented Solange with the gown of white, and the other woman had been smiling as well, the pale-skinned beauty who spoke to her in French. She had not remarked upon it then. It had seemed the most natural thing in the world to respond to their warmth in the blurred mixture of languages that they had all understood.

The most natural thing in the world.

With sudden insight she recalled the voices that had comforted her after Damon discovered her scars, remembered the familiar cadence of them from long ago, in fact, so long ago she had almost forgotten. . . .

The solitude of her sickness had driven her further into the fever that had taken her at Wellburn, further from the nightmare that had been her reality then and into the soothing darkness of someplace she had no name for. It had been apart from anything she had known, and yes, Damon had been there, too, talking to her, guiding her, but now she remembered these other voices, feminine reassurance in that darkness. The

French and the English had been mingled then too, but not confusing. Just loving. Just the solid consolation of a sort of love that she had never known in her life, but that was not unfamiliar to her, nevertheless. It had been instinctive, maternal. . . .

Jazel had died long ago, but it seemed she had never truly left her daughter after all. No wonder none of the women at Wolfhaven had known of the two mysterious women with the gown. Perhaps no one but she believed in ghosts.

Solange lifted a branch of the lavender and inhaled it, catching a hint of summer warmth again. She stared down at the portrait.

"Solange! Solange, are you up there?"

The voice was muted, as if it traveled over a long distance, but the worry it carried was distinct. Before she could answer she heard the footsteps running up the stairs and so decided to stay where she was and wait for Damon to come in.

"Here I am," she called when she heard him reach the top.

"Solange? Good God, what are you doing in here? We've been searching for you! Why didn't you answer our calls?"

"I didn't hear you," she replied. "I didn't mean to worry anyone. I didn't think I had been up here that long. I thought you were to be gone for the day?"

Instead of answering her, he shouted down the stairs. "I've found her, she's fine!"

Damon pushed the door open as wide as it would go before a stack of trunks behind it stopped him. It was enough to let him squeeze through the opening.

He looked upset. Seriously upset. She put the lavender down. "Are you well, Damon?"

"Am I well? I have just spent three of the most harrowing hours of my life imagining all sorts of grim endings for you! You were lost outside, you were drowned in the ocean, you had fallen from the turret—"

"Really, my lord, I would never be so clumsy as to fall from a turret. I have had a plethora of experience in climbing them, if you will recall."

"I did recall! Why the hell do you think I thought of it in the first place?"

She stood. "As you may see, there is no cause for alarm. I have not fallen, or drowned, or been lost at all, except lost in my own thoughts up here."

He enveloped her in a fierce hug, cutting off her breath and lifting her feet off the floor. "Do not leave again without giving someone word of where you are headed, Solange."

"But I only—"

"Unless you wish for me to die young from acute distress."

"Of course not! I just—"

"Promise me."

He kissed her cheek. His breath warmed her ear, making her smile in spite of herself. "Very well, Damon. I promise."

"Thank you." He released her and took a look around the room. "Now, be so good as to tell me how you managed to pick the lock to this place. None of our attempts have met with success."

"Pick the lock? I didn't. The door was unlocked."

His gaze was sharp. "Impossible."

"I assure you, it is very possible, since it is true."

"I'm sorry, I didn't mean to imply otherwise. But there is no key to be found for this door anywhere. It has remained shut up tight since before I took over the estate. Some of the serfs even swear it's haunted up here." He gave a short laugh. "Which is why, I suppose, I've left it alone for so long. I'd been planning on knocking out the door sooner or later."

Solange went back to the trunk she had been going through and knelt again. "I'm glad there's no need for that. Come look what I have found."

She showed him the miniature. He studied it in silence, then knelt beside her and handed it back. "Where did you find it?"

"Here, underneath these clothes. Damon, this was her trunk! These were your mother's things, I'm sure of it."

Once she said the words, she felt better immediately, as if by voicing her thoughts aloud they had come true. She picked up the black bliaut, wanting to show him the wolf embroidered on the shoulder, but he had seen the twigs of lavender and raised one to his nose.

"I remember this," Damon said slowly. "I remember this smell."

"Yes," said Solange. "I remember it too."

"No, I mean from long ago. From before I came to Ironstag."

"Ah, well," she said, "I have discovered it much more recently than that."

"She loved lavender. She always did." He seemed

far away, twirling the little stick of dried flowers between his two fingers. Solange sat by quietly, giving him time to capture the memory. His profile was handsomely intent, a purely masculine version of the painted lady's features. She loved them both, mother and son, and the ache in her heart now was bittersweet. At least he has this, she thought, at least there is this small thing for him. For us, she amended, when she saw the smile he gave her.

"What else is there?" he asked.

The next few hours flew by again, lost in the discovery of scrolls and bits of jewelry, of old saddles and spurs and ragged cloaks. They were forced to leave when even the little candle sputtered in the vase, its glow becoming dimmer in the advancing darkness. Before they left he scooped up the sum of the gowns Solange had discovered, saying, "Why don't you take these until we can get some new ones made for you? I don't think she would mind your having them."

"No," Solange replied, opening the door for him, "I don't think she would either."

IT WAS THEIR SECRET PLACE. She was scrambling away from him, laughing, almost choking on her laughter, while Damon chased her, scolding her.

She was young, very young, with Damon still a full head taller. He almost caught her but at the last second she danced out of his reach, giggling, waving her fist playfully in front of her face. The green of the grass around them was very rich.

No, no, said Damon in his stern voice, and she didn't

understand yet that his anger was real, not play. She hadn't understood.

She clutched her prize tighter in her chubby fist, loving this new game. Again she moved it toward her mouth.

No! cried Damon, leaping for her again, and he had Redmond's face, and Redmond's blank eyes, and it was Redmond's hand reaching out for her, trying to hurt her—

"No!" cried Solange, waking with a start.

Damon was with her instantly, holding her, murmuring to her in a soothing voice. "'Twas only a dream, my sweet." He wrapped his arms around her and kept her close, stroking the hair off her forehead until she relaxed again. She turned in his arms and lay on her side next to Damon so that she could see his face.

The bed was soft and deep. Eventually his caresses slowed and faltered as he slipped back into sleep. It was not so easy for her.

He liked to keep her in his room at night after they made love, claiming the bed was wider. She hadn't minded. Her room was close enough for convenience, but she would have been happy beside him wherever he lay his head. He slept heavily these past few days, worn from working from dawn till late in the evening. Yet when she expressed concern he claimed he was content enough as long as he had her to come back to.

Tonight he had loved her with the fervent, almost violent passion that had become his hallmark lately. No matter how late he came to their bed, no matter how hard he had worked that day, he would kiss away her worries for him, kiss her until she had no choice but to respond to him.

He could not let a day pass, he said, without making love to his wife. It would be a grievous sin, he was positive.

So he always joined her in the bed, else playfully captured her and dragged her over to cover her with himself. His intensity soon erased any playfulness, however; she couldn't help but be a little awed that such a man would worship her body with his own in this manner.

He claimed her as his own again and again, holding her, stroking her, bringing them both to the height of passion so many times, she felt as if she might die from the pleasure of it all. This was Damon, the lover of her dreams, who had shattered those inexperienced musings with the power of his actuality. He had proven to be so far beyond her initial comprehension. He had shown her a new universe.

"I love you," Solange breathed, watching him. "I love you, I love you. I have always loved you."

He didn't stir; she had not expected him to. Indeed, her whispered confession had not been intended for him to hear awake. She wasn't ready for that step yet.

But soon. She wouldn't be able to stop herself from declaring it soon; she came closer every day. The only thing that held her back was her husband himself.

She *thought* he loved her. He acted as if he did most of the time. He showed her a courtesy that was reserved only for her. His actions toward her publicly had been nothing but kind and chivalrous, sparking lively gossip from the other occupants of the castle, she knew. Here was the dreaded Wolf of Lockewood, treating the woman he had been forced to wed with not only mercy, but all showings of consideration!

Her lips curled up at the memory of the disbelieving stares whenever he held her chair for her, or stood when she did, or the way he tended to hold her hand without thought while talking to others.

Not that any of it had taken away from his intimidating reputation as a warrior. Instead, she noticed many of his men began to imitate his manners, showing a marked improvement in the tempers of the castle populace that reached well down into the village. She had overheard one wife remarking to another that she barely recognized her own husband anymore, and hoped his lordship intended to keep up his fine example for the sake of the womenfolk!

There was also that goodly portion of the castle population that had known of her through the legend. In fact, it seemed to Solange that she heard the muted gossip wherever she went now: There she was, the woman who had left their master to despair while she married another, yes, it really was she, and was she so fair as she had been painted? Some said aye, others sniffed disdainfully, still full of offense for the sake of their lord. But whether they approved of her or not, her mere addition to Wolfhaven heaped more reverence upon the story of the Wolf. The marquess must indeed be magic, they whispered, to have lured back the one who left him those many years ago. His powers stretched beyond comprehension, they said.

And she heard the other hushed tales as well, those of the man she had previously been with. Black stories laced with bloodshed and wickedness that followed her down the halls of her new home, constantly at her heels, it seemed. It was a wonder to her that such gossip could be told at all, for she felt the same unpleasant chill creeping over her skin whenever she heard the name of Redmond as the speaker did who told of it. Who would wish to rekindle such a presence here, under the protection of their lord? It seemed she must reconcile herself with the knowledge that the shadow of her former life would ever cling to her, no matter how much she wished it gone.

She could live with that, Solange decided. For casting that shadow was the bright sun of her true love, and, after all, who could have light without darkness?

As far as she could tell, Damon had ignored all the rumors, and she had tried to emulate him. But privately she agreed with his admiring people. Yes, Damon was magical. She discovered a little more of this every day she was with him.

He was a fine, noble, amazing man, a man filled with light and goodness, which made the darkness in him all the more noticeable to her.

And it could be very dark, indeed. Often he avoided her company when these moods struck. She tried not to be hurt when he left her abruptly, or lingered over some work that could have waited until later.

Solange saw past his tightened face and the anger in his eyes to the pain that was the root of it all. It was no consolation to her that the root seemed to be a perfect image of herself.

She knew she was not perfect and had never been. This particular darkness stemmed, she perceived, from the fantasy image of a life that never was. If they had actually married those nine years ago, if they had actually defied her father and Redmond, where would they be today?

What if he had stayed with her a little longer in her room before the wedding, what if he had kissed her just once more? Would she have been able to resist him? Would she have found the strength to send him away? Would they have run away together to find their own happiness and not endured nine years of separation that had threatened to consume them both?

Would Wolfhaven have been theirs sooner? Would the land have been more settled, the people more at peace?

Would they have a family now?

What if there were no scars on her body, and there were no secrets to her past? It was a siren's song, pondering those thoughts, a deceptively harmless fantasy that was not harmless at all.

She knew this darkness because there were times—not often, no, she fought to ignore the seductive lure—but definitely times when it tantalized her.

What if, what if . . . It was the magic phrase that was no friend to her, yet plagued her relentlessly in her husband's eyes.

It was ironically amusing that her worst enemy seemed to be a ghost Damon had created of her true self. He would not let go of that other Solange, no matter how false. She could see him struggle not to let go of it. He didn't care how much it hurt him. He was torturing himself with different endings to their story because it was a cover for what truly hurt him.

She could guess what that was, but was still helpless to stop it.

Guilt was a powerful emotion, she found.

The darkness in Damon was an unpredictable thing, arriving without warning, vanquishing his charm and any apparent good humor with a blistering heat. She would even swear she could feel it come over him as a change in the air, much like she could feel the weather's shifting moods.

Oh, she knew well enough now which subjects to avoid. Anything about the past could set him off, so she took care to answer his questions indifferently, as if it no longer mattered to her. She never brought up the topic herself. It was a constant struggle to balance the darkness with light, but she would not stop trying.

And always, always she endeavored to cover her arms and her legs from him as unobtrusively as possible.

In the depths of his self-torturing he became incapable of helping her fight her own demons. Perhaps this made her stronger, having to deal with it alone, she didn't know.

But she did know a part of her would have liked to share it with him: the humiliation, the betrayals, the emotional pain that dwarfed whatever physical pain she might have had. Part of her wanted relief from that past, but the only relief she could rely upon was the passage of time. Someday, she hoped, someday she would look upon it all with nothing more than gratitude that she was no longer in that place.

And then, perhaps, time would heal Damon as well.

But as for now, she was alone in this battle with her

past choices. At the same time, she didn't feel she could afford to leave Damon alone with his. It made her more guarded than she liked with him. It made her think of old times when she had felt as free as a sprite around him, had trusted him with everything about herself up until that very last day.

Nothing stays the same, Solange thought firmly. Change is good. I will make it be good.

In his sleep Damon sighed and rubbed his chin.

I love you, she thought again, and then closed her own eyes.

Chapter Twelve

The hart seemed suspended between the mist and the water. It was a large buck, handsome and ruddy, with a full rack of antlers and very calm eyes.

It was looking right at her.

A rosy line of sunlight was slipping up the pond, illuminating the depths to a mossy green glow. The sun was rising fast and the hart was about to vanish into the woods.

"Go on," she said softly, "I won't tell them you were here."

With a sudden brilliance the hart leapt from the edge of the pond, where he had been standing to drink, leaving a shimmering arc of water behind him as the only reminder that he had been there at all.

Solange watched the arc fall back into its element, creating ring upon ring on the surface of the water. The sunlight picked out the ripples in a glittering celebration.

She had ridden ahead again, something she absolutely was not supposed to do, but Iolande was impatient for a run and simple human logic could not convince her mount to wait for the plodding pace of Godwin and the rest. The monastery was not that far, after all, and what harm could come of her traveling around a bend a few minutes before the others? She always reined in and waited for them before she got too far.

Even riding sidesaddle she could outpace them. That had been the first long and serious argument between her and her husband. She wanted to ride astride all the time, but Damon finally had to insist she use the proper form when in anyone else's company. His argument was that she had an obligation to set an example for the other noblewomen, but his real reason was that she looked just too damn alluring riding astride. It was shocking and provacative all at once, and there was no way in hell he was going to allow any of his men to see his wife in that position again.

Solange grimaced, adjusting her leg around the horn of the saddle for comfort. The reason for the slow pace of the others was the long, flat farm cart being pulled by a team of plow horses. The road from Wolfhaven to the monastery was fairly well traveled by now, but there were plenty of ruts and ditches along the way. She didn't expect the team of horses to work harder to keep up with her. She merely wanted to let Iolande have her head for a brief stretch at a time.

"My lady, whatever it is I have done to so offend you, please allow me to offer my most sincere and abject apologies."

Solange turned laughing eyes to Godwin, who had just ridden up behind her on his own mount. "Why, sir steward, you have done naught to offend me, as you must know."

"Indeed? Then, alas, I must conclude my lady has a black heart with no just cause, to wish me dead at the prime of my youth."

"It was only a little gallop, Godwin."

"Your husband has expressly charged me with your welfare on this trip, as you know, Marchioness. I doubt very much he would be so blithe if he knew you did your best to leave the rest of us behind at every opportunity."

"Then I do owe you an apology. I have no wish to bring trouble upon your head."

"It is not my head I am so worried about. It is my neck."

"I shall ride with the rest of you, Godwin."

"Thank you. I was so looking forward to living another day, you see."

It was turning out to be relatively warm, considering the past week had been frosty with snow. Iolande was not the only creature among them who was heartened by the unexpected temperature. All the horses picked up their feet a little higher, and the rest of the men were trading jokes and stories back and forth in glad voices.

It was a good day for a ride, and conveniently timed. Damon's herbal supply was in sore need of restocking after the autumn and winter of early colds and maladies that had swept through Wolfhaven. He had established a small trade relationship with the monks, who agreed to grow some of the more essential herbs he needed in addition to their own in exchange for gold.

Damon had ridden ahead of them all in order to prepare the monks for their arrival. The head abbot, Father Ignatius, was a cantankerous old fellow, he had explained to her, who would not deal with anyone but him and never took kindly to unannounced visits. He also flatly refused to read missives, Damon continued with a wry smile, and was known to turn back his party at the gate for any number of reasons, from protests over the color of their horses to disagreements over Scripture. His favorite method, however, always involved quizzes about angels.

"Once he denied Aiden entry because he could not answer the question of which angel governs fruits and vegetables."

"Is this the same monastery that sent over the priest to marry us?" she asked.

"Aye. Father Ignatius was taken to bed that day, thank God."

The monastery was smaller than the other ones she had seen, but had the same solid stone wall surrounding it as was usual, with a coarse wooden gate that was heavily barricaded. It swung open readily enough, however, when their group arrived and announced themselves.

Damon was there to greet them. He immediately walked over to Solange to help her off her horse, and gave her a resounding kiss. There was a chorus of disapproving sounds from the string of monks standing behind him. Damon smiled against her lips, and then released her.

"My lady," he said, turning them both around to the monks, "allow me to introduce to you the good friars of the Most Holy Grounds of Lockewood. Brothers, my lady wife, the Marchioness of Lockewood."

Solange sank into a graceful curtsy. The monks nodded, and one came forward nervously. "My lord, Father Ignatius said to load up your cart as quickly as we could manage. May we begin?"

"Aye. All is ready. My men will assist you."

Everyone but Solange had done this before, and the mass of monks and soldiers moved off as a group to a separate stone structure from the main building. Damon took her arm.

"Would you like to see some of the grounds?"

"Is it all right?"

"I don't think anyone will stop us if we just walk outside. I've already inspected the crops, so all they need to do is load them. Godwin knows what to do for the herbs, he's been with me every time I come here. It won't take long."

The monastic grounds were plain in the wintertime, but the inner fields still held many signs of cultivation. Narrow wooden stakes dotted one plot with the nubs of the pruned vines still visible. All the plots were neatly plowed, if empty, and were scattered randomly among the buildings making up the order.

"There doesn't seem to be an abundance of space for the crops," Solange observed as they stepped around another tiny square of land jammed up against a wall.

"No. The order here is very small, and so was the

space allotted to them. It's a difficulty for us. I was fortunate enough to be able to negotiate a deal with the Father for what little we can obtain here."

"Really?" A hare scampered across one of the brown fields, a silver streak diving into a burrow.

"Although the monks could use more land, what the church wants is more gold. That's why they were willing to talk to me at all."

"You pay them in coin?"

"Aye. It's the best of a bad bargain for us. For all the wealth Wolfhaven represents, we're almost always poor for gold. Edward's tax for Ironstag has effectively depleted us, at least until the next wool shearing, or harvest."

"Here now! Here now, you young impudents! What do you think you're doing over here?"

Coming toward them on an angled trail was a bent old man in a monk's habit, waving his fist in the air.

"Father Ignatius," Damon greeted him. "How delightful to see you once more. May I introduce you to the marchioness? My lady, our good Father."

The friar came up to them with a belligerent air. "So, this is she, eh? Well, that gives you no leave to go tramping about my grounds! Uncivilized heathens! Tell me this, Marchioness, tell me who is the Angel of Destiny, eh?"

Damon began to speak, but Solange cut him off. "I believe that would be Oriel, Father."

"Eh? Oriel? Well. Ahem. Very well, get on with you, then. I don't have all day to be talking to the likes of you! On with you!"

"Good day to you, Father," said Damon cordially. He was smiling as they walked away.

The cart was fully loaded upon their return, with Damon's men standing by. None of the monks were in sight. "It's all here," said Godwin, indicating the piled bushels of dried herbs tied in bunches.

Damon walked over to the cart. "It's less than last year."

"Just so. I inquired, but the monks declared it was all they could spare."

"I know. I had a conversation about it with Father Ignatius." Several of the men rolled their eyes at the name. "He told me the demand for their liquors and spices is rising, so that our humble crops must come second."

"And what question did you have to answer for the pleasure of that conversation, my lord?" asked Robert with a wink to the rest of them.

" 'Which hour of the night does the Angel Farris govern?' By the way, it's the second hour, in case it comes up again."

"I've learned more of angels than swordplay, dealing with this place," grumbled Aiden.

"I'm certain our Father would say it's good for your soul, my friend," replied Damon. "And I am not sure that I would disagree. Let's be off."

Damon rode beside her on the way back, pointing out the barren stalks of wild herbs he would harvest in the summer, or a family of quail hiding under some fallen leaves. Solange listened and nodded, but the question that kept nagging her finally had to be voiced.

"Damon, even with what you buy from the monks

and what you may find yourself in the wild, you still don't have enough herbs?"

"We don't have enough of the *right* herbs. Some of the rarer ones, such as anise, I get from traders in the cities. Those I replenish as I need to, usually about once a year. But some of the more common herbs, as you know, are used much more frequently than others. I keep those in a separate room that is better able to hold larger quantities. Even still, I run out very quickly."

"Well, why don't you just grow them yourself?"

"I have thought of that. But we've needed all our farmers and fields for edible or tradable crops. Right now Wolfhaven cannot spare the men for a field of medicinal herbs."

"I could do it."

"What?" She had taken him by surprise, she could tell.

"Give me a small plot of land. I could tend to your herbs for you."

"Solange, don't be silly. I don't expect you to work in the soil."

"I want to."

"You are the Marchioness of Lockewood."

"I'm still Solange, my lord. You grew up with me. You above all know of my lavish skills in such fascinating pastimes as sewing and lute playing."

He shook his head. "I know your skills for getting what you want, my lady."

"You need the crops. I want to do it. What harm is there?"

She was so serious and so earnest at once. How

could he deny the reasonableness of her request? She had defined his problem and pinned down a solution with the cool logic that marked most of her convictions.

"It would have to be a small plot to begin with," he said cautiously.

"Oh, of course. I have seen a stretch of land out by the line of the forest—"

"No. I'll rebuild the wall around the abandoned garden next to the buttery. It's fallen in many places, but the damage is not irreversible. I do not want you working unprotected, or far from home."

"Thank you, my lord." She gazed serenely ahead. "'Tis a wise decision from all sides."

He tried a small joke. "Wisdom is one of my specialties, you know."

She gave him a sideways look, suddenly awash in sunlight. "Yes, I suspected as much. Your clever attempts to hide it did not fool me."

He gave a shout of laughter, drawing amazed looks from the seasoned soldiers riding behind them. Few had ever heard him laugh so loudly before, and none had seen such open affection from him to any woman. It was still new to them, this lighthearted side of their Wolf, but none begrudged him it.

Damon's soldiers knew of the years he had endured, for they had been there beside him. Every one of them had a story to tell about him, how he saved this man's leg with a poultice, or that man's life with a mace in battle. He had collected friends the way most men in court collected enemies, scattered and brought together from every corner of the empire. Each one would have gladly repaid him with their lives, for they figured they owed it to him in one manner or another.

They were those who were cast aside, men without homes or allegiances, most enlisting in Edward's forces for lack of any other means to earn a meal. Sullen and suspicious when Damon had joined their ranks, one by one they had been drawn to him, to his ruthless fighting style, his easy way of treating all men as equals, and perhaps most significantly, to the shadow of pain that lived in his eyes that the men recognized as a spirit kindred to themselves.

Before long, soldiers were waiting on lists to serve under the Wolf. He would take any who wanted to come and fight with him, did his best by them, and always regretted their loss.

When Edward finally granted his petition for Wolfhaven—with much grousing about being deprived of his best warrior—Damon announced to his men that anyone who was free to come with him was welcome. He made it clear the castle was in ruins, the land was raw and remote, but this stopped none of them. Many had wives already, a few with children. They all came.

It had instantly transformed the abandoned castle into a home, albeit a ramshackle one. Local peasantry at first abhorred the intrusion, then embraced it and the new system of work Damon brought. Farmers were eager to cultivate their lots, supplied with the seeds that the marquess gave them. The herds of sheep began to slowly multiply, bringing back the wool trade that Wolfhaven had been known for.

There was still so much more to do. And now

Solange wanted to help, Damon realized. She wanted to be a part of it all, and had come up with this way to be useful. A tendril of something uncurled in his chest, something he had not even been aware of before. It let him breathe easier, a little deeper than he had been used to.

Solange wanted to help him. She wanted to stay and build up their home.

He sat back in his saddle and let the mild warmth of the sun soak into his bones.

Up on a hill, far from the caravan of people going down the forest path, was a broad oak tree no different from any of the other trees that composed these woods. But behind this tree hid a lone man who watched the group go by with sly elation, and then vanished into the woodland.

"MARCHIONESS?"

Solange looked up from the paper she had been studying and making periodic notes upon. She placed her quill upon the table. "Yes?"

It was one of the women; Solange racked her mind to think which one, but couldn't remember. The one with the brown hair and blue eyes who liked to sing? Or was it play the lute?

The lady smiled shyly. "I am Mairi, my lady, we have met a few times before."

"Yes, of course. Please do come in." Her fingers were stained with ink and she had nothing to wipe them on but her skirts, which she couldn't do because they were one of the new outfits sewn for her, and she hadn't the heart to ruin it just yet. "Oh, bother," she muttered, looking around for her tattered handkerchief.

"Allow me, my lady." Mairi produced a white square of cloth from her sleeve.

"Oh, no, I couldn't," Solange said awkwardly, envisioning the permanent black smudges.

"I insist." Mairi held the cloth out, still smiling. "I have many."

"Ah. Thank you." Solange took it carefully between two fingers.

The other woman appeared to become shy again, gazing down at her feet. Solange stared at her bent head, somewhat taken aback.

It was the first time one of the women of the castle had sought her out, certainly the first time any of them had been to her personal chamber.

That afternoon she had turned a corner by the window into a workplace for her garden, setting up a comfortable table and chair to take in the view as she planned. It was considerably more complicated than she had first anticipated, but instead of being daunted, she was excited. She was going to work with living things, nurturing them. She was going to be useful.

"I know the rug is of intricate design," said Solange gently, "but I don't think it warrants such a flattering inspection. Won't you sit down?"

Mairi gave an embarrassed laugh. "Thank you, Marchioness."

"Please call me Solange."

"Solange. Are those the plans for your garden?"

"Oh, yes! Have you heard of it, then?"

"Indeed I have. It's the reason I have come to see you."

Solange raised her eyebrows. "Have you gardening experience, Mairi?"

The lady leaned forward in her seat. "I grew up on a country estate, my la—Solange." She took a deep breath, as if to deliver bad news. "I am the daughter of a gardener."

"That's wonderful! Can you help me, then? I have no gardening experience at all, you see, merely a great deal of enthusiasm."

"You don't mind that I'm not nobility?"

"I should think not! If you were nobility, for one thing, you would probably know just as much about gardening as I. How lovely that at least one of us knows what to do. Will you help?"

"Why, yes, I would be pleased to." They exchanged happy looks. Solange indicated her papers on the table.

"You could help me map it out if you like, and tell me which plants would best grow where. I don't think you'd much like the sowing part, however," she continued doubtfully.

"Oh, no, quite the contrary," replied Mairi in her soft voice. "Sowing is the best part, I find. My father taught me from a young age to appreciate the miracle the Lord has made our soil. I'm afraid I'm very much the peasant, for I do still long to plant and seed. That is why I came to you when I heard the news of your garden."

"Well, then I am just as much peasant as you, for I

am very much looking forward to it also. Would you care for something to eat or drink?"

The afternoon passed in pleasant degrees; a new friendship began unfurling between the two women. For Solange it was a novel experience, and one she was to forever cherish. As the light faded into dusk and they parted for supper, each was aware of another like herself nearby, one more friendly soul in a world that should be filled with them.

At the great table during dinner Solange mentioned to Damon her meeting with Mairi. "Which one is she?" he asked, scanning the faces of the women in the crowded hall.

"There, next to Robert. The pretty one in the yellow gown."

"Oh, yes. I recognize her. She's Robert's sister, in fact. Came here last summer."

"As recently as that?"

"She is a widow. Her husband died and she had nowhere else to go."

Solange leaned around Damon to take a better look at Mairi, who was eating quietly next to her brother at a table near the end of the room. She glanced up, and their eyes met. Solange waved happily. Mairi waved back.

"She's very nice. I think she'll be a great help with the herbs, my lord. I am surprised you have not prevailed upon her knowledge yet to cultivate some."

"I had no idea of her background, Solange. I never inquired into it. Robert simply told me he wanted to bring his widowed sister here, and I approved. That was all."

Solange turned back to him. "You'll take in anyone, won't you?"

The kindness in her voice embarrassed him. "I could not refuse her. She was a woman in need."

"Not many would care about that."

"Nonsense, my wife. Any true gentleman has a care for his fellow creatures."

"You are correct," she agreed. "But perhaps you are unaware of how few *gentlemen* there are."

Damon took her hand. "Nay, I know too well."

"Then you understand why I am the most fortunate of women, my lord."

His focus on her sharpened, creating that familiar fluttering in her stomach. He raised her hand to his lips. "Come upstairs with me, Solange," he said huskily.

"In the middle of the meal? What will everyone think?"

He stood, raising her with him. "Only that *I* am the most fortunate of men, my dear."

In the bedroom he stripped her slowly, uncovering her layer by layer, as if in search of a greater treasure behind each movement. She was so perfect, so damn perfect for him, Damon thought, and the way she kissed his fingers, his knuckles, his arms whenever they passed near her lips had him shaking already with desire.

When at last she stood before him in the discarded pool of her gowns, she showed no shame at her nakedness. Calm and trusting as a doe in the wild, she watched him with glowing eyes, followed his movements as he tore off his own clothes and then knelt before her. Her hand came to rest upon his head, her fingers threaded through the shimmering black waves in a lingering caress. He cradled her body with his palms, running over the smooth muscles in her legs, the sweet curves of her buttocks. He slipped one hand between her thighs and parted them, then ran the edge of his hand higher, massaging her until her hips arched toward him and she was gasping.

Keeping his hand in place, he traced the roundness of her navel with his tongue and traveled downward, amazed again at the contrast of her shapely lines imbued with purity, cnthralled with the pattern of her breathing as he kissed her lower, past the dark triangle that marked her apex, until he had her parted before him and she clutched at his shoulder and begged him to rise.

He wouldn't. She tasted like nectar and Solange, a unique thing he had never experienced, and but for the driving ache in his loins, he wanted never to end. Over and over he massaged her tender nub with his lips and his tongue, using both hands now to cup her bottom and bring her closer to him.

She stood with her eyes closed, wanting him to cease his tormenting and yet not wanting him to.

"Damon," she gasped. The world was him, only him, and the pleasure jolted her so much that she thought she might fall, but she didn't care, because he was there, ready to catch her.

As the last tremor shook her, he stood and picked her up in his arms and carried her to the table, because it was closest to them, and he had to have her then, right then.

He sat her on the edge of the table and then placed himself before her. He was stiff and throbbing with need for her, which made his hands a little rough as he pushed her legs apart and entered her wetness.

The urgency made him thrust deep with a single stroke, penetrating her as far as he could. Her legs were spread wide to accommodate him, her arms back on the table to support herself as he withdrew, and came again, and again, a heavy rhythm that rocked them both to the core.

Her head tilted back. Her eyes were closed again, but he couldn't stop looking at her face, at her breasts, at their joining, his beautiful wife, his haunting Solange, who panted now and licked her lips and moved her hips to take in more of him.

And the rhythm filled him, controlled him, flooded his senses until he was the rhythm and nothing more, a simple, powerful thing that was dark and salty and painfully exquisite.

He bent over her and buried his head in her neck, letting the passion empty him, spilling himself into her with a glorious abandon. She arched into him with a small cry, and he felt the rapid pulses of her own climax, squeezing the last ounce of ecstasy from him.

For a long while they remained locked in that position, neither willing to end the embrace. Only when he noticed the skin on her arms began to grow cold did he separate from her.

"You are incredible," he said, pulling her off the table to stand in his arms. She had no reply to this but to shake her head, smiling in a bemused sort of way that made him kiss her once more.

"Come, I don't want you to take a chill." He took her to the bed and left her half buried beneath the largest fur he could find while he gathered up her clothing. She looked ridiculously young, with flushed cheeks from love and sparkling eyes; she reminded him vividly of the girl he used to know who thought nothing of stealing out at night to count the stars, or climb the highest turret, or whatever it would have been at the time.

But she was different now. She was his, for one thing, and only his. No man could pull them asunder again, only God, and Damon hoped the Lord had seen enough of his misery without her to take pity upon him and not separate them again.

"Here." He handed her the crumpled clothing and she burst into laughter.

"Oh, dear. I suppose I could tell people I fell asleep in them, or perhaps became caught between two very large stones while wearing them . . ."

"Put on a fresh gown if it matters."

"Yes. I think I should."

But she didn't move out from under the fur, only peered up at him owlishly. He realized, uncomfortably, that she was waiting for him to leave, or at least move away from her.

Ever since he had discovered the faded scars marking her, she had gone to great pains, he perceived abruptly, to ensure he did not see her body so plainly again, except when they were making love.

And since they usually made love at night, he had not noticed any flaws on her. He always insisted upon keeping at least one candle lit, true, but it was a timid glow by any means, and afterward he extinguished it with no thought at all, only utter exhaustion and satisfaction.

A flash of guilt streaked through him. This was his fault. He was doing this to her; he was the one making her pull into herself because of his anger at another person. She should not have to hide herself from him. She should be able to trust him at least that much. His guilt grew.

He joined her on the bed. "Solange. I want to thank you for what just happened between us."

She was all blushes and modesty, ducking her head. "You don't have to thank me, my lord."

"No," he said thoughtfully. "I think you are wrong about that. It is the greatest honor and privilege to be able to make love to the most beautiful woman in the world. Therefore it would be a gross insult to you if I did not thank you."

Her look said she couldn't decide if he was teasing, and that gave the guilt another spurt of growth. He pretended affront. "Do you mean to suggest by your doubtful silence that I am anything less than a gentleman? Although there are numerous persons who would agree with that assessment, I would hope that my own wife would see through to my heart of gold."

Her face cleared, the shadow of disappointment so fleeting, he almost didn't see it. "Oh, you are joking. How silly you can be, declaring me beautiful."

"Nay, my lady wife, I am sorry to point out that you are wrong once more." He searched her eyes, willing her to believe him. "I said you were the *most* beautiful woman, and I by my honor I mean that. No woman on earth compares to you, Solange."

To his consternation, her lower lip began to tremble, and her eyes filled with unshed tears. "You are mocking me," she said. "I will not be mocked." She struggled to free herself from the fur. Damon was appalled that she had misread him so completely. He moved to keep her beside him.

"Solange! No, no! I would not mock you, how could I? How could you even think such a thing? How could you, when you are my life, when you are all that's rare and precious and good to me? You are a drop of perfection in this imperfect, sorry world, don't you see that? You are all that has haunted me, and all that has sustained me in my own weaknesses." He took her hands and would not release them. "When I tell you that you are the most beautiful woman in the world, I say it with all the truth I can find, and I know I must say it poorly, to have you take me so wrong. I will show you, then."

He let go of her long enough to take up the jeweled stiletto she kept close on the table by the bed. Her breath drew in sharply, but she didn't cower from him, not even when he took her hand again.

He turned the knife around, closing her fingers around the hilt and raising her arm, pointing the razor-sharp end into his bare chest. "By my vow, and my oath, by my honor and my love for you, fair Solange, I speak the truth. Never have I broken my word, my lady. You are the most beautiful woman in the world to me, in all of creation, and nothing, not time, nor place, nor man nor woman shall ever change that.

Your body is but a small part of your beauty, and I cherish it. God, I cherish it. You should know that by now. Sometimes it is all I can think of, the joy of making love to you. It consumes me; I cannot think or eat or sleep until I am with you again. You must know this, how could you not?

"But the rarest thing you have is the depth of beauty that lives only in the best of us, and usually only in scant portions. In you, however, it lives with vibrancy, in you it overflows into all that you do, into all that you choose to touch. It is this beauty I truly treasure, my love, for this is the best gift of all. Your sweetness, your goodness, your wit and virtue and all those things you are blessed with bless me also, because I am the man you are with. I am the man whose life has been permanently intertwined with yours. And I am the man who has always loved you, Solange."

Her tears were unchecked now, silver trails of silent passage and a message of eloquence in her eyes.

"I have always loved you," he repeated simply. "If you still doubt me, my life is better ended now. It is up to you. I cannot live without you again."

She pulled her hand out of his and flung the dagger across the room to clatter against floor.

"Stop," she cried, and buried herself in his arms. The love came fiercely upon him, a fiery need and a comforting relief to hold her like this, to have her cry into his chest, to rock her and never let go again.

"I cannot bear it anymore, I cannot," she hiccuped against him. "I love you. I love only you. And I don't care about beauty, or goodness, because if any of those things mean I have to give you up again, I won't do it! I'll be wicked and sinful and selfish, I don't care. . . ."

An amazed laugh rumbled in his chest. "My tigress," he said, half stunned by what had happened.

"Yes! I'll be a tigress. Tigers are never afraid, and neither shall I be." She raised her head. "I love you, Damon of Lockewood."

"And I love you, Solange of Lockewood."

And for a short while, just a glinting bubble of time, there was nothing else in the universe, and there was no reason to stop the kiss between them that mingled their tears and set their hearts to beat as one once more.

Chapter Thirteen

"I PREFER APPLES TO GARLIC, Lady Solange."

Since this was at least the third time she had been informed of the seven-year-old's culinary preferences, Solange merely smiled as she stepped over a dry clump of grass and replied, "Yes, Miranda, I know."

"Apples go in tarts," the girl continued thoughtfully. "I like tarts."

"I like tarts too," her younger brother piped up anxiously. "Can I have tarts as well, Lady Solange?"

"Yes, William. I believe that when we are finished, there will be enough tarts for all of you."

"Garlic is nasty," said another girl. "Why do we have to have garlic at all?"

Solange had to pause to lift her skirts over a low stone wall that had long ago crumbled to its base in the pasture. "Well, Jane, we need garlic for lots of things." She began to aid the children over the wall, one by one, with the help of the two other women in the group. "The marquess uses garlic in some of his medicines. And I think garlic tastes rather nice with some meats."

"Me too! Me too!" said William.

"And I like it roasted with butter, on bread with supper," Mairi volunteered.

"And in stews," added Carolyn, the mother of two of the children.

"There, you see? Garlic can be quite nice." Solange surveyed the meadow with a practiced eye.

"I prefer apples," Miranda said stubbornly.

"Yes, I know." Solange walked over to her and pointed to one corner of the field. "That is why you are going to have your very own apple tree, right over there. What do you say to that?"

"Oh, yes! My own tree!" The girl clapped her hands together and began to race to the corner. The other children scattered after her in a ragged tail.

Only William remained with the three women, looking forlornly after the others. He shifted his weight onto his good foot, using the small carved stick he had been given as a cane.

He had been born lame, Carolyn explained earlier, the physician had said it was because her pregnancy had been cursed.

"Cursed or no," she had said, "William is my delight, and he does so want to be a part of the garden project like the other children, my lady. Could you not find a little something for him to do? He is very quiet and won't be a bother, I promise."

The "garden project" had rapidly grown beyond a simple field of herbs, due much in part to Mairi's very vocal enthusiasm for the plan. One by one the other ladies at Wolfhaven had offered to become involved, and this often meant their children had asked to help as well.

Solange had not the heart to turn away a single one of them, especially since it seemed to be the perfect way to get to know the others, a way that she had been seeking for some time. Soon she had more help than work, and that had led to the discovery that Wolfhaven had no formal orchard to speak of. Most of the old trees had grown heavily gnarled from the years of neglect and died in the ground. Creating a new orchard seemed a natural extension to the herb garden, and Damon had reluctantly approved, unable to deny that they could always use more fresh fruits. But, he added, she would not plant too far from Wolfhaven.

His determination to keep her close to home filled her with a kind of amused exasperation. Nevertheless, she didn't want him to have to worry about her. The strip of field by the forest she had first noticed, she had argued, was the ideal solution, being neither too small nor too far from the castle. Damon had been forced to agree.

Now Solange knelt beside the lame boy, giving him a cheerful smile. "What kind of tree would you like, Willie?"

"A garlic tree?" he suggested hopefully.

"Hmm, that might be a bit difficult. If you like, you may help me with the regular garlic in the herb garden though."

"Yes," he said promptly.

"But I was thinking of something special for you. Do you see that little mound of grass over there, right next to this wall?"

He nodded his head.

"Well, I was thinking that it would be the perfect spot for a cherry tree."

"A cherry tree," he echoed worshipfully.

"I found a beautiful cherry sapling in the old grove, growing right where no others could grow. As soon as I saw it I knew it was yours, since it must be a magic tree. Your own magic tree, growing out in the old orchard."

The little boy's eyes were wide with wonder. Solange leaned closer. "I'll tell you a secret too," she said conspiratorially. "I much prefer cherry tarts to apple tarts."

"Me too!" William exclaimed.

"Me too," said Mairi.

"Me too," whispered Carolyn, and then gave her son a hug.

There were children running rampant over the wild field, shouting out questions to the women and instructions to one another, each eager to discover the perfect spot for their own part of the orchard.

Mairi shook her head, smiling. "Good gracious, what have we done?"

"I only hope they'll be so enthusiastic when it comes time to do the real work," Solange said.

"Oh, no, my lady," Carolyn said. "I don't think you need worry about that at all. They are good children, all of them, and eager to please. There really isn't enough for them to do at the castle yet, since the boys are too young to be pages still, and the group of them too young for more than the briefest of instructions in the schoolroom. This will be a wonderful lesson for each of them. Although," she added ruefully, "I do fear they will require rather strict supervision. If we are not careful, we shall end up with a forest of fruit trees instead of a grove."

"Yes, Mairi, I believe that will be your area," Solange said casually. "You have such a way with the children, plus you know the lay of the land. And, of course, Sir Godwin will need someone here to tell him where to plow."

Not surprisingly, Mairi colored up to the roots of her hair. It hadn't taken Solange long to notice how her friend grew awkward and stilted whenever Godwin's name was mentioned in conversation, or how she tended to follow him with her eyes whenever they were in a room together. She had not broached the subject with her yet; she didn't want to intrude on what might be a sensitive subject to a woman who had been widowed not that long past.

But the romantic in her had been delighted with the discovery. Godwin was unattached. Mairi was unattached. Solange liked them both very much, and hoped there might be a match for them somewhere in the future. No, she would not intrude. Well, she would not overtly intrude. But since the opportunity had presented itself . . .

"Will that be all right?" she continued. "I could supervise it myself, but you are so clever with the map, and I have promised the marquess to concentrate on the herb garden first."

"No, I would be happy to take up that duty," said Mairi. "You are very kind to offer it to me."

"Let's see if you still think me kind this spring, when your nose shall be blistered from the sun and your gown muddied every day."

"My opinion shall not change," Mairi said firmly.

"Nor mine," added Carolyn. "Have you given thought to the Christmas celebration, my lady?"

Solange grimaced. "I cannot believe I only have just heard of this. Christmas is less than a sennight away, and now I discover I am expected to plan an entire celebration!"

"It was the tradition for the Marchioness of Lockewood to organize the party," said Carolyn. "As I said to you yesterday, these past five years have been somewhat haphazard celebrations, and before that, as you know, there were none at all. You should not feel pressured, Marchioness."

"Carolyn, I cannot even convince you to call me by my given name! How could you possibly think I have the skills necessary to host a party for all of Wolfhaven?"

Mairi gave an easy laugh. "We will help you, will we not, Caro?"

"We would be delighted to," said Carolyn, "Solange."

"Me too!" threw in her son.

As they rounded up the children and headed back to the castle gate, none of them noticed the pair of watching eyes that followed them from the woods, marking their exit just as carefully as they had marked their entrance.

GOOD BOYS," Solange said softly. "My brave fellows, what handsome boys you are."

She knelt in the soft dirt that made up the floor of

the kennel, heedless of the fine layer of dust that coated the hem of her gown. Around her stood seven fully grown mastiffs, all of them sniffing the bowls in her hands eagerly.

"Here you are." She placed the two bowls of meat down in front of her, and the dogs crowded closer.

She had come across their kennel by casual design, for she had been keeping an eye out for it for days. She hadn't told Damon of her intent to meet the dogs. She rather thought she could imagine what he would say to that, and none of it would be anything she would want to hear.

They were hunters, mighty warriors of their breed, and necessary for the survival of the castle. They had been trained to attack upon command, and usually such an attack was fatal.

So she had taken a good week to get to know them before she entered the gate to the kennel. A week was enough, she had decided that morning, to allow them to become familiar with her scent.

Fortunately the kennel was placed at another odd angle of the castle, an afterthought, Solange guessed. Twin pine trees shielded it from the excesses of the sun, and from prying eyes. For the past week she had made a point of going there at least twice a day, a good break from the garden planning, and talked quietly with the hounds.

They were wary at first, a few showing fangs, but she had expected this, indeed was used to this, and knew it was only a matter of time before they trusted her enough to let her come in.

"You see, Jane?" Solange called in a low voice. "Nothing to fear."

Jane and her friend Miranda both watched the marchioness with eyes like saucers. Jane gave a little moan.

"Oh, they will eat you up, my lady!"

"No, silly. See? They are my friends." Solange patted a large brindled male beside her. "If you are gentle with them, there is nothing to fear."

"My lady," said Miranda in an awed whisper, "are you magic?"

"No. You must simply treat them with respect, and they will respect you in turn."

She had brought these two girls with her to prove to them that the dogs were not as hideous as the nursery tales she overheard whispered about with gleeful horror made them out to be. When she had heard the children's stories of the mastiffs' fearful teeth, she had been amused. But when she had seen these two girls scream shrilly when one of the hounds had gotten loose in the hall, she had decided to take action.

The dog had just returned from the hunt, and her jaws had been bloody. True, the sight of the huge female headed toward them, mouth dripping with pink saliva, was probably unnerving. But at their age Solange had already made great friends of the hounds at Ironstag, and the piercing, unnecessary screams from both Miranda and Jane were enough to set anyone's teeth on edge.

Solange had decided to woo the dogs to gentleness and then bring the girls to witness it. These two were the natural ringleaders of the rest of the children, and if they could be emboldened to like the dogs, so would the rest.

And it was working. Jane had already come three steps closer to the kennel gate, and Miranda was only a step behind her.

The dogs had devoured the meat scraps and began to sniff around for more.

"It's true they are big," Solange said. "And they do have sharp teeth. That's one of the reasons you must respect them. But all creatures desire love, and the hounds are no different."

"May we come in, my lady?" Jane was already working the latch on the gate.

"No," Solange said firmly. "Not yet. They do not know you well enough to let you into their home. You must promise me you will not come in here unless I give you permission."

Jane paused, a hand still on the latch. She opened her mouth to argue, but then the largest of the hounds looked up, it seemed right at her, the hair bristling on the back of his neck and his lips curling back, revealing a full set of sharp white teeth. A low rumble shook the air.

"I promise, my lady!" squeaked Jane, and backed away quickly.

The other dogs lifted their heads as the first one did, all of them growling now, all of them looking toward the gate.

But no, Solange saw, standing up to see better. They were looking beyond the gate and the girls. They were looking into the woods not more than fifty feet away.

She felt the hair on her own neck stand up as she

searched the line of trees with her eyes, but she could see nothing, nor hear anything either.

"Girls," she said mildly. "Go back inside the castle. Walk, don't run."

They picked up their skirts and ran. Solange crossed slowly to the kennel gate, but still she could see nothing. The solid, muscular bodies of the dogs pushed at her as they all crowded close to the entry. She was very glad she was on the inside of the gate, with them.

Probably a boar, she thought. A wild boar.

But there were no other sounds, no birds singing, no scuffling in the leaves on the ground, nothing but the steady, deep-pitched growls from the dogs.

The dark greens, browns, and grays of the forest muted the light, created illusions with shadowy shapes that drew the eye, then vanished.

There was nothing there. Not a boar, not a hare, nothing.

But the dogs knew better, and she trusted them more than her own vision.

From nowhere a man came into view at a half-run, and the dogs erupted into a frenzied barking, some of them leaping up to push their paws against the gate.

It was Damon, and he was furious. Again.

"Oh, dear," she said under her breath.

He walked up slowly to the kennel. The dogs were still barking, but it was different now, there was no menace to them. Their hackles were no longer raised. She sincerely hoped Damon could tell the difference.

"Solange," he said conversationally. "Come out right now."

"Yes, my lord," she responded in the same tone. "But only see how the hounds are delighted to have you here. You must quite be their favorite."

"Solange," he said again, and the edge of steel she heard was not her imagination, she knew.

"Yes," she muttered. Before she left she made a great show of petting the heads of the nearest hounds, who responded with happy pants. Damon was opening the gate.

She slipped out through the wedge of the opening and he shut it behind her with more force than necessary. She paused just behind him, searching the trees one more time.

An ordinary view. Nothing unusual. Nothing to make the mastiffs give the warning of danger. Yet there had been something out there. Of that she was certain.

Damon grabbed her arm and pulled her into his embrace.

"Don't," he said, and that was all, because he was kissing her hard and squeezing her ribs until she had to pound on his shoulders for air.

He lifted his head from hers and loosened his grip, but not by much.

"Don't do that again," he said, and he sounded odd, his voice remote and shaken. She tried to relax in his grip.

"There was nothing to fear," she started to say, but before she could finish her thought he was kissing her again, as hard as before, and she wondered if her lips were going to be bruised.

He pulled away again and took a deep breath of air.

She decided to say nothing, letting the tension in him spin itself out before trying to reason with him.

He released her but kept his grip on her arm and began to pull her back to the castle. Near the gate with the guards were Miranda and Jane, both pale and fearful looking, and to reassure them she gave them a cheerful smile and waved with her free hand.

They did not wave back.

Damon pulled her past them and into the great hallway. It was difficult to pretend that all was normal, since he had the look of a man with death in tow, and not his own wife, she thought somewhat indignantly. Servants scattered, men ceased their conversations, women gave little gasps as they went by, and still he did not stop until she pulled out of his grip in front of her chamber door.

"I am not some piece of mutton, my lord, for you to drag about at your whim," she said, attempting a tone of command.

He stared down at her and she felt a distinct chill.

"After you" was all he said, however, and pushed open the door for her.

She realized that unless she wanted an audience for this scene, she had better retreat inside. She lifted her chin and went in. Damon followed.

She stopped in the middle of the room, fully prepared to handle the argument she was certain was about to occur. But when she turned to look at him, what she saw was fear on his face, plain and simple. Fear, something she had never thought to see on him. It drained away her anger, left her feeling uncertain, confused.

He stood by the door, making no move to approach her, only looking at her.

She lifted one hand in supplication, then let it fall to her side.

"There was no harm," she said.

He said nothing.

"They are quite tame," she tried again.

"They are killers. They are trained to kill strangers."

His voice was even, calm. She saw that he held his hands in fists at his sides, that his knuckles were white.

"I took a full week to let them know me first," she said gently.

"A week?" He gave a short, mirthless laugh. "A week, how prudent of you. One entire week." Something in his voice cracked, and the emotion was there, raw and powerful. "Those mastiffs are not your pets, Solange. They will kill you. It's what they do."

She knew right then that he was not going to understand, that he would never understand, that the deep and chilling thing in him would not let him. He was afraid for her. He was afraid to lose her.

It made her walk over to him and pull his face down to hers, seeking his lips. He stiffened, resisting her, but she was persistent, reaching up and kissing him until his arms came around her in a sudden move, and he was kissing her back with all the passion and fear and desperation she had seen on his face an instant earlier.

He was a brave man, but it seemed she had become his inadvertent weakness. She would keep this secret to herself, guarding it carefully, and then, over time, perhaps wean him away from this fear. She couldn't let him control her, but she would help him somehow.

It might be best, she thought with only a twinge of guilt, not to tell him of what the dogs heard in the woods. No need to worry him unnecessarily. It had only been a boar. . . .

"Stay away from the hounds," he said against her lips. His voice was more normal now.

"Aye," she replied. "For now."

"Forever!" he said, and then realized how foolish it sounded.

She leaned back and looked up at him, a mysterious gaze full of golden smoke, then favored him with a slow smile. "For a while."

He wasn't going to get her to agree with him, and he knew she wouldn't lie to him to get her way.

"If anything ever were to happen to you," he began, but couldn't finish, because his throat closed at the thought.

"I know," she said. "I know, my love."

The Christmas celebration at Wolfhaven was a huge success.

It had taken frantic planning, a scrambling together of people and resources that had Solange half mad by the end and wondering why anyone would bother with such a thing at all. But it was worth it, she knew.

She knew it that morning when she attended the Cristes Maesse in the little chapel and listened, as enthralled as everyone else was, to the priest who had married her speak in his calm voice of peace, and joy, and hope.

She knew it when she saw all the people who made up Wolfhaven sit together and laugh and sing, regardless of class, regardless of history.

She knew it when she heard the familiar and dear songs of Christmas being played by any who could find an instrument or carry a tune, aided by the jongleurs.

She knew it when she saw the children screeching with delight over their gifts of wooden toys, from dolls to miniature lances.

She knew when she could sit back and smell the spices from the wild boar and goose, the pies, the fresh breads mingled with the clean scent of pine boughs.

She knew it as she watched the Yule log burn and pop in the grate of the main hall, illuminating the cheerful faces around her, warming the entire room.

And she knew it most of all when she sat beside her husband, her lover, and felt his quiet happiness become her own, saw with his eyes the joyful gathering of his people in his home, each and every one of them a testament to his life, to his successes.

He looked magnificent, wearing his black tunic with the silver wolf, and although the color was not typically festive, she wore her own to match it. It seemed appropriate enough that they would wear the heraldry of Lockewood to mark the event.

They sat together at the main table. The feast was long past, but the celebration continued late into the night, sometimes with dancing, sometimes with shared tales of the season. Solange kept a close watch over Damon; it was a constant delight to see him, even still. And tonight he laughed with the others, joined in the conversations, and even refilled drinks when the serving maids were busy exclaiming over their gifts.

At Solange's persistent urging, Mairi came up to the main table and sat beside her. "You are a fortunate woman," she said in a quiet voice.

Solange didn't have to ask what she was referring to. "I know. More fortunate than I deserve, no doubt."

"I must wonder about that, my lady. I find we usually get what we deserve in this life, eventually."

"Do you really think so? A rather sobering thought. I would hate to think I deserved getting dunked in the creek this afternoon."

"Ah, but you have proven me right, Marchioness! You received exactly what you deserved. Anyone could see the branch was not nearly strong enough to support your weight."

"Anyone but me, you mean. Well, I could not help it."

"You could have. Jane should not have shown you the nest."

"Jane was perfectly correct in coming to me, and I told her so after I had dried off and changed. If she hadn't told mc of the birds, they would be dead by now, since their mama died. Thank goodness I was able to hand them down to Jane before the bough snapped. And I got only a few scratches in the fall."

Mairi shook her head. "It was a foolish risk, Solange. You might have been far worse off than getting a few scratches, you know. They were only birds."

Solange gave a delighted smile. "Yes, but now we have three of our very own hawks! Even you must confess, my dear, that the men were rather pleased with the outcome. Three young hawks to train. Godwin was ecstatic."

"But your husband was not."

As if he sensed their conversation, Damon paused in his discussion across the room with a group of his men and threw the two women a considering look. Both of them smiled at him in return. Solange picked up her goblet and continued.

"He will be fine. He didn't really mean that I couldn't go out any longer."

"Hmm. As I recall, he seemed very serious indeed about it."

"Yes. He meant it at the time, I know. He was a trifle upset."

"A trifle?" interrupted Mairi. "His scowl could have melted stone! Women and children ran for cover, even the men found somewhere else to be while he was yelling."

"But he'll be fine, you'll see," said Solange. "He was worried about me. That's all."

"I believe you are right about that. He *was* worried about you. He cares about you a great deal."

"Yes."

Knowing that was what gave Solange the courage to face her furious husband that afternoon in her room, when he had stormed in while she was still drying off from her plunge into the frigid creek. Knowing that he did care, that he *loved* her, made her patient during his lecture, made her quiet while he vented his worry and fear through anger, and finally made her grateful when it was over and he hugged and kissed her and then begged her to be more careful.

He was getting better, she thought.

"Which brings me back to my original observation." Mairi nibbled at a sugared plum. "You are a fortunate woman, Marchioness."

"Yes, I am."

But did she deserve it? To accept that would mean that she had somehow deserved to have Redmond as well. And nothing could convince her that she had been bad enough to deserve that.

For a while, yes, for too long a while she had half-heartedly believed the things he had told her: that she was a poor wife, that she didn't realize how lucky she was to have him, that she was ungrateful and unwilling to try to please him. He was so convincing, so sincere. And she had tried harder and harder to please him, no matter how strange his behavior, no matter how demeaning his demands. He told her that she was weak, and in response she had tried to prove herself strong, only to have her efforts mocked and held up as an example of her weakness.

He would tell her that he loved her but then went on to prove his love was only a reflection of that twisted thing inside him, false and hollow as sin.

If she had known as a small child that there could be such a man waiting for her in her future, would she not have tried to change that path, to change herself in some way? Solange thought so. She hoped so. There would be no going back, of course. Perhaps that child could never have been convinced, anyway, of the evil that lurked in the heart of a man so fair in appearance. He had never quite been able to hide the flatness of his eyes, though he had managed the rest well enough.

The curly yellow hair, the slickness of his smile, were a bright disguise to what she knew he really was.

Solange sometimes wondered not how she survived Redmond, but rather how she survived her childhood without the knowledge of human nature that Redmond later provided. Had she been that isolated, that unassuming?

She was unable to be her own judge. Those days at Ironstag had long ago taken on a faded quality she had never fought to revive. She had kept the memory of Damon alive, yes, but the rest of it had been welcome to leave her. After the first few weeks at Wellburn she had wanted nothing to do with any of it. The contrast between the maiden Solange and the Countess of Redmond had been too great to bear. Something deep inside her had told her quite strongly that if she chose to cling to the girl she had been, she would surely die.

And she had not been ready to die.

She had killed the girl instead. Well, she actually did not quite manage to kill her completely, for the girl still showed up in various drugged dreams, especially during that long, long year in bed, wishing, hoping, pining . . .

But when she was herself, Solange abandoned that futile path and steeled herself to become a changed woman. It took time. It took too much time. More than that, it took anger, and fear and loneliness, and made them her allies, and she thought that was perhaps her greatest victory.

There came a day when she had been able to stand up and look into a mirror, and see a strong person there. That person was trapped, yes, and afraid, certainly, but with good cause. She was not weak. And she was not a bad person. She did not deserve this.

On that day Solange said no to Redmond for the first time. It had seemed to gain her nothing; no was a word that the earl had been astonished by, and eventually had laughed off. But she had said it nevertheless. It was a tiny thing of power and it braced her in some way she didn't even fathom. From that moment she grew, and she continued to grow no matter what he did to her. None of that sordidness could touch her again, even if they struck her, even if they tied her down, even if they forced her to do things.

Solange blinked and became instantly surrounded by the goodwill of Wolfhaven once more. The agreeable noise of the crowd filled her ears again, the music, the laughter.

"Solange? My lady, are you well?"

Mairi was looking at her with concern. She had put her hand on Solange's arm.

"Oh, yes, I am fine. Silly of me, I became lost in thought while staring at that torch there. It has quite blinded me, I fear. I don't suppose you have another handkerchief about you?"

Mairi reached into her sleeve and pulled out a linen square. Solange began to laugh. "You are always prepared, aren't you?"

"A handkerchief is an excellent thing to keep close by, I find. Do wipe your eyes, my dear, before your husband sees you weeping and assumes I have put you out. For although you seem able to handle his fearsome temper, I think to have him yell at me would make me faint on the spot."

"He would not yell at you. But he might raise his voice somewhat."

"So you say. I for one would prefer not to find out. There, you look much better. Quite restored. Do you wish to talk about it?"

"Why, no, there's nothing to discuss."

Mairi adjusted the hem of her sleeve. "Perhaps not." She kept her eyes down. "But I could not help but notice that the torch is not near enough to us, my lady, to warrant such tears, even if you were to stare into it for half the night."

Solange had no reply to that; it was perfectly true. Around the room, one by one, voices became lifted in song, a lilting and surprisingly delicate harmony emerged. She saw Damon join in, adding his baritone to the lot. She could hear him above all the others.

"Mairi, do you ever miss your husband?"

The other woman sighed, then looked around the room absently. "Yes, I do sometimes. Richard was basically a good man. He could be kind and caring. Occasionally he would lose his temper. It didn't happen very often. I suppose I most like to remember him in a happy way."

"How long were you married?"

"Four years. We did not see each other much after he joined Edward's army. He would go off on the campaigns and I would stay in London. I was very sorry that he died in battle. I don't like to think that he suffered."

"I'm sorry," Solange said.

"No, it's fine. It's been long enough so that I can talk of it without feeling lost. It's odd in a sense, we were matched from childhood, but neither of us really knew the other. Both of our families served on the same estate, both held the same rankings on the estate, so that was considered enough."

"Did you . . . want to marry him?"

Mairi gave a little laugh. "What girl doesn't want to be wedded? He was handsome and likable. Our parents, of course, arranged it." She paused. "I don't think I ever loved him, however. I don't think he ever loved me. But we muddled through."

Solange nodded, lost again in her own thoughts. Mairi ran her finger around the rim of her wineglass.

"Do you ever miss the earl?"

Solange lifted her head. "No," she said. "I never, ever miss him."

Mairi nodded sadly. "It's like that sometimes."

That was all there was to it, thought Solange. It was just like that, for some reason. There was no sense in lingering over past injustices, because nothing could be done to change them. In fact, she knew she had a great deal to be thankful for, and some of that knowledge could indeed be put at the feet of Redmond.

If she had not experienced Redmond as a husband, for example, she might never have fully appreciated the gift of Damon now. Oh, she would have loved him no matter what. That would never have changed.

But perhaps she would have thought nothing of a husband who treated his wife so tenderly. Perhaps it would have seemed simply normal to have a man be strong and gentle all at once. She might never have given a second thought to the fact that Damon could lead an army to victory after victory, yet still care enough about a trio of helpless baby birds to ensure that they were tucked safely away in a warm nook of his castle.

It would have seemed perfectly natural that a man with a reputation as a fearless fighter would also be a dedicated healer, willing to help any man, woman, or child who came to him.

She might have thought all men were as good as he. She might have never known there was anything other than his goodness in the hearts of husbands. He would have been all of her world, all of her experience, and so maybe it was better that she knew enough of the other side now to appreciate him.

Maybe.

It had to be. Because this was what she had, for whatever reason. She would make the best of it.

Damon sang the last bars of the song to her, locking her eyes with his own. When it was finished, he didn't move away from his friends. But he was watching her, and he was smiling.

It was enough.

THE HAWKS WERE STILL TOO YOUNG to do anything but squeak blindly and open their beaks for food. Their down was soft and fluffy, giving them a rather absurd appearance that suggested nothing of the glory that their adulthood would bring.

"The fire in here should keep them warm enough. I think they'll make it," said Damon. He was carefully feeding them scraps of raw meat. One of the birds nipped his finger when he didn't move it fast enough.

"They are eager to live," Solange replied ruefully, examining his finger.

"It's nothing. I'm glad they're hungry. It's a good sign."

He fed them the last scrap, then wiped his hands on the wet cloth they had brought along with them for that purpose. "Just think, we have the beginnings of Wolfhaven's rookery," said Solange.

"Aye. We'll have to wait a while before they're old enough to train."

"I believe you had several offerings for the job, however."

Damon laughed, which startled the birds into momentary silence. "Suddenly it seems I have men aplenty with hawking experience."

They were quiet, watching the birds flounder about in the makeshift nest they had created out of bundles of old cloth in a wood box. After a while they settled down into a common ball of fluff, each tucking a wing here and a head there, until they were completely content and indistinguishable one from the other.

Solange glanced out the window of the small room. The night sky was patchy with silver clouds racing each other high above. It was very late, and everyone else had already retired, but she had wanted to check on the hawks one last time.

"Was it a good celebration, do you think?" she asked. "Did everyone enjoy themselves?"

"If you could measure it by the amount of wine they consumed, I'd say it was a very good celebration."

"No, really."

"Really." He came and put an arm around her shoulder. "It was splendid. Everyone loved it. The only criticism I heard all night came from a five-year-old, I believe, who was complaining about the lack of a dancing bear."

"That would be Bertram. He was very disappointed that I could not procure him one."

"Thank God. I can't imagine where we would house a bear."

"Oh, I found a perfect room right off the main hall," she began innocently.

"Don't even think about it. I'd have to keep a guard on the bear at all times to keep you from sneaking in to feed it and getting eaten yourself."

"Just a little bear," she implored with sparkling eyes.

"Have pity on me, lady. My heart cannot bear such worry."

He joined in her laughter at his sally, then finished it by pulling her into his arms and giving her a hungry kiss. He had been forced to watch her all night, resplendent in her black gown, consumed with pride that she wore his mark upon her shoulder, wanting her every moment, knowing they could not leave until everyone else had.

So he had made himself wait for her, allowing her to revel in the culmination of her hard work in preparation for tonight. She deserved to enjoy the party. He thought that she had. He hoped that she had, because now that it was over, all he wanted to do was take her back upstairs and make love to her all night long.

Half the night long, he amended to himself. Dawn was not that far away.

"Come away with me, my lady," he said, drawing her arm through his. She gave him no argument, just leaned her head on his shoulder and walked with him out of the room.

He thought, for perhaps the hundredth time, about how she was just the right height for him, which led him to think about how her hair was just the right color, her voice just the right pitch, her mouth just the right shape, her body just the right softness. . . .

In his chambers he began to kiss her slowly, thoroughly, lingering on her lips, tilting her head with his fingers and then drawing them down to her shoulders, to her breasts. Her arms started to slide around him.

"Oh!" she exclaimed, then pulled away from him. "I almost forgot! I'll be right back."

He pulled her back to him, letting her feel his arousal. "It can wait."

"No, no," she said, smiling. "I'll be right back, I promise."

He released her and she ran from the room into hers. Damon began to pace, then raked a hand through his hair, impatient with anticipation. Whatever it was, he ordered himself, be pleased. Act happy. It was still Christmas.

And it would be only a few minutes until he could resume the delightful activity of making love to his wife.

Solange appeared again through the doorway, holding both hands behind her back. She looked very excited, and very gorgeous.

"Are you ready?" she asked.

"Oh, yes."

She brought her hands forward and walked over to him. "Merry Christmas," she said softly.

Cupped in her hands was a miniature carving of two wolves sitting side by side, their heads tilted toward each other. They were cleverly carved from the same piece of polished wood; the narrow pattern of rings in it echoed the shapes of their bodies, giving the little wolves the illusion of movement.

He took it from her carefully. "Where did this come from?"

She gave a happy smile. "I wish I could tell you I carved it myself, but I think you know my skills better than that. I had it made for you though. There is a very talented woodcarver in the village. Godwin told me of him."

The more he examined the carving, the more lifelike it seemed. Both wolves had tiny chips of ebony for eyes. He thought they might even be smiling.

"Thank you," he said. "It's a beautiful piece."

"I was hoping you would like it. I know it's not a sword, or a mace, or even something useful, but I, well, I wanted you to have it."

"Solange, I will treasure it always," he said sincerely.

"And there's one more thing." She was gone before he could protest, then back again with her hands hidden. "I came across the opportunity to get this for you, and I knew you would like it, so . . ."

She brought forward a book, bound in leather, thick and heavy in her hands. He put the little wolves on a table and then picked it up carefully.

"Plantarum Medica," he read aloud from the cover page. "A book on herbs." He turned a few of the pages, noting the detailed illuminations, the clarity of the text. He was astonished. "Solange, where did you find this?"

"At the monastery," she said smugly. "I won it from Father Ignatius."

He thought he hadn't heard her correctly. "You *won* it?"

"Yes, well, I had to buy it as well. But I had to win the right to buy it first."

"When did you go to the monastery?"

She came up and examined the book beside him, ignoring the ominous warning in his voice. "Don't worry, my lord. I didn't go alone. You may be certain I had a full accompaniment of men with me."

"Which ones?" he asked smoothly.

"Don't be annoyed, Damon! I was perfectly safe. It wasn't their fault, I told them it was to be a surprise to you. And I went out only once, just to fetch the book. Aren't you pleased with it?"

She leaned up and kissed him on the cheek, then turned another page in the book. It showed a delicately illuminated drawing labeled *Tussilago Farfara* in flourishing script. Coltsfoot, his mind automatically translated, good for coughs. Damon looked up at her. "It's wonderful. I must confess I am at a loss to imagine how you got Father Ignatius to part with it."

"It wasn't easy. First of all, I sent an inquiry to the monastery to see if they had any books on herbs, and if they did, if I could purchase one."

"Which Father Ignatius declined, of course."

"He was rather curt in his refusal. He did mention, however, that the monastery had several fine volumes on herbs, and none of them were for sale."

"I cannot believe he read your note at all," said Damon.

"I remembered what you told me, so I picked an herb from your collection, sorry, it was a very little amount, and wrapped the note around it. I prefaced it with a question to him, asking him if he could identify it."

Damon went over to the bed with the book and sat down. "You appealed to his vanity. Very resourceful."

"Thank you. Over the next few days I sent more notes, and still he denied me. Finally I hit upon something. I proposed that if I could answer any questions he put to me regarding angels correctly, he should sell me the book."

"He couldn't refuse the temptation to show you up."

"Of course not! So I rode to the monastery and answered the questions, and then bought the book."

"How many questions did he ask?"

She rolled her eyes. "A whole list's worth. I had to study for a week."

Damon began to chuckle. "My poor Solange. What you went through for me."

"I am pleased you appreciate it," she said primly, and then broke down into laughter. "He was quite furious at the end, I'm afraid, but he couldn't go back on his word. It's a good thing we are going to grow your own garden."

Damon placed the book gently aside and then went over to a trunk. "I have something for you as well."

Her laughter ceased, replaced with a fragile look he couldn't define. It made him uneasy, as if she were afraid that what he had for her was something unpleasant or frightening. He banished that thought, telling himself he was reading something into nothing. Nevertheless, he approached her slowly, then placed the necklace in her hands. "I hope you like it," he said awkwardly.

She bent her head and lifted her hands, cupping the delicate chain and pendant in her palms. The pendant was a string of flowers, she thought, but no, more abstract than that, golden petals with rounded, polished garnet hearts, and small pearls separating each. It was a perfect match for the ring he had given her so long ago.

"Merry Christmas," Damon whispered. He drew her down to the bed with him, nestling her beside him in the warmth, noting the stillness of her features, the glimmerings of tears in her eyes. "What's wrong, beloved? Does it not please you? I'll find you something else, it's not important, don't cry, my love. . . ."

"No," she said, clutching both him and the necklace. "It's wonderful. It's perfect. It's just that"—her voice broke—"it's just that I love you so much."

His unease disappeared with her words, replaced

with a humble feeling that was still new to him: his unabashed love for her, reflected in each of her tears, in the warmth of her body curled trustingly next to his. He kissed the top of her head and she turned her lips up to meet his, and they began to celebrate that love in their own fashion.

Chapter Fourteen

"Do not," Damon repeated for the fourth time, "attempt to feed the hounds while I am gone. They are too wild for you yet."

"I won't," Solange sighed.

"You said that before." He crossed over to where she was leaning against the window, half in sun and half in shadow against the bright sky.

"I won't attempt to feed *or* water them, my lord," she amended. "But I do think you are wrong in this, Damon. Those dogs are very willing to be friendly."

"Nevertheless," he continued. "Do not—"

"Yes, yes, yes. I won't do this and I won't do that. You would think I were a child of five, not a woman of five and twenty."

This was an argument they had been having with growing frequency over the past week, ever since Damon had been informed that a journey to Ironstag could no longer be put off. A messenger had arrived, informing him that the steward there sent his greetings, and the most humble request that the new lord arrive soon, *very* soon, he prayed, to sort out the growing problems of an estate with no master in residence.

It was a scant month into the new year, but Damon supposed he had had longer than he deserved in avoiding this duty. He assembled his men with reluctance and prepared to leave as soon as possible in order to return to Wolfhaven, and thus Solange, that much faster.

She wasn't pleased that he was forbidding her to go. He had tried to explain to her that it was not a pleasure trip. It was going to be rough and rapid, cold and wearing. She had responded with the acrid comment that he must have mistaken her for some feeble thing, to think she could not handle a galloping pace and a brisk wind. Perhaps he had already forgotten, she had continued, that she was the one who had been ready to journey from France to England alone, weather be damned!

He had not forgotten. She had a wild spirit and a brave heart that led her places most rational men would fear to tread. God in heaven, how could he forget that? It was a constant worry of his, that her next escapade would be her last, and there would be no one but himself to blame. He was more than half tempted to bring her along just to keep an eye on her. He would miss her sore enough.

And there was no denying that he could not shake off the strange apprehension that gripped him whenever he thought of her alone, and therefore vulnerable. He told himself it was irrational, worrying over her when it was plain to see she would be well protected while he was gone. But the feeling did not abate.

He did not want to leave her. He was almost willing

to include her on the journey just to eliminate this unpleasant sensation that ate away at his stomach, this acidic anxiety for her.

But then he would see her as he was seeing her now, a slight figure framed against the window. No matter what she said, no matter how free her spirit, she was still a woman, his beloved, and his responsibility. She was small and delicate, determined and yet seemingly unaware of her own fragility. She had survived the journey to Wolfhaven, but it had not been easy on her. He had seen the signs of exhaustion in her from the beginning but had been incapable of changing their path once it had begun.

She needed pampering, not a week-long rough ride. It had not been, after all, long a period since they had arrived here. He would not risk her health on such a routine trip as this. Chances were very good it would snow, perhaps several times, before they reached Ironstag, and so they would not have the luxury of time in putting up full tents at night, with all the servants and cushions and fine foods that she deserved.

Still, it was not an easy decision for him to go without her. He couldn't take her, he didn't want to leave her. The best he could do was surround her with the thick walls of the castle and a contingent of his men while he was gone. She would be all right. She had to be.

Her face was pensive as she stared up at him now, the amber light in her eyes bright in the warm stroke of the sunlight.

Damon gave up his lecturing and instead pulled her into his arms. "If you would allow me to go with you," she said, muffled against his chest, "you need not worry about all the things you have forbidden me to do."

"I told you, we will go together in the late spring, perhaps, or early summer. When the weather is fairer and we may travel at our leisure. Remember, Aiden will remain here to supervise while I am gone. You must go to him if there is any trouble."

"There will not be any trouble, husband."

"No, because you will obey my commands. Won't you, wife?"

"Hmmph." She rubbed her face into him, sweet and pliant despite her protest.

"Solange. Have I told you yet today how much I love you?"

She turned her face up to his. "I believe you have, my lord, but only once or twice. It has not been nearly enough."

"I do love you, my wife, more than all of this earth itself."

"And I love you, my husband, more than all the stars above."

Through the panes of the glass window came the faint sounds of men shouting good-naturedly at each other, and horses stamping their hooves against the stone courtyard.

"They are waiting for me," he said regretfully.

"I will be waiting for you as well," she replied.

He kissed her, wishing all over again that he did not have to go. She kissed him back with her whole heart, clutching the shoulders of his leather jerkin, wanting to hold this memory with her until he returned.

"Damn," he breathed, breaking away. The men outside were shouting for him now. There was no time for what he really wanted to do. Someone would be at their door any second.

"Have a safe journey, beloved." She had a saucy smile.

"I will, if I am able to concentrate on anything but you," he said bluntly.

As if on cue, there came a heavy knocking on the door. "My lord?" It was Braeden's voice. "The horses are growing impatient. The men have bid me to come and ask you how much longer you will be."

"Tell them I am coming now." Damon reached down and brushed a strand of hair from her face that had escaped her elaborate braid. She sighed and patted his arm reassuringly.

"Do not fear, my husband. I will follow your instructions, at least until you come home to me."

"I know you will. And I will be back sooner than you think."

She walked him down to the outer bailey, where a group of people had gathered to see the men off. Damon mounted and saluted her good-bye, and then they were gone in a moving army of horses and men past the portal. Solange watched until she could see nothing of them any longer, until the sterling trunks of the woods enclosed them completely.

Mairi stood beside her, watching as well. At length she turned to her. "Come, Solange. Let's go work on the plan for your garden. A good distraction is what we need today."

"It is not my garden, it is our garden."

"Wolfhaven's garden, then." The group of people had already split up and gone to their various chores. The two women walked alone into the castle.

IT WAS ODD HOW THE DAYS seemed so empty without him. It was odd because it was such a new feeling to her; even the years without him had not seemed so vivid with loss.

She supposed it was because she had grown accustomed to his company again, but rather more his loving company. It made her dreamy, something she had not indulged in for a good while. The sewing circle of women had become used to her frequent pauses in mid-stitch, the faraway gleam in her eye.

And she in turn had slowly become accustomed again to the casual company of others. She had not wanted to go back to the circle until she felt fully prepared to interact with these women, but Mairi had insisted that she join them the day after Damon had left, saying it was her duty now, as the mistress of the castle, to demonstrate a social grace to others.

Solange had conceded that point with much doubt. Part of her was still terrified of those others, illogically, stupidly, she scolded herself, but still, terrified.

It had taken time and repeated exposure to them to convince that shaken part of herself that these were not the women of Wellburn or Du Clar. Planning the garden and the Christmas party had set the roots to easing her fears. Everyone had been cordial and helpful; no one had an unkind word that she heard.

It opened up that shrunken space in her, let it blossom slowly beneath the honest congeniality of the people surrounding her now. Mairi's insistence on the sewing circle had shown an uncanny perception of what Solange needed and would not take for herself. The women there were gentle with her, gradually growing bolder with stories and jokes until Solange was laughing openly with them, encouraging them to tell more until the light failed or it was time to attend to other duties.

Mairi didn't even have to convince her to visit the nursery. She wanted to go on her own, and was placidly welcomed by the mothers and nurses there.

The children were more enthusiastic in their welcome.

"Lady Solange! Lady Solange! Are you here to take us to the field?" cried Bertram, bouncing up and down on his mother's lap.

"Why, no, I'm afraid not, Bertram. The field will have to wait for another day." Solange sat down on the floor beside William, who had been playing with a toy sword.

"Why not, Lady Solange?" A little girl ran up to her and tugged on her sleeve. "I want to go see where my tree is going to be again."

"Yes!" said another girl. "I do too!"

"Me too!" said William, staring up at her hopefully.

"The field has not changed since we were last there," Solange laughed. "And you all remember where your trees will go, I am certain. But if you like, we could bring out the chart, and I can show you on the paper where each of you has marked your spot."

This plan was met with resounding approval, and so Mairi produced the chart and the children pored over it, each declaring their own tiny dot of land the best, the most beautiful, the highest, the lowest, the closest to the castle, the farthest from it, or any other title they could think to bestow.

Children climbed up on her, over her, around her, all seeming to want her attention, her affirmation of whatever they could think to ask her. She answered as many questions as she could until their mothers took pity on her and announced it time for their supper. In a flurry of small, plump arms and legs they left her for the table set up just for them.

"Do not be offended by their fickle affections, my lady," said one mother. "Cook promised them each a pudding at the end of the meal."

"A pudding! Well, naturally they would run for that. I would as well."

How cozy it was, she couldn't help thinking. How nice, to grow up with all these companions, sharing meals, and toys, and adventures. It made her wonder why her own childhood had been so lacking in these things, except for her constant companion of Damon.

"A rare handful, isn't it?" asked Mairi, surveying the group fondly.

"A rare treat," Solange declared, "to see so many happy young faces."

"Don't be fooled, Mistress," called out one nurse who had overheard the remark. "More than half the time they're busy fighting, if they're not all the best of friends."

One by one the mothers left to seek their own meals, leaving Solange and Mairi to follow. They walked slowly down to the main hall.

"You know," said Mairi, "I was thinking about the schooling of the children. They neither read nor write. There hasn't been anyone here to teach it to them, save the marquess, and of course he is much to busy for such a thing."

Solange looked at her askance. "You know how to read and write, I notice."

"Barely. I learned what I did from my father, and only infrequently, since most people disapproved of it. I had to beg him quite horribly for the lessons I did receive, on the basis that I wanted to learn the spellings of plants and something of gardening."

"Something should be done to remedy this," Solange said.

"Aye, and you are the woman to do it."

"You are a woman full of excellence, Mairi."

"Only practicality."

"Excellent practicality, then. I think it a delightful idea to teach the children to read. Do you think the mothers will mind?"

Mairi laughed. "Mind? They are far more likely to join in the lessons. You'll see."

It took not even a day for word to get out that the marchioness was going to hold lessons for the children. She made plans to begin the next morning, in fact. As Mairi wryly pointed out, one of the benefits of being the mistress of the castle meant she could establish a domestic routine anytime or anywhere she wished.

But nothing had prepared her for the sight that greeted her that morning as she walked into the schoolroom, laden with scraps of paper and a box full of quills and ink bottles.

Sitting in a neat half-circle on the rug in the center of the room were the children, all quiet and large-eyed. That they greeted her happily without running to climb on her was a surprise enough. But behind the children were over a dozen adults, mostly women, with a sprinkling of men as well, sitting on benches or on the floor.

Solange stopped at the entrance, afraid there had been some sort of trouble. She couldn't imagine why all these people were here, unless it was to protest her plan.

Mairi stepped forward. "We are all ready, my lady."

"Ready?" She saw no looks of anger, only anticipation, mingled with a sort of embarrassment from some of the adults.

"Ready for your lesson, of course." Mairi came up and took some of the materials from her hands. "I warned you," she whispered.

"Oh. My lesson. Really?" She surveyed the crowd. "You all wish to learn to read and write?"

"Yes, my lady," called out Carolyn. Many of the others nodded.

"Well. I see." Solange walked over to the table that had been set up for her, where Mairi had already put the box of quills. She stared down stupidly at the paper scraps in her hands.

What was this feeling that came over her, this bittersweet ache that flooded her chest suddenly? It left her dumb and blind, but it brought a kind of strength with it, a hot, welcome feeling that made her look up at the faces in spite of herself.

No one was mocking her. No one was laughing at her. Everyone she saw had only a look of patient hope.

"I'm afraid I didn't bring enough paper," she said into the silence.

"Then we shall get you more," said Mairi.

And they did.

The lessons progressed slowly, for Solange was unused to teaching as much as any of the other adults were unused to sitting in a schoolroom. Of all of them, the children fared the best, being both enthusiastic and easily accepting of ideas just beyond their grasp, for such was their world.

As the days passed, the classes grew, and a routine became established. Solange was given the comfort of knowing that a good many people had come to depend upon her for something that only she could supply. For the first time in her life, she was learning to become a part of an extended family, and thus closer to the life Damon had created.

She had been able to convince almost all the women, and a few of the men as well, to address her by her given name rather than by title, and in turn she learned each of theirs.

It made life at the castle much more comfortable. It was not her imagination, she told herself, that people were calling out greetings to her as they passed now. Women were coming to her for advice. Even Cook sought her out to consult on the menu for the night of the men's return.

The days now were brisk with a biting wind that

scattered the brown leaves left on the ground and left her cheeks apple-bright from the ride she wheedled Aiden into allowing her to have every so often. He would always accompany her, however, with two other men, the three of them surrounding her.

She was more than a little annoyed with them all, even though she knew they were acting only on Damon's orders. Despite his progress, she supposed, he was still overprotective of her. But these rides with the men beside her smacked too closely of the supervision she had endured at Du Clar, the stifling restrictions that had been forced upon her for years.

Damon was just going to have to learn that she would not stand to be coddled, she decided. She was not a child. She had already lived a lifetime, it felt, of having her every move scrutinized when she had been under Redmond's rule. She was heartily sick of it.

Before she had left Du Clar she had made a silent vow to never submit to such control again, and the fact that—quite the opposite of Redmond—Damon meant well did not negate the element of control he still tried to exert over her.

Out of consideration for the men, she never tried to outrun her accompaniment; she had no wish to bring the wrath of her husband down upon their heads should she actually manage to escape them. But it irked her, this constant vigilance, and in her irritation she convinced herself that everyone was overreacting, that even the wild boar had not existed, that it had been naught but the wind through the trees that had spooked the dogs. . . .

Solange felt an exuberance and daring she had not

recalled since her youth. It meant she retired each night with a smile that lasted until she lay down in Damon's bed alone.

Nights were the hardest, she decided, for there were no distractions from the fact that he was not lying beside her, kissing her, making love to her. At night she often spent hours staring up at the ceiling, over at the herb rack, out the window at the midnight sky. Sleep would woo her eventually, but never quickly enough. He will be back soon, she told herself. Very soon. Every day that passes is a day less I have to wait.

This night was no different from the others, except a light snow had begun to fall outside, dusting the landscape with an icy frosting. She arrived in the room after supper, weary from the day, yet wide awake, wondering what Damon was doing now. Was he on his way back? Was he warm? Was he safe?

The weaponry mounted on the far wall gleamed with a metallic dullness against the stone. Each lance, each sword, each lethal piece, gave mute testimony to the years her husband had endured without her. He was a knight, he was a skilled warrior. She should not be worrying about him like a mother hound over her pups.

She walked over and touched a finger against the sharpness of a morning star, noting the scratches on the iron, each pit in the metal representing a returned blow.

He had endured all this. Surely he could endure such a routine thing as a small journey from castle to castle. She was fretting over nothing.

A quiet knocking came on the door to her chamber. By the time she walked back to her room to answer it, it had grown to a rapid pounding, and a woman's voice was calling her name. Solange swung open the door.

It was Carolyn. Anxiety was etched across her face. "My lady," she began, and had to take a gulp of air.

"What is it?" asked Solange, drawing her into the room. "Calm down. Tell me the matter." A dreadful thought took her. "Is it the marquess? Did something happen to him?"

"No, my lady. It's William!" she blurted out. "He is missing from his bed. I cannot find him anywhere."

"Missing?"

"Aye! Oh, my lady, I am so worried for him! He is so small, you see, and so—" A sob caught in her throat.

"Who else knows?" Solange was thinking quickly.

"His nurse, a few of the other mothers. I went to them first, thinking maybe he went to play with one of his friends." Carolyn grasped Solange's hands. "What if he is hurt? What if he has fallen somewhere and he can't—"

"Carolyn, stop imagining things. We're going to find William. I want you to go get Mairi, tell her to gather the other women and form a search pattern in the castle, do you understand?"

"A search pattern," Carolyn repeated gratefully.

"Mairi will know what to do. I am going to get the men. They will search outside. Now, go. Go quickly."

"Thank you, my lady." Yet she stood still, as if frozen.

Solange gave her a brief hug. "We will find him, never you fear."

The other woman smiled tightly, and then she was gone.

Solange roused Aiden and quickly explained the situation to him. "We don't know how far he could have gotten, since we don't know how long he has been gone. But I think the first place to look would be the field by the woods, where the orchard is going to be. William liked to go there."

Aiden slung his cloak over his shoulders. "Don't worry, my lady. We'll take care of it." He led the pack of men outside and began issuing instructions.

Solange began to climb the stairs to locate the other women and help them. Something was bothering her. She had forgotten something important. Something . . .

A cherry tree, William had said to her.

A magic tree, she had told him. *Your own magic tree, growing out in the old orchard . . .*

"Fool, fool," she cursed herself under her breath. He had been asking her for weeks to take him there, and she had not, because there had been no time for it, and then she had not been able to leave. In a heartbeat she weighed the option of running up to find the other women and tell them where she was going, or just saving time and going.

She had grabbed someone's cloak from the hall and was already out the door before the thought could complete itself; the vague notion of finding the men and telling them instead trailed away completely when she couldn't immediately see any of them.

The old orchard was not near the field. It was in the opposite direction, and the snowy wind that grabbed her borrowed cloak convinced her not to waste the time to hunt them down. Either the boy was there or he wasn't. If he wasn't, she would run back and tell them to search the area more thoroughly.

She ran along the old stone walls of Wolfhaven with both hands holding up her skirts, ducking her head against the flakes that drifted down into her eyes.

The woods were dark and silent when she arrived, and there was no answer to her calls. There was hardly any light to see by. Cursing herself again for not thinking to bring a lamp or even a candle, she wove her way through the old bent branches, black with wetness, to the spot where she had found the cherry sapling.

William was not there. There were no little footprints in the new fallen snow to indicate that he had been there at all. The sapling stood untouched between the massive old trees, lightly covered with virgin snow.

Solange hugged her arms around herself and stood up from examining the little tree. "William!" she called, more out of repetition than hope. She looked around blindly. "William!"

A sound reached her, the smallest of sounds, from off to her left. She blinked against the snow, and called out the name again, then paused, listening.

"Lady . . ." came the whimper.

"William!" She ran a few steps, then stopped, listening again. "Call to me again, William!"

"Lady." The voice was stronger now, or perhaps just nearer. Solange wiped the gathering snow off her hair and listened again, taking cautious steps in what she hoped was the right direction.

She almost missed him, the little lump huddled beneath the limbs of a dead tree. "Here," he cried, when she had walked past him, and she picked him up and kissed his cheek, then hugged him close with all her might.

"Willie, what were you doing out here?" she cried in mingled anger and relief, brushing the snow off him.

"My t-t-tree," he chattered through frozen lips. "M-magic tree."

"You should have waited for me to take you there." Guilt and remorse filled her.

"I'm s-sorry." The little boy began to cry. "I got l-lost. I got s-s-scared."

"No, no, it's all right, my sweet. Don't cry. I'm not mad at you. But I've got to get you home. You're chilled to the bone." She settled him on her hip, wrapped the cloak around them both, then set about finding her directions again.

"Wait," William said against her neck. "M-my cane."

Without letting go of the child, she knelt down and searched the snow with one hand until she came across the smooth outline of it. "I have it now, don't worry."

He wasn't too heavy, but the cold was beginning to affect her. The snow abruptly stopped, which helped her to see, at least, where she was headed. William had gone limp with his head tucked down between her jaw and her shoulder, a trusting little life in her arms she suddenly felt fiercely protective of.

"Don't worry," she repeated between heavy breaths. "Don't worry."

But it seemed much longer on the way back than it had going. It was more difficult dodging the outstretched branches that snatched at her hair and pulled at her clothing. She was fairly certain she was headed in the right direction. Eventually she found the path of her own footprints that led into the woods, and followed them with relief. William stirred beneath her chin.

Behind her came the sharp snapping sound of a twig breaking, which ceased as soon as she stopped walking.

She waited in the darkness, clutching the boy close. She heard only silence.

Solange swallowed her fear and went forward again, walking as lightly as she could. Was that another noise behind her, that ghostly breathing, almost like laughter? She stopped, and so did the sounds.

William was looking up at her fearfully; he had heard them too. She forced herself calmly to start walking again, trying to hear how close the sounds were behind her. She imagined she had a good twenty feet.

It wasn't nearly enough for her to escape. But it would have to do for William.

"My gracious," she said in a bright, clear voice. "You are a growing lad. I think I'm going to have to let you walk on your own."

She knelt, putting him down carefully, and handed him his cane. "That's better," she said loudly as she rapidly removed her cloak and bundled it around him. Then, in a whisper: "Follow the trail, Willie, do you see it? Follow that trail as fast as you can, and it will take you back home."

"But—"

"Do as I say! You must be brave, William, and tell the others that I am coming right after you. Hurry!" Behind her, the silence waited.

She stood up. "Go. I am depending upon you."

Her heart squeezed as she watched the little figure limp away, the cloak trailing ridiculously behind him.

God keep you, she thought, then turned around and walked back into the darkness of the orchard.

She made an effort not to follow the original path exactly, but wavered slightly off course, as if she were confused. It would buy William a few minutes more, not much, but hopefully enough to get him within sight of one of the searchers.

The loss of the cloak brought the wind more sharply to her, but she paid scant attention to this discomfort. She was listening as hard as she could, waiting for the sounds she had heard before to begin again.

When she paused to free her hair from a grasping branch, she caught the echo of the sounds, then they faded away as she freed herself and moved forward again.

The game continued until she was almost back at the sapling. It has to be enough time, she thought, it has to. I cannot wait any longer.

Neither could he.

"Good eve to you, my angel," came the familiar mellow voice. He stepped out of the shadows and walked slowly over to her, both hands outstretched to show them empty.

She said nothing in reply. There were no words to be said, they were smothered by the emotions. Fear. Anger. Wild, irrational fear.

There had been no boar, after all, no, not at all. . . .

"You took a foolish risk to come back into the

woods alone." Redmond gave her his wide, handsome smile. "Why, what if it had been wolves trailing you?"

"Wolves would not hurt me," she said. "I know the sound of vermin when I hear it."

Anger slashed across his face and was gone. The smile stayed as wide as ever. "As much as I look forward to conversing with you over the habits of certain animals, I'm afraid I simply don't have the time for it now." His eyes flicked over her shoulder.

She felt the movement in the air behind her but didn't turn, so the blow was clean to the back of her head, and she crumpled gracefully to the ground.

Chapter Fifteen

IT WAS THEIR SECRET PLACE. None of the adults knew they were there, and so her laughter had a ring of freedom and joy. She waved her fist about her face teasingly.

Damon was yelling at her, reaching for her. No, no, he said, but he leapt at her and missed, she was too fast for him, for all of them, even when she was laughing so hard.

No, Solange, stop it right now, he cried to her, and with the quickness of a cat he was up again, knocking her hand aside with all the force that three extra years over her gave him.

Belatedly she realized it was no longer a game, he was not playing with her, he was yelling.

He was yelling at her, but she was watching her hand open up from the impact of his, watching the small yellow berries fall harmlessly out of her palm and into the green, green grass. . . .

HER HEAD ACHED. It ached with a kind of thudding regularity that indicated she had not been unconscious very long, although she was stretched out on something soft, and covered for warmth.

"Hello, hello," said a singsong voice beside her ear. She winced without meaning to, causing the voice to grow louder.

"Wake up, my angel. Time to wake up."

The voice reminded her of her dream, of those pretty little yellow berries she had found one day.

"Solange," said the voice. "Wake up."

Such a cheerful color, she had thought, attractive enough for a child of five to want to taste, for surely something so pretty would be sweet as well.

A light slap across her cheek snapped her head to the left. It wasn't hard enough to really hurt. Not yet.

But the berries had fallen, lost in the thick green grass. She had never forgotten them. They came from a plant she had discovered all alone that day, such a strange plant with a green and purple stem and leaves—

The next slap was slightly harder.

And the name of that plant, she had certainly never forgotten that.

The name was hemlock.

She opened her eyes. "I am surprised to see you," she said.

Redmond lifted his brows. "I imagine you are."

Solange looked behind him, seeing that they were in a cramped dark room that smelled of sod and smoke, a burrow carved into a hillside. Outside the low hole that made up the doorway to the room stood at least two men. Everyone, it seemed, had recovered quite nicely. She was sharply sorry for it.

Although the common henbane she had discovered that day in the French countryside would have been enough to stop his breath, she had decided to settle on something a little more poetic, something a little rarer in the woods, a private joke of her own. She had found it accidentally one day on a supervised outing, no one but she had noticed it. But her mind never let her forget the location of the little mottled plant with the pointed white flowers and cheerful yellow berries.

She had gone back under the cloak of night and collected them as soon as she had been able; for although Redmond was still in England at that time, she had no doubts he would seek her out again one day. After all, he had promised her he would, after the last time he had visited Du Clar. That time he had killed her mare, Gytha.

So in preparation she had dried the berries and stored them in the passageway behind her walls, in the cool darkness where there was no light or warmth to leach away their unique properties. And sure enough, Redmond had returned. But this last time, she had been ready for him.

Or so she had thought. Alas, she was not the herbalist that Damon was. Apparently she had not used enough of them on Redmond.

"I had no idea you were so resourceful and creative in the kitchen, angel," said Redmond now. "Who knew you had access to my dinner?" He gave a brief laugh, then leaned down close to her face, so close, his rust-colored beard pricked her skin. "You will have no chance to be so resourceful again, of course. It took me long enough to recover from your last effort."

"My husband will come for me," she said.

"My poor darling, you have hit your head too hard,

I fear. Don't you understand, Solange? Your husband has already come for you."

"He will come, and he will kill you. I am warning you now."

"Do you perchance mean that man who has stolen my lawful wife? That man who aided in my attempted assassination, that man who will be tried and hung for his crimes against me? That man?"

She made no attempt to move in any way, knowing that it would only draw attention to her in the midst of his madness. Strangely enough, the fear was completely gone. All she felt now was calm resolution. It was going to be finished one way or another. It was finally going to be finished.

"I wish the weather were a little nicer, of course," Redmond was saying, calmer now. "I find London so dreary in the wintertime."

He had moved away from her and was uncorking a flask of liquid. His shoulders were hunched over as he pulled out the cork, giving him the illusion of some hump-backed imaginary beast with long, curly hair. A yak, she thought, wasn't it a yak that had all the hair . . .

"And I'm afraid you won't have the opportunity to see any of the famous sights while we are there," Redmond continued. "Except the court, of course. Perhaps the Tower, as well, if you are very good. Oh, and I know of the most delightful little apothecary shop. I must take you there. The owner has the most interesting little room in the back, filled with all sorts of devices."

He took a long swallow of the contents of the flask.

"I am not going to London," she said.

"Oh, but you are." Redmond came over and sat beside her on the pallet. He made a show of pulling a blanket up to her chin. "For if you don't go to London, you won't be able to testify against Lockewood, will you? You won't be able to describe to the court how he seduced you, persuaded you to harm your devoted husband and then run away with him. And," he added softly, "we can't have that. I want the world to know what a devil that man is. I want the world to know of his wickedness before they torture him to death for his crimes."

"You know he had nothing to do with my plan. You know I acted alone."

"I know nothing of the kind! I do know my sweet wife was corrupted and stolen from me! That is what I know!"

She said nothing, just watched him, watched the empty eyes become shuttered, considering her.

"Although," he said, and she heard a world of meaning in his voice. She heard the cunning there, and the laughter. "Although you did seem more than a trifle disturbed that last day, that very day I had arrived to take you back to Wellburn. Do you recall that, Solange? Yes, you did seem angered about something. I wonder . . . I wonder, could it have been what I told you of Lockewood? Could it have been that pathetic little story of how he came to me at Ironstag and offered me everything to have you?"

She kept her breathing steady, refusing to allow the words to hurt her again. The earl smiled fondly.

"Yes, I believe that might have been it. I told you of

how the sniveling boy came to me that night before our wedding, offered me his gold, his lands, why, everything he thought he had in this world in exchange for you. I told you how I laughed at him."

She focused on the dim outline of the sod ceiling above her.

"Had I but known what tender emotions you carried for him all these years . . . How much easier it would have been for both of us. I would have convinced you right away that you could belong to no man but me. It's not too late. You are still mine, Solange." The richness in his voice drew shivers down her skin. "Nothing will ever change that. Lockewood will never change that."

"I was never yours. I was his before any of us were born. You may try, but you will never change that."

Redmond narrowed his eyes. "You will tell the court the man is possessed of a devil. You will tell them he has practiced black magic upon you, that he is a sorcerer, spiller of innocent blood. That he is an alchemist."

"I will not."

He placed both hands beside her shoulders, pinning the blanket tight across her body, trapping her. "Why do you fight me so, darling Solange, when I am the one who loves you, who has cared for you these past years? Even when you scorn me, even when you run away from me, don't you realize how much I love you? How much I"—his eyes traveled down her form—"need you?"

She turned her head away from him. "You know nothing of love."

"Nothing? Surely you have wronged me once more! I am wounded! See the power your mere words have over me? Nothing of love! Why, would a man who did not love his wife follow her across the ocean when she fled from him, after she had tried, indeed, to poison him? Would such a man take the pains I have taken to follow your trail, questioning peasants and children and tavern wenches to piece together the tale? Would such a man, instead of going straight to his lawful discourse with the king, choose to follow the trail of his wife, to haunt the woods outside of where she stays, living like the lowest peasant in this squalid hut, waiting for just a glimpse of her again? Waiting for the opportunity to become reunited with her, waiting so patiently for her to appear alone at last to come back to him?"

Redmond's hands released the blanket and began a slow trail down the outline of her arms. "Would such a man forgive his foolish, weak little wife of her insanity, of her willful defiling by another man, and bring her back into the fold of his arms? Such is love, Solange, the love I have for you."

His fingers curled over her hands, pulled her upright so quickly that her head was left spinning. Redmond forced her to lean into him, speaking low into her ear.

"You have the gift, Solange. Only you. You know it, and that is why you torment me with it, because you can."

He smelled like the room, fetid and sour. She tried not to breathe too deeply. "I have nothing for you."

"No." His hands moved restlessly over her back. "You know you do. You know yours is the only essence that will work. I have tried others, yes, so many others. But yours is the only one I can use. It is your natural gift, designed to please me. And, oh, it does, Solange. It does. It will again, very soon."

Somewhere, far away, a wolf howled into the night.

"My lord," announced one of the men standing outside. "We have no more time to waste. We must be off."

"Yes," he said to the shadow by the door. "Mount up. We are off."

Solange had gathered her spinning senses by now. She pushed away from him. "I am not going, Redmond."

His smile was ferocious, slick and glittering in the dark. "How many times must I instruct you to call me by my name? Stubborn little wife. After all I have done for you, after I have taken every consideration for you. Yet I see I have not taught you well enough. Perhaps I was wrong in allowing you to leave Wellburn in the first place. You were docile enough there."

"I was almost dead there," she said flatly. "Your precious experiments were in danger of dying with me."

"Allowing you to reside at Du Clar has only increased your rebellious spirit. Your ladies were quite correct in their reports to me. I must remember to reward them when we return."

She sat still, keeping her head proudly upright even though it hurt. "I am not going. You will have to kill me first."

Redmond stood up, impatience marking his movements. "Do not think such mad thoughts. I have no plans to kill you. You are worth nothing to me dead, as you well know."

"I am not going."

"But I have no unease about bringing you in a sleeping state, Solange, if necessary, for the whole journey. You know that as well."

"The reason you didn't go to the king first is that you have been warned about the rumors, not because you care so deeply for me."

Redmond said nothing, but she knew by the way he paused in putting on his cloak that she had touched upon the truth. She kept talking, keeping her voice even and steady.

"You knew if you showed your face in the court there would be a goodly chance you would be arrested, didn't you? You know what they're saying about you. You know what would happen if you arrived with no proof of your innocence. You know the punishment for what you have done."

She had his attention; he was listening to her. Solange slowly began to stand up.

"You knew that unless you arrived with someone to testify for you, someone close to you, a member of the peerage, you would be held until enough evidence was mounted against you. You would be interrogated until you confessed, and then you would be hung. But if you arrived with your wife to defend you, the daughter of a respected marquess . . ."

The wolf howled again, closer now, and an answering *yip, yip, yip* from another echoed away. The earl gave a short laugh.

"You know, there were so many times I regretted the only thing you kept close to your heart was that middling mare of yours. I regretted that I killed it so quickly, because it brought forth such a magnificent fury in you. I'll never forget it. You were alive again, vibrant, an angel of rage. You were stunning. It kept my experiments going for weeks. How much richer it will be now, knowing you will be forced to watch Lockewood maimed and killed. All this time there was something you had managed to hide away from me inside your heart. How delightful."

Outside, the urgent voice of the man came again. "My lord! It is time! We cannot tarry longer!"

Redmond showed no signs of hearing. "You have made all my dreams come true," he said happily. "The death of a man I despise on top of your agony. It is almost too much to bear."

"Do you smell lavender?" she asked softly.

The horses began to scream, the two men were suddenly shouting, a tangle of noise and streaking shadows past the doorway made Redmond turn and run over to it, sword drawn.

There were snarls and guttural cries; she heard the horses pound away in a panic. After that there was only silence.

The earl took a few steps outside the door. "My God," he said, for once sounding shaken. "My God, did you see them?"

"I am not going anywhere with you." Redmond looked back at her, seeing her with the brightness of the moonlight that had just cleared the clouds. She stood upright and calm in the middle of the dirt room, wild, unbound hair, eyes like flames he had not seen before. "You won't be going to London either."

He gripped his sword more tightly. "You are coming with me. You will testify for me. You have no choice."

"You are wrong. I am staying at Wolfhaven. And"—she tilted her head, giving the appearance of listening to something he could not hear—"you will not be here much longer to say anything, one way or another."

"Quiet, slut! Do you think because you have let another man touch you that you may speak to me this way? Do you think that because these two idiots are dead that I have no others behind me? I have an army behind me! I am the Earl of Redmond! No one will dare accuse me to my face!"

"No one will have to. I shall testify against you after you are dead."

He walked over to her and leveled the tip of the sword against her chest. "You tempt me too far, my dear. I have been much too soft with you. I will not make the same mistake in the future."

"There is no future for you," she said simply.

"Step away from my wife," came the icy command from the doorway.

Redmond stilled; she saw the past and the present and the future blend, she saw the three of them from outside of herself and from within: violence, then a calm that portended all was ending right now. It was ending, and she knew how it would end.

Then Redmond smiled at her, a gentle smile she had seen countless times before, and so knew what it meant.

In the instant before his hand moved, she flung herself to the ground and rolled without hesitation, avoiding the deadly drive of his sword but still feeling the sting of it as it sliced at her arm. In the next heartbeat Damon had let out a bellow of outrage and was upon him. Redmond used his momentum to carry himself forward, but it was too late. As he swung up and around, Damon had already delivered the fatal thrust, piercing Redmond's leather jerkin as if it were nothing but spun cotton.

Solange scrambled out of the way as his body fell to the ground with a heavy thud, a lifeless shape with a spreading stain of blood on the ribs.

Damon stood immobile, sword still poised in the air. He was breathing heavily, though not from exertion. He was lithe and taut and ready to fight again, even though the battle was over and the enemy was defeated. The point of the sword began to quiver ever so slightly.

She went over to him and put both her hands over his.

"Put it away now, my lord. This work is done."

He resisted the light pull of her hands at first, not seeing her, not hearing her. She kept her back to the thing that had been Redmond, and stepped in front of Damon, trying to catch his eyes.

"My love, my beloved. It's over. Let us go."

His eyes remained fixed behind her. Over his shoulder Solange saw Godwin walk in, give the body a dismissive glance and her a longer one. "The marchioness is injured," he said dispassionately.

That brought Damon back.

"Where?" He dropped the sword and brought her into the jagged line of moonlight creeping into the room.

"'Tis nothing," she said hastily. "A scratch."

His hands carefully pulled apart the torn cloth around her shoulder, revealing the razor thin cut Redmond had given her as she had rolled away from him. It had to be deeper than it looked. The crimson of her blood was smudged black in the darkness.

"We should get her back to Wolfhaven," Godwin suggested in his diffident voice.

"Aye," Damon agreed. "Have the others take care of this." He gestured to the form on the floor. "And the rest of them."

He could barely think of what he was doing. All he knew was he had to get her to safety. She was bleeding, dear Lord, and he had to staunch it, he had to think of what he could do to staunch it. He would fix her at Wolfhaven. Wolfhaven was the key.

When a party of his men from Wolfhaven had ridden out to meet his own group returning three full nights ahead of schedule from Ironstag, he had fought the rising panic in his gut with a steely force. When they had told him she was missing, that a child had babbled of a monster in the old orchard and that she had gone back alone to fight it, he had heard enough to push Tarrant forward into the run of his life, thinking only of her, of saving her, of fighting whatever she was facing.

Somehow there was no doubt in his mind who that monster might be. A part of him had known all along that Redmond was not dead, that he could not have been dead, and now he had Solange again. The thunder was coming again, that old familiar ally. The thunder of the hooves and in the sky were blending together to drown everything else, bringing out the warrior's instinct until it burned away every other part of him, until it left him as honed and sharp as his blade. The Wolf was alive in him once more.

The warrior met with the men at the gate of Wolfhaven, found the tracks that led to the woods, found the two sets that had followed hers, doubled back, and then followed her again, and then found the place where his wife had collapsed into the snow, leaving the clear imprint of her body where she had fallen before they had picked her up and carried her away.

The thunder had been a stone in his heart until then. At that moment he came closer than any other in his life to letting go of his reason altogether. He could trace her outline in the pristine white snow where her arms had been outflung, where her head had lain to the side. But there was no blood, as Godwin had pointed out. No blood.

Not yet.

It had been remarkably easy to find the old sod dugout, even though he had not guessed it existed before now. Easy to follow the trail of the two men. Easier still when he heard the wolves attacking, guiding him right to her.

And it had been easy to kill Redmond. The thunder had been silenced when he had drawn the life out of that body.

He didn't know what was wrong with him now. It

should have been over. The anger should be gone. It *was* gone. But what was this new thing?

"I am fine," Solange was saying over and over. "I am fine."

She was not fine. He could see that there was blood soaking her arm, coming down in blackened ribbons, making his hands tremble again as he held the reins of his stallion, making him push the horse as hard and as safely as he dared in the snowy night to get them home.

They were waiting for him at the gate, those who had not ridden with his search party. They were men with stony faces, women with weeping ones, all of them converging upon them as Damon brought Tarrant to a halt.

"I am fine," Solange assured them, but he didn't allow her more than that. He issued a curt command for his medicine bag to be brought to him, then carried her in, ignoring her protests, to the great hall.

He put her in a chair next to the fireplace, fed her the warm soup the servants brought for her, pushed back her hair, and then ripped the gown from her shoulder to expose the wound.

It's not that bad, his logic told him. You've seen far worse.

But it's *her,* howled his heart, it's *her* bleeding, it's *her* flesh that is torn. He stared at the cut, at the flow of blood, and tried to think of what he should do next, but he couldn't. He had no idea. Everything, all his field experience, all his learning, was banished. It was her blood. It was her *blood.*

One of her hands touched his cheek. It was like ice. "Damon. Drink the soup."

He didn't want any damned soup. He wanted to fix her arm. He had to fix it, but he just couldn't think of how. He looked up at her blankly, hoping she could help him. She smiled. "A sip, my love. For me."

He slowly became aware that there was a crowd gathered around them both, and that someone was holding a bowl of broth beneath his nose. He hesitated, then took the bowl and drank it and handed it back. The bracing warmth of it allowed him to breathe a little better.

"Hot water," he said suddenly. "I need hot water and clean cloths."

"Here, my lord," said a woman he knew, Solange's companion, pointing to the basin of steaming water at his feet. "And here are the cloths, my lord." She put two into his hands and held on to the rest, standing ready.

"'Tis only a scratch," Solange said.

"You were lucky," he said gruffly as he began to clean the cut.

"I know," she replied.

SHE SLEPT THROUGH THE NIGHT and past the next day and night, making him fear she had slipped into a fever somehow when he was not watching her closely enough. But no, her forehead remained cool to his touch, even though she didn't stir, not even when the child she had rescued had to see for himself that she was alive and came into the room that night with his mother in tow, gulping down tears until he saw the covers rise and fall with the rhythm of her slumber. She did not stir when Damon at last lay beside her, on top of the covers, nor when he got up the next morning. She did not stir when he changed the bandage on her arm twice, checked on the fine stitches he had sewn himself to close the wound, and replaced the herbal poultice he had mixed for her. She slept on.

But the afternoon of the second day brought a sunbeam to drift across her face, warming it and gradually brightening the redness behind her closed eyes until she was squinting. When she tried to raise an arm to cover her face, she found she could not move either of them, and this caused her to open her eyes and turn her head.

On her right she could see a thick white padding secured to her arm, and felt the streak of pain when she attempted to lift it. That explained that.

On her left were no bandages, but rather the sleeping figure of Damon, sitting on a low chair but bent over the bed so his head rested on the covers, one of his hands holding fast to hers.

What she could see of his face was drawn and haggard, though she thought, blurrily, that the rough stubble of beard gave him a roguish charm.

The irrelevance of the thought tickled her mind and made her smile a little. Damon stirred, tightening his grip on her fingers before moving his head, blinking wearily into the brightness of the light. He looked up and caught the remnant of her smile, then blinked again, as if to clear his vision.

She said nothing, but kept her smile in place, allowing him the moment of adjustment. Immediately he was up, placing a hand over her forehead. "How do you feel?"

"Most excellent," she said. "And you?"

His reply was to sit on the chair again and bow his head low over the hand he held. With a great deal of effort she managed to lift her other hand and bring it over to rest on top of his head, letting her fingers comb through the luxuriant strands. He didn't move to stop her. He didn't move at all, just allowed the caress, breathing shakily down into the covers of the bed.

There were no other sounds she could hear, no noises from the hallway, no birdsong outside the diamond-glass window; only him, only the sweet sound of his breath filling her room, the beauty of him overflowing in her.

"I tried to kill him myself," she said, still stroking his hair. "Right before you came."

Still he said nothing, but moved his head to rest his cheek upon the back of her hand. He stared off into someplace she couldn't see.

"I didn't want to deceive you." Her own voice sounded somewhat strange to her, as if she were listening to someone else speak. "I thought he might have actually been dead when you arrived. It certainly seemed as if he were about to die the last time I had looked in on him. I was going to wait one more day before leaving, but then you came, and I . . ." She trailed off momentarily, then continued, stronger. "I wanted to leave with you. I knew you didn't want to accompany me, but I had to try to get you to come. I was so glad that you did."

"You didn't tell me any of this," he said, still not looking at her. "You should have told me."

She felt a faint amusement. "What, my lord, that I had attempted to murder my husband not three days before, and that now I needed to flee the country before I could be formally accused? Oh, yes, I can imagine how receptive you would have been to helping me then."

"You should have told me. You should have trusted me to help you."

"Perhaps you are right." There was no hostility in her voice, only her typical calm reflection. "But I could not take that chance. I had to leave Du Clar. By my life, I had to leave."

"Aye, by your life you did!" Damon raised his head and looked at her fully. Anger tightened the lines around his mouth. "And now I know full well why! You risked your life to end that of a man who should never have been allowed to live in the first place! You were left to fend for yourself against that monstrosity, who cut and maimed you—"

"He had not touched me for an age, Damon. It had been years since I had seen him last. And I did not give him the opportunity to hurt me again. By the eve of his return I had already taken care of him."

It felt remarkably good to talk about this to him at last. The words flowed from her tongue and she let them out, breaking loose the last of the chains of the past. "It was the blood, you see. It was what he wanted, for his tests. The experiments. The alchemy ruled him, it had always ruled him, and he needed me, he said, something in me made them better. But after that time at Wellburn, when I was ill . . . he sent me to France to recover, and I refused to return. I threatened to do whatever I could to foul his experiments. For a while, it worked."

Damon was staring at the back of her hand. "And then?"

"And then, one day, he came back." She left the rest unsaid, because the memories had taken her back to that brutal day two years ago, and once again she could not speak from the fury within her, she could not voice the keen despair that had swept her as she had watched Gytha die at his hands. Within that memory grew the newer one, that of Redmond laughing at her, laughing at the memory of a good man offering everything for her. It mingled with his laughter as he taunted her with the blood of her horse still splashed on his boots.

The most wicked of men was always laughing, she thought, and wondered what he had laughed about over his dinner that night she had given him the hemlock.

"He was a killer," she said finally, "in love with death. He killed Gytha, and then he told me he would begin to kill the serfs next if I would not do as he wanted. So I did what had to be done. That was all. I had to do it."

Damon kept his silence, watching the shadows play across her face. She had again that brittle look, the one he had not seen since they had been on the boat to Dover. It imbued her with a remoteness that belied her feminine beauty. It was the splintered detachment he had seen in the eyes of a hundred different men since the beginnings of the war.

She listed without inflection the sins of the man she

tried to murder. Damon couldn't touch that detachment, he knew that from experience. He wasn't able to heal the wound within her that separated the woman he loved from the creature who had acted to survive. He could only offer her himself. His support, his love.

It could be that he would never be able to know what thing lived in that look she carried now; it could be that he would not be able to ever bear the full truth of it. He didn't know. But she was here now, safe with him. He would keep her safe for the rest of their days.

"Do you hate me now, Damon Wolf?" she asked lightly in a voice designed to hide her true self. But now he could recognize the worry in her eyes.

"Hate? Is that what you think?" He shook his head. "How could I hate the woman I love most in this world? How could I hate the one who is the other half of me? And although I think it is not a difficult thing to do, she is the better half, at that."

She gave him that uncertain look, the one that hurt him the most. There were tears hovering on her lashes. "God help me, I do not deserve a man as good as you."

"Then God help me as well, for I certainly do not deserve a woman as good as you."

"Do not tease me!"

"Tease? You would think that I would tease after all this?" He gave a broken laugh. "You would not say such a thing if you could see into my heart, dear love." He moved to sit beside her on the feather bed, sinking them both deep into the center of the mattress. "I have a love who is brave as a warrior, clever as a puzzle, beautiful as no other woman could ever hope to be. I would not dare tease such a one."

She shifted over to allow him more room in the bed, then nestled down to lie in the crook of his arm. He kissed her forehead. "My heart is forever gone to you. Nothing can change that."

She was quiet for a while, a long while, and he thought she might have drifted back to sleep, until she spoke again in a small voice. "What will become of us now, my lord? We are not married, I suppose. It seems I am a widow all over again."

"I have already sent a messenger to Edward, bearing most of the news. I have informed him of the earl's . . . inclinations, and requested that he formally annul your marriage to him."

"Do you think he will listen?"

"Edward is no fool. He will have heard the rumors, and he trusts me. I think he'll do as I ask. He has incentive. I told him you would grant Redmond's estates to the king's treasury as a gesture of goodwill, should it be in your power to do so."

"He may have them all and burn them to the ground, for all I care."

"I doubt he will burn them. But I do believe he will do all he can to ensure you have both the right to will them to our sovereign and to obtain the annulment. He is wily enough to find a way."

A silence again, both of them considering this. Solange took a deep breath.

"So, it is done," she said.

"Yes, Solange, it is done."

The purport of his words were just beginning to sink in. It was done. Those nightmares that had possessed him could now be buried with their bitterness.

He wanted no more of that agony. The lady was at last here beside him, truly his in every sense that mattered, just as he had always known she was meant to be. It was done.

She squirmed a little beside him, then slid one of her legs over his. "Perhaps, just to be certain, we should get married once more."

The bright sunlight encompassed the room, casting a golden glow all around. Damon smiled up at the ceiling. "Is that a proposal, my lady?"

"Well, yes. I suppose it is. Wilt thou have me, my lord?"

"Aye, beautiful lady. I will."

Epilogue

THE ROAD TO RECOVERY was formed of simple things—the rush of wind from a bird's wings, the pristine color of the noon sky, the steady reassurance in the eyes of the man who truly did love her. Or now, the wondering face of a child as he tasted the first sweet bite of a late summer—in this case, a long-anticipated cherry tart.

Solange smiled down at the boy. "Well, William, what do you think? Was it worth waiting for?"

William continued thoughtfully chewing, then nodded his head. "Although," he added seriously in between bites, "three years is an awful long time to have to wait."

"But your little tree has borne fruit before all the others," reminded his mother.

"Yes." He brightened. "And Miranda has been so cross!"

This made the women gathered around the table in the buttery burst into laughter as they passed the tray of tarts around to the rest of the waiting children, drawing the attention of the tall man who had just entered the room.

"And what is the cause of such mirth, my lady wife?" Damon asked, walking over and artfully stealing a tart from the tray. "Has my daughter done something new to amuse? Has she spoken a new word? Made an inventive new pattern in her food?" He walked over to where Solange stood, holding the toddler in her arms, and kissed them both before biting into the tart.

"Papa!" cried the child, reaching her arms out for him. "Mine!"

"No," said Solange ruefully. "She has the same words as always."

"I will share with you, Kathryn, but you cannot have it all." He broke off a piece of the tart and handed it to her. The little girl gave a gleeful chuckle.

"I am lost, I fear," Damon said half seriously.

"And how is that?" Solange wiped up the cherry juice from her daughter's chin.

"Kathryn will be my undoing. She has her mother's eyes, her mother's sweetness. How can I say no to her?"

"She has her father's smile and charm," Solange replied firmly. "And yet I find myself saying no often enough."

"Where was your no last night when she wanted to bid a good night to the hawks before she went to sleep?"

Solange laughed. "That was different."

Kathryn echoed the laugh, releasing the last bit of the pastry to put her fingers in her mother's mouth. Solange gently extracted the little hand, gave it a kiss, and then began to wipe up again after the tart.

As he watched the two heads bent to each other, one black and the other darkest brown, the two profiles so similar, Damon felt a sense of completion as he had never known. It was a good feeling, a surprising one even still, though the nights were becoming fewer and fewer that he woke up in a panic that Solange had been just another dream of his. She was always there beside him, day or night, real as the black castle itself, sweeter than life.

The past three years had brought to Wolfhaven a multitude of blessings, a gradual increasing of the estate in every area, from financial to geographical to population. The marriage of Godwin and Mairi had begun the cycle. . . .

No, Damon amended to himself. It was Solange herself who had begun the cycle, and who steadily improved upon it by bringing forth their first child, and soon another. Within her the light of Wolfhaven shone the brightest, tending her gardens, teaching her classes, watching over every living thing she could while still showing him she was grateful, each night, to be his love.

But Damon Wolf did not think, deep in his heart, that she could possibly be as grateful as he was to have her. He did not truly think that such a thing could exist. Damon knew, beyond all mortal doubts, that he was the most blessed of men. The mirrored faces of his wife and daughter were proof of that.

Solange placed Kathryn in his arms, and then the three of them walked outside to enjoy the enduring fairness of the summer day.

About the Author

SHANA ABÉ lives in Southern California with her husband and three house rabbits. Yes, the rabbits really do live in the house. Shana can be reached at ShanaAbe@aol.com

If you loved

A ROSE IN WINTER

Look for Shana Abé's next enchanting medieval romance

The Promise of Rain

to be published by Bantam Books in the fall of 1998

Turn the page for a sneak peek into this spellbinding new release. . . .

ENGLAND

MAY 1117

SHE THOUGHT the whole thing had been rather too easy.

First there was the serendipitous coincidence that the very lord Kyla sought had not bothered to leave the rustic English border town since the massacre at Glencarson last month.

But she had explained that away as a commonsense move on his part, to keep his base entrenched on his own English soil while hunting for her up north. She thought she would have done the same thing.

And how quickly she had been able to pinpoint the inn where the soldiers were staying. To give herself credit, the town only had two inns. It had to be one or the other. The soldiers constantly milling about The Hound's Taile had resolved that issue.

But perhaps she should have taken a longer look at the arrangements before leaping forward with her plan. She had only given herself a day to scout the area. It had seemed simple enough. A small inn, a courtyard with easy access to the stables and the main road . . .

Oh, it had been so sweetly arranged. That tiny twinge of warning was all but vanquished once she had seen the man she sought himself, strolling so casually across the courtyard.

And it had to be him. It had to be.

No other man in this remote little town could have walked with such a manner of confidence, seeming to part the very air in front of him with a wealth of power and grace.

The day was cloudy, so when she first spied him what she noticed was the presence of him more than anything, an overall impression of complete and absolute command.

Then the woolly clouds blocking the sun lifted. With breathtaking abruptness clear sunlight spilled all around him, leaving her almost to gasp out loud.

What twisted fate had endowed a man who had the soul of a devil with a person so blessed? It was bitterly unfair, watching such perfection move across the yard without any acknowledgement of its own beauty.

Honeyed hair fell in casual waves. He had a firm jaw, wide shoulders, and she could swear a crooked smile curved those sculpted lips, a smile given to no one but the birds in the trees, it seemed. She could even make out the color of his eyes, a vivid greenish blue, bright against the tan of his face.

They were an exact match to the color of a small stone she had seen once at court, set in the ring of a Moorish prince.

Turkeis, the prince had called it, with a knowing smile at her, and then translated the strange word: turquoise.

She hated Strathmore with sudden force, hated that he lived and Alister died. Hated that the man who would have had her in marriage would now have her in chains, yet still walked as a free man without a care to trouble him.

But mostly she hated him for who he was, the man who had hunted what was left of her family to death.

Kyla, crouching behind some empty ale barrels in an alley, closed her eyes then, willing him to go away.

When she opened them again, he was gone.

She faded back into the shadows of the building to wait until nightfall. After that, she had merely chosen the most auspicious room—the largest one, of course, the only one with its own balcony—and had no trouble at all scaling the stripped branches of a summer vine that had buried its roots in the walls of the inn. It had only taken a minute.

Yes, it had been so easy.

And that was what she got for using her heart and not her head, for now he had caught her, and she would die without even the revenge she had been nursing since Glencarson. He had trapped her in this little room with him, and in an instant he would hand her over to Henry's men. Hound of Hell, indeed.

Her hand ached from the punch she had delivered to his jaw. She sincerely wished she could do it again.

He was standing there, almost grinning at her after having made that ridiculous formal introduction, as if they were at a ball and not toe-to-toe in the darkness of an inn where she had come with half a mind to kill him.

"Give me the letter," she said in a low voice, rubbing her knuckles slightly.

Roland took a careful step away from her before replying. "Sorry," he said. "Don't have it."

He watched with interest the despair that flickered across her face and was then gone. Her eyes narrowed in the half-light. He really couldn't see what color they were, something light. Green, he would guess, or robin's-egg blue, perhaps, to go with that cherry hair . . .

"You lie," she hissed.

"I'm afraid not, my lady. The letter is not here."

She hesitated; he watched her fight the urge to look at the wooden box on the table, the corner of paper sticking out.

"It's blank," he said gently.

She shifted on her feet, allowing a thick fall of hair to cover half her face. With abrupt intensity Roland found himself wanting to touch it, wanting to feel for himself the fire of its color. It almost caused him to miss the forward leap she made for the window.

He caught her, but not without a struggle, and he was desperately afraid they were making too much noise. For lack of a better idea he forced her over to the thin pallet that was the bed and made her sit still while he sat beside her, holding her against him.

Again he felt her tremble, but he couldn't be distracted by that now. He was going to save her even if she didn't want him to.

Roland placed his lips close to her ear.

"Take me to your brother. I will promise you both safe passage to London. I will speak to the king for you."

She said nothing in response to this, but he thought he felt the trembling increase.

"I can help you, Kyla. You know that. I can help you both."

He felt the moment stretch out, growing longer and thinner with an undefined emotion that hummed and sang between them.

"Spawn of the devil!" she burst out loudly. "Leave me be! I'll kill you!"

Instantly he was on top of her, smothering her with his body as he clapped a hand over her mouth. Her eyes widened, she twisted her body beneath his with surprising strength, but he was able to hold on to her as the door opened.

"My lord?" came the gruff call. "All is well?"

"Aye, Gilchrist," Roland said with lazy humor. "This wench and I are having a bit of sport. She's a saucy thing." He kept his arm down by her face, blocking the view of the soldier in the doorway.

"Ah," said the man with dawning understanding and a chuckle. "Good sporting, my lord."

"There is no doubt of that," Roland said pleasantly.

"Good eve to you, my lord." The soldier shut the door.

Kyla bit the inside of his palm.

"You are not endearing yourself to me, my lady,"

said Roland in the same pleasant tone he had used with the soldier.

She didn't care for that, it was clear. If possible, her eyes got wider, then narrowed again. She tried a mighty heave to throw him off her.

As interesting as the position was, he was going to have to do something to calm the lady. He didn't want her to hurt herself, not to mention him. He would try reason one more time.

"Kyla," he said quietly. "I can help you. Let me. I can take you and your brother to London under my protection. No harm will come to you, I swear it."

He lifted his hand from her mouth.

In the gloom she stared up at him, eyes wild and her mouth a little bruised from the struggle. It came to him then that she was not merely beautiful, as he had first thought, but that she was amazingly beautiful, fantastically beautiful, quite the most incredible thing he had ever seen.

If her face was a little too thin, her mouth a little too sensual, her brows too straight, her neck too long, none of it mattered when the sum of the parts made up the whole. He found himself caught in the spell, mesmerized, and she allowed him this, seemingly diverted in her own perusal of him.

Roland came back to himself with a slight shake of his head. It was unlike him to play the part of a smitten boy, no matter how bewitching the woman. He was her protector, not her lover.

Not even her betrothed.

But embers in the fireplace let him catch the movement of the tip of her tongue as she moistened her lips, and he felt himself respond with an immediate rush of passion.

He sat up abruptly, scowling. This was not supposed to happen.

"Where is the real letter?" Her voice was husky. She didn't move from the pallet, a sweet temptation with her hair spilling around her face and her body not nearly concealed enough in her black tunic and hose.

He heard the question. Yes, he heard it; it floated out into the room, and certainly she deserved a response. But what he wanted to do was hold her, hold her tenderly, and break the news to her as gently as possible.

"There is no letter at all," he said instead. "I made it up."

Her lips parted slightly in shock. She shook her head mutely.

"It was a trick, to trap you," he said ruthlessly, trying to slay this soft, unfamiliar thing inside of him she had found. "It was successful."

Her eyes closed, squinted shut, as if to fight off the words.

The weakness inside of him rolled over, horrified at his callousness. She looked so helpless. How could he do this to her?

"Kyla. It's over. Take me to your brother."

She opened her eyes, looked past his shoulder to the ceiling of the room. "All those lives lost," she whispered. "For a lie. For nothing."

The weakness exploded into life again. He fought it, he didn't have time for it, weakness would not help anyone. Weakness would leave them vulnerable, and Roland had spent the last hard years of his life making sure that vulnerability would never be a factor for him again. He stood.

"We need to get back to London. I know your father is dead. Take me to Alister, and we will go."

She came back from someplace far away, looked up at him, and he saw her focus sharpen on him again. Saw the loathing she had for him. It was such a contrast to the immediate memory of the lushness of her body beneath his. . . .

"You knew I would come if you lied," she said.

"Well," he conceded. "I thought it might be your brother instead. I thought he might be the more impulsive of the two of you."

There had been no news of either Kyla or Alister after the massacre of Glencarson. An entire village of people had vanished, seemingly without a trace, save those left in the field. By the time Roland arrived, those that had been left behind had been too long dead to identify. He had a feeling that the Warwicks weren't there anyway. Searching the hills would have been an exercise in futility; the villagers were far more experienced than his own people in surviving in the Highlands. He had pulled back here to rethink his options.

Roland wasn't about to let anyone know, least of all this angry young woman, how lucky for him it was that she had been spotted that day by his squire, who had seen her before in London and alerted him immediately.

He knew one or the other of them would show up tonight. He knew it in his bones, and these feelings were never wrong.

"Where is Alister? Is he ill?" he asked now, already making plans to surprise the boy before he got wind of his sister's capture.

Kyla ignored his questions. "You made up the story of the letter. You made up the proof of my father's innocence."

Roland said nothing, just watched her, waiting for her to accept it.

"You sent word to me that you had a letter to prove he didn't murder my mother." Her voice cracked slightly. "You told me you would give it to me—"

"If you met me at Glencarson," Roland concluded. "And you did not."

She was silent, contemplating him. Then:

"I don't know why I should be surprised that you would lie. You are naught but a slave to the king, everyone knows that. You have no soul. You have no remorse. Of course you would lie."

"Of course. Take me to Alister, Kyla."

She gave a muffled laugh, then turned her head to the side. Roland felt something in him freeze, go numb.

Damn, he thought, *damn, damn . . .*

"How did he die?" he asked.

"How do you think?" she spat, sitting up quickly and scrambling to the other side of the pallet.

"The cold," he said, following her form with his

eyes, wanting to believe what he said. "The Highland snows—"

"It was not the cold, my lord Strathmore. It was not the snow. It was you. It was your command to attack at Glencarson that killed my brother."

There was a surfeit of pain in her voice, calm as it was. It spoke measures beyond a scream or a cry. It sliced him to the core, hearing that pain come from her.

But perhaps more of his torment came from within himself. He wanted to deny he was responsible for the attack. He wanted to deny the indecency that had taken place in his name. He wanted to, but he couldn't.

He had not been there at Glencarson. But he should have been.

"I'm sorry," Roland said. "I'm very sorry. What happened at Glencarson should never have occurred. It was a mistake, and I will always regret it."

Kyla took a heavy breath and let it out slowly, staring at him all the while. She seemed to make up her mind about something.

"I'll be going now." She walked over to her dagger, which had landed on the floor amid the rushes.

Roland crossed the short distance and took the knife from her hand before she could close her fingers around the hilt. "We're all leaving soon. Have you any other supplies to take?"

He saw her shoulders stiffen beneath the tunic she wore.

"I would sooner travel with the devil himself than with you," she said flatly. "Leave me alone."

"If this is all you have, I suppose it will have to do. I'll see what I can do about getting you some proper clothing. Perhaps the barmaid has something you could wear."

He tucked the dagger into the heavy leather belt he wore. Kyla shook her head at him. Her eyes were shadowed.

"Again, my lord, you manage to astonish me with your audacity. Perhaps I have not made myself clear to one as thick-skulled as you. I came here to kill you. By the grace of the Lord I have decided not to do that. But now I am leaving."

He blocked her way by stepping in front of her without touching her, maneuvering her until she was backed up almost against the wooden wall.

"Forgive me, my lady. I think I have been the one who was not clear. You are accompanying me to London." Roland kept the threat in his voice to a velvet purr. He had found that this usually had the maximum effect. She was so much smaller than him. He wanted to smile at the fierceness of the look she threw up at him.

"I will die first!"

"No," he said softly.

"I will kill you, then!"

"No," he said again, then waited. He listened to the raggedness of her breath, felt the tension radiate from her to him with almost physical force, then felt it begin to wane. *Good,* he thought, *almost there.*

"Give me back my dagger," she said tonelessly.

"I think not, my lady. Not just yet. Perhaps later."

She moved one hand a fraction.

"It's mine."

"I'll keep it safe for you."

Again that tense silence from her, that blaze of emotion he could almost feel for her, the anger, the uncertainty.

"When we are in London," he said, placing one of his hands on the hilt of her dagger, "we will look for that proof of your father's innocence."

"Oh yes," she said scornfully. "*Now* I believe you. There's certainly no reason for you to lie to me *now*. Everyone knows the Hound of Hell would offer his word to keep a village safe, even as he burned it down."

He turned the anguish her words caused him into a careless shrug, backing away slightly.

"If you wish to leave, Lady Kyla, you are free to do so. The soldiers outside will retain you, of course. I will see to that. My men would never harm a lady." He gave a fearsome smile in the shadows and had the satisfaction of seeing her take a step back. "Some of the soldiers here, however, are Henry's men. And they have been promised a fortune to bring you back, living or dead. Although I think they might prefer you living, at least for the next few nights. There are more than forty of them, after all."

He turned away from her indignant gasp and walked back over to the table by the door. "It matters not to me which path you choose. As you say, the Hound of

Hell has no soul, and certainly no reason to regret the foolish choice of someone who does not recognize her redemption when it is offered to her."

He let her see him take hold of the door handle. "I offer you my protection. Whatever else you may think of me, I *will* keep you safe. It is my mission to do so. What say you, my lady? Where will you cast your fate?"

Surprisingly, an ember in the fireplace popped with a brief flowering of golden sparks, illuminating her for a fraction of a moment. It was enough for him to catch the look of resignation shrouding her, and although he should have been happy with the turn of her thoughts, he was slightly ashamed of himself, of his blatant manipulation of her fears.

Another irksome quality she had unearthed in him. How inconvenient. He would have to see what he could do about banishing this new sensation inside of him as soon as possible.

"I cannot trust you," she said in a frustrated tone. "You would as soon have me dead, no doubt."

"Oh no, my lady," he said quietly, so quietly she had to strain to hear him. "Not I. I would have you live a long and fruitful life."

She made a sound of disbelief. Roland turned the door handle, opened the door a crack.

"And in the final outcome, what does trust matter, Lady Kyla? It seems to me your choices are quite clear. Either come with me peaceably, or come with me forcibly."

She watched him toy with the handle, then glanced

over longingly at the balcony window. Her hands were balled into fists.

"You have tricked me, made it impossible for me to leave. I cannot win."

"That's what I do," Roland said, and opened the door wide.